KING OF ASHES

KING
OF
ASHES

A NOVEL

S. A. COSBY

PINE &
CEDAR
NEW YORK

KING OF ASHES. Copyright © 2025 by S. A. Cosby. All rights reserved. Printed in the United States of America. For information, address Flatiron Books, 120 Broadway, New York, NY 10271.

www.flatironbooks.com

Flame art by PiximCreator/Shutterstock

Designed by Donna Sinisgalli Noetzel

Library of Congress Cataloging-in-Publication Data

Names: Cosby, S. A., author.
Title: King of ashes : a novel / S. A. Cosby.
Description: First edition. | New York : Pine & Cedar, 2025
Identifiers: LCCN 2025000748 | ISBN 9781250832061 (hardcover) |
    ISBN 9781250832078 (ebook) | ISBN 9781250408822
    (international, sold outside the U.S., subject to rights availability)
Subjects: LCGFT: Gangster fiction. | Novels.
Classification: LCC PS3603.O7988 K56 2025 | DDC 813/.6—
    dc23/eng/20250210
LC record available at https://lccn.loc.gov/2025000748

Our books may be purchased in bulk for promotional, educational, or business use. Please contact your local bookseller or the Macmillan Corporate and Premium Sales Department at 1-800-221-7945, extension 5442, or by email at MacmillanSpecialMarkets@macmillan.com.

First Edition: 2025

10 9 8 7 6 5 4 3 2 1

This one is for Todd Robinson.

Long live the thugs.

Memory believes before knowing remembers.
Believes longer than recollects,
longer than knowing even wonders.

—WILLIAM FAULKNER

All empires are created of blood and fire.

—PABLO ESCOBAR

KING OF ASHES

CHAPTER ONE

H e dreams of his mother.

Her mahogany skin is deeper and darker in the sepia-tone filter that diffuses the cinematography of his dream. Her eyes, deep and wide, sparkle at him like fireflies. Her hair, cut short in the back and curly on the top, seems to glisten as well. She is wearing the nurse scrubs he last saw her in that day. The cuff of her left pants leg has minute drops of blood like an abstract henna tattoo.

In his dream he reaches out his hand, not the hand with the twelve-thousand-dollar watch but his sixteen-year-old self's hand. And before he can touch her, she fades away like an instant photo moving in reverse.

And then he wakes up with her name on his lips.

The taste of the woman lying next to him waits there too. Waits for his tongue and shame to find her flavor. She turns and throws one finely muscled light brown thigh over his own and murmurs his name.

"Roman."

It comes out with the solemnity of a prayer. He rolls over, away from her. He knows her stage name, but it escapes him at the moment.

"Hmmm?"

"We getting breakfast?" she asks. They shift in the bed, changing positions until her back is against his chest and her legs are drawn up nearly to her chest.

Roman closes his eyes and takes a deep breath. "Hmm," he murmurs.

He puts his hand on the small of her back and makes light circles with his fingertips.

"Can we go to Mammy's? I'm starving," she whispers. Her name escapes him, but he can see it in his mind. The letters are jumbled, like one of the puzzles in the paper his mother used to like to solve.

She turns to him and he sees the delicate curve of her chin and fullness of her lips. She smiles, and her bright blue eyes seem to sparkle at him. He'd asked her if they were contacts and she'd playfully punched him. Her eyes were as bright as . . .

Saffire. Her name is Saffire. Her friend's name was Genesis. She was in his guest room with his friend Khalil. All of them had been guests at a release party for Lil Glock 9's new single. A party put together by his label to gin up interest for his new song that was debuting on all major streaming platforms. Roman knew the party was more a formality for Lil Glock's fans. An excuse for them to prostrate themselves at the feet of their idol. There wasn't really any money in streaming. It was the concerts and tours where he really cleaned up, and even that wasn't the gold ring it used to be. Roman's wealth management firm had helped Lil Glock 9, whose real name was Franklin Parrish, maximize his earnings while keeping him out of the crosshairs of the IRS. That maximization required more and more creative accounting over the years as record labels took more and more of the pie from recording artists, and recording artists like Lil Glock went to great lengths to pretend they were still at the head of the table.

Roman vaguely remembered Khalil introducing Saffire before they were zooming down Decatur in Roman's Porsche heading for his condo.

My 2012 Porsche, he thought. He preached fiscal responsibility to his clients, but not many of them wanted to drive a ten-year-old Porsche or use rented jewelry for social engagements or video shoots. Roman knew he had to present a certain persona as a money manager in one of the richest cities in America, but he didn't intend to put himself in the poorhouse in service to that image.

"I ain't renting a damn thing. I wanna own my shit," Lil Glock had said, even as Roman tried to explain the concept of depreciation.

Roman heard a man's voice, then a woman's laughter, from the living room. Khalil and Genesis were awake as well. A few seconds later there was a knock on his bedroom door.

"Hey, Rome, we about to dip and get something to eat. Y'all wanna come with?" Khalil said. Roman could envision him on the other side of the door rapping his huge tattooed knuckles against the wood, his wide frame nearly blocking out the door. Khalil did security for many of Atlanta's upper-class elites. He moved through their world like a dolphin gliding through water playing savior for a lost sailor, but Roman knew what those tattoos stood for, and knew Khalil wasn't a dolphin. He was a shark.

"Yeah, just let me get—" he started to say, but the ringtone from his phone cut him off midsentence. He extricated himself from Saffire's thighs and got his phone off the nightstand. The morning sun was climbing over the downtown Atlanta skyline, lighting it like the flame from an oil lantern. He looked down at the touch screen as "Für Elise" played.

It was Neveah.

Roman took a deep breath and answered the phone. It was going to be bad. She never called unless it was bad. He could count on that like the rising of the sun that was now casting his shadow across his king-sized bed.

"Hey. What's up?" he said.

"It's Daddy. He's been in an accident. He's in a coma. You should probably come home, Rome," she said, her voice not rising above a whisper.

Roman left Khalil and the girls at his penthouse and went downtown to where the offices of Carruthers and Associates held court among the numerous financial investment firms that seemed to spring up overnight in Atlanta like magic beanstalks.

"Have Simon take my meeting with that new singer from Sony," Roman said to his assistant Keisha as she furiously took notes on a tablet. "Have Gary and Nick take on the meeting with the two new Housewives of Atlanta. Reschedule the meeting with Elian Rhodes. I don't want anyone but me talking to him. The Falcons have serious concerns about his spending habits. Cancel my follow-up with Lil Glock 9. Postpone my meeting with the Kee Law Group. And don't let anyone talk to the president of Morehouse until I get back."

"How long do you anticipate being gone?" she asked.

Roman had paused. "Long enough to make sure my daddy isn't going to die."

His flight didn't take off until 8:00 P.M. That was the earliest one he could get, even though he lived in one of Delta Air Lines' major hubs. He'd had time to pack, he'd handled his work responsibilities, and he'd given Khalil his spare key. He was all set to go home.

He just had one more stop to make.

He checked his watch. He'd arrived on time for his appointment, but it was now ten minutes past the time they had agreed on. He knew it was all part of the experience, but it still annoyed him a little.

He was sitting in the exquisitely understated anteroom of a high-end two-story classic colonial-style house at the end of an exclusive cul-de-sac just off of Peach Tree Road in Buckhead. A New Age instrumental song was playing over hidden speakers as barely noticeable incense burned in both corners. Roman tapped his knee with his index finger as the music reached a crescendo.

Finally, Miss Delicate came through the door.

She was tall, nearly as tall as Roman, which made her close to six feet. Her dark skin was smooth as a night gone black. A long, thick black braid spilled down her back to her firm, rounded backside. Roman pegged her age at around forty-five or fifty. It was hard to tell. Her face was bereft of wrinkles and her body was more toned than the woman he had spent the night with just a few hours ago. If she was fifty, that made her exactly fifteen years older than him.

He liked that. Or, more accurately, he needed that.

"You can come back now," she said. Her voice was conversational in tone but direct and implacable.

"Yes, Mama," Roman said with a tongue that felt like a roll of cotton.

The cuffs bit into his wrists just enough so he knew they were there. They didn't hurt, not really. The pain, real pain, would come later. The sting from the restraints was an almost welcome sensation. A familiar feeling that made him comfortable even as his breath began to come in rapid-fire gasps. He wasn't afraid. They had a firm safe word. Miss Delicate would release him the moment he uttered that word. The moment it flowed from his lips he'd be free.

Physically, at least.

But there was a place in his mind, between the shadows of his desire and the sunset of his self-loathing where time slowed and the real world fell away, where the safe word didn't work. Where Miss Delicate ignored his protestations. Where he was given what he craved in the deepest, darkest caverns of his heart.

Penance. Punishment. Absolution.

Usually he only had an appointment here once a month, unless he was having a particularly stressful week, like when one of his clients tried to convince him to invest all his savings, nearly forty million dollars, into a cryptocurrency corporation. It was during those times, when he felt like Atlas carrying the full weight of his clients' lives, their legacies, their earned or unearned prosperity on his shoulders, that he came here for a "supplemental" appointment.

He knew that in many ways he was the stereotypical client for someone like Miss Delicate. A rich businessman who wants to give up the power he wields so blithely during his workday and surrender to the control of another. And, if he was being honest, that was definitely a part of it. But in reality, that was a small part of why he came here, why he sought out a place like this. It wasn't about sex. It was sexual, yes, but it wasn't sex. Sexuality was just the pen they used to write the story he needed to read again and again.

The story where he stops his mother from leaving the house that day and vanishing without a trace. The folktale where he is the classical hero that stops his mother from disappearing like the morning dew in the light of the rising sun.

Miss Delicate walked around the Saint Andrew's Cross, her stiletto heels making a sharp report with every step. When she stopped, she was behind him. He could feel her breath on his neck.

"Are you sorry? Are you sorry for being such a worthless son?" Miss Delicate said. Her voice was deeper than it had been in the anteroom. It was melodious and rich.

An angel with a black halo.

"I'm sorry, Mama," Roman whispered.

Miss Delicate walked back in front of him. She was carrying a cat-o'-nine-tails. She unfurled it and the leather straps sounded like the dry, whispery wings of a bat.

"I don't believe you," she said.

An hour later, Roman was buttoning his light blue Blugiallo shirt as Miss Delicate, not her Christian name, was putting away her toys under the soft pink LED lights that lined the ceiling along the cove molding. Roman often thought her setup was less Gothic dungeon and more salacious boudoir.

With a cat-o'-nine-tails.

Roman cleared his throat. "I need to cancel next week's session. My dad was in a car accident. I need to go back to Virginia. I don't know for how long," he said softly.

Miss Delicate sucked at her teeth.

"And yet you came here before getting on a plane and going to your father's bedside?" she asked.

Roman felt his cheeks begin to burn. "Yes. I . . . There's just . . . I don't go home a lot. There are bad memories there. This helps me deal with them," he said.

She walked over to him, black stiletto heels tapping. She stood in front of him, staring into his eyes. He could smell her sweat. He'd asked for and had received an intense session. Beneath her sweat he could smell her body wash or soap. And beneath that was her natural scent. Raw and intoxicating.

"The session is over, but consider this a professional courtesy. You will never forgive yourself if something were to happen to your father while you were here. And you already have a problem with forgiveness," she said in a low voice.

She leaned forward and whispered in his ear.

"You like to create situations where you need to be punished. Even if you have to punish yourself. This isn't one of those situations. This is your father. Go. Now," she said.

"I am, I just wanted to . . . I needed—" he started to say, but she cut him off with one raised eyebrow.

"It wasn't a request," she said sharply.

Now, hours later, he was sitting in first class sipping a Jameson on the rocks from a plastic cup as the flight attendants went over the safety protocols, which always struck Roman as a bit ridiculous. Seat belts on a plane were like helmets during a skydive. They mainly existed to make you feel better about this incredibly dangerous journey you were embarking upon. When it was the human body versus the ground, the ground was undefeated.

He finished his drink and closed his eyes. He thought about the power of tragedies. How they came into your life unbidden and upended your world without any care or concern. He'd once dated a woman who was a theoretical physicist. She would lie on his chest after making love and tell him about her kids, who were nearly his age, or her latest article in a scientific journal, but one night she started talking about the nature of the universe in almost biblical tones.

"I used to be afraid the universe was evil. Now I almost wish it was. Because evil can be bargained with, evil has a purpose, no matter how horrible it may be. But what I've come to realize is the universe is indifferent, and that is so much more terrifying," she had said.

As the plane taxied down the runway, Roman thought he disagreed with her assessment. The universe was both evil and indifferent. It was both horrific and idiotically apathetic. It was like a god that strode through time and space full of anger and bereft of concern.

Behind his closed eyes a movie played starring his mother, missing now for nineteen years, and his father. He saw them both fading away, turned to dust and lost in the wind as the universe shrugged and continued on its way.

CHAPTER TWO

A s soon as the plane landed at the Richmond International Airport,
he called Neveah. She answered on the first ring, her voice raspy as
eighty-grit sandpaper.

"Yeah."

"It's me," Roman said.

"Oh, I didn't even look at the phone. Thought it was the hospital.
What time is it?"

Roman looked at his watch.

"Nine forty. You at the house?" Roman asked.

"Yeah."

"Dante there?" Roman asked. His sister made a noise halfway between a grunt and a groan.

"I haven't seen him since the accident. I don't know where he is. That
ain't nothing new," she said. Roman heard the acrimony there, ignored
it, and moved past it, because he knew she had some for him as well as
Dante. Dante was just a closer target.

"I'm at the airport. I'm renting a car. You want me to come pick you
up, or you wanna meet me at the hospital?" Roman asked.

"Rome, it's past visiting hours," Neveah said.

"Nev, I'm going to see him. You wanna come or not?" Roman said.

Neveah didn't say anything for a few seconds. What wasn't said in those
moments spoke volumes. Roman could hear what she wasn't saying.

Oh, now you're concerned about him?

Oh, now you wanna come into town like Big Willie big-money grip?

You haven't been home for five years. Five fucking years.

None of that came through the cell phone towers or across the phone signals. All he heard was a heavy sigh. A sigh his sister had seemed to utter since the beginning of time.

"I'll meet you there."

Roman got off Interstate 64 at the Jefferson Run exit behind a tractor trailer blowing black smoke out of the vertical pipes that ran along both sides of the cab. He felt his stomach tighten as he guided the four-door sedan around the gentle sloping curve of the exit and merged onto Harper Street. He passed the abandoned bus station, went through the first of the four stoplights in this part of Jefferson Run, and passed two adult video stores, anachronisms that survived off the prurient needs of the citizens of Jefferson Run. The two stores, across the street from each other, also sold sex toys, costumes, and fake boner pills. A veritable cornucopia of items that catered to the basest desires of the flesh.

Hypocrite much? he thought as he adjusted himself in the seat of his rental and felt the welts on his back. He drove past the plethora of Mexican restaurants and check-cashing places, on past a consignment shop and then more abandoned buildings, more abandoned warehouses. He turned left onto Lillyhammer Street and past Church's Chicken, a business that stubbornly refused to go under, with a staff that were well versed in serving you chicken or fists.

He came to a stop sign. There was a hospital to the left. But if he turned right, headed out to the city limits, he'd come upon an industrial park, one of those brutalism-inspired monstrosities. Most of the businesses that were there when he was a kid were gone now. He knew that from conversations with his daddy. But the Carruthers crematory was still standing, a dusty red-brick monolith set against the crumbling skyline of the city of Jefferson Run.

Roman thought calling Jefferson Run a city was as generous to the formerly bustling hamlet as it was insulting to real cities across the Old

Dominion. When he had been a senior at Jefferson Run High (home of the Mighty Stags), he'd done a paper on the once-vaunted manufacturing history of his hometown. Situated at the junction of two rivers and two interstates, Jefferson Run was once a manufacturing center. The city had been home to a large automotive brake pads factory, tobacco warehouses, a mason jar factory, and was home to one of the state's oldest HBCUs, Prosser State University. They were also called the Mighty Stags. Roman always thought that was hilarious.

As he drove toward the hospital, passing boarded-up buildings and broken streetlamps, he thought Jefferson Run, or Jefferson Got the Runs, as he and his friends had called it back in the day, was like a patient on life support who was too stubborn to realize they were dead.

It wasn't lost on him that the same analogy might be applied to his father, lying in bed trapped in that nether region between life and whatever comes after life. But Keith Carruthers wasn't a dying city. He was a man who had sacrificed everything for his family. More than most could even imagine. He wasn't dead yet, and Roman wasn't ready to let him go. Not by a long shot.

He saw Neveah standing in the lobby of the hospital, squeezing herself tight. His sister had their father's frame. Thin but wiry, with a light brown complexion. A close-cropped haircut accentuated her large eyes and full lips. His sister was a beautiful woman, but Roman could see the years on her face, creeping in around the edges. Years of helping their daddy run the crematory while Roman was down in Atlanta, that new Black mecca, establishing himself while learning to deal with the bougies who called A-Town home, and Dante . . . well, Dante played the role of the little prince.

"Hey," Roman said.

Neveah turned and set her mouth in a tight line that you might call a smile if you squinted hard enough. Roman went to her and put his arms around her, and after a beat she returned the embrace. Yes, there was bitterness between them, and yes, he hadn't shared the weight the way he should have, but they were sister and brother. The three of them, Dante, Neveah, and Roman, had shared the same womb, been brought into the world with the same alchemy of love, passion, and need that had lived between their parents. That magic united them for all time even if it didn't give the same solidarity to their parents. They were siblings, flesh of the same flesh. What they knew, no one else could possibly know or understand. They kept each other's secrets. Much the same way it was with most families.

"What happened?" Roman asked.

Neveah rubbed his back before releasing him from her embrace. Roman tried not to flinch as her hand moved over the still-fresh welts there.

"Truck ran him off the road near the train tracks. Train hit his van. Doctors say both hips broke. Nine broken ribs. Bleeding on the brain. He even got a broken pinkie, Rome," she said as she started to cry.

"Let's go see him. I need to see him," Roman said.

"They won't let you. It's past nine," she said.

"I'm going to see my daddy. Which room is he in?"

"Two forty-five, but I'm telling you, they won't let us go in."

Roman didn't respond, but walked down the hall past a sign that said ROOMS 201–245 toward a semicircle nurses' station. A tanned white woman with her blond hair pulled back in a severe bun was working at a computer as he walked past.

"Excuse me, sir, visiting hours are over," she said.

Roman stopped and turned to face her.

"I just flew in from Atlanta. My father is here and I've been told he is in a coma. I'm not trying to be difficult, but I'm going to see my father. Now, if you want to call security or the police, well, that's a decision you can make. But my sister has a cell phone and I'll make sure she records the entire exchange. By eight tomorrow Jefferson Run Memorial will be on every social media platform going viral because you accosted the son of a local business owner when all he wanted was to see his father. Is that the road we want to go down?" Roman asked.

The nurse turned red under her tan. "Please keep it under five minutes," she choked out.

———

The fluorescent lights in the room were low and emitted a bluish hue. They gave the room a submerged appearance, as if they were all underwater. His father was lying on his back with his eyes closed but his mouth slightly agape, with a thick clear tube extending from it. A ventilator pumped up and down in the corner. Roman went to the bedside and gently grabbed his daddy's hand. He felt the scars there, the burned places, the nicks and divots. Hands that told a story of determination and setbacks. Of success and sorrow.

Roman squeezed his daddy's hand. He hoped he'd receive a squeeze in return, but the hand remained inert. Neveah moved to the opposite side of the bed and put her hands on the railing.

"The doctor says we should talk to him. That people in comas can hear us. I don't know if I buy that," she said.

Roman squeezed his daddy's hand again.

"It's Rome, Daddy. I'm here," he said.

His daddy's face remained impassive.

"How long you gonna be in town?" Neveah asked.

Roman shrugged. "I don't know. I've got a lot of stuff going on back home."

"I guess it is your home now," Neveah said. Roman ignored the comment. "I was asking because I got like six bodies that gotta go in the oven over the next few days. Dante is supposed to help, but I ain't heard from him since Daddy had his accident. I mean, that's what they calling it," she said.

"What do you mean, 'that's what they calling it'?"

Neveah licked her lips. "About two weeks before this happened, somebody slashed all the tires on both of the vans. A week before that, somebody spray-painted '187' on the front door. Now Daddy gets run off the road? Just seems like too many coincidences to me," Neveah said.

"Who would want to hurt Daddy? It ain't like he competing for business with other crematories. Like he says, long as people dying, he gonna be in business," Roman said.

"I don't know, and that's what's bothering me. But like I was saying, you think you can come up to the shop tomorrow? I got one guy who I know is every bit six hundred pounds," Neveah said.

Roman let go of his daddy's hand. He wiped at his eyes even though there were no tears to be found. He wanted to cry, but it felt like the shock of seeing his daddy hooked up to all these tubes and machines had locked the door to his heart and barricaded his tears behind a dam.

"Yeah. I'll come up."

"Thank you," Neveah said.

"You know you don't have to thank me for anything," Roman said.

Neveah's phone buzzed. She pulled it out of the pocket of her jeans. "Hey, I'll be right back."

"Is it Dante?" Roman asked.

"No," she said as she stepped out the door.

Roman squeezed his father's hand, then touched his father's face. The skin felt cool and damp. His father's left eyelid was partly open, exposing a sliver of white.

Roman winced, took a deep breath, then turned to follow his sister into the hallway. She was leaning against the wall murmuring into her phone. Roman paused to give her some privacy, but he still heard her end of the conversation.

"Yeah, well, I'll try. Just text it to me. I said I'll try. I'm here with my brother visiting my dad. Yeah, okay. 'Bye," Neveah said before putting the phone in her pocket and turning to face Roman. There was a look on her face that he couldn't completely decipher. It wasn't anger, but it wasn't joy either. It was more like resignation.

"I'm going to the house," he said.

"Here's the key. I have something to do. Just leave it under the planter on the porch," Neveah said, pulling a key ring out of her pocket and slipping one off the metal circle. She handed the key to Roman.

"Okay. You all right?" he asked.

"No. I can't stand seeing him in that bed. I can't stand thinking of running the crematory by myself. This feels like losing Mama all over again. I'm not all right at all, Rome," she said.

Roman touched her shoulder. "I didn't mean it like that."

Neveah patted his hand, then waved him off.

"I know. It's just been a rough year. We're busier than ever. Covid damn near broke us. And it was just me and Daddy for most of it. Things have just marginally let up." She sighed. "I just been stressed, Rome," Neveah said.

Roman wanted to tell her everything was going to be all right. That he was home now and they were going to right the ship and this time he would do his part. Tell her her big brother was here to lay the crooked places straight. But he didn't, because that would be a lie. He'd help her tomorrow because that was the right thing to do, but if he was being honest, and he knew among family honesty could be a rare commodity, he didn't want to work at the crematory. He didn't want the scent of burning flesh in his nostrils or ashes in his hair. He wasn't ungrateful for the life flames had given him and his brother and sister. But he had no desire to be the King of Ashes. That title belonged to his father, and Roman was content to let it live on through him or burn with him.

CHAPTER THREE

Roman parked the rental in the asphalt driveway of the house his daddy shared with Neveah and Dante, a two-story modern farm-style house with a porch that ran from one corner of the house to the other. He grabbed his bags from the trunk and carried them inside to the guest room. This house was three times larger than the one they had grown up in while his father and mother scraped and saved to open the crematory. That was when his daddy worked as a grave digger for Bama Mathews Vault Company, out of Petersburg, and his mother was a surgical tech at the same hospital where his daddy now hovered over the border between this world and the next. Roman could remember the suffocating heat that enveloped him like a shroud and the bitter cold that stole his warmth when they had stayed in a single-wide mobile home near the outskirts of Jefferson Run in the Shady Hill Trailer Park.

Time and perseverance had taken them from that aluminum rect-angle to this twentieth century manor on the hill in the land of HOAs and gated communities. A beautiful four-thousand-square-foot house his mother lived in for all of six months before she disappeared after her night shift at the hospital.

According to the police, June 6th, 2003, Bonita Carruthers walked out of Jefferson Run Memorial and vanished like a cloud of dust caught in the summer breeze.

Roman went to the kitchen, dropped to his haunches, and opened the cabinet below the sink. His daddy's bottle of scotch was still there, like it had been when he and Dante used to sneak sips back when they were both less than teenagers. He poured himself a drink over two ice cubes.

As he took his first sip, he stared at a ceramic teddy bear cookie jar that sat on top of the fridge. That bear had been there since before his mother disappeared. A smiling light brown teddy bear with a bright red bow. The head of the bear was the lid. Roman used to tell Dante they were cutting the head off the bear whenever they pulled a chair from the dining table to grab some cookies before dinner. After what happened with their mother, Neveah didn't think the joke was funny anymore.

"What if somebody killed her, Rome? Cut off her fucking head and—" Neveah had said once.

"Stop it, okay?" Dante had pleaded.

They never went in the cookie jar again.

Roman closed his eyes. Tried to shake from his mind the image of his mother dead in a shallow grave without her head.

He took another sip and went out to the porch. Roman sat in one of the rocking chairs there and stared out into the rapidly darkening night. Stared out across the front lawn, down across the hill that ran parallel to the train tracks. At the bottom of the hill a sidewalk started that ran right through the heart of Jefferson Run. But out here, where his daddy had built his vinyl-covered castle, the city was more of a whisper than a shout. In the backyard, past the bricked-in barbecue grill his daddy and his uncle Harold had built, the woods waited, ever encroaching, waiting, perhaps, for the day men flipped a switch or dropped a beaker and snuffed out the light of human existence like a child blowing out a candle. Waited to reclaim the land, the sky, and the night.

Roman took another sip of his daddy's scotch. Twenty-five-year Macallan. It went down smooth and easy, like a woman or a man desperate for all the things that make men or women drop to their knees. Roman took another sip.

Maybe the woods should take it back, Roman thought. He imagined what Jefferson Run, what Virginia, had looked like before the time of men. A Garden of Eden that men had spoiled.

"You thinking too deep, kid," Roman murmured.

A set of headlights lit up the night at the bottom of the hill. A red Dodge Challenger parked next to Roman's rental. The headlights shone bright, then were extinguished. The driver's door opened and Dante stepped out onto the asphalt. He shut the door, grimaced, made a half step to the right, then back to the left, straightened himself, and headed toward the house. Roman noticed the faraway look in his eyes.

Dante was as high as the price of gas.

Roman took a last sip and set the glass on a side table next to the rocking chair. He stood as his brother put his foot on the bottom step of the porch. Dante didn't seem to have noticed him yet. His brother was dressed for early fall in the Old Dominion. A light black leather jacket over a black-and-white T-shirt for the Roots. Skinny blue jeans that stopped just above his old-school Timbs. In the five years since Roman's last visit Dante had grown a wispy goatee. Roman thought it was more like the suggestion of a goatee, so thin it looked like he could wipe it off with his thumb and a few drops of spit. The faux-'hawk/Afro Dante was sporting completed his nouveau-Black-hipster look.

"Dante," Roman said.

Dante snapped his head up and his eyes widened slightly.

"Rome! When you get here?" Dante asked. He didn't slur. If anything, his voice was clear and jubilant.

"Came in today. Just got back from seeing Daddy," Roman said.

Upon mention of their father, Dante flinched. "Oh," was all he said.

He moved up the steps as Roman moved down them, and when they met in the middle Roman wrapped his arms around his brother. Dante returned the embrace ferociously. Roman thought his brother felt as brittle as a baby bird. His bones like candy glass, his skin as thin as crepe paper. When was the last time he'd eaten? Roman thought.

But his embrace was bear-trap-tight.

"It's good to see you, man," Dante mumbled against Roman's chest.

"Good to see you too. Let's go in," Roman said. They walked in the house and Dante went into the kitchen. The bottle of scotch was still on the counter. Roman watched as his brother eschewed a glass and took a long swig straight from the bottle.

"So what happened with Daddy? Was it a hit-and-run? Nev said the cops think it's an accident, but she talking like she thinks it was on purpose," Roman said.

"Shit, I don't know. You ain't gonna ask me how I'm doing? We ain't talked in a year," Dante said. He took another swig from the bottle.

"I texted you last week. You never answered. And, I mean, don't take this the wrong way, but Daddy's the one in the hospital. You still upright," Roman said.

"I know he in the fucking hospital. I know that. I was just saying you could ask about me. Ask how I'm doing too. You can do both. You can do both, nigga. Fuck, try multitasking. Damn," Dante said. He laughed, but his laughter had an undercurrent of despair.

"You're right. I can do both. How you doing? You good?" Roman asked.

Dante leaned against the counter. He rubbed his pants vigorously, like he had something fetid on his hands and was doing his best to wipe it away.

"I'm . . . okay. I guess. This thing with Pop. It's a lot. Then me and Thalia broke up a few months ago. I guess I been kinda bouncing around in my own head. Just a lot of things going on. None of them good. I don't know." Dante stopped talking, and Roman watched as he looked at the cookie jar.

"Sometimes I wonder what things would be like if she was still here. Seems like all Daddy knows is hard work. He don't never tell me that I've done good. He don't never say he proud of me. Shit, he don't even act like he likes me. But Mama . . . Mama could say it. She could tell you she loved you more than the sun and the moon and all the stars." Dante rubbed his face. "She could say it and she'd mean it. And you knew she meant it. She wasn't saying it because she felt like she had to because she'd hurt your feelings and was trying to clean it up. She'd just say it from her heart. Not a lot of people like that in my world anymore, big brother," Dante said.

Roman felt a lump form in his throat that felt as hard and sharp as a piece of obsidian. He missed their mother just as much, but he never pulled off the bloody bandages and exposed himself so naked and raw as Dante had just done. Not even with the many women he took to his bed or to the woman he paid to exorcise his demons with leather and screams. Dante's simple declarations cut to the quick of what they had all lost that day. They had lost a mother, their father had lost a wife, but more than that, they'd all lost a guiding light. A beacon in the darkness that showed them the way home. A beacon that was also a fire that warmed them and made them feel safe in the way that only a mother's arms can.

"I know Daddy is a hard man to love sometimes," Roman said. "Growing up, it felt like the crematory was his fourth child. But he built that place brick by brick, him and Mama. He put us here in this house. Put me through the University of Georgia. Got you that Challenger. He sacrificed everything for us. He might not be a kind man, but he's a good man, and that means something. You need to go see him. Like, yesterday. He's in rough shape. You don't want something to happen and you don't get to say goodbye."

Dante looked down at his Timberlands. "I'll go, okay? I'll go. You ain't gotta try to make me feel bad," he said in a low voice.

Roman didn't respond to that statement. He didn't know what words would come out of his mouth that wouldn't seem pedantic and infantilizing. Dante was a grown man. Roman shouldn't have had to guilt him into visiting their father, and yet that was exactly what he had done, because in the end guilt was a powerful motivator and he couldn't stand to think of their father leaving this world without all his children at his side. They'd lost that opportunity with their mother.

He would not let that happen again.

"All right, I'm going tomorrow. Right now I'm going out. I gotta get out of here," Dante said. He pushed off from the counter.

"Going out? You almost drove the car up in the house. You sure about that?" Roman said.

Dante rolled his eyes.

"I've come home way worse than this. I'm just going over to Millicent Avenue," Dante said.

"What's on Millicent Avenue now? That used to be where the big laundromat was and that country bar, what was it called, the Cactus Spur?" Roman said.

"Nah, it was called the Golden Spur, but they had a big light-up cactus on their sign. They been gone, man. Now there's a club over there. Candy's. It's a chill spot. I'll see you in the morning," Dante said.

"You determined to go over there tonight, after you stumbled up in the house?" Roman said.

"One of the good things about being an adult is I don't have to ask permission to do shit," Dante said, laughing. He started for the door, then paused. "You know, if you so worried about me, why don't you drive my car? I know a little ol' club in Jefferson Run can't compete with Hotlanta, but, shit, you get to have a drink with your brother. Can't do that in Atlanta," Dante said. He bit his bottom lip and raised his eyebrows.

"So, to save your license and possibly your life, I have to go drink watered-down brown liquor at the latest juke joint?" Roman said.

"When you say it like that you make it sound terrible. I mean, it is terrible, but you ain't gotta make it sound like that," Dante said.

Roman stared at him.

Dante stared back.

Roman burst out laughing. It was the first time he'd laughed since before Neveah had called him this morning. It was real and genuine and, he had to admit, despite everything that was going on, it felt good.

"Come on, fool, let's go drink cheap liquor and have a whole chicken thigh on two pieces of bread and call it a sandwich," Roman said.

"See, now you talking like you from Jefferson Got the Runs, not some pretty boy from Atlanta," Dante said as they headed out the door.

CHAPTER FOUR

Candy's was located in a weathered stand-alone former warehouse that was the site of the aforementioned country bar on the corner of Millicent Avenue and Lady Smith Boulevard. Roman wondered, not for the first time, what manner of beautiful women had inspired so many of the names for streets in Jefferson Run. He also wondered what they would think if they could see the ruin of the roads that bore their appellations.

There was a huge empty lot behind the warehouse that served as a parking lot for Candy's. Roman turned off of Millicent before he hit the corner, and drove down an alley between the club and the moldering former laundromat. Kudzu and honeysuckle had embraced the laundromat like long-lost lovers, the kind of lovers you feared would find you after you moved halfway across the country.

He guided the Challenger to the far end of the lot and parked. He liked the car. He didn't know if it could beat his Porsche, but he didn't think he'd bet against it. The engine seemed to balk at merely doing the speed limit as they drove through town. Khalil had told him once about a good ol' boy he'd run across when he was working "security" for some clients who ran guns up the East Coast on the Iron Pipeline. He had said that ol' boy could drive through the eye of a needle backward doing a hundred miles an hour. He'd been some kind of infamous getaway driver. Roman thought a guy like that could probably beat you in the Challenger no matter what you were driving.

"Like I say, it's laid back in here. Not like that place near the train tracks. People get shot up there so much they should hand out bullet-proof vests when you pay the cover charge," Dante said.

"Things that bad around here now? No wonder Daddy's staying busy," Roman said.

Dante went quiet again. He'd been vacillating back and forth between joyful exclamations and slack-jawed silence. Roman knew his brother was struggling with so many things. Dante wasn't just the baby of the family chronologically, but emotionally as well. Roman could remember him sobbing at seven years old when their father killed a copperhead in the backyard with an ax. Dante was convinced the copperhead's family would wonder what happened to him. He and Neveah had fallen over giggling at their little brother and his concern for the family of a poisonous reptile.

When their mother disappeared, Dante's concerns didn't seem so funny.

Dante shook himself, snorted, coughed, and regrouped. "Yeah, it's rough out here. Come on, let's go in. I can introduce you to the current crop of Jefferson Run nines. They be sixes in Atlanta, but beggars can't be choosers," Dante said. He smiled, but it seemed forced.

They paid the cover and walked into Candy's.

The club was decked out in LED lights on every conceivable edged surface. Red LED rope lights ran along the bar. Blue ones ringed the quarter-round that ran along the perimeter of the ceiling. The tables in front of the bar had soft white lights billowing from underneath. Behind the tables, the small dance floor was surrounded by pop art in neon and LED. Words like DON'T DO COKE IN THE BATHROOM or STOP DRINKING BEFORE YOU SEND THAT TEXT shared space on the walls with hearts made out of stretched tubes of neon that had been pulled and teased like lengths of taffy.

"Come on, let me buy you a drink," Dante said. He cut through the crowd and made his way to the bar. He slid his slight frame onto one of the stools as Roman did the same.

The club was actually a pleasant combination of down-home atmosphere and small-town aspirational sophistication. The music evoked red clay roads and the blues filtered through a Dirty South hip-hop prism.

A few people recognized him, more than he thought would. He had

avoided visiting for half a decade, yet here were people giving him familiar back slaps and awkward handshakes that didn't seem to know when
to end.

The fact that he recognized so many faces was comforting and a little
sad. Jefferson Run was a difficult place to leave, and even harder to leave
behind.

Dante ordered two shots of Jameson and two Crown-and-Cokes.
Three lovely sisters sidled up to Dante as he was ordering.

"Big D, you gonna get me and my friends something to drink?" one
of the women, who was sporting a powder-blue Afro, asked. She had
gold fronts on her first four teeth and light eyes like drops of liquid plati-
num. She was wearing a pair of jeans that were so tight Roman thought
she might have been born in them, and a baby-doll T-shirt cut off at the
midriff that barely covered her pendulous breasts.

"Trina, you know I got you, boo!" Dante said.

He ordered three shots of Hpnotiq for the ladies. When the drinks
came, he handed the ladies their blue liqueur absentmindedly. He didn't
even turn his head to watch them melt into the crowd.

"They still drinking that up here?" Roman asked.

"Trina likes it because it matches her hair. Here, let's toast. To my
Rome, he got a big head and a big brain and his feet used to smell like
three-day-old fried onions, but other than that, he all right, I guess,"
Dante toasted.

Roman picked up his shot of Jameson and clinked his glass against
Dante's.

"And to my little brother Dante, who believed in the Easter Bunny
until he was fourteen," Roman said with a little smirk.

"Shoot, fool, you ever been to a furry party? Easter Bunny a straight
freak," Dante said. They downed their shots and Roman chased it with
the unsurprisingly weak cocktail. While he was sipping, two couples
came up to Dante and asked for a round of shots. Dante obliged them
almost immediately.

"You know, I usually advise my clients against trying to buy the bar
when they are socializing. Playing big-money grip ain't a solid retirement

plan," Roman said, a little shocked at how quickly the cadence and jargon of his hometown had returned to his speech.

"Good thing I ain't one of your clients, hoss," Dante said, chuckling.

Roman shook his head. "I'm just saying, with Pop in the hospital, you might want to keep it tight. Neveah say he got good health insurance, but medical bills will pile up quick. They are what we call an 'unpredictable expense,'" he said.

Dante's shoulders sank. "I know, man, okay? You think I'm not thinking about Pop? I think about him every second of every day. I think about him laying there bleeding down on them train tracks, the same tracks where they found Mama's car. You think I don't think about him? Fuck all that, man. I just want to hang out with my big brother for a minute. I know you and Neveah think I leech off of Pop, but I love him, ya know? He wants me to be my own man. I wanna be my own man, but I ain't smart like you and Neveah. I can't run the business. I can't be no financial adviser. I'm good at spending money, not telling people what they should do with it, ya know? Like these people here, I know they only like me cuz I come in here spending dollars, but that ain't why I love Pop."

In the blood-red glow of the LED lights that surrounded the mirror behind the bar, Roman could see tears slowly making their way down Dante's cheeks.

Roman put an arm around his brother's thin shoulders.

"Hey, hey, I know you love Pop, I was just—"

"Trying to look out for me. I know. You always do," Dante said. He put his arm around Roman's broad shoulders. He pulled him close.

"I missed you, Rome. I missed you so much. I'm so fucked up, big brother. I fucked up so bad," Dante said.

"Hey, everything's gonna be all right, okay?" Roman said. He turned on the stool and hugged Dante. "I'm home. You hear me? I'm home."

It was not lost on him that he had deigned not to tell Neveah a version of the benevolent lie earlier. But he thought anyone who knew his siblings would agree Dante needed the lie more than Neveah did.

After their third drink, Roman checked his watch and saw that it was past 1:00 A.M. He yawned a bit and tapped Dante softly on the shoulder. His brother's head was lolling gently side to side.

"Hey, come on, let's settle up and go home. I'm getting up and going to help Neveah at the shop in the morning. And you need to get some sleep. Shit, I need some sleep. I'm tired as hell," Roman said.

Dante turned to him and was about to protest when Roman saw his eyes get wide.

Roman looked over his shoulder.

The crowd had not thinned at all, even though the night was edging toward morning. In the varied light he saw people gyrating on the dance floor, couples and groups of friends at the tables. Then he noticed how the dance floor was parting like a river flowing around a stone as a group of men with a few gorgeous women made their way through the club. The two men who seemed to be leading the group were both slim but wiry. One had a large Afro and the other had long twisted braids that hung down his back and fell into his face. They were both wearing button-up white shirts opened to the throat that exposed tattoos that seemed to glow from the black light in the ceiling. The one with the Afro was also wearing a thin leather jacket and a gold pendant of a skull in a top hat.

The man with the braids looked at Roman and Dante as they moved toward the front of the club to an area off to the right of the bar that was what passed for a VIP section and sat down. Roman wasn't sure, but he thought the man with the braids winked at them.

"Come on, Rome, let's go home. I'm ready to go home. Give 'em your card and let's go." Dante said. His voice sounded shockingly sober.

"Dante, what's wrong?"

"Can we just go, please? Come on, man, let's just go," Dante said. Roman pulled out one of his credit cards and paid the bartender, even though he hadn't been the one handing out free shots all night. He got the tab, signed it, and hopped up off the stool. Dante was already moving toward the door. They got outside in the chill night air. September in Virginia was often balmy as June, but this year autumn was asserting her authority. They got to the Challenger and Roman got in the driver's seat as Dante hopped in the passenger side. Roman started the car. A man was walking past the Challenger holding a glass beer mug. As Roman looked down to click his seat belt into place, Dante started yelling.

"No! No!"

Roman snapped his head up just in time to see the man light the liquid in the beer mug on fire and pour it all over the hood of the Challenger. The man dropped the mug and nonchalantly walked away as blue flames raced across the hood.

Roman jumped out and pulled off his shirt. He frantically slapped at the flames, only for the fire to wick up his shirt and set it ablaze. He dropped it and stomped it out as the flames died down and eventually extinguished themselves on the hood. Dante turned his face to the window and closed his eyes.

Voices from the parking lot exploded in a cacophony of mockery as Roman stared at the crowd over the roof of the car, breathing in the cool night like a locomotive.

"Rome, let's just go. Come on, man. Please," Dante said.

Roman got back in and tore out of the parking lot, the sickly sweet scent of burned liquor and scorched metal filling the car.

CHAPTER FIVE

When they pulled back into the driveway, Dante hopped out before the car came to a complete stop. He shambled up the steps, unlocked the door, and tripped inside. By the time Roman came through the door and locked it behind him, Dante was in the kitchen throwing the bottle of scotch to the head.

Roman tried to snatch the bottle from him.

Dante held the bottle loosely by the neck with his right hand and wiped the back of his mouth with his left. He stumbled backward and reflexively put out his empty hand to steady himself. His left hand slid along the counter and fell into the dish rack on the sink. The whole apparatus fell to the floor. The plates and bowls and glasses in the rack shattered against the tile floor.

"Shit," Dante said as he tried to right himself while still holding on to the bottle of scotch. Roman stepped over the shattered crockery, and this time he did take the bottle from Dante's hand.

"You've had enough."

Dante pushed him. Roman outweighed him by nearly thirty pounds. CrossFit four times a week had put a lot of muscle on his lean frame. Roman barely moved.

"Fuck you, man. You think you can just tell me what to do? You ain't been here for five years. You don't tell me shit. You don't know nothing. You don't know nothing about me, and you don't care. Mama gone because I fucked up. Daddy's in the hospital because I keep fucking up, and you don't even care. Nobody cares," Dante said, tears streaming down his face like tributaries.

Roman set the bottle down and put his hands on Dante's shoulders. He leaned forward until their foreheads were touching. He spoke, and his voice lost the deep Atlanta high society accent and took on the lilt and rhythm of central Virginia. He wasn't Roman Carruthers, CEO of Carruthers and Associates, now. He was Rome. He was Dante's big brother. The firstborn. He stepped back into that role and took on all that it entailed.

"I'm your brother. Believe me when I tell you this. I care. Talk to me. Tell me what's going on. Tell me why you haven't been to see Daddy in the hospital. Look at me. Tell me why some joker threw a fireball at your car tonight. Tell me why you looked like you were going to shit your pants when those other guys came in the club. The ones with the braids and the Afro. Tell me. Whatever it is, I got your back. Always."

Dante pulled his head away from Roman's and gazed up at the ceiling.

"It's bad, Rome. So bad. I'd kill myself, but that wouldn't fix it," Dante said. The tears still flowed. Roman gazed into his little brother's eyes and saw the ghost of regret, the specter of despair, but more than anything he saw fear.

After they swept up the broken dishes, they moved to the living room. Roman sat in his dad's easy chair and Dante sprawled across the sectional couch. Roman leaned forward and let his hand dangle between his knees. Dante ran his hand across his face. Silence lived between them for what seemed like hours, until Dante finally spoke.

"So, um . . . I been hanging out with my boy Getty and his girl Cassidy. You know, she go to Hempstead College over in Richmond. She knows a lot of the Beckys and Tylers over there. Getty was talking about how they be into Molly and shit. So Getty was like, ya know, we should get something and flip it. He was saying how them people at Hempstead love to party and shit. Said it would be easy money," Dante said.

"Dante, you *have* money. Daddy gives you three grand a month and pays your car note and insurance. You live here rent-free. You don't even have to pay for your food," Roman said.

"I know that! That's why I got on. I'm thirty. I gotta go to that fucking firepit every day. Gotta walk in there and smell that shit. See the bodies with flies on them. Taste the burnt air. And I can't say no, because Daddy do pay my car note and he do give me money and he do buy the fucking groceries. You got to go away. You got to leave. I wanted my own money. Wanted to do something on my own," Dante said. Now he was standing, waving his hands as he talked. Roman let him pontificate without pointing out that he knew that Dante in fact did not go to the crematory every day. Not the one in Jefferson Run or the other one out on 301 near Red Hill. He let Dante tell his tale with all the caveats and reimaginings he needed. Because, despite the revisionist history Dante was indulging in, despite the editorial license he was employing, Roman thought he knew where this story was going. He could see the end coming like a clairvoyant.

"All right. You and Getty got some Molly and tried to sell it. Then what happened?" Roman asked.

Dante walked to the end of the couch and turned his back to his brother. "Yeah, we got some Molly. Got some brown too. A lot."

"How much is a lot?" Roman asked. He'd known for a while that Dante was self-medicating with both legal and illegal drugs. The last time Roman had been home Dante had been walking around with an Altoids container full of Percocet while drinking Lean. He didn't chastise him then, nor did he feel the need to do so now. They were all living in the shadow of loss. She didn't light up at the hospital, but he knew Neveah smoked a pack and a half of Newports a day. She'd taken up the habit a month after their mother disappeared. He didn't know what her other vices were, and he didn't want to know. He had enough of his own to contemplate. If Dante wanted to dull the pain, to find a way to float among the detritus of their shared grief, then who was he to judge?

But this, this was something else entirely. This was like swimming with sharks when the water was full of blood.

"It was like fifty grand worth of Molly and . . . two hundred fifty grand worth of heroin," Dante said. Even as Dante spoke, Roman felt incredulity rise in his chest like bile. He couldn't have heard him correctly.

There was no way his little brother had gotten into the drug game as a neophyte and just been given three hundred grand worth of product to sell at a nearby liberal arts college whose most notable graduate was a guy who'd won in a reality TV game show.

"Dante, how did you get so much product? Have you been dealing all this time?" Roman asked. He did his best to keep his tone steady, but rage and fear were magnificent vocal instructors.

"No. This was my first time, I swear to God. They just . . . they knew who Daddy was. They was like, 'You're good for it,'" Dante said.

Roman closed his eyes.

"You and Getty and Cassidy used your own supply, didn't you? Y'all partied it up with the Molly and heroin and now you in debt," Roman said.

It wasn't a question.

"Yeah," Dante said.

"How much?" Roman asked. He noticed he was now gripping the arms of the easy chair. His long narrow fingers digging into the smooth velour fabric like he was gripping a stripper's ass.

Dante responded, but Roman was again struck by the words so fully that he was sure he had misheard him.

"How much?" Roman asked again.

"All of it. We owe all of it. Three hundred thousand. Cassidy and Getty used up the brown, shared it with their friends, then some frat boys just jacked us for a lot of the Molly. Like they took almost twenty grand. We tried to sell the rest, but nobody wanted to pay when they could get it free from Phi Delta Zeta, so we just popped it ourselves."

"What the fuck do you mean, they jacked you?" Roman said. Now he was shouting, and he didn't care. He found himself nearly apoplectic.

"Getty went to sell them a chunk, and they beat him up and took it. We told Torrent and Tranquil, but they was like, that wasn't their problem," Dante said.

"Okay, okay . . . first, was you with Getty when he got jacked? Because that whole situation sounds suspect as hell. And second, two hundred and fifty thousand dollars' worth of heroin is about two and a

half kilos. You really think Getty and this Cassidy chick used that up and
didn't die? Your friends played you, D."

Dante shook his head.

"*No*. Why would Getty lie? He owe the same debt as me. Torrent and
Tranquil ain't the type of niggas you play with. They run the Black Baron
Boys. Rome, they're bad. They just . . . they bad, man. We should've
never fucked with them dudes. They crazy, and they . . . just ain't the
ones to fuck with. They were the ones in the club tonight. The ones with
the Afro and the braids," Dante said.

"Getty don't owe the same debt as you," Roman said in a full-on
Virginia cadence.

"What? Didn't you hear me? We got it from—"

"No. You got it from the Black Baron Boys. They fronted y'all based
on *your* family ties, Dante. This is your debt, not Getty's. Now can you
see why it might be plausible that he lied to you? Like, can you stop and
think about it for a minute? Think hard," Roman said. Dante turned and
faced him. His eyes were wide as hubcaps. His pupils seemed to fill their
sockets.

"He wouldn't do that. He wouldn't put me out there like that."

"Why wouldn't he? Because y'all are friends? I work with money every
day. Money is like acid. It burns through everything. Friendships, family,
lovers, husbands and wives. Whatever bond you think you have, money
will make that shit dissolve. It's acid. Don't ever lie to yourself and think
it ain't," Roman said.

Dante collapsed on the couch. Roman let go of the arms of the chair.
He let his mind absorb all that Dante had told him and he filled in the
blanks where his brother was holding back. Because he knew Dante was
holding back. No one ever told the whole truth, not even with their hand
on a Bible.

"These guys, what was their names? Torrent and Tranquil? They
slashed the tires on the vans, didn't they? They ran Daddy off the road
too?" Roman said. He thought, once it was out in the world, living and
breathing between them, that it wouldn't be as bad as having the thoughts
in his head, but he was wrong. It was worse. Seeing the way the words

tore into Dante's face was worse. Feeling the words in his mouth like soiled pennies was worse. Having that knowledge out in the ether was like uttering a curse.

Dante didn't answer. He just nodded. Tears came again, but Roman wasn't as moved this time. His wrath was warring with his love for his father and compassion for his brother. He wasn't sure which emotion was going to win.

"Okay. Obviously Nev doesn't know. Let's keep it that way. She doesn't need anything else on her plate," Roman said. He realized they'd all filled that plate over the years.

"Did they give you a timetable to come up with the money?" Roman asked.

"Two weeks. That was three weeks ago," Dante said.

Roman felt his stomach drop to his knees. "D, why didn't you call me?" he shouted.

"For what? You got a spare three hundred grand? I was just . . . I needed time to think of something. Then Daddy got run off the road, and I just . . . I froze."

"Okay. Can you get in touch with these guys?" Roman asked.

"For what? So they can tell me how they gonna cut me up in sections and put me in a hole in the woods?" Dante asked.

"No. So we can talk to them. So I can talk to them and make some kind of deal," Roman said.

Dante blanched. "Rome, these guys ain't like your clients. They are straight killers. They not gonna take a fucking payment plan. Did you not see what they did to the car?"

"If they were serious, they would have shot the car up tonight with both of us in it. They were sending a message. Well, message received. We gonna fix this. I got some savings, I'll get the money. You just set up the meeting," Roman said.

"Yeah, but last time we tried to fix things it didn't work out so well," Dante mumbled.

Roman felt Dante's comment slip in between his ribs like a stiletto, but he ignored it.

"Contact them. Tell them to meet us at the crematory tomorrow night," Roman said. He got up and stood at the end of the couch and put his hand on Dante's shoulder.

"I don't know about this, Rome," Dante said.

"I do. Make the call," Roman said.

CHAPTER SIX

Neveah heard the doorbell ring just as she was positioning the body lift next to the stainless-steel table with the large waxed cardboard box on it. Her daddy had set up the doorbell to ring in the lobby, the supply room, and the main oven room. He did the same with the telephone when they still mainly used the landline. He used to say a missed call was missed money. Neveah thought it was funny he didn't seem to mind missing her school plays or track meets when she was in high school. Of course, after their mother disappeared, school plays and track meets and school dances had become things she used to do. She had been a child who had been tasked with putting away childish things. Their daddy had needed help at the shop, as he called it, and with Roman halfway out the door and headed to college, and Dante too much of a wreck to deal with life, let alone the dead, it had fallen on her to become her daddy's right-hand man.

Neveah thought it was funny how their father never missed a call, but he had missed his own life passing him by. And he had given her the same kind of myopia, it seemed.

She went through the door that led from the oven room to the lobby and opened the front door.

Roman was standing there in a crisp white button-down shirt and khakis.

"I almost thought you wouldn't show," Neveah said.

"I said I would, didn't I?" Roman said.

"People say a lot of things. You might wanna take that shirt off. We got a couple of slushies back there," Neveah said. Slushies were what their father called bodies in an advanced state of decomposition. Funeral homes that didn't have their own crematory often brought those bodies to Carruthers Cremation Services weeks in advance of a memorial service. Mortuaries were an amazing amalgamation of art and science, but even they had their limits. When a body had moved from just human remains to the outer edges of putrescence, it was beyond the skill of most morticians. Daddy liked to say this was where they stepped up to the plate.

"Sometimes you just gotta burn everything. Nobody ever complains about the scent of ashes," Keith Carruthers liked to say, as if he were imparting mystic yet homespun wisdom.

Neveah thought her daddy was wrong. She'd gone on more than one date where a man swore up and down he could smell the scent of burned flesh on her skin. Half the time she thought they imagined it once they found out where she worked. Half the time she thought she could smell it herself no matter how many showers she had taken. And she took a lot of showers. Used gallons of sickly sweet shampoo. And even then she thought sometimes she could still smell it, under the strawberries and vanilla and orange blossoms. A harsh, acrid aroma, like meat left on the grill too long.

"I figured I'd change into scrubs," Roman said.

"Hold on, let me take a break," Neveah said.

"I'll come with you."

They stepped outside and Neveah closed the door behind them. In one smooth motion she pulled a pack of cigarettes out of the pocket of her own scrubs and lit one up with an orange disposable lighter. She inhaled deeply and let the smoke trail out the corner of her mouth like the plume from a steamboat.

"I thought maybe Dante would come with you. Sometimes when you come home it makes him act like he wanna do some work," Neveah said. She leaned back against the brick exterior of the crematory. They stood under a small awning as the early morning breeze stirred the air around them. Dust and debris from the junkyard across the road engaged in dog-fights as the wind picked up speed. The crematory itself was a two-story windowless brick cube. It had a front door and a roll-up garage door on the left side of the building. On the right side of the building, the exhaust for two massive crematory ovens dominated the architecture. When the floating detritus reached those exhaust vents they were blown skyward by the enormous fans.

Roman shook his head. "By the time I woke up he was already gone. House was empty this morning."

"That sounds like Dante. Early bird gets the weed, or Molly, or what-ever he on these days," Neveah said.

"You didn't come home last night, did you?" Roman asked.

"No, I didn't," Neveah said. She didn't plan to elaborate. And why should she? He was her brother, not her daddy.

"You think Dante got a problem?" Roman asked.

"Daddy do. He sent Dante to rehab last year. He stayed a week. Daddy kept threatening to cut him off, but he never did. He the baby, ain't he?" Neveah said. "Shit, he ain't been right since Mama went missing. None of us have."

Roman sighed. "I don't think we're any more messed up than any-body else. You should hear some of the conversations I have during con-sultations," Roman said.

Neveah took one last drag off her cigarette, then dropped it on the asphalt and ground it out with her heel.

"Yeah, but how many of those people got a mama who went missing and a whole town who thinks your daddy burnt her up?" she said, before going back inside, leaving the door open partially.

Roman stared at the front door of the crematory. Slate-gray, with a wide brass doorknob made smooth from decades of use, it stood mute as a palace guard, yet it seemed to speak to him in his mind.

Abandon all hope, ye who enter here.

To Roman the crematory was a kind of hell. Full of fear and fury and the ghosts of thousands of souls consumed by flames.

After he changed, they spent most of the morning moving bodies from the cooler to the two ovens, then packing the remains in plastic bags that were then sealed with metal ID tags before being put in disposable heavy cardboard containers about the size of a Bible. It took him about an hour to get back into the swing of things. It had been a dozen springs, summers, falls, and winters since he'd operated the hydraulic body lift with its scissored erector set, interconnected arms, or the electric bone grinder that crushed the immolated remains into a fine sandlike powder. When the cremains dropped down through the flame grate into the ash pan, they resembled gray chunks of gravel. The skin and flesh and blood were all burned away, but fragments of bone and minerals remained. An average adult male could be reduced to six pounds of cremains in about two hours.

Roman ran the body lift into the wall a few times and he almost dropped a bag of cremains after taking it off the grinder, but eventually a latent form of muscle memory took over. He'd spent too many Saturdays and Sundays in this brick-and-mortar citadel of the dead to completely forget its rituals.

Roman thought about Dante. He knew his brother liked to party, liked to get high from time to time, but in light of their conversation last night he'd begun to suspect Dante's drug use had gone from recreational to intractable. Because Roman didn't believe for a minute Dante hadn't helped Getty and Cassidy shoot up a big chunk of that horse.

Dante was falling apart while Neveah tried to hold them all together. Guilt, something he was well acquainted with, increased his empathy for his sister exponentially. When she talked about Dante, Neveah sounded like the brother of the prodigal son. He also thought she had a right to sound that way.

Finally, as the clock clawed its way toward seven, Neveah paused long enough to have another smoke break. He knew the state had rules about smoking on the premises, but it seemed to him to be the height of irony that his sister had to step outside to indulge in her vice of choice.

"That one that's in there now is the last one for the day. We gotta let the ovens cool off before we clean them out for the night anyway," Neveah said. Her scrubs, like Roman's, were soaked through with sweat. Even though they kept the garage door open and had two huge five-foot-wide shop fans blowing and the temperature outside was in the low sixties, in the oven room the thermometer still got to over a hundred degrees.

"Why don't you go on home? I'll shut things down," Roman said. Neveah looked at him. A sardonic smile unfurled across her face.

"What, you feel bad about all these years I've had to do this with Daddy?" Neveah said.

"Maybe. Maybe I can see you just need a break," Roman lied.

"Okay. Don't forget to cut off all the gas valves and leave the exhaust on."

"I know."

"Daddy's always been afraid of a fire. He always saying he don't want the flames to turn against him," Neveah said.

They stood side by side under the awning as Neveah smoked and Roman checked his phone. He'd told Dante to get the Black Baron Boys to come over around nine. He figured the crematory afforded them the privacy they needed while arousing the least amount of suspicion. Unless The BBB rolled up in tricked-out Caddies and Bonnevilles with twenty-four-inch rims. Then even the woeful Jefferson Run Police Department might take notice of their meeting.

"You ever wonder where she is?" Neveah asked.

"Not anymore," Roman said. He put his phone away. The sun had set and the first stars of twilight were appearing like bulbs on a string of lights being turned on one by one.

"I used to think about it all the time. It was like it was all I could do was try and figure out what had happened to her. Like it never made sense to me how the cops found her car down by the train tracks. What would Mama be doing out there?"

"Meeting somebody?" Roman said, sharper than he intended.

"I used to think Oscar did it, but I don't know. After she went missing and people started to talk and Daddy fired him, I asked Daddy did he think Oscar had anything to do with it. He told me he didn't want to think about it. Wasn't worth talking about, he'd say. Oscar died a few years ago, and when Chester Harmon from Jackson Brothers Funeral Home brought the body over here, Daddy wouldn't even look at him. Had me put him in the oven," Neveah said.

"I mean, I can't even imagine how hard it was for him . . . Everybody knew. That's all they would talk about in school for years. How Mama was messing around on our daddy," Roman said. His jaw felt stiff and robotic, like he was a tin woodsman in need of oil.

"That don't mean he had to kill her," Neveah said.

"Who?" Roman asked. It came out on the back of a gasp.

"Who the fuck do you think?" Neveah said.

Roman pushed himself off the wall. "I know you not talking about Daddy," he said.

Neveah blinked her eyes rapidly five or six times.

"That's the first time I've said it out loud. It's like, him being in that bed, I'm not afraid to say it. You know, when she first went missing and the cops came around, I told myself the way he was acting was because he was scared. Back then I thought he was scared she would never come back. But now, now I think he was scared they'd find out what he did."

"You can't believe that. You can't believe he killed her," Roman said.

"I been doing the books since I turned nineteen. Her name is still on one of the accounts. All these years, and she ain't never dipped into that account. No phone calls. No birthday gifts. No Christmas cards. Never sent Daddy divorce papers. No invitation to meet her new man. Nothing in nineteen years."

"That don't mean he killed her. Not Daddy. He doesn't have it in him to kill the mother of his children. They built this together. Her working at the hospital, him working part-time for Jackson Brothers, part-time at Trout's Restaurant. You don't remember? They put their heart and soul into this place. Together. I remember the day Daddy got the loan. He piled us all in that Suburban and took us to Old Country Buffet. Mama said this was the fanciest place in Jefferson Run and Daddy said one day he'd take her to Richmond for a real fancy dinner, but until then this would have to do," Roman said, his voice cracking.

Neveah took another drag, expelling smoke through her nostrils like a drake. She peered into the gathering dark. At the stars, ceaseless and ancient in the night sky, the quarter moon like the sliver of a fingernail rising behind redolent clouds.

"Our mother was cheating on our father with the man who helped them run the business they had built. The mother of his children and a man he trusted like a brother. Our daddy, who's heard whispers all summer long that his wife is fucking his employee, who worked himself to the bone getting this place off the ground, owns a crematory. And one day, that wife, that mother, just up and goes missing? What do you think I think? Everything you just said is the reason why I think he did it. The more you love somebody, the more a broken heart turns that love to hate. Of course I think he did it. Matter of fact, why don't *you*?" Neveah asked. She took a last drag on her cigarette. Roman saw the tip flare red like the end of a bullet.

"Because I know Daddy," Roman said.

"I'm going home. Don't forget to turn off the valves," Neveah said. She walked over to her truck and climbed inside.

As if on cue, her phone vibrated. It was a text message.

Im free again tonight.

She typed with one hand while lighting another cigarette with her free hand.

Not tonight Chauncey. Family stuff.

She hit send and tore out of the parking lot. She reached the end of Industrial Way and turned right toward downtown. She wanted a drink. She wanted ten. She wanted to wash the taste of what she'd just said out of her mouth. Not because she thought she was wrong, but because she was afraid she was right.

———

Roman went upstairs to the private area and jumped in the shower. He turned the water as hot as he could stand it before it would be scalding and let it wash away the remnants of the bodies they had incinerated and the lives they had reduced to dust. Once, before his mother disappeared, he'd asked his father why he'd chosen to open a crematory rather than get his mortuary license.

"You run a funeral home, you got to be a counselor, a lawyer, an insurance agent. Hell, sometimes you gotta be a detective. Too many jobs, not enough reward. But here, we let the fire do all the work. We ain't gotta dress no bodies, we ain't gotta put no makeup on 'em. We ain't got nobody complaining they don't look like themselves. There's no questions or complaints here. We just let 'em burn. Everything burns," his daddy had said.

As the years had gone by, Roman would sometimes reflect on his daddy's stark mercenary business philosophy. As a child he didn't know the word *nihilism*, but over the years it had become the best way to describe his father's worldview. Everything burns. His marriage, his friendships, his relationship with his children. Everything was set on a pyre to be sacrificed to his ambition. And yet Roman still loved him. Loved him for those sacrifices. For his will. If it weren't for his daddy, where would he be? Flames paid for his degree from UGA. Fire gave him the life he lived in Hotlanta. It was his daddy who allowed him to be the man he'd become. Not his mother, no matter how much he missed her. No matter how many times he dreamed of her.

The doorbell chimed through the building.

Roman hopped out of the shower and put on his khakis and his shirt. He slipped his Rolex on his left wrist. He'd had his shirts specially tailored to be shorter on the left arm so he could show off the twelve-thousand-dollar timepiece. He'd purchased it secondhand through a jeweler who did work for some of his clients. He liked nice things, liked to wear the nicest clothes, drive the most extravagant cars, eat at the most exclusive restaurants, but there was still a frugality borne from the same fountain of wisdom his father drank from.

Everything burns.

Cars depreciated the moment you drove them off the lot. Jewelry was only as valuable as the market deemed it. Anyone who watched *Antiques Roadshow* could tell you that. Even tailored shirts tore and unraveled eventually. It was all a charade. An act, and the material things were a part of the costume. He liked playing dress-up, but he liked having an offshore account in the seven figures range more.

He wiped his face. Saw a man worth over a million dollars on paper staring back at him. But for the moment he might as well be worth thirty thousand. Most of that money was in accounts he couldn't touch. He had set up a complex byzantine system of financial maturation that required patience and planning. This was not the advice he gave his clients, people who wanted immediate returns on investments. For them, he made the money they'd made work for them like serfs. He invested in high-yield accounts, hedge funds, and high-end precious metals. Tech stocks. Real estate, and on and on and on. Items that could be flipped with a moment's notice when a client needed bail money for a public transgression that had gone viral or hush money for a private one. His clients were the type of temporary celebrities and nepo babies who wanted to retire to an island, when they thought of retiring at all.

Roman wanted to own one.

By the time he got downstairs, whoever was at the door had given up on the bell and was banging on it. The sound reverberated through the building like a drum in a museum.

Roman checked the peephole.

There was a man standing there in a brown UPS uniform.

Roman opened the door.

"Package for Carruthers Cremation Services," the UPS man said. He handed Roman a box the shape and size of a large Bible, like the one they used to have on the pulpit of First Abyssinian Baptist Church out in Taylorville, where they had attended church as a family before his daddy had built them a house in Jefferson Run proper.

"Sign here," the UPS man said. He handed Roman a stylus and held out an electronic tablet for him to sign. Roman did as he was asked.

"Have a good night," the UPS man said.

"Hopefully," Roman said as he clutched the package.

He put the package on the desk in the oven room and then went back upstairs to wait for Dante.

An hour later he heard the Challenger pull into the parking lot.

He went back downstairs and unlocked the door. Dante pushed the door open and slipped inside. Roman noticed his eyes didn't have that glassy sheen he'd noticed last night. He went to the wooden chair next to the coffee table in the lounge and sat down in front of the office door.

"I went to talk to Getty. Asked him about what you said," Dante said.

"And what did he have to say?" Roman asked.

Dante ran his hand through his hair. "You were right. He was all like, man, that's on you, man. You the one they trusted. Rome, this motherfucker looked me in my face and said that shit."

"Okay. Okay, we use that when we talk to these boys," Roman said.

"Use it how? Rome, what am I gonna do? Them Gilchrist brothers gonna kill me," Dante said.

Should have thought of that before you tried to be a dealer, Roman thought. "They're not going to kill you. How are they going to get paid? We just have to offer them a good deal. One that ensures they get their money back with interest."

"Rome, you still not getting it. These boys is monsters, man," Dante said.

Roman crossed his legs. "No, they're not. They just gangsters. And gangsters are just CEOs who work the streets. I've dealt with CEOs and I've dealt with some doughboys before. I can speak their language. I can make this work."

Dante licked his lips. "Let me tell you something about these boys. You remember Eva Willis? Ran track? These boys are her sister's children. Torrent and Tranquil Gilchrist. They call him Torrent because he washed away all his competition in Jefferson Run. Tranquil, well, that's about an oxymoron, because he crazy as shit. Only you can't never tell it on his face. You don't never know when that boy mad, sad, or glad. Couple of years ago a boy named Quaran came up here from Richmond trying to make moves. He was tied to the Crips or the Bloods or some shit. Tried to move in here without understanding the rules. Just started running around town hitting they stash houses. They run a couple of car washes and vape shops and he ran up on them too. Eventually he ran up on Torrent at Trout's Restaurant. Knocked the plate of chitterlings Torrent was eating on the floor 'by accident' on purpose." Dante paused, gathered his reserves, then went on with his tale.

"About a week later, his baby mama gets a whole dinner delivered to her house. Dude comes up like DoorDash. She told people later she told him he had the wrong address, but he wouldn't listen. So she takes the food, right? What harm is it? And it's good, man. Cornbread, mac and cheese, turnip greens, big jug of iced tea, and a plate of chitterlings. She gives some to the kids, she has some herself. You know, put some hot sauce on them chitterlings and go to town. Now she eats 'em all up. Rome, she got to the bottom of that plate and somebody had taped a page from a book to the plate. It was a page torn from the Quran. They fed that nigga's guts to the mother of his children. Whatever you thinking about saying to these boys, think about it real long and real hard," Dante said.

Roman flicked his fingers in a dismissive gesture. "Dante, that's an urban legend they probably started to make themselves sound scary. You can't pay any attention to that. They not gonna cut you open. We just have to negotiate an agreement where both sides walk away feeling like they won."

"Rome, these ain't the kinda boys that want everybody to win," Dante said.

Roman was about to respond when the sound of a pair of dual mufflers filled the night. Dante and Roman both looked toward the main work area at the back of the building. The sound of the mufflers reverberating originated back there. Roman nodded toward the door marked PRIVATE at the back of the lobby. Dante went first, then Roman followed him. Dante went to the roll-up garage door and peered through one of the four windows that ran the width of the door.

"It's them," he said. His breath started to come in rapid bursts. Roman got up and went to him. He put his hand on the back of his neck.

"It's gonna be okay. You introduce me, tell them who I am, then let me talk, okay?" Roman said.

Dante nodded.

Roman squeezed his hands into fists while flexing his toes in his shoes. He tried to project an aura of cool confidence. The kind of confidence he took into his conference rooms. He'd said he'd handle these men and he was sure he could, but now the moment was upon him and his nerves tried to wreak havoc on his body. His deeper brain, his animal self, begged him to run. Run from this place and perhaps even set it on fire before he fled.

But he couldn't leave Dante. Not again.

"Open it," Roman said.

Dante pressed a red button near the garage door and stepped aside.

As the door rolled up, Roman saw two cars in the tiny parking lot. One was a money-green big-body Bonneville with huge twenty-four-inch rims and a paint job like melted candy that shimmered under the sodium arc lights on either side of the lot. The other car was a simple, understated black BMW. Three brothers spilled from the Bonneville. Roman felt his chest tighten. They were big dudes, wearing baggy blue jeans and loose-fitting white T-shirts. One of them sported a wave cap and had a long black chain with a pendant in the shape of a skull wearing a top hat. They all had tattoos that matched the pendant running up and down their arms in various permutations.

Two men exited the BMW with the smooth, easy grace of athletes. They were both lean, like collegiate basketball players. The driver was the shorter of the two. He sported long, loose locs. His neck tattoos sported the same skull-and-top-hat design as the pendant the driver of the Bonneville was wearing. His white shirtsleeves were rolled up, showing even more art on his muscular forearms. He wore skinny black jeans and was rocking old-school red-and-white Jordans.

The man who emerged from the passenger side was taller, but Roman could see the familial connection to the driver. Their faces had the same permanent scowl. It was like the metal handles of a cauldron that had slowly but surely melted infinitesimally over the years, only to become rigid again as it cooled. But Roman didn't think these men ever cooled. Their wrath was an eternal flame. He could feel it coming off them like heat from a woodstove.

The passenger had a full Afro with a razor-sharp part that ran horizontally across the left side of his head. He was wearing a long black blazer over a white button-down shirt and black pants. He had the same skull-and-top-hat tattoo on his left hand, but it was subtle compared to the ink of his driver or the men from the Bonneville.

Torrent and Tranquil. The Gilchrist brothers. The soft light in the club last night had given their faces a childish countenance, but under the pale white light of the overhead fluorescents the dark roads they had walked and the terrible things they had seen were stamped on their faces like a brand. In the club, they appeared to be wannabe players. Now, in the quiet gloom of the crematory, they looked like unrepentant stone killers.

Roman swallowed hard.

"Rome, this is Torrent and Tranquil," Dante said, nodding toward the two men from the BMW. "This here is D-Train, Splodie, and Yellaboy."

"I like that chain, man," Roman said.

The man in the wave cap nodded. "Yeah, man, just got this piece. They call me Yellaboy 'cause I had jaundice as a kid, not 'cause I'm light skin 'cause I ain't," he said with a laugh that cut off like it had been sliced by a katana when Torrent looked at him.

First thing Roman had learned in business school was establishing a rapport wasn't just about opening dialogue, it was also determining where one was on the social hierarchy. Yellaboy was at the bottom. Roman determined this by his need to explain his nickname.

"Y'all come on in," he said. More hierarchical maneuvering. He was the one extending the invitation, not Dante. A tacit acknowledgment that he was the one in charge. The group of men entered the work area en masse.

"Pat them down," the man with the Afro whom Roman had pegged as Torrent said. Yellaboy moved forward and without asking permission ran his hands over Roman's chest and stomach, up and down his legs, and around his waist. He did the same to Dante. Torrent fixed Roman with a heavy-lidded gaze. He silently stroked a goatee, cut with precision, for a few seconds before putting his hands in the pockets of his coat.

"Your brother told us you had something to say," Torrent said. His voice was low and even. Tranquil leaned against the body lift and crossed his arms over his chest. Roman noticed the other three members of their coterie had spread out around him in a loose semicircle.

Roman took a deep breath.

"My brother and his friend Getty got you to front them an enormous amount of product. Three hundred thousand dollars' worth, to be exact. Molly and heroin. Now, Mr. Getty told my brother a story about getting jumped for fifty thousand dollars' worth of Molly that I don't believe any more than I believe in Santa Claus. I'm not trying to tell you your business, but I'd take that issue up with Mr. Getty personally, if I was you. Now, that leaves the two hundred fifty thousand dollars' worth of heroin. My brother made two serious mistakes. He tried to get in this game, and he tried to get in it with someone like Getty. Now—"

"I don't need a recap of how he fucked up. What I need to hear from you is how you gonna pay us our money," Torrent said. His eyes landed on Roman like a hawk eyeing a rabbit.

Roman tried to give the gaze right back to him, but there was an emptiness in Torrent's eyes that made him drop his own and start talking again.

"Okay. I have two hundred thousand dollars in that package over there on the desk. That should satisfy part of his debt. I can get the other fifty grand by the end of the month. This should take care of his whole debt. In the meantime, if you maybe want some help putting it in some less . . . risky investments, I'd be glad to assist you. That's what I do for a living. I make people's money make more money for them. And I'm really good at it," Roman said. He felt his heart vibrating in his chest like the wings of a hummingbird. He'd thrown that last bit in there just to soften the blow of not having the full amount ready for this gang of killers and thugs to pick up and then ride off into the sunset. He'd called Khalil last night at 2:00 A.M. and gotten him to go into his safe at the condo, grab all his emergency cash, and then drive to South Carolina and send it to him through a UPS drop-off box.

He'd given him the crematory's address. He'd prayed the package didn't arrive until after Neveah had left, and he'd lucked out that his particular UPS driver must have been running late. He'd been checking his phone for alerts all day with his stomach twisting until he'd heard the doorbell chime.

Torrent held up his hand. Roman stopped talking. Behind him the ovens clicked and pinged as they cooled. Dante was gnawing on his bottom lip.

"You think I don't know what to do with my money?" he asked. Roman watched as the rest of his crew straightened their postures. Tranquil pushed himself off the body lift. Something in the atmosphere had shifted almost imperceptibly. Except Roman was perceiving it. He kept his eyes forward but licked the roof of his mouth as he chose his next words.

"That's not what I meant. That was not an insult," Roman said.

"You know, you saying a lot. But I'm still not hearing the part where your brother pays me back my money," Torrent said.

"I'm saying I have the two hundred thousand right here; if that's not enough, I offered my services. That's all I'm saying." Roman spoke slowly and clearly. He felt as though he were walking on the edge of a knife and that knife was sharp enough to slice him in half.

"I understand what you're saying. You want me to wait, what, three months? While you play three-card monte with my money while your brother keeps walking around like he don't owe me a grip?" Torrent walked across the concrete floor until he was a foot away from Roman.

"I said . . . the end of the month," Roman whispered.

Torrent leaned his head forward.

"Your brother and his friend came to me talking like they knew what they were doing. But they didn't. They came talking to me like they knew how to step on the product. But they didn't. They came talking like they was gonna double their money and pay me back my part plus interest for me fronting them that much. So in reality they owe us four hundred and twenty thousand dollars."

"That's . . . forty percent interest," Roman said.

Torrent put his finger to his lips in a *shhh* motion.

"That's what they agreed to. That's what they said they would do. But they didn't. They just walking around Jefferson Run playing in our faces. Even after your vans got sliced. Even after your pops got his brains scrambled on that train track. So what makes you think I think you better at keeping your word than your brother? You think I'm stupid?" Torrent asked.

Roman felt his throat go as dry as desert sand.

Torrent snapped his fingers in front of Roman's face. "I asked you a question."

"No. I don't think you're stupid. I was just—"

"Yeah, you do. You think I'm some fake-ass Nino Brown who hides money under a mattress while I wait for Johnny Law to come break down my door."

"No, that's not it at all. I mean, look me up. I know what I'm talking about. I was just trying to explain to you . . . like finance . . . a lot of people have a hard time . . . I . . ." Roman said, but it seemed as if he were running out of words. His heart was jackrabbiting all over his chest.

"This is what's gonna happen. We taking the two hundred. Then next week we want the fifty. Then you can pay us every month until I feel like you and your brother done paid up the price for my patience. That's the playing-in-our-face tax," Torrent said.

"I . . . look, we don't have fifty thousand dollars a month for an undetermined time. I can pay you what he owes. I can. That two hundred is a good faith payment. Another two-twenty at fifty K is four months, give or take. That's what he owes. That's what we can pay," Roman said. His mouth was now watering, slick saliva filling it like someone had turned on a faucet. He was going to be sick, but he refused to let it come up. He had to make them understand what he could do and what he couldn't do. They might appear to be just common gangsters, but Roman could see they were far from stupid.

"Tranquil," Torrent said. His brother strolled over to where Roman and Torrent were standing. He fixed his eyes on Roman. They were a dull, muddy brown that looked black under the dirty yellow lights in the ceiling.

"Look, I don't how this got sideways, but—"

The blow came so fast and so quick, later he would think it was like watching a cobra strike on a nature program. Too fast for the eye to register, but the results were plain to see. And, just like a rodent stuck by that cobra, Roman was on the floor writhing in pain. Tranquil grabbed him by his hair and pulled him up until he was on his knees. He took the barrel of the gun that he'd struck him with and put it in his mouth. Roman tasted gun oil and metal as his teeth brushed the sight at the end of the barrel. He heard Dante yell, but he couldn't see what was happening to his brother. All he could see was Tranquil and Torrent looking down at him, backlit by the bulbs in the light fixture hanging from the cavernous ceiling of the oven room.

"I hate a smarty-arty nigga that think he can come and school me like my ass rides the short bus. Get him up on his knees," Torrent said. His cadence was unbothered, his manner unhurried. Tranquil pulled Roman by his shirt collar to a kneeling position. Blood spilled down his face from the wound at his temple.

"You come here grinning at me in your fancy shirt and your fancy watch and your fancy white-boy shoes just to tell me how you not gonna pay me. That's not how we get down in the J," Torrent said.

Roman felt tears at the corners of his eyes. The taste of the gun oil was making him gag.

Torrent moved behind him.

"This how we get down in the J," he said.

Roman tried to speak, tried to cry out, but his tongue couldn't make its way around the barrel to perform its magic.

Then he was struck again. This time on the top of his head. Hard. He felt his ears ring as his teeth broke against the barrel of the gun. For a moment the pain was so intense that it seemed not to exist. In its place for the briefest of moments was a sense of coldness like he'd bitten into an ice cube. But that only lasted for a millisecond. And when the pain came, it was like slamming face-first into a fence post. It was sticking his

finger in a light socket. It was taking a punch to the mouth with a handful of quarters. It was all these things all at once.

Tranquil pulled the gun from his mouth. Roman fell forward onto
the floor. Blood filled his mouth with its bitter coppery taste. His tongue,
now free, instinctively ran across his top teeth. What he found there
horrified him. Jagged shards of teeth that were cracked and split like
splinters. Roman rolled onto his side and let the blood flow out of his
mouth and down his chin. He felt something hard and sharp trying to
slip down his throat, and so he reflexively spit and coughed. He could
see a small splash of red on the concrete floor, and swimming among
that crimson puddle were white bits stained red. He realized they were
pieces of his teeth.

Torrent walked around his prone form and dropped to his haunches
in front of Roman's face.

Roman tried to think. The pain in his mouth was like he'd kissed a
live wire. Death was as close to him now as it had ever been. A couple
nights ago he'd been lying in bed next to a model whose claim to fame
was being Ass Shaker #2 in an Usher video, and now he was bleeding on
the floor of the building his father had built brick by agonizing brick. It
was now at this moment, with a mouth full of blood, that he recognized
his mistake. He'd gotten so accustomed to the larger-than-life cartoon
characters that passed themselves off as tough guys in sound booths in
Atlanta, spinning tales of a life they had only observed from the edges,
taking that bystander's knowledge and creating tales of imagined street
cred that got downloaded millions of times by similarly false thugs who
wanted to believe they were about that life, that he'd forgotten there
were *real* gangsters out there. Men for whom murder was just another
part of the job. Business as usual. What had Dante called them?

Monsters. They were monsters, and they were eating him and his
brother alive.

"You too soft and pretty to talk slick out your mouth, you know that?
Too many places on your face to get fucked up. You like a stained-glass
window. All bright and colorful and shit, but ain't really no use to nobody. A church catches on fire, you have to break that window to make

it useful. Now, as far as I'm concerned, your brother's debt is now your debt. The way I see it, I can get rid of him and his little buddy and still get my money. I can't just let him walk around disrespecting me. You understand, right? You a businessman, right?" Torrent said. He stood and wiped his hands on his pants.

"Splodie, shoot that nigga. You got till Friday to get me the rest of my money. Then the first of every month, fifty grand. If you don't, then we come by here and visit again. Only this time we talk to that sister of yours. And then, if we don't get the month after that, we'll take you to the farm. Let you meet my pooches. But you gonna pay. You a smart boy, ain't ya?" Torrent said. Roman saw Splodie pull a gun from his waistband and put the barrel against Dante's head. He forced himself up to his knees. He spit out what felt like a gallon of blood and saliva and teeth and screamed.

"*Wait!* I can get you another hundred thousand. Now. But I meant what I said about helping you with your money. I'm good at this. I'm one of the best. I can triple what they owed you. I know folks. I get inside leads on good stocks. I know people that know when companies going public. I know how to make this money do magic. We work for you. One month. I triple what he owes you. And . . ." Roman paused. He was out of breath. His head felt like it was about to crack open like a walnut. He knew he was making a bargain with the devil, but this was his last card to play. Otherwise they were both dead and on their way to hell. "And you can use our building to make your problems disappear," Roman said.

Torrent held up a finger and Splodie pulled the barrel of his gun away from Dante's head. Torrent made a go-on motion by twirling his index finger.

"You get full use of the facilities. We make your problems disappear. Nothing but ashes. No DNA. No fingerprints. Even the bullets melt. Everything burns. And I know you got people you need to make disappear. You don't build what you've built without people wanting to take it away from you," Roman croaked.

Torrent stroked his goatee. "Triple it? And we get to use this hotbox anytime we need it?"

"On my mama, I swear. One month."

Torrent looked at his brother. Tranquil shrugged.

"Okay. One month. Remember you said triple."

"I won't forget," Roman said. He stared at Torrent.

"All right. Fuck it. But I still can't let Dante walk around without addressing his disrespect. Grab his hand," Torrent said. Splodie and Yellaboy grabbed Dante by his arms and forced him to his knees. D-Train grabbed his left arm and pulled it away from his body. Torrent pulled a pair of garden shears that their daddy used for trimming the few box-wood bushes in front of the crematory off a pegboard near the cooler.

"What are you doing?" Roman moaned.

"Rome! Help me!" Dante cried.

Roman started to rise, but he felt the barrel of Tranquil's gun against the back of his head. So Roman just stayed there on his knees. A penitent to a slumbering god. There would be no divine intervention for either of them. The terror in his little brother's cries hurt him more than his ruined teeth. He pitched forward and vomited as he watched Torrent cut off Dante's pinkie finger with the garden shears and then crush it under his heel.

CHAPTER SEVEN

The dentist, a jowly specimen with the broken capillaries in his nose of a man who made a whiskey neat three times a night, every night, shone the overhead light into Roman's mouth and clucked his tongue.

"We can put in a partial bridge. We could do implants, but they can be more expensive. A lot more expensive. Now, it usually takes insurance companies a few weeks to approve the charges, but—"

Roman cut him off. He'd rinsed his mouth out last night with antiseptic mouthwash. The sting actually dulled the pain for a moment. The coppery taste of his own blood still lingered in his mouth, though. He thought it gave him a metallic rasp.

"Implants. Run my card. I need it done today," Roman said.

The dentist frowned. It made his jowls look like two extra sets of lips.

"Mr. Carruthers, implants can run you as much as—"

Roman cut him off again.

"It's a Black Amex. Run it."

In his mind he saw himself as a child. A child with a crocodile-shaped toothbrush and a little red pill the school nurse gave you in fourth or fifth grade. You were supposed to crunch up the pill and then it would stain the areas on your teeth that had a buildup of plaque. These sections would show up bright red like you'd taken a bite out of some raw meat. He saw himself looking in the mirror as his whole mouth glistened in red. His father and mother had worked so much when they were trying to get the crematory off the ground, they often didn't have the time to make sure he and Neveah and Dante were brushing properly.

Once his firm had taken off, he'd invested thousands in veneers and routine polishings and cleanings. Rich people who were going to trust you with the money they were trying to hide from Uncle Sam or their wife or their husband wanted to tell themselves you were one of them. Any hint that you had ever lived below the poverty line sent them scurrying like mice back to their elite ivory towers. They didn't trust one of the poors to handle their wealth.

They looked at your clothes, they listened to how you talked, they looked at your teeth like you were a horse for sale. Tranquil and Torrent had scattered all those thousands of dollars across the floor of the building his father had given everything to build.

Dante had been right. Roman had underestimated them. Torrent and Tranquil and their crew looked at him and saw his fancy watch and his nice clothes and thought he'd never known hard times. They thought he was soft.

Roman thought there were many things you could say he wasn't. He wasn't a gangster. He wasn't a good son or a good brother. He wasn't a good boyfriend.

But he wasn't soft.

Torrent and Tranquil only saw the surface of what he was or who he'd become. They couldn't peer into his eyes, into his soul. See the rock that lived there. Immutable and immovable as the pyramids. They only saw Roman Carruthers, money manager. They didn't know what he was capable of or what he was willing to do to achieve his goals.

That was their mistake.

He was the one who remembered when his family lived on the south side of town near the transfer station for CSX in a part of town called the Skids. A place where an oily film constantly floated in the air from the diesel train engines. The Skids were where the Pink House was, Jefferson Run's brothel. It was a lost highway of check-cashing places, freestanding cinder-block sheds that served as the homes of neighborhood convenience stores, single-egress juke joints and scrapyards that grew like amoebas in the shadows of abandoned tobacco warehouses and empty storefronts. He remembered living there while his mom and dad worked to raise their credit score to qualify for the loan that would allow them to build the crematory. Living there was a bit of revisionist adjudication. They survived there. They fought there. The Skids either broke you or possessed you. Unless you got out. And their father and mother had gotten them out, but not before the Skids taught them certain lessons.

Roman poked the jagged pieces of his front three teeth with his tongue. These weren't the first teeth he'd lost. Lomello Green had hit him in the face with a forty and knocked out one of his molars when he was a kid. Lomello hadn't liked losing a pickup game to Roman's team. He had gone home and told his father and his mother, but they both seemed to be distracted.

"You're the oldest, Rome. You gotta learn to look after yourself," his father had said.

"But I'm only fourteen," he'd whispered back.

Three hours later Roman was pulling into the driveway. Dante was at home laid up on the couch with a huge bandage on his left hand. Roman had taken his brother to the hospital after scooping up the remnants of his pinkie and putting it in a bag of ice. It was all for naught. After they cleaned his wounds and addressed Dante's hand, the doctor had told them the finger was too damaged to reattach.

"Whoever jumped you did not want you to get that finger back." The doctor, a young brother, stitched up Roman's scalp and Dante's stump and sent them on their way. Roman thought it wasn't irony but something close to it that they had spilled blood in the building their father had built, and were being tended to in the hospital where their mother used to work.

"Should we . . . go see Daddy while we here?" Dante had asked after getting his first dose of the pain meds.

"I don't want to see him like this," Roman had said before pulling his lips back and showing off his broken smile. Dante hadn't pressed the issue any further.

Roman went to his brother now and patted him on the shoulder. The television was on the cartoon channel and Dante was eating a huge bowl of cereal. Roman felt that this wasn't some expression of nostalgia for Dante. His brother was in many ways still a child. A babe lost in woods that were exponentially more dangerous than he could comprehend.

"How you feeling?" Roman asked.

"Like shit. The meds that doc gave me ain't doing nothing," Dante said.

"You hurting?" Roman asked.

"Nah, just my finger tingling and I know it ain't there," Dante said.

"If you ain't hurting, then the meds working. Where's Neveah?"

"She said something about going to the cops. Us getting jumped, the thing with Daddy and the vans, got her thinking we being stalked," Dante said. He put his bowl down on the coffee table. "Rome, don't you think we should tell her what's going on? She has a right to . . . you know, protect herself."

"How?" Roman asked.

"What do you mean, 'how'? I mean she should know somebody out to hurt us," Dante said.

"And then what? What is she gonna do? How does her knowing anything about this put her in a better place than she is right now? Neveah already feels responsible for you, and she is worried about Daddy, and she still trying to keep the shop running. She doesn't need anything else. We gotta handle this so she doesn't have to put this on her list of things to do," Roman said.

"Handle it? They cut off my finger, Rome!" Dante shouted. He put his hand against his face and began to sob. Roman pushed Dante's legs out of the way and sat next to him on the couch. He put his arm around his little brother and rocked him slowly back and forth.

"That motherfucker stomped on my finger like it was a goddamn roach, Rome. You got your teeth fixed, but my finger is gone," Dante said through his sobs.

"Look, I know it doesn't feel like it, but we got lucky last night. They were going to kill you. Just to make a point. Their greed is what saved us. It's what we can use against them," Roman said.

Dante wiped his face with his T-shirt, an old BORN IN THE USA tee.

"Rome, what are you talking about? Did you see what they did to us last night? What you talking about, using something against them?" Dante said.

"You heard them last night. You owe what they say you owe. They are gonna bleed us dry, then break us down into parts to use for a grist mill. There's no number that's gonna get them off of us. I triple, they gonna want me to quadruple it. I pay them fifty K every month for a year, they gonna make it a hundred K next year. They are never going to let us go. We want to be free of them, we got to get rid of them. Permanently," Roman said.

"And how you plan on doing that? Because your plan last night was pretty fucking terrible," Dante said.

Roman took his arm from around Dante's brittle shoulders. "Did you forget I'm trying to fix something you fucked up? Yes, I made a mistake last night. I let my pride in my salesmanship cloud my vision. They are monsters. And a monster ain't nothing but a beast that you don't understand. But I understand them now. Their greed is the thing that drives them. It's their weakness. Now, I have a new plan, but since you doubting me, let's hear what you gonna do. Tell me how you plan on figuring your way out of this. I'm listening," Roman said.

Dante didn't say anything for a while. He reached for a pill bottle next to the remote. He grabbed a pill and dry-swallowed it. He took his cereal bowl and resumed eating. Finally, after a few minutes, he spoke.

"I'm sorry. I know you sick of looking out for me. I just bring bad shit to you all the time and then you try to clean it up. It's like trying to clean up a lot of blood. We just make a bigger mess," Dante said.

"That's not how it is. You're my brother. I love you. I love Neveah. I love Daddy. I'm not supposed to let anybody hurt you. And I did. Doesn't matter how we got here, I'm still not supposed to let that happen. But I'm fixing it. I promise you that. I'm going to fix it," Roman said.

Dante nodded. Roman punched him lightly in the arm. "I got some phone calls to make. You good? You need anything?"

"I mean, a spare pinkie would be nice," Dante said. Roman stared at him until Dante smiled. Roman closed his eyes and shook his head. When he opened them he was smiling, just not as wide as Dante.

"I'll be back," he said, before heading for his father's study.

Dante watched Roman until he turned down the hall and he heard the door to the study shut. Once he was sure his brother was out of earshot, he pulled out his cell phone and dialed Getty's number.

It went to voicemail. Like it had been doing all morning.

"Hey, man, it's me. You need to dip. Like now. Call me when you get this," Dante said. He ended the call to Getty's phone and dialed another number.

This one also went to voicemail.

"Listen, Cass, stay away from Getty for the next few days. That thing we was doing is going south. I don't want you to get hurt. I . . .'Bye," Dante said.

What he was doing with Cassidy wasn't really cheating. The three of them had spent more than one night together. It was all casual and open and progressive, but he'd be lying if he didn't admit he didn't really want it to be open or casual. He supposed he loved her, as much as he was able to focus on and love anyone since his mother had vanished. He wasn't sure why Roman had seen fit to mention Getty to the Gilchrist brothers, but even a goofball wannabe like him knew that if the Black Baron Boys didn't make an example out of him, then his partner was next in line.

Maybe Getty had gone down to Virginia Beach. He had family there, or so he said. The tattoo shop where he worked didn't open until noon. He'd call them in an hour and see if Getty had shown up for work.

Dante ate another spoonful of cereal. He forced it down his throat even as his stomach protested.

Because he didn't think Getty was going to show up for work. Not today. Not ever again.

Roman dialed a familiar number from memory and waited. After two rings, Khalil's deep voice filled his ear.

"What up, man? How's your pops doing? You get the package?" he asked.

"About the same. Yeah, I got it. I need you to do me another favor," Roman said.

"Hit me on WhatsApp," Khalil said, and ended the call. Roman pulled up the messaging app on his phone and sent Khalil a brief explanation of his situation.

I need you to talk to Sasha Billings. Tell her I want the full treatment. Then get her to transfer the funds to a crypto acct. Then come on up. I'll comp u for your time, Roman typed.

Got it. be there by tomorrow night, Khalil replied.

No questions, just a confirmation.

Roman thought having a friend like Khalil was often the best thing and the worst thing to ever happen to him. Khalil was a former Army Ranger turned mercenary who then transitioned into a security specialist for the rich and infamous in Atlanta, and they'd first met when a client of Roman's, a famous NFL running back on the down-low, needed someone to handle paying off a blackmailing lover who was a semi-well-known male stripper.

Roman had arranged the funds and Khalil had taken care of the actual transaction. A month after the payment, the blackmailer had mysteriously disappeared. The blogs and gossip sites said he'd gotten lost in the California hills hiking. Roman was fairly sure someone had paid the bloggers to spread that story far and wide. The police didn't seem inclined to investigate. Eventually even his memory was consumed like red raw meat by the zeitgeist of Hotlanta.

That was what kind of great and terrible friend Khalil could be. Right now he was convinced it was more of the former and only a bit of the latter. Khalil would come, no questions asked. He would be here by tonight and then Roman would have to tell him which direction he was pointing him. Because Khalil was like a loaded gun. You pointed him at something, whether it was planning security routes for the Grammys or putting the fear of God in the boyfriend of a famous influencer who was too handsy with the moneymaker, and he moved forward like a bullet.

Roman wanted to point him at the Gilchrist brothers and pull the trigger until it went *click*.

Neveah sat in the front waiting area of the Jefferson Run Police Station tapping her foot to a nonexistent beat. After a few minutes, the desk sergeant motioned for her. She went up and he gestured toward a door with a sign on it that said INTERVIEW ROOM 1.

"Detective Mansfield is waiting for you," he said.

"Thanks," she whispered as she headed for the door.

She entered the room and closed the door behind her.

Chauncey was sitting on one side of a faux-wooden table. She sat in the plastic molded chair across from him. He steepled his fingers in front of his face and stared over the tips at her. His light hazel eyes seemed to burn like whiskey-soaked embers.

"What are you doing? Why would you come here and ask for me?" Chauncey said. The fluorescent lights over their heads gave his brown skin an ashen patina. His close-cropped low-profile flattop was sprinkled with flecks of gray.

"My brothers got jumped last night. Somebody cut off my little brother's finger, I—"

"Then have them come file a report! Or call 911. What you don't do is come down here and ask for me! What, you thought I was gonna make your brothers a priority because we have a friendship? You know how many people get jumped on the daily in Jefferson Run? How many people get murdered? I can't just drop all my current cases to investigate what happened to your brothers when they didn't even make a goddamn complaint!"

"I just thought you could ask around or something. My brothers got hurt. Bad. Rome's teeth got knocked out. They cut off Dante's fucking finger. I thought the least you could do for me is check into it. You know, seeing as we are routinely gobbling each other's private parts," Neveah said.

Chauncy clapped his hands together. The sound echoed through the room like a rifle shot. He put a finger to his lips, then pointed it at Neveah.

"Stop. Don't come down here again. I'm married."

"I'm well aware of your marital status, Chauncey."

"And you knew I was married when we met. So you ought to understand you can't come down here asking for me like I'm your personal Judge Dredd."

"Look, I'm not asking for special treatment. But somebody tried to kill my daddy, and now my brothers got fucked up. Somebody is after my family. And all I'm asking is for you to look into it. Hell, I'll make a report. But somebody is out to get us, for some reason. You ought to understand how terrifying that is, seeing as you a family man and all," Neveah said.

"Keep my family out your mouth. God, we have a good thing. Why would you wanna mess that up?" Chauncey said.

Neveah looked at him. But we don't have a good thing, she thought. We have a thing that makes us feel good. And even that is debatable at this point.

She rose from her chair. "Do I need to file a report?"

"No, there doesn't need to be a record of you being here. Jesus Christ. Look, I'll ask around a little bit. I got a few CIs I can talk to, but don't come back down here asking for me. You're smarter than that," Chauncy said.

She thought back to when they'd first met six months ago. Chauncey and his partner Vega had come by to take a look at a body they had in the cooler. Victor Dearborne had been ventilated by the latest advanced weapon in the arms race on the street, an AR-15, while sitting in a barber chair on High Point Street. Chauncey had told her the medical examiner had accidently deleted photos of the tattoos on Victor's body. He and his partner needed to take new pictures and try to decipher the cuneiform that covered the young man's body to determine if he was a captain in the Black Baron crew or just an innocent bystander.

"But if we being real, not many innocent bystanders get lit up in a barber chair while everyone pretends they were looking at their phones,"

Chauncey had said with a sly smile. That smile wasn't what won her over, but it was like the first drop of water that wears away a boulder. They'd taken their pictures and then he'd asked for her number, in case he had more questions.

She'd known any further questions the detective with the cute eyes had were not going to be related to the demise of dearly departed Victor, but she didn't mind. What was wrong with a little flirtation? A little fun. God knows she deserved it. And, yeah, she saw the ring on his finger, but he was the one married, not her.

By the time he started telling her how his wife didn't understand him, that he loved his kids but craved his freedom, how their marriage was just in name only, she realized he might have been the one married, but they were equally yoked in their sin. And for what? Fifteen or twenty minutes of moans and sweating and the crystalline rapture that exploded in her body and then faded like the last notes of a sad love song she knew had to end sooner rather than later? She'd told herself this was for her, this affair was a gift to herself. Chauncey wasn't creeped out about her job. He never joked that she smelled like burning skin. He caressed and touched places on her that hadn't felt the touch of another person for years. It was that pleasure, so deficient in her life but white-hot like the burners when they ran the ovens all day, that kept her coming back again and again. He'd touch her, kiss her, and she'd close her eyes and pretend she didn't know what kind of man phoned you for a booty call while your father was on life support fighting for his life and his wife was out of town visiting her sick mother. Pretend she didn't know what kind of woman that made her.

But with each interlude her postcoital clarity revealed more and more about the man to whom she was giving her body. And the more she saw of him, the more she realized he was honestly and truly a bad person. Not that that was absolving herself, mind you. But she was doing something bad, she wasn't actually a bad person. There was a difference, no matter how minute.

Therefore, his reaction wasn't so much of a shock as it was sadly predictable. Of course he wouldn't help her when she needed it. Like a lot of men, Neveah was slowly realizing that Chauncey regarded his partner in adultery with contempt. Well, that was fine, she was learning to regard him the exact same way.

She walked to the door. "I'm beginning to think I'm too smart for a lot of things."

CHAPTER EIGHT

Roman pulled into the parking lot of the Save-U-Moore convenience store and killed the engine. The dusk-to-dawn security lights were just coming alive one by one like fireflies. Roman got out and went inside.

He walked up and down the aisles and was mildly shocked at how little they had changed since he was a kid. There was still more malt liquor than water or fruit juice in the coolers. The candy and cookie racks were overflowing, while the bread shelves were coated with dust. Roman thought when folks talked about a food desert, what they really meant was that the food available wasn't any good. Instead of a desert, he thought of it like an ocean. All that water, but if you drank from it you would die. Little stores like this were the flotsam and jetsam in an ocean of junk.

He was only in there to grab a can of biscuits and some cheese. He already had the ground beef and the tomato sauce. He was going to make Neveah and Dante an old favorite from their teenage years. Cheeseburger casserole. It was a fairly simple recipe he'd gotten from the back of a Hamburger Helper box. His parents never explicitly said he was going to have to be responsible for his siblings. It became an expected duty. When the children got home from school there was no food waiting, and so Roman would be the cook. Often when they woke up there was no breakfast, for the same reason. He remembered how it seemed like his folks were both married to the crematory more than to each other. It took up so much space in their lives it felt like there were times it left little room for them to be parents.

Roman put the biscuits and the block of cheese on the counter. A young brother with cornrows started to ring him up without asking if he found everything he needed, for which Roman was silently grateful. Whoever had done the kid's hair was a talented hairdresser. There was an S-wave pattern to the cornrows that Neveah had never been able to master when she'd do his hair back in the day.

"Roman Carruthers, that you?" a ragged voice from the shadows said. Roman watched as Leslie Moore, the owner of Save-U-Moore, came shuffling up to the counter with a walker. His dark skin appeared almost blue under the overhead lights.

"Yes sir, how are you?" Roman asked.

Leslie grinned, showing two rows of yellowed teeth.

"They never did find your mama, did they? Bet your daddy killed her and spread her ashes in the river," Leslie said before turning around and shuffling back to the darkness behind the counter.

"My granddaddy got Alzheimer's pretty bad. He don't mean nothing by what he say," the young brother said. Roman paid for his food and left the store without responding.

When he got in the rental, he started the car and turned the radio all the way up until the bass made his ears hurt. He lay back and closed his eyes. He took deep breaths, deep from his core, and expelled them through his nose. It was a technique he'd picked up when he was doing yoga three times a week before his firm really took off. He'd been gone from this town so long he had let his guard down. He forgot how the disappearance of Bonita Carruthers was still the most infamous story in Jefferson Run. Never mind the violence in the streets, the hundreds of murders as gangs rose, then fell, in their bid to control Jefferson Run's criminal subculture. Forget the cheating scandals at Prosser State, or the utter incompetence of the city council when it came to bringing legitimate business to Jefferson Run; the disappearance of Bonita Carruthers and the possible involvement of her husband was still the main topic of conversation even for someone with dementia.

Because the kid hadn't asked who Roman's mother was, had he? He hadn't asked what his doddering old grandfather was talking about, had he? Roman's mother had moved from infamy to legend. She was the Bigfoot of Jefferson Run. The Cropsey of High Point Street. He understood it in an intellectual way. His father had never moved. The police had never been able to pin his mother's disappearance on Keith. She was Roman's mother, but she was Jefferson Run's ghost. Their phantom that they called upon when there was a lull in the gossip or a sermon went on too long.

He could hear them in his mind.

Remember Bonita Carruthers?

Wasn't she sleeping with Oscar Conley?

I mean, if it was me I'd burn her ass up too.

Roman sighed.

Memory is a powerful thing. It's a spirit we willingly call upon to whisper lies or help us punish ourselves. For the people of Jefferson Run, remembering Bonita Carruthers was their hobby. For him it was his penance.

"What you cooking up in here?" Neveah asked.

Roman was standing by the stove sipping some more of his daddy's good scotch while he waited to pull the cheeseburger casserole out of the oven. Dante was asleep on the couch. Neveah got a can of soda out of the double-door refrigerator and leaned against the counter.

"Making a cheeseburger casserole for dinner, unless you had plans," Roman said. He sipped his scotch. He watched his sister take a long swig of soda. She loved to drink from an ice-cold can but didn't like ice cubes in her drinks. Roman thought it was funny how the most random insignificant things burrowed into your brain when it was about your family. Especially when it was about your siblings.

"Nah, I don't have plans. But I can't believe you still know how to make that. I figured you eat out seven days a week down in Georgia," Neveah said. She set her can on the counter.

"I advise my clients to cook at home as much as they can. You spend all your money at Ruth's Chris, you gonna eventually be asking for a job application there," Roman said.

For the briefest of moments he saw it. A real smile on his sister's face. The first one he had seen since he'd landed. It appeared and disappeared so quickly he thought she must have surprised herself.

"Before we wake up Dante and he eats half the damn casserole in one bite, I want to talk to you," Neveah said.

"Okay."

"I went to the cops. They didn't seem that interested, because neither one of you reported getting jumped. But I know somebody down there and they told me they were gonna ask around," Neveah said.

"I appreciate that," Roman said.

Neveah pinched the bridge of her nose.

"Rome, I know it might not seem like it to you, but I ain't stupid. Me and Daddy have walked out the shop at three A.M. on a Saturday night when High Point Street was going off like Chinese New Year, and ain't nobody ever jumped us. Because nobody in the street thinks a crematory got money like that. So why don't you tell me what really happened before D wakes up? Because it ain't a coincidence that the tires got slashed, Daddy got run off the road, and you and D got fucked all the way up."

"Neveah, I'm telling you the truth. Dante stopped by, he helped me clean up, then when we walked out we got jumped. They wanted our wallets, but I don't carry cash and D didn't have but a twenty. They got D's debit card and my Amex. Now, he had some other stuff on him, I think it was Molly. They didn't believe us when we said that was all we had, and they flipped out. That Molly was why Dante didn't want to go to the cops. I swear that's all there is to it."

"Ever since we was little, you do this thing where you stare the person you lying to in the eyes. Like you doing now," Neveah said. "Dante is involved in something. Something that almost got you and Daddy killed. Talk to me, Rome. Let me help. Tell me what's going on before they take more than your teeth or his fingers."

Roman dropped his eyes. He studied the pattern of the porcelain tile in the kitchen.

"I swear, Neveah. That's what happened."

Neveah let out a long sigh. "No, it's not. But you not gonna tell me. That's another thing I know about you. Once you've made up your mind about something, not even an act of Congress can get you to change it. Wake Dante up. I'll get the food out the oven. I'm hungry and tired and I just don't have the energy to argue with you about why you lying to me."

"Neveah, I swear—"

"Stop! Stop saying that. Stop talking to me like I'm stupid. I don't know if you noticed, but the shop is my whole life! I don't hardly have any real friends. I don't have a real man. It's all I've got. You and Daddy and Dante saw to that. So, if Dante has gotten into something that puts that in jeopardy, I should know about it. You know, Daddy does this same shit. Oh, I'm qualified to do the books or help throw a body in the oven, but when it comes to the 'serious' issues, he doesn't let me in on it. Doesn't want to trouble my pretty little head too much. I've learned to expect that from him. Hell, I've learned to expect that from most men. I just didn't think I'd have to deal with that from my own brother," Neveah said. She opened the oven door and pulled the casserole dish out bare-handed before slamming it on the range top.

"Don't do that! Get an oven mitt or something!" Roman said. He rushed to her and grabbed her hands.

"I've been working those ovens at the shop for a long time, big brother. I don't have much feeling in the tips of my fingers. They been dead for years," Neveah said. She pulled away from Roman and started grabbing plates from the cupboard.

Roman felt like there were things he should say, but he wasn't sure if they'd widen the gulf between him and Neveah or close the crevasse that existed between them.

In the end, he chose silence. That was the only way to be sure he didn't say the wrong thing.

———

After dinner as he lay in his old bed, Roman got a text from Khalil.

> Just landed. Want me to come to the house?
> Or get up tomorrow?

Roman texted back.

> Tomorrow. Got a lot to go over.

> k. hey got the email, the thing went thru

> Good.

Roman put his phone back in his pocket. That email meant Khalil had gotten in touch with Sasha Billings. Sasha was another financial adviser he knew who dealt exclusively in high-yield cryptocurrencies that she could pump up, then dump, with the quiet alacrity of a practiced broker who lived on the outer edges of the new financial Wild West. He didn't like dealing with her unless one of his clients found themselves in a situation where they had an exorbitant fiduciary surplus that needed to be "refreshed."

Money laundering were dirty words in the circles he ran in.

He kept an open account with a hundred thousand dollars in it at her firm. A sort of escrow under a corporate name that couldn't be traced back to him or his clients. When he asked for the "full treatment," that meant she would take all that money and buy a really strong stock that was prime to be pumped-up. Then she'd help him dump it. He always thought that would be his final contingency plan if things went south with his firm or one of his clients did something so illegal and fiscally irresponsible he'd have to start over. It was his own personal fail-safe procedure.

Last night he had failed. And until he fixed it, no one was safe.

CHAPTER NINE

R ome, wake up."

Roman opened his eyes slowly. He saw Dante standing in the doorway to his bedroom holding a phone. The pale green light from the phone's screen lit up his face.

"What?"

"It's Torrent. He wants us to meet . . . there," Dante said.

Roman sat up and swung his legs around until his feet touched the cool wood floor. He took the phone from Dante. "Hello?"

"Time to fulfill part of your promise, homie. Meet two of my boys at your place. Twenty minutes," Torrent said.

The line went dead.

"What does he want, Rome?"

Roman stood. "Get the car, Dante."

They didn't speak on their way to the crematory. Roman drove Dante's Challenger through the cracked streets of Jefferson Run with the grim determination of an executioner making his way to the gallows. He tried to mentally prepare himself for what was waiting for him and Dante at the shop. Some enemy of the Black Baron Boys wrapped in a blood-soaked sheet. Some mother's son, some father's child, who would never see another sunrise or breathe the fresh air that seemed so unique to the Old Dominion.

"Everything burns," Roman murmured.

When he pulled up to the shop, there were two cars waiting with their parking lights on, casting weird shadows across the pavement and past the pavement into the trees that stood sentry over this part of Jefferson Run. One was the old-school ride with the big rims. The other was a hyper-stylized Honda Accord with an obnoxiously large spoiler and smoked-out windows and glittering chrome rims.

Roman parked the car in the front parking lot. When he got out, the drivers of the two cars exited as well. One was Yellaboy and the other was Splodie.

"Cut off your parking lights. Don't need the cops stopping by because they got curious about why there are so many cars here," Roman said. Splodie and Yellaboy complied. Roman unlocked the main entry and walked through the shop to the rear garage door, with Dante on his heels like a lost puppy.

When he got to the garage door, he unlocked it using Dante's keys and rolled it up. Yellaboy and Splodie went to their respective trunks and, after some struggle, emerged from behind the raised lids with two figures.

Two live figures with pillowcases on their heads.

Yellaboy and Splodie hustled them through the roll-up door, while Roman, despite his shock at seeing two alive-and-kicking individuals, hurriedly brought the door down behind them. Once the door was closed, the two individuals were pushed to the floor as Yellaboy and Splodie stood over them.

Roman walked around the gangsters and their charges and stood next to Dante. He could feel his brother trembling as if his spasms were affecting the air currents between them.

"How you do it? Do you just throw them in the stove?" Yellaboy asked.

"This . . . this isn't what we agreed to," Roman said. He let each word hang in the air for a moment before he let another one escape his lips.

"Yeah, Torrent thought you might say that. That's why he had us bring 'em like this. He wants you to get dirty on this. He said something about you getting dirty so you can't rat on us later," Splodie said. Roman was trying to think, trying to calculate his way out of this. He wouldn't have the rest of Torrent and Tranquil's money until he talked to Khalil. When he was lying on the floor bleeding, he had never even considered the possibility that giving Torrent and Tranquil access to the shop to eradicate their enemies would entail said enemies walking through the door. He'd just assumed they would be bringing a body, not a person. His father always emphasized the difference.

"A body is just the meat and bones. By the time they get to us, the person they used to be is long gone," Keith would say when they rolled a box into the oven. Even when they had to put his friend Donny Riggs on the rollers.

The idea of the living coming to this place to be incinerated was so far removed from his understanding, it was like a wolf not considering a trap would grab his paw.

"What? Why would I snitch? I'm trying to work for you, trying to pay off my brother's debt," Roman said. He was careful not to say he wanted to work *with* the Black Baron Boys. He'd learned the weight of words with these boys when he watched his teeth skittering across the floor.

"I don't know. Motherfuckers snitch for all kinds of reasons. Anyway, Torrent said for you to do these two," Yellaboy said as he pulled out his phone and looked at it. For one gut-churning moment, Roman thought he was going to record the murder of these two people, but instead he just typed a message and put the phone back in his pocket.

"You got this? I gotta dip," Yellaboy said to Splodie.

"Yeah, I got this, but . . . man, you better watch yourself. I know where you going. I hope it's worth it," Splodie said.

Yellaboy stared at him.

"Sorry."

"When it's done, text me," Yellaboy said.

He gestured to Roman and Dante.

"They bitch out, Torrent said to cancel them."

"I got it, but . . ." Splodie said. He and Yellaboy had a silent conversation before Splodie turned his head away and Yellaboy nodded.

"All right. Holla at me," Yellaboy said. He went to the roll-up door, raised it, exited, then rolled it back down behind him.

Splodie pulled the pillowcases off of the two figures on their knees.

"Oh my God," Dante whimpered. He stumbled against Roman. Roman had to put his arm around Dante's waist to keep him from falling over.

There was a white boy with white-boy dreads on his knees in front of Roman. His face was a Jackson Pollock painting of blood and bruises. Next to him was a woman who might have been Latina or mixed, Roman wasn't sure. They both had duct tape on their mouths and their wrists were bound in front of them.

"That's Getty and Cassidy," Dante whispered to Roman.

Roman stiffened.

"Hey, just so you know, this white boy tried to throw you under the bus. Said you stole the product from him and he didn't know what you did with it. Just saying," Splodie said.

"Why'd you bring the girl?" Roman asked. He tried to keep his voice as nonchalant as Splodie's seemed to be at this moment.

"Nigga, she was there. She saw us snatch him up. Torrent said both of them gotta go. He don't like people playing in his face," Splodie said.

Roman looked at Getty. Getty's eyes were wide and rimmed in red. There was a bruise on his left temple the size of a fifty-cent piece. Tears ran down his cheeks and splayed over the duct tape over his mouth like diverted rivers. He was talking or trying to talk behind the tape. The way he was shaking his dreads told Roman he was probably trying to say, *No, please don't kill me.*

Roman had a feeling that wasn't an option.

Splodie raised his football jersey and pulled a gun out of his waistband. Roman didn't know a lot about guns, but it was big and silver and looked like it might be a semiautomatic. It resembled Jules's gun from *Pulp Fiction.*

"You gonna do this, man? Or do I have to put in some work?" Splodie asked.

Roman took his arm from around Dante's waist. He licked his lips. He felt like he might be sick again. He dealt in numbers, equations. Were there times when his mathematical manipulations caused someone to be erased from the census? Did he make money appear and disappear for folks who regularly buried people in the woods surrounding Stone Mountain? Yes and yes, but this was different. There was a distance that was unique to his position that shielded him from the ugliness that was drawn to wealth like flies to piles of shit. Numbers didn't beg for their lives.

Roman's eyes darted from side to side. His father had a gun in the office, but he couldn't see himself actually putting the gun to Getty's head and pulling the trigger. There was a crowbar and hammer on the tool chest to his right. There were a few rolls of duct tape similar to the strip on Getty's mouth on the work desk where the funnel and bone grinder sat covered in ashes. He could maybe put a strip over Getty's nose, but as soon as the thought entered his head he knew he didn't have the fortitude to stand there and watch a grown man suffocate.

He turned his back on Splodie and put his hands on Dante's shoulders.

"It's him or us. You hear me? It's him or us," he said in a low harsh murmur.

"What about Cassidy?" Dante said. He had his head down and spoke into his chest.

"We can talk to him about that, but either way, Getty's not walking out of here. You know that, right? Little brother, it's him or us." Roman put two fingers under Dante's chin and raised his head. "I choose us."

He turned back to face Splodie.

"Help us get a cremation box down off the rack here," Roman said. Splodie grunted but put his gun back in his waistband. Roman, Splodie, and Dante grabbed a flat, heavy cardboard square from the short cantilever racks in the corner. Then Dante and Roman went about folding it and snapping the cardboard tabs into small slots until the flat piece of cardboard became a long rectangle box.

"Let's put him in," Roman said.

"I can't. I can't do it, Rome. I know he double-crossed me and lied to me, but I can't do it," Dante said.

"You ain't gonna pop him first? Damn, nigga, that's cold," Splodie said with a laugh.

"Him. Or. Us," Roman said.

Dante shook his head.

"Okay. It's okay," Roman said.

He took several deep breaths until he thought he might start hyperventilating, and then he went to Getty and grabbed him from behind under his arms. The man was shockingly light. He started dragging him to the box that was sitting on the body lift. He'd lowered the lift until it was almost on the floor. Getty started to fight, kicking his feet and trying to twist his way out of Roman's grip, but until recently, Roman was working out four times a week. He gripped Getty's T-shirt and in one swift movement he pulled him up and dumped him in the box. When Getty tried to sit up, Roman punched him in the nose. He felt something give way in the man's face as he fell back against the bottom of the box. He sat up again and Roman hit him again, harder this time, throwing all his weight into the blow. Getty fell backward into the crate. He moaned from someplace in the back of his throat and struggled to sit up again. Roman, nearly crying, hit him again and again until Getty stopped moaning, stopped moving, and was still.

Roman flexed his hand. Blood decorated his knuckles. He hadn't thrown a punch in years. Not since he'd caught up with Lomello Green three years after he'd been hit in the face with that forty. But his body didn't forget how to deliver the blow.

Roman grabbed the cardboard lid of the cremation box and, quick as a cat, he ran a heavy strip of duct tape around the box and under it at the foot and the head and the middle, securing it in place. Without saying a word, he raised the platform of the body lift and pushed it up to the oven entrance. He raised the door and then he pushed the box off the lift onto the rollers that carried it into the yawning maw. He moved the lift and pulled the door down until it locked. He stared through the heat-treated tempered glass window in the door.

He's unconscious, he thought. I knocked him out. I knocked him out. He closed his eyes tight.

He opened his eyes and walked around to the control panel and laid his hand on the ignition switch. It had a large green plastic cap over it that would glow from the small light bulb inside it when he pushed it and lit the flames that would bring the oven to life.

Roman looked at Dante. He was leaning against the wall with his head down again. Dante, who as a kid cried when their dad killed a copperhead in the backyard.

For all his faults, Dante was a good person.

Roman thought he was a good person too.

Maybe he was wrong. But did it make you a bad person if you did a horrific thing for a good reason? Like saving your brother's life?

He swallowed hard.

Then he pushed the button.

The flames came alive with a whoosh that sounded like a dragon breathing fire over a doomed village. As the flames engulfed the crate, the sound of thunderous kicking erupted from inside the oven.

Roman covered his mouth with the back of his hand and took a step backward. He thought he could hear Getty screaming.

Cassidy, who until this point had seemed to be catatonic, hopped up and took two running steps toward the back door before Splodie backhanded her, almost absentmindedly. She collapsed to the floor in a heap of long black hair and long legs.

"You wanna get a box for this bitch too?" Splodie asked.

Roman was about to answer when he noticed Dante was standing behind Splodie. He couldn't remember seeing him move off the wall, but now he was standing behind Splodie holding something in his good hand.

Splodie must have felt him there, because he'd started to turn when Dante hit him in the head with the ball-peen hammer from the tool chest. The sound of the stainless-steel head of the hammer cracking against Splodie's skull was a dull thud that seemed muted, softer than Roman would have imagined. Splodie went down to one knee while simultaneously trying to reach for his gun. Dante hit him again. Harder this time, across the back of his head. Blood flew up and landed on Dante's face. Splodie fell face-first onto the concrete. A crimson pool began to envelope his head even as the sounds from the oven ceased.

Roman felt like he was frozen in place.

Dante dropped the hammer. He blinked his eyes, flecks of blood dripping down his face. "I couldn't let him do it. Make you do it. Not to her," he said as he shook his head side to side.

Would Roman have done it? Would he have burned this girl alive, whose only crime was dating a man who didn't understand that he was chum swimming with sharks?

Roman decided he didn't want to answer that question.

CHAPTER TEN

The glow from the fire of the ovens bathed the three of them in a harsh orange light that flowed through the specially treated view windows. They had stood there in front of the ovens for an hour as the flames devoured both Getty and Splodie with avaricious abandon. Dante had his arm around Cassidy, holding her close in a way that Roman thought was too tender to be the first time.

It seemed like Getty had screamed for hours before he finally, mercifully, went quiet. Dante had covered Cassidy's ears, but she cried all the same. Great wailing sobs that echoed through the oven room like a banshee's call. Roman thought the heat must have made the tape melt. He didn't understand how Getty had been able to scream that long. He should have run out of air long before then. Maybe it hadn't been ten minutes. Maybe it had only felt like it. He knew he'd hear those screams endlessly in his dreams.

At the hour-and-a-half mark, Roman had turned up the heat past the regulatory parameters set forth by the state, to speed up the process. The ovens roared like demons who stood sentry at the gates of hell.

We'll see hell one day, he thought. We'll march right down to those gates.

There was a pathway open to him that he could follow that would allow him to assuage his guilt with false piety. They had saved Cassidy. They had saved themselves, for the moment. If Roman let himself walk down that road, then the horrors of tonight would just become the latest in a long collection of terrible deeds done for the greater good that he had to force down into a deep, dank hole in his heart.

But he thought he was running out of room in that particular crypt.

"He didn't get jacked," Cassidy said quietly.

"What?" Dante asked.

"He didn't get jacked. He sold it, the Molly. He said he cut it or something and sold it for double. He just didn't want to share," Cassidy said.

Color me surprised, Roman thought. But maybe knowing that Getty had betrayed him would make the shock waves of this night a little easier for Dante, and for a moment Roman was deeply grateful.

Cassidy speaking seemed to break the collective spell of paralysis they'd all been enthralled in since Roman had locked the second oven's door.

He turned and faced her and Dante.

"Cassidy, it's time for you to leave," Roman said.

"Rome, she's been through a lot. We been through a lot. Can you wait a minute?" Dante said.

Roman squeezed his fists. "Dante, she has to go. We have to clean this up and she has to get on the road and get far away. Now. Right now."

"Get on the road?" Cassidy asked. Roman looked at her, and he felt a hitch in his chest as he studied her naïve eyes. She had no idea what was happening to her. She looked like a doe in the eye of a hurricane. She didn't ask for this, but now they were all inexorably tied to a millstone that could drag them to their graves.

"Cassidy, they're going to think you're dead. You should be dead, if not for what Dante did. You have to leave town. Tonight. Now. Or they'll kill us all. You have to leave and you can't ever come back," Roman said. He spoke softly, but with resolve. He needed her to understand how precarious their situation was at this moment, and for all the moments in the future.

"But . . . my mom, I gotta talk to my mom . . . I can't just leave," Cassidy said.

"Rome, she can at least go talk to her mom," Dante said.

"So they can roll up on her mom and ask her where she is? How you think that's gonna go? Or did you forget about your finger?" Roman put both his hands on Cassidy's shoulders.

She was trembling.

"Was you gonna burn me up like that?" she whispered.

"No," Roman said, and in his soul he thought he meant it. "But you gotta go. I'm gonna give you some money. I took Splodie's keys out his pockets. You gonna take his car. You can use your phone for now, but you need to get somewhere far away and get a new phone. Don't contact anyone; don't call your mom. Don't use your ID. Get a job waiting tables or something. Get paid under the table. I'm going to give you my number. You get a new phone, you call me and I'll help you start a new identity. But that's for later. Right now you have to leave," he said.

She looked from him to Dante.

"D, what . . . do I have to go?" Cassidy asked. Dante looked past her to Roman. They locked eyes, and in that entwined gaze they had a silent conversation.

Dante pulled her away from Roman and hugged her tight.

"He's right. They'll kill us all if they find out you're alive. You just get out of town. We'll stay in touch. Tell you when it's safe to come back," Dante whispered in her ear. He stared at Roman the entire time he spoke. Roman gave him a look when he mentioned Cassidy coming back, but he didn't contradict him now. That would have to come later, when they were alone. If they were able to get her into Splodie's car before someone from the Black Baron Boys saw them and decided to relieve them of their gray matter.

"Okay. If you say so. I'll go," Cassidy whispered.

They walked her out to Splodie's car. Roman gave her a thousand dollars from the petty cash box in the office. He made a mental note to replace it before Neveah found out it was missing.

Cassidy got in the driver's side and Dante closed the door for her. She started Splodie's car, and powder-blue running lights came up from the undercarriage. Cassidy lowered the window and Dante dropped to his haunches.

"You get far away, okay? Then you get a new throwaway phone and you call me. Let me know you're safe," Dante said. He leaned through the window and kissed her on the forehead.

"Don't tell anybody about what happened here. Just keep quiet and keep to yourself. It's going to be all right. We'll get you some more money soon," Roman said. He thought about the idea of relativity. At work he moved around millions of dollars, shuffling huge amounts from one account to another. Hiding, combining, dividing more money than some people made in their entire lives. And now his life depended on ensuring that a naïve girl had just enough cash to eke out an existence for the foreseeable future.

"Who am I gonna tell?" Cassidy asked.

"Why don't you get on 95 and head to D.C. for right now? They got cheap hotels in Chinatown. We'll talk soon, okay?" Roman said.

Cassidy nodded. Dante kissed her on the forehead again, and then she raised the window. They watched as she backed up, turned, and headed out of the parking lot and onto the street. The taillights of the Honda blinked once when she came to the end of the street, then disappeared as she turned right and headed out of the industrial park and toward the I-95 exit. The wind came up and stirred debris in the street into little dust devils. Sandwich wrappers, old flyers for long-defunct clubs, stray packing materials, all danced in the pale moonlight for an audience of two.

"You think she gonna keep her mouth shut?" Roman asked.

"Like she said, who she gonna tell?" Dante said.

"You think she gonna stay away?" Roman said.

"The only person she got is her mom, now that Getty's . . . gone," Dante said.

Roman sighed. "Let's go back inside. We have to finish it."

They scraped the ashes out of the collection bins and then bagged them up in one bag, which he dumped in the hazardous-waste bin in the back of the oven room. He and Dante got a bucket and two mops and cleaned up the blood from Splodie's head wound. They worked quietly if not efficiently. Dante kept dropping his mop. When they finally got up the blood, they dumped the water in the bucket down the drain in the maintenance closet. Roman opened the oven doors to let them cool while Dante rinsed off the mops.

It was like Splodie and Getty had never walked through the door.

"Let's go home," Roman said.

"I'm not going home right now. I need to go . . . do something," Dante said.

Roman took a deep breath. "You can't go out getting high. Not tonight. We need to go home and stay there. You get high, and one of Torrent's boys see you, and then you panic or you talk—"

"Do you think I would really say anything about tonight to *them*? Fuck me, I wouldn't do that to you or Cassidy. I do need to get high. And drunk, and then maybe I'll get some cough medicine. I just can't go with all this in my head. I can't. I killed a guy. I killed a guy, Rome. I can't close my eyes tonight with this in my head," Dante said. He was breathing fast and shallow.

"I didn't say you would tell on purpose. Let's just go home. I know Pop got another bottle around there somewhere. You don't need to be alone tonight," Roman said.

I don't want to be alone tonight either, he thought.

Dante shook his head. "Ain't gonna cut it, big brother. You take the Challenger. I'm gonna get an Uber. I need to get out of here. This fucking place. I hate this fucking place! Goddamn it! I hate it!" He rushed past Roman, but Roman grabbed his arm. Dante twisted from his grip in a shocking display of strength and headed for the lobby and then went out the door.

Roman stood in the center of the oven room, breathing harder and harder. He closed his eyes. He felt like his heart was going a hundred miles per hour. He ran his tongue over his new implants.

"This is not who you are. This is not who you are. You're going to get them out of this and then you're going to go home to Atlanta and forget all about this. This isn't your home anymore. This is just a place where your family lives. This is not who you are. This is not who you are," he whispered.

He said the phrase again and again as he turned off the lights and headed for the car. When he got outside he looked for Dante, but his brother was already gone. All he saw were the sodium arc lights of the junkyard down the street, the swinging traffic lights at the intersection, and the last of the dancing detritus in the gutter. He thought about his father's favorite saying and how his father was wrong. Not everything burns.

Some things end up in the gutter where they belong.

CHAPTER ELEVEN

B y the time Roman pulled into the driveway, the sun was coming up over the back corner of the house, sluicing through the trees like water coming through a sieve. He climbed the steps up the porch and found himself in his old bed before instantly falling asleep.

He dreamed of his mother.

Her face floated in front of him like an untethered balloon. It moved just out his reach. In the dream he could see his hand, and it was the hand of his sixteen-year-old self, thin fingers, soft palms. Her face was so close, just a hairbreadth away from his fingertips.

In his dream she smiled at him. Smiled at him and said something, but it was indistinct. She said it again, and then she said his name.

"Rome, my summer child."

Then he woke up.

He walked downstairs and tried to find some coffee in the cabinets. Instant or some beans, he didn't really care, either would suffice. He checked his watch. It was just a little past ten. He heard the stairs creak, and then Neveah appeared like a wraith by his side.

"Dante didn't come home. Where'd you two go after dinner?" Neveah asked.

"Went to have another drink together. Catching up for lost time, I guess. Then he met some girl and dipped. I stayed, drank more than I should have, and then I came home and crashed," Roman lied. The ease with which that lie ran out of his mouth shocked him, but he told himself it was all in service to a greater good. Keeping Neveah far away from this rotting morass he and Dante found themselves swimming in.

It was enough that he and Dante had blood on their hands. Neveah didn't need those same stains on the tips of her dead fingers.

"You gonna be a damn drunk if you keep hanging out with Dante every night," Neveah said as she reached over his shoulder and pulled down a box of instant coffee. She moved around him and grabbed a kettle. She filled it with water and set it on a burner on the stove, then leaned against the counter. Her stance was so similar to Dante's, Roman felt his throat knot up for a moment. They were all more alike in their unconscious movements and actions than most people outside the family would ever realize. The way they laughed, the way they leaned against a counter, the way they chewed their food. Last night, eating dinner, he noticed how they all sipped a drink after taking a bite of the casserole, to help them swallow. Ancestry stretched marionette strings down through a genera-tion of couplings, of sighs, of long winter days and champagne Saturday nights, to make them move with unpracticed synchronicity.

Their family tree had deep roots that bound them all together in its grip.

"I'm gonna be okay. Been a minute since me and Dante got to hang, even if it's like this. And, just for the record, you get to ask us where we been, but we can't ask you nothing? Is that how it works, because I want to make a note in the family handbook," Roman said. He smiled at his sister, who shook her head.

"Okay, I deserve that, but I didn't come home with stitches in my face or missing a finger. I'm not going to get in it with you this morning, but whatever is going on with you two, it's got something to do with Daddy. You can go ahead and tell me now, or just wait till I figure it out. And I will figure it out," Neveah said.

Roman knew that she was right. Eventually she might figure out what he and Dante were doing with the Black Baron Boys. But not be-fore he figured out how to extricate them from this hornet's nest Dante had put them in.

"Ain't nothing to figure out, I'm telling you. Anyway, what you got going on today? Only a few bodies left in the cooler. You gonna need help with that?"

"I always need help. You want to come in a little later after your hangover eases up? You can man the office while I go up to Richmond. Gotta pay the license fee today, and I do it in person because during Covid it got lost once and that was all kinds of hell to get straight," she said.

"I can do that. Say I get there by one?" he said.

"Yeah, that works."

Neveah lowered her chin and then raised her head and stared at the ceiling. "So, I'm friends with this cop named Chauncey. He might want to talk to you about what happened with you and Dante, and before you say 'Nothing,' he just wants to ask around, see if he might be able to help. You gonna have to file a report if you want him to do something official. This would just be an informal kind of thing," she said.

Roman's chest went tight. The last thing he needed was a cop coming around and talking to him at a murder scene that just happened to be his family's business.

"I mean, he don't really need to worry about it," Roman said, and immediately regretted it.

"Rome, are you and Dante doing something illegal? Because that's what people doing illegal shit say about talking to the cops. And don't give that shit that 'we Black and we don't talk to cops,' because I guarantee if somebody in Atlanta stole your Porsche you'd be running down a meter maid to help you out if she could," Neveah said.

He shifted gears. "No, we ain't doing anything illegal. It's just . . . look, I think Dante was messing with somebody's girlfriend or wife, and . . . it's just . . . I ain't trying to kick that hornet's nest. Not saying I wouldn't like to see them fuckers that jumped us get what's coming to them, but the cops don't really seem to have a handle on things here in town and, well, what if them boys figure out we pointed the finger at them? Look what they already did. Me and Dante ain't Omar and Stringer Bell," Roman said. He watched Neveah's face pinch up like a raisin when he unspooled this tall tale.

"You really think it was a jealous husband?" she asked.

"Or boyfriend. Dante likes to play with fire," Roman said.

The teakettle began to whistle.

"I'm going to go get ready for work," Neveah said. She didn't wait for Roman to respond before she stomped back up the stairs.

Roman called Khalil.

"Veni, vidi, vici," Khalil said when he answered the phone.

"Hey, man, I'm gonna text you my pop's address. Can you come over around five? I want to lay some things out for you and get your opinion. You got that thing from Ms. Billings?" Roman asked.

"Negro, I ain't doing nothing but sightseeing and waiting. And, yeah, I got that thing. I'm at the Edgar Allan Poe Museum right now. Did you know he married his cousin? Was that why he always looked so sad?"

"Probably because she died young," Roman said.

"Damn. He looked creepy and had bad luck. He didn't have no choice but to write scary stories. Yeah, shoot me them deets and I'll meet at *el numero cinco*," Khalil said.

"All right, talk to you then."

"Bet," Khalil said, and hung up.

One of his girlfriends had described Roman as a habitual problem solver. His mentor at the firm he worked for before he opened his own business, Emil Sarlentanias, an Armenian economist, had called him a crow.

"You're funny and slick, but you're constantly watching, constantly learning, always ready for an opportunity. Like a crow."

He'd learned a few things about the BBB and how they operated the last few days. They were the problem he needed to solve. He had a few ideas, but he wanted to run them by Khalil.

Roman knew money.

Khalil knew strategy.

With those two things, you could put a crack in any foundation.

CHAPTER TWELVE

Dante woke up.

He was disappointed that all that oxy he'd done didn't take him to the great hereafter. His mother was there. He wanted his mother. No, scratch that. He wanted his mommy. He wanted her to hold him close. To say he wasn't an abject failure. To lie and say he wasn't a perpetual disappointment.

But apparently today wasn't the day for a one-way trip to the ether.

He pushed himself off the couch he was sleeping on and sat up. Last night after . . . everything, he'd gotten a ride out to the Skids. There was a white boy named Tug who lived there in a double-wide that served as a trap house, party spot, and general den of iniquity. He lived with his girlfriend Raynell, who was related to Torrent and Tranquil through their aunt. She'd been the egress through which he and Getty had walked into the worst mistake of their lives.

When he'd arrived last night, he wasn't greeted as an exile as he'd expected. Apparently his status as a debtor to the most dangerous two men in the city hadn't scared off his drinking buddies. They asked what happened to his finger, he lied about it, and they moved on to more pressing matters. He came in and bought six oxys, drank them down with a bottle of cheap malt liquor, and to complete the trifecta of stereotypical bad behavior, he had sex with Raynell's friend Dulsi while the rest of Tug's guests played video games on his big-screen television.

Just as he was about to put it in, he stopped himself long enough to realize he needed a condom. When he questioned Dulsi about procuring one, she had giggled.

"Just pull out. It's okay. I wouldn't mind having a Carruthers baby," she had squealed.

He'd almost crawled away from her. A Carruthers baby. Even out here among thieves and addicts and the beasts of ill repute, he wasn't Dante. He was just a Carruthers, just a scion for what passed for wealth in this part of the Old Dominion. Not a person, no, never that, just a means to an end. A rope bridge from poverty to prosperity by way of his seed.

For a moment he actually thought he was going to grow a bit of self-respect, but then he sank himself into her and felt her body quiver, felt her wetness splash across him, felt her teeth bite into his shoulder. Felt himself do what he did best and give in.

He pushed himself off the couch and rose to his full height. He didn't remember getting dressed and leaving the bed he'd shared with Dulsi, but he must have, because he was back in his boots and his pants and his hoodie. He ran one hand through his hair, then stared at his other hand, the one that was short a pinkie, and grimaced. The oxy must still be in his system, because he couldn't feel the stump throbbing. When he and Getty had first gotten that big bag of brown from the BBB, he'd imagined flipping it and making enough money to pay his car off and rub it in his daddy's face. He didn't want to be Pablo Escobar, he just wanted to show up his daddy. Prove he didn't have to suckle at his teat. Show him that he could do something on his own. Wash the taste of his father's sacrifices out of his mouth.

Now Getty was ashes and he was missing a finger and his brother was tied to him like the last men on a sinking ship lashed to the sail's mast.

"Hey, you up?" Tug said. He was still playing video games, while everybody else was still passed out like mannequins in various states of distress. Arms and legs all akimbo on his ratty sectional sofa that sat at a right angle to the couch. Dante thought he'd probably been up all night. His eyes had the red death stare of a connoisseur of the best meth available in J-Run. He was manipulating a controller with practiced dexterity.

"Yeah, man. I'm 'bout to bounce. Appreciate you letting me come over."

"Always welcome, brother. Can't say the same for Getty, though."

"Huh?" Dante was suddenly wide awake and alert like a gazelle at a watering hole.

"Getty, man. Streets saying he's a snitch. Somebody saw Johnny Law at his house last night. Word is it look like he got run up on. Door was knocked down, and cops was snooping around," Tug said, as he put a little body English on the shot he took in the video game.

"Huh, well, that don't mean he a snitch. Cops was investigating?" Dante said. He felt like he was going to hyperventilate.

"Yeah, but they trying to act like they ain't. Only thing, you know Jamir Paige? Anyway, he was in lockup, and when they came back to the station they was complaining about a CI going missing. Jamir got out this morning and been telling anybody who listen that the CI gotta be Getty. Like they had four squad cars and two detectives at his place. When the last time that many cops came out for a missing white boy with dreads? Nah, Jamir swear it's true. That's good enough for me," Tug said.

"Man, that's crazy. I just talked to him last night. He was talking about going farther down South, like maybe Georgia or Alabama," Dante lied. The lie appeared in his mind crystal-clear and unbidden, but here it was, so he decided to use it.

"If he know what's good for him, he won't never come back. He was always shady as fuck, but this getting him in some deep water. He think he the big dog, but he running with some fucking wolves," Tug said as he guided his character through a dystopian cityscape. Dante thought it resembled what Jefferson Run was going to look like in a few years.

"Aye, I hear you. Well, I don't get down like that, and if he do, he can suck a whole-ass donkey dick and go back for seconds," Dante said.

Tug howled with laughter. "Man, you crazy. You sure you don't wanna hang around? Raynell went to Church's to get us some lunch. You welcome to grab something."

"Nah, I gotta get going. Wait, what time you say it was?"

"I didn't, but it's like one."

Dante checked his phone. He had one missed call from Roman and one from Cassidy. He resisted the urge to slap himself on the forehead.

"Yeah, let me bounce. I'll holla at you, Tug," Dante said.

"Be breezy," Tug said as Dante walked out the door.

Dante called Roman first so he could ask him what he should say to Cassidy. Rome answered on the first ring.

"Where are you?" he asked.

"Was at a friend's. Where are you?"

"I'm heading to the hospital, then I'm going to relieve Neveah so she can pay the license fee," Roman said.

"Shit, that's today? Damn, that ease up on you quick," Dante said.

"You coming by the hospital?" Roman asked.

"Nah, we need to talk, but not on the phone."

"What's wrong?"

"I'll tell ya in person."

Roman was quiet. Dante could hear him breathing, imagine the rise and fall of his broad chest as he seethed.

"What did you do?"

"It's not what I did. Look, we just need to talk, okay? I'll meet you at the shop a little later. I'm going home now. I think I need to take a shower. Say by three?" Dante said.

Roman didn't respond immediately.

"Yeah, okay. You sure you don't want to come to the hospital? We can just ride to the shop together," Roman said.

An image of his father filled his mind. Tubes and wires encasing him while his mute form lay still and the machines that were keeping him alive whistled and rattled and hummed with cold impartiality. All because of him. Because of what he did.

He couldn't do it. Not yet.

"I'll just meet you at the shop at three," Dante said.

"You gonna have to come here eventually. Don't make it when they tell us to pull the fucking plug," Roman said.

The line went dead.

CHAPTER THIRTEEN

Roman sat next to his father's bed and slid his hand between the rails to grab his father's chilly paw.

The afternoon had turned brisk, another rarity this soon in September for Virginia. He didn't believe in signs or portents, but this early cold snap felt eerie. It was as if Mother Nature herself were turning her back on them and giving Old Man Winter early entrance to the body of Gaia. Night, winter, and death were at the gates.

"Stop it," he said.

He looked at his father. He searched his face for even the slightest hint of responsiveness, but it was slack and smooth as a piece of obsidian.

Neveah said his insurance should cover up to six months of catastrophic care but after that they were on their own. The great American health system would let them down like it did countless other families across the country. Or maybe it would grant them mercy and let his father slip away. Was that mercy? Roman didn't think Keith Carruthers would think so.

He wondered what Oscar Conley's family had done with his ashes.

The man his mother had turned to for comfort, for affection, when her own husband could not give her the warmth she craved. Roman thought it was ironic a man who commanded fire could be so cold. Not just to his wife but to his children as well. He wished he could find Conley's ashes. Take them to an old outhouse out in the Skids and pour them over the maggots. It wouldn't avenge his father's cuckolding, but it would make him feel better, if only for a moment. His mother was gone. He couldn't confront her.

Roman thought if he ever had children, he'd do his damnedest to make sure they never knew if he or their mother was taking company with someone else. Children shouldn't know where their parents extinguish their passions.

Was he still angry at his mother?

If he was, that anger smoldered under the weight of his love for her in much the same way his disappointment in his father lay buried under his gratitude for the man.

He pulled his hand away.

He stood and touched his father's brow. It was cool. He leaned over the bed and kissed his forehead.

"I love you, old man," he said.

His father remained mute.

That wasn't out of character for him. Roman could count on one hand how many times Keith Carruthers had said he loved him. Once at his graduation from college. Again when Roman survived a car accident in Atlanta, and once . . .

That day. It was on that day when the word first crossed his father's lips.

Roman left the hospital and drove to the crematory.

He pushed the bell and Neveah came to the door almost immediately.

"Where you been? The state office closes at three. Damn," she said as she grabbed her truck keys and a manila folder.

"Went to see Pop. Sorry, guess time got away from me," he said.

"Okay, well, I got two in the oven. And Weldon Travis from Jackson Brothers Funeral Home is bringing a big one over for direct cremation. He gonna need some help. I'm out," Neveah said as she headed for the door.

"You not gonna ask how he is?" Roman said.

Neveah paused.

"If he was doing better, you would have said something," she said.

Then she was gone through the door.

Roman had cleaned out the second oven and packed the cremains when he heard the doorbell for the front door ring. He assumed it was Weldon. Maybe he wanted to make sure someone was here before he backed up to the garage door.

When he opened the door, it wasn't Weldon.

There was a thin, wiry brother with a close-cut salt-and-pepper flat-top standing in the doorway. He was holding a badge.

"You must be Roman. I'm Detective Chauncey Mansfield. I'm a friend of your sister's. She told me you were here. Can I come inside for a minute?" he said.

Roman studied him.

He was wearing a brown blazer over a black turtleneck and a pair of jeans with brown loafers. He had a gun on his belt; but for that detail, he resembled a tenured philosophy professor. He wasn't intimidating like most cops Roman had encountered, especially cops in Atlanta who investigated his clients from time to time. Big, 'roided-out behemoths who got their beaks wet like it was a standard operating procedure they taught you in the academy. Ten thousand could buy their silence for a DUI. Domestic abuse was fifty, and anything short of murder was low six figures.

But Chauncey had the hungry eyes of a predator. Eyes that tried to take in everything without giving you anything in return. He had said he was Neveah's friend. And Neveah had called him her friend. As innocent a designation as one could imagine. But Roman couldn't help but suspect this man with the gold wedding ring was sleeping with his sister.

Neveah had a type.

Emotionally unavailable "bad boys." She'd told him once when they had been closer than they were now that you couldn't get hurt if you didn't fall in love. He wondered if she still believed that, or was she now deluding herself too?

"Sure, Detective. Come on in," Roman said.

He sat on the recliner in the rear of the lobby. Chauncey sat on the love seat across from him. He put his badge away and took a visual tour of the lobby.

"You'd never think a place like this was the lobby for a crematorium. Feels like I'm in my doctor's office," Chauncey said. Roman could tell he expected a polite chuckle, but he didn't give him one. He didn't often take an instant dislike to someone, but something about Chauncey instantaneously aroused his disdain. Roman had spent enough time in boardrooms and offices with men like Chauncey. They thought they were hiding their egotism behind their velvet patter, but that actually exposed it. The velvet was moth-eaten, and he could see the real Chauncey through the holes.

When Roman didn't laugh, Chauncey pushed on.

"So, your sister told me you and your brother got jumped the other night. "

"Yeah. Three guys jumped us as we left the shop. He'd stopped by to help me finish up here. We were trying to give Neveah a break. My dad's in the hospital," Roman said.

"Yeah, hit-and-run, right? My colleagues are still working on that. Did you get a look at them? The assailants?" Chauncey asked.

"No. It was dark. They rushed up on us. Punched me in the mouth and broke four of my teeth. Then they cut my little brother's finger off and stomped on it," Roman said. He used the truth to build his lie.

"Were they wearing masks?"

"I don't know. I don't remember," Roman said.

"You don't seem very concerned, Roman. These men beat you like a runaway slave, then they amputated one of your brother's fingers, and you're recounting the story like you're reading your grocery list," Chauncey said.

"I've got some distance from it," Roman said.

Chauncey leaned forward.

"Okay, let me be straight with you. Until today, I wasn't really interested in looking into this. You and your brother didn't file a report and it seemed like the two of you either, A, wanted to handle it yourselves, which is a terrible idea, but, hey, that's your right, or, B, you wanted to let it go, which has its own set of problems, but so be it. But then I got a call that John Paul Mathias Getty has gone missing. Do you know Mr. Getty, Roman?" Chauncey said.

Roman kept his face rigid, but his mind was reeling.

"I've heard my brother mention him once or twice. I think they're friends. I just got into town the other day, though," Roman said.

"I know. You're visiting from Atlanta, where you run Carruthers and Associates. Gotta say, your client list looks like the front row of the BET Awards," Chauncey said.

Roman gave him a light shrug.

"Okay, well, Mr. Getty did some work for us from time to time. The only reason I'm telling you this is because I don't think we are going to see Mr. Getty again. Looks like someone broke in the house he rented over on Sledmore Street; some people call that part of town the Skids. Someone busted down his door, and then it looks like they rearranged the décor with his face. So, let's cut the shit, shall we? Your sister is a good friend of mine, so I'm giving you a break here. Your brother is a known associate of a CI who went missing right around the time you and your brother got your shit absolutely rocked. So, why don't you tell me what you know before you really get hurt?" Chauncey said.

Roman could tell he thought he sounded tough.

He didn't.

He sounded like a child playing cops-and-robbers.

Roman leaned forward.

"Did Neveah tell you about our mother? No, why would she? Everyone knows the story. Well, when our mother disappeared, we promised to take care of each other. We wanted to make it easy on our dad. That autumn after our mom disappeared, this kid started stealing my sister's lunch. Me and Dante tried to let her take care of it, but eventually she let us help out. Because it's we three, and just us three. We look out for each other."

Roman sat up straight.

"So, this kid, he was bigger than me and Dante. No way even if we both jumped him we could take him. That's why me and Dante found the next-biggest kid, a walking amalgamation of trauma and psychosis named

Roland Rundgren, and stole his bike. Then I took his bike over to the kid who was stealing my sister's lunch and rode it past his house, and because he was a stupid bully he knocked me off the bike and stole it from me.

"This was about nineteen minutes after I told Dante to tell Roland that he saw who stole his bike. The kid who was stealing Neveah's lunch ate through a straw for a month," Roman said.

He stood.

"We three, and nobody else but us three. I love my sister. I love my brother. We'll be okay. People who hurt us, who hurt my brother, who hurt my sister . . ."

He lingered over the word *sister*.

"Those people tend to meet a Roland Rundgren."

Roman went and opened the front door. "I'll tell my sister you stopped by. I appreciate your time."

Chauncey grunted and stood. "Okay, tough guy. I hope I won't have to get your sister to ID your bodies. You have a good afternoon," he said.

Roman shut the door behind him, and then once it was locked he slid to the floor. Getty was a snitch. But he must have been picked up before he got to snitch about his deal with Dante.

That little bit of luck might just keep them alive for another day. It also might let Roman defuse the mayhem Dante's naïveté had unleashed. Might let him get back to his actual life. Because this wasn't it.

Roman sat with his back against the cool metal of the door and nodded. He thought of an engineering class he had taken as an elective. The first step in moving a great weight was finding the fulcrum. The first step in cracking a great rock was finding the fault line. The natural place where the rock was weakest.

Khalil could be his fulcrum.

Yellaboy running off the other night.

Getty being a snitch.

He thought maybe he'd found the fault line in the Black Baron Boys.

He thought maybe he'd found where they were the weakest.

Now all he had to do was figure out how to push that fault until it split.

JUNE 6, 2003

MORNING

Dante comes downstairs and blows by Neveah as she is grabbing her bag for the track meet.

"*Hey!* Where you going?" Neveah screams at him as he heads for the door.

"I'm going to the basketball court. Gonna meet Charlie and Stefan," Dante says.

"Not before you get your breakfast. Daddy said we all have to eat our breakfast. Mama's not gonna be home until ten. Now, eat some cereal, 'cause you know you gonna get sick if you don't," Neveah says.

"You better eat it. You don't want to throw up when you playing basketball. Again," Roman says from the couch. He's playing video games and has a giant bowl of cereal on the coffee table in front of him.

"Make sure he eats," Neveah says.

Dante begrudgingly sits down at the table and pours himself a bowl of milk and cereal and starts shoving the spoon into his mouth.

"Mama gonna be tired when she come home. Y'all wash your bowls up, please and thank you," Neveah says. She double-checks her bag to make sure her cleats are in there along with her track uniform and her warm-up suit. Her top has a red outline of a stag on the front under the words JEFFERSON RUN TRACK TEAM.

"I got it. You gonna miss your ride," Roman says.

"Don't forget the bowls," Neveah says as she hurries to the door.

"Hey! Good luck today," Roman yells.

"Yeah, good luck, goober," Dante says.

Neavah looks at them, searching their faces for something she doesn't have a word to describe yet. Later, she'll think the word she was looking for was *disingenuous*.

But she'll remember she didn't see that in their faces. They'd meant it. They wanted her to do well. To win.

"Thanks, knuckleheads."

It's the last track meet of the year. Her mother can't be there because she is just coming off her fifth straight overnight shift. Her father can't be there because he is still working part-time for Jackson Brothers as he gets the crematory off the ground. They don't have enough contracts yet for him to leave the funeral home, but all three of them know it won't be long now.

Their father is determined.

They know their mother will sleep for a few hours, then go to the crematory to help their father and Oscar. Oscar, who calls Roman "chief" and Dante "squirt" and Neveah "Miss Lady." Oscar, who Roman sometimes catches staring at their mother longer than he, even at sixteen going on seventeen, thinks he should. Neveah says he just has a crush. And why wouldn't he?

Their mother is beautiful.

Their father's nickname for her is "Stuff," short for Hot Stuff. It's the closest any of them have heard him come to being loving. But it's genuine. They can all feel it. It's bright and shining and comes from a place inside their father that few people can ever hope to touch.

After Neveah leaves, Dante goes to the door and peeps through the sidelights. He sees her walk down off the porch and he sees Susie Pettigrew's dad's car pull up. It's an old sedan, even though Dante doesn't know that's what it's called. He watches Neveah climb in the backseat. He sees her laughing at something Susie says.

He doesn't know it, but it's the last time he'll see her laugh for a long, long time.

"I'm going to the basketball court," Dante says.

"You finish your cereal?" Roman says. He is only half paying attention to his brother. He is concentrating on his video game, but he's only giving that a quarter of his attention. What is really on his mind, what has taken over his waking thoughts and his nocturnal dreams, is Delia Cochran.

She lives four houses down the street in the part of town where he and his family are relative newcomers. Delia has long braids like Janet Jackson in that movie about poetry his Mama loves so much. Delia is darker than Janet but she has much the same proportions, and Roman thinks her smile gives Miss Jackson a run for her money.

Delia is going to be home alone in an hour. Her father works at the sheet metal plant near the crematory. Her mother is away taking care of Delia's grandmother.

Her father won't get off work until five.

They have all day.

He's nervous. Delia claims she's done it dozens of times. Roman has never done it. But he can't stop thinking about it.

"I ate enough. I'm gone," Dante says.

"Hey, be back before dark. Mama gonna whoop my ass and yours too if you let them streetlamps catch you," Roman says.

He is just getting used to streetlamps. When they were still living in the Skids, the streetlamps were haphazard at best.

In the years to come, Dante will forget he ever lived in a place where the streetlamps didn't come to life like sentries for the Fae. The memories of the Skids will fade away until he can only access them in his nightmares. He won't remember them even then, because his nightmares are filled with horrors that fill the space where those memories might reside.

"I'll be back before then."

Roman doesn't know it yet, but a series of events have been set in motion that none of them can foresee. A die has been cast and a Rubicon has been crossed that will cast a shadow over their lives that will never lift, never cease, a blackness that will envelop them all like the cold embrace of an endless night.

Roman looks up and sees his little brother, heading out the door and grabbing his bike off the porch.

The morning sun baptizes both sinner and saint alike.

Before the day is done, they will encounter both.

CHAPTER FOURTEEN

oman heard someone backing up to the garage door. He went and opened it and saw a dark blue van with the words JACKSON BROTHERS FUNERAL HOME on the back glass.

He waited, and Weldon hopped out the driver's side.

"Well, look what the cat dragged in! Good to see ya, man," Weldon said. He held out his hand and Roman dapped him up with a little chest bump.

"This a big ol' boy, man. He ain't miss many meals. We had to get him up off the floor in one of them little row houses near the Skids. He owe me two vertebrae," Weldon said. He raised the rear door of the van and Roman saw a wide wooden skid with a three-inch-high lip around the length of the six-foot-five-inch-long rectangle. A body with a large white sheet thrown over it was in the wooden crate. The belly of the body seemed to rise up like Mount Kilimanjaro. The skid had fabric handles screwed into the foot, the head, and the sides.

Roman went and got the body lift and positioned it so if they were lucky they could drag the skid out and let it slide onto the body lift.

"You kept your certifications up? You don't need the state boys coming through here and popping y'all for a violation. They live to put they foot on the neck of a Black business," Weldon said.

"Neveah keeps it paid. So that when I come home I can help," Roman said. After their mom went missing, their father's eighteenth birthday gift for each of them was a state crematory worker's certification class. Roman got his the summer before he went to college.

"Good. Man, I'm glad you up here. I mean, I know it's for a terrible reason, but she needs the help, man. Your pops, he like my pops. Don't want to admit he fighting Father Time, and that ol' boy is undefeated," Weldon said.

"Yeah. Trying to get Dante more involved too," Roman said. Weldon didn't comment, which was a comment in itself. Weldon and Roman were both the "good" sons of the men who made their livings from death. Roman knew Weldon's brother Jaimie was doing ten years for manslaughter for accidentally shooting his girlfriend while playing around with a gun. Roman could never understand how someone who saw the grim realities of the fragility of this human shell could have been so cavalier about handling a gun.

Accidents happen, though, don't they? a voice said in his mind.

"I guess we better pull this boy out of here," Roman said.

Together they pulled the crate onto the body lift with as much care and respect one could muster when moving a four-hundred-pound body.

Roman engaged the motor on the lift and rolled it to the far end of the room near the ovens. Weldon pulled some papers from the inside of his jacket pocket. Roman knew they were the cremation authorization and the death certificate. He thought it was ironic in this age of digital footprints and ethereal social media existence how much paper still defined someone's life. Whether it was dollar bills or a death certificate, paper and ink still gave our lives more meaning than terabytes and data points.

"When'd you get into town?" Weldon asked as he handed the documents to Roman.

"A few days ago. Came up for Daddy. Think I'm gonna hang around for a minute. Help Neveah out," Roman said.

"Terrible about your daddy. How's he doing?"

"Still in a coma. They say it could be another ten days or ten years," Roman said.

Weldon sucked his teeth.

"You know we just picked up Jacob Pettigrew," Weldon said.

"He related to Susie Pettigrew?" Roman asked.

"Yessir. He's her son. They called him J-Rock. They found him down by the train tracks. Somebody worked on him real good. All the meat was gone from his legs. Medical examiner said it looked like he been mauled by a pack of wolves. Except, ain't no wolves in Virginia," Weldon said.

Roman felt his bile rise up like magma in a volcano, but he kept it down through an act of will.

"What you think happened to him?" Roman asked.

"Somebody set some dogs on him before they put a bullet in his head. Fourth body I seen like that this year. You know, I buried his daddy Ronnie Byrd, and his uncle Sonny, and granddaddy Huck," Weldon said.

"Damn. That family has used ya'll for a long time," Roman said.

Weldon scratched at his chin.

"That was all the last three years. They was all in that life. That shit keeps us busy, but goddamn, it feels like we blinked and every factory in this town pulled up stakes and left boys to start slinging like it's a family business. The Black Baron Boys versus the Ghost Town Crew versus the independent doughboys versus the cops. Every night round here sounds like the 4th of July. You know Jefferson Run used to be the number one producer of Mason jars? Was the number one producer of Mason jars from 1901 to 1987. Now all we make is orphans and widows," Weldon said before retrieving a flask from his other jacket pocket.

After Weldon left, Roman started to put the body Weldon had brought in the oven. Because of the weight it took an extra hour before he could pack the cremains into a container and put them in the cabinet to await Weldon's return. Once he'd done that, he opened the oven and let it begin to cool as he shut down the shop. He stopped the process of shutting down for the night just long enough to find an ATM and take out two five-hundred-dollar withdrawals from his checking account to replace the money he'd given Cassidy.

He went home and pulled into the driveway at half past five.

When he walked in the house, Khalil was sitting in his father's recliner. Dante was face down on the couch, snoring so loud it sounded like he was handsawing a redwood.

"I knocked for a long time. He never woke up, so . . . I got myself in. He's all right, just knocked out. That's your brother, right?" Khalil said. He was wearing a letterman jacket with the logo of a long-defunct clothing designer on the back and the left side of the front of the jacket where a high school's first initial would have gone. His locs were pulled back into a loose ponytail. He had on a black pair of Timbs and Roman knew he had at least two guns on him and probably that many knives.

"Yeah, that's Dante. My baby brother. Come on, let me get you a drink and I can tell you what's going on," Roman said.

"Well, I figure since you had me send you two hundred grand by UPS and then had me bring up another hundred and ninety grand, yes, your investment has matured, according to Ms. Billings, and that some folks need killing," Khalil said.

He laughed.

Roman didn't.

Roman poured himself a drink. He got Khalil a water. In all the time they'd known each other, he'd only seen the big man drink alcohol twice. Once during a raucous New Year's Eve celebration at a party thrown by a one-hit wonder hip-hop impresario who was holding on to his fifteen minutes of fame like the grim grip of death. The other time was when they took a shot to celebrate the birth of Khalil's niece. Neither time did Khalil allow himself to get intoxicated.

He placed the drinks on the kitchen table.

"Dante, get up, man," Roman said as he tried to rouse his little brother. Roman suspected it was an opioid-assisted slumber, but he needed Dante to be a part of the discussion he was about to have with Khalil.

"Five more minutes," Dante mumbled.

"Dante, get your ass up!" Roman said. He grabbed Dante by the collar and physically sat him up on the couch. Dante blinked his eyes and put up his hands in defense of a blow that was only raining down in his dreams.

"Hey, Rome, I gotta tell you something." Dante paused as he stared at Khalil with sleepy eyes. "Wait, who the fuck is that?"

Khalil nodded at him as he sat at the kitchen table and began to drink his water.

"That's my friend. Come on, we can talk at the table," Roman said. Dante got to his feet and shuffled over to the table. Roman sat down across from Khalil, with Dante at his left. Roman took a sip of the bourbon and let the ice cubes clink against his new teeth. His upper jaw still had a dull ache, but the ice and liquor helped to quell it a bit.

"Khalil, this my brother, Dante. Dante, this my friend Khalil. We can talk in front of him. He's gonna help us with this situation," Roman said. He and Dante shared another unspoken conversation.

What can we tell him?

Everything.

"Okay. What's up, man?" Dante said.

"Not much, man. Just here to help. You could say I have a special set of skills," Khalil said. He gave Dante a small smile.

"Okay, Liam Neeson," Dante said. Khalil laughed and Dante laughed but Roman did not. He took another sip of his bourbon.

"So, what's going on up here, man? What you need?" Khalil said.

Roman set his drink down and rubbed his face.

"My brother here got in debt to some people you don't want to be in debt to. I tried to help, but things just got worse. Let me tell you the whole story," Roman said.

Thirty minutes later he'd finished his bourbon but Khalil was still sipping on his water. Dante was laying his head on the table.

"All right, fifty grand a month is a steep tax. How you thinking about handling this?" Khalil said.

Roman shook the ice cubes in his glass. "I think the weakest spot these boys have is fear. They rule through fear. Because they are afraid themselves. They got these rival gangs coming at them, the, what is it, Dante?"

"Ghost Town Crew. Mostly Mexican dudes. There ain't a lot of them, but they don't mind popping off. Black Baron Boys keep them in check mostly, but it ain't easy," Dante said.

"Yeah. Ghost Town Crew. They don't want to give up any territory. Jefferson Run isn't a big city, it's really a glorified town, but people here work at Prosser State, they got jobs in Richmond. A lot of people here don't have a lot of money, but the ones that do like to spend it. The Black Baron Boys are running things here. I'm assuming they got a hand in drugs, sex trafficking, maybe gambling. They're scary, but they're scared of things too. Jail, losing respect in the street. Getting pushed off the block. It's their weakness. It's why they're so violent. Creating this reputation makes people less inclined to cross them."

"Except for Getty," Dante said.

"He thought he was protected," Khalil said

"He was wrong," Roman said.

Khalil leaned back in his chair until it was up on two legs. "The way I see it, you have two roads you can take. When I was doing some private work out West I heard about a white boy that got into it with some Aryans. They put a greenlight on him and his whole family."

"A what?" Dante asked.

"A hit. Anyway, this old boy went to war on them. Hit a bunch of stash houses and fucked up a lot of the Hitler Youth. He racked up a lot of bodies, and eventually he made it so expensive for them Aryans they canceled the greenlight. And then he rode off into the sunset," Khalil said.

"Really?" Dante said.

"That's the story anyway. Nobody ever saw him again, but nobody ever fucked with his daughter again either, so I think there's some truth to it. Anyway, that's one way," Khalil said.

"We can't just start a war with these boys. We have too much to lose. We got Neveah, we got my daddy. The business. No, that's not gonna work. What's the other way?" Roman asked.

Khalil undid his hair tie and let his locs fall past his shoulders. "The other way is we bust them up from the inside by pushing them from the outside. We used to call it counterinsurgency in the military," he said.

"That's what I was thinking. I get inside. I tell them about Getty being a snitch. That's a good-faith gift. We in this together now anyway. That's what they wanted. I make them some money. Make them see me as valuable. Make them think of me as an asset. Someone they can trust."

"Then you use your position as the trusted consigliere to turn them against each other. Move them around like pawns. Exploit their paranoia. 'Cause all gangsters are paranoid as fuck," Khalil said.

"We already got one pawn. Yellaboy. I don't know where he went that night, but I don't think he wants Torrent and Tranquil to know about it. That's leverage."

"I can help from the outside. Make some moves that only you see coming. Maybe throw a grenade or two in some of their stash houses. Go at places where they feel safe until they don't know which way is up," Khalil said.

"We play on their insecurities. We make them nervous. If I make them enough money, if they see enough of it on the table, they'll turn on each other. You spread enough money around and the Pope will stab somebody in the back," Roman said.

Khalil let his chair sit back on all four legs. "Paging the de Medicis," he said with a chuckle.

Dante let out a deep sigh. "Y'all talking about this like this is *Goodfellas* or some *Casino* shit. These motherfuckers are murderers! We can't just play undercover brother with these boys."

"Dante, I don't know if you realize this, but everybody at this table has killed someone," Khalil said. "Some of us more than others. What that means is that you can't go to the cops. Especially since your friend was a CI. There's no way to clean that up for the police. Now, I just met you, and I'm not trying to be disrespectful, but I haven't heard you say one word about how you think you and Roman should extricate yourselves from this situation that you created. One thing I know for sure.

You don't have to pay a debt if the person you owe the debt to is dead. But if you have a better idea, I'm all ears." Khalil leaned forward and took another sip of his water.

Dante sat back in his chair. "I think . . . I just think we should pay them. Just pay them and eventually they will let it go," Dante said.

"Dante, that's not going to work. They are never going to let this go. They are going to bleed us like vampires until we're broke. Until we run out of blood," Roman said.

"Well, then maybe your friend here can just get rid of them," Dante said.

Khalil grunted. "To go at guys like this, to quote *The Wire*, you come at the king, you best not miss. I could take them out, but I need to get close to them to do that. That takes time. Besides, gangs like this are like a hydra. You got to cut all the heads at once. Debts die with the people that they're owed to, but you gotta get 'em all. Or it just moves down the line. Do you understand what I'm saying?"

"Then let's just . . . go away. I'll go away. I'll leave," Dante said.

"So they can kill Neveah and then make me sell the business and pay anyway? Put Daddy in some backwater nursing home with one aide for twenty people where he lays in his own piss till the morning shift comes in? Is that what you want? Because that's what happens if you leave. You think you and Cassidy gonna run off into the sunset together? Look at me," Roman said.

Dante raised his head and looked at Roman.

"They tried to kill Daddy. They took your finger. They knocked out my teeth. They're trying to take everything our father built. What he dedicated his life to. What Neveah has dedicated her life to. You just want to let them get away with that?" Roman said.

Very quietly, Dante said, "I just wanna live, Rome."

"*What kind of a life is that?*" Roman screamed.

The house went silent.

Dante dropped his eyes.

Khalil finished his water.

"I'm sorry," Roman said. "I'm sorry. This is just . . . this is the way we get out of this. This is how we do it. We can win, we just have to be smart. Okay? We stay on the same page and we just work together. We can do this."

"Okay," Dante said. His voice barely made it above a whisper.

"Speaking of being on the same page, this girl Cassidy, is she gonna be a problem? Because you going to have to explain where Splodie went. And if she shows up, how long do you think it will be before she tells somebody how Dante saved her life?" Khalil asked. There was no whimsy in his voice now. He was sitting straight, with his chin on his folded hands. Roman had seen him adopt this demeanor before when he was about to guard a local celebrity. He was transforming from Khalil, the guy who liked to party with video models, to a jaguar that stalks the dark. The shadow's shadow. That was what he'd called it one time.

"When I'm on with someone, I'm their shadow's shadow. I'm seen but not seen, ya know?" Khalil had told him once before he'd escorted a notorious local politician to a volatile social appearance.

"We tell people that after him and Yellaboy dropped off Getty and Cassidy, they dipped. We don't know where he went. Yellaboy can't contradict us because I get the feeling he wasn't supposed to leave. Splodie is the first chess piece. We use him to control Yellaboy. We're in a MAD with him," Roman said.

"What's a mad?" Dante asked.

"Mutually assured destruction pact. He can't tell on us, and we can't tell on him. Except I can leave little hints. Make Torrent wonder what happened between him and Splodie," Roman said.

"Okay. Okay. What do you need me to do?" Dante asked.

"You keep doing what you doing. Partying. Drinking. Just, if you talk about Splodie, make it seem like he could be in the Witness Protection Program or he got taken out by the Ghost Town Crew. Keep it loose, but keep talking about it. We get them to start looking over their shoulders, it's like pushing a snowball downhill," Khalil said.

"We wait a few days, then I meet with them. I give them half the hundred thousand. I tell them I can take the fifty and make it one fifty in two weeks. Which I can. I know how to move money around. They want fifty grand a month. I can triple that. Make them see me as not only valuable but indispensable. I can invest in volatile stocks, use Ms. Billings to pump and dump, make a few phone calls the SEC doesn't need to know about. Once I do that, I'm in," Roman said.

"What happens then?" Dante said.

"Remember what Pops said when he taught us how to play chess? The king is the most important piece in the game. We move the pawns around the board until they take the king out for us. Then we flip the board over and get rid of the pawns too. Everybody has a weakness. Theirs is greed." Roman said. He turned his glass up and crunched down on the ice cubes with his bright new shiny teeth that replaced the four Torrent had knocked out.

The pain was exquisite.

CHAPTER FIFTEEN

Neveah pulled in next to Dante's Challenger and behind Roman's rental car. The porch lights were on, covering the front yard in a sallow sheen. Neveah got out of her truck and walked up the steps. Every time she came home there was this faint hope that one day she'd walk through the door and her mother would be sitting there in the living room waiting for her. Older, maybe with her hair now a soft shade of silver. Perhaps a few lines around the corners of her mouth that creased when she laughed. Their mother had a wonderful laugh. A full-throated exclamation that used to ring throughout the house like a church bell. There were nights, when she was particularly stressed, when she heard that laugh in her dreams. Of course, her mother was never waiting for her, she never came home, she was never there to hold Neveah when she cried.

Eventually she stopped crying. It was like the flames from the crematory had finally made her tears evaporate, like a pot left boiling on the stove.

When she walked through the door there was someone there with Dante and Roman, but it wasn't her mother.

"Hey, Neveah," Dante said.

He was sitting at the table. Roman was pouring himself a drink. Sitting next to Dante at the table was a tall handsome brother with long locs. She could tell he was tall because even sitting down he was taller than Dante.

"Hey, Neveah, this my friend—"

"Khalil. Me and Roman went to college together. I was in Richmond visiting some family and he told me to come by for a drink. But I'll get out of your hair. I'll get an Uber to take me back to my hotel," Khalil said. He stood and shook Neveah's hand. His grip was strong, almost frighteningly so, but he kept it light and gentle as he raised, then lowered her hand.

"Rome, I'll hit you up tomorrow if you wanna get lunch. My treat. Y'all have a good evening. Nice meeting you, Dante," Khalil said.

"You too, Khalil," Dante said.

"You don't have to leave on my account. You boys wanna have me go upstairs so you can continue your meeting of the He-Man Woman Haters Club, that's fine," Neveah said.

The man chuckled. "Nah, meeting's been adjourned. Rome, I'll hit you up tomorrow. Y'all be good," he said. He headed for the door, then stepped out into the crisp night air.

"You get the business license stuff straight?" Roman said. He sipped his bourbon.

"Yeah, seven hundred dollars for the state to tell us our floors ain't clean enough. So, how long your buddy gonna be in town? I know you been gone a long time, but I can still turn up in the kitchen. I can make us dinner one night if you want," Neveah said.

Roman gave her the barest of smiles.

"I forgot you had a thing for locs. That's got to be it. Because I've been home four days and you ain't offered to cook me shit," Roman said. Neveah smacked him on the arm, then half-heartedly swung at his head, which made him laugh. Dante joined him, and suddenly they were all guffawing.

For a moment Neveah thought it felt like they were all kids again. Then she remembered what had happened when they had been children. What had been taken away from them by fate and circumstances beyond their modest control. She remembered how all their hearts had been broken that Saturday in June and all they had been left with were the shards.

The laughter died in her throat so quick it was like a door had been slammed shut.

"You get that body done that Weldon brought by?" she asked.

"Yeah. Packed him up and racked him," Roman said.

"All right. I'm going to bed. I'm tired. I'll see y'all in the morning," Neveah said.

"We should go see Pop tomorrow. All of us," Roman said.

"Yeah, I'll let you know," Neveah said.

"I mean . . . what you got to let me know? I did all the bodies that needed to be done today. Everybody else is waiting on the ME to clear them. We got time in the morning. We should go," Roman said.

"I said I'll let you know. Maybe you should drag Dante's ass up there. He ain't seen him since the cops called us and told us he was spread all across the CSX railroad," Neveah said.

"Why you getting mad? All I'm saying is we should all go see Pop. I think it helps him," Roman said.

"I'm not mad, but, Roman, you can't drop in every five years and then just start giving out orders. You might be the oldest, but you ain't Daddy. You ain't the patriarch. This ain't one of them plays Mama used to watch on DVD where the big brother rolls into town and fixes everything, then at the end we all have a big cookout. You here because daddy is half-dead. When he dies or he comes out of the coma and somebody gotta wash him and feed him while he has to go back and forth to rehab, you'll be gone and Dante will be high and I'll do what I always do. *I'll do it*," Neveah said.

"Nev—" Roman started to say, but Neveah was already stomping up the stairs.

"You gotta give her some space, man. She does a lot. She keeps everything moving. Shit, last month Pops forgot to make the house payment and she had to run down to the bank to get it straight on her birthday. She don't mean nothing by it. You just gotta let her be," Dante said.

"We're not good brothers. But we gonna make sure none of this Black Baron Boys shit touches her. I mean that. She doesn't need that in her life," Roman said.

He started to walk up the stairs.

"I telling you, man. You need to leave her alone," Dante said. Roman paused, looked back at him, and then continued up the stairs.

"Don't nobody listen to me, I guess. But then, why would they?" Dante said out loud. He fished around in his pocket and pulled out a pill bottle. His bandage began to seep as he twisted off the cap and dry-swallowed two Percocets.

Roman knocked on the frame to Neveah's open bedroom door.

"I don't want to argue with you, Rome," she said as she lay on her stomach across her bed. A lamp on the nightstand cast strange angled shadows on the far wall. Her posters of Usher and Ja Rule had been replaced with framed photos of lions, cheetahs, and gazelles. There was also a map of Africa next to the photos. A night-light that projected a galactic scene on the ceiling, complete with blue pinprick stars and a swirling red and blue black hole at the center, hummed quietly next to the lamp.

"Where'd you get those pictures?" Roman asked.

"I bought them at a flea market before Covid. A guy who'd been to Kenya took them. He said it was the greatest moment of his life, seeing them in the wild," Neveah said.

"I believe it. Seeing something free that you've only seen locked up makes you think. Makes you reassess things," Roman said. He wondered if his sister knew he was talking about her. He'd never seen her free. He was trying to fix Dante's fuckup, but it was Neveah who carried the family on her back like a modern-day Atlas. It was true what she'd said. He was trying to be like their father, but he was a poor substitute. But Neveah had assumed the mantle of mother and had worn it like armor against her own pain. But that armor also weighed her down like an anchor plunging to the deepest depths of the sea.

What would she look like if she were free? Would her eyes find that spark that the lion or the cheetah had? Would the wrinkles on her face melt away in the bright light of peace? None of them had known peace since their mother vanished, but Neveah deserved to feel some modicum of that elusive state of being.

"You ever thought about going?" Roman asked.

"Going where?"

"To Africa. To Kenya," Roman said.

"And who's gonna take care of everything here? Dante? You? Definitely not Daddy now."

"Maybe it will be me. I'm here now. If we get this thing with Pop sorted out, I can always come back. Stay for a couple of weeks while you take some time off. Get out of Jefferson Got the Runs," Roman said.

Neveah turned over and propped herself up on one elbow. "What's wrong?" she asked.

"Why something gotta be wrong? Look, you don't . . . I'm not Pop. But you ain't Mama. And you don't have to be. It was wrong what we did. Me, Pop, and Dante. We let you try to be Mama when you should have just been Neveah. I mean, Pop pushed it on all of us, but you . . . it wasn't right. So, if you ever want to get away, I'll come here and make the lights stay on. It's kind of my job, paying bills," Roman said.

"You mean that, don't you?" Neveah said.

He was about to answer when her phone rang. She grabbed it off the nightstand, looked at it, and then silenced it before placing it back on the nightstand.

"Your friend came by the shop today," Roman said.

"He's just a guy I know who happens to be a cop," Neveah said.

Roman leaned against the doorframe. He crossed his arms and lowered his voice.

"Look, I ain't trying to get in your business, but that dude's a dick. No matter what, you're my sister, and you can do better than that guy," Roman said. He didn't mention noticing the wedding ring on Chauncey's hand. He didn't mention the sneer on Chauncey's face when he said he was Neveah's friend. He didn't mention that Chauncey reminded him of the boy who stole Neveah's lunch when they were kids. He didn't have to say it. He knew she could read it on his face.

"Yeah, he is. And I ain't trying to get in your business, but what's up with your friend Khalil? I ain't never heard you mention him before. He said y'all went to college together. But I didn't see him at your graduation. I would have remembered him," Neveah said.

"He dropped out. Went in the military. Was a Ranger for a few years. I think he does private security work now," Roman said. He'd read a book by a famous con man called *Catch Me If You Can* once. An ex-girlfriend had told him it would help with his sales skills, but all he took from it was if you were going to lie you should sprinkle in a little truth to season the story. Khalil did drop out of college. He did join the Army. He had been a Ranger. He did do private security. That was all true.

Khalil's also made people disappear, he thought. He's killed at least four people in what the police were advised to call self-defense. I think he could kill someone with his bare hands. He's my friend, but he's also as dangerous as those big cats on your wall. He's the jaguar. All that was true too.

"Okay. Well—"

The phone rang again.

"I'll let you get that. I mean it, though. You'll never regret traveling. Mark Twain said it's fatal to ignorance," Roman said.

"Mark Twain never met a hardhead from Jefferson Run," Neveah said.

.

Roman slipped out of the room and Neveah answered the phone.

"Yeah," she said.

"I'm calling you. You know that means I'm free," Chauncey said.

"What'd you say to my brother today?" Neveah said.

"Roman? He don't have no idea how much trouble he is in. Your other brother's friend was a confidential informant that was hooked up with the Black Baron Boys and was double-dipping with the Ghost Town Crew. If I was you, I'd get your brother Dante to come in and talk to us. Black Barons are rumored to be hooked up with Shade Sinclair. Ghost Town has ties to MS-13. Neither one of them would have a problem putting your brothers in a box. But that's not why I called," Chauncey said. "Sharon's gone for the rest of the week, and she took the boys. You want to come over?"

Neveah thought the fact that he so blithely talked about her brothers being murdered by a mythic gangster or a deadly Los Angeles–based gang, then switched to getting in her pants, was indicative of what kind of person Chauncey really was at his core. The news about Dante's friend confirmed for her that whatever happened to Dante and Roman the other night was worse than what she thought but also sadly not surprising. Dante stayed in a perpetual state of semi-inebriation or drug-induced intoxication. The idea that he'd be friends with a drug dealer was not shocking to her in the least. That didn't mean the news didn't frighten her deep inside. She loved her brothers. Even if they didn't help with . . . anything, most of the time. She loved them in a desperate, nearly blind, fanatical way. She loved her father, yes, but the way she loved her brothers was different.

Her father's wife had disappeared.

They had lost their mother.

In her mind there was a chasm between those two sides of the same event. She and Roman and Dante were on one side of that chasm and their father was on the other. They stood side by side in the dark on the precipice of that undiscovered country called the Unknown.

As the years had washed over her she became more and more convinced her father stood at the border of a country called Secrets. In between them, in that valley, was the truth.

She took care of her father. She made sure the bills were paid. She ran the business with him, but every day she felt herself growing more distant from him. When their mother's birthday came around and their father sat on the porch and drank until his eyes were floating, he'd talk to her about how much he loved their mother, how much he missed her.

"She was my Hot Stuff. The best thing that ever happened to me. We wouldn't have the crematory if it hadn't been for your mother. I didn't have no credit to get that loan. Your mama helped me build what we have brick by goddamn brick. Shit. She made mistakes, but so did I. I'd give anything to have her back. I'd burn it all down just to hear her voice again," he'd say. Then she'd have to help him up to bed. Every year he repeated the same soliloquy and every year she believed it a little less. By the time he'd said it this year she had to bite down on the inside of her mouth to stop herself from calling him a fucking liar.

Her brothers were all she had. Not her father, she could barely lie to herself about that anymore; not the crematory, she honestly didn't give a fuck about that outside of needing it to pay the bills; and not her mother, who was a wraith gone silent except in her dreams.

She would find a way to fix this mess even if they didn't want her help. It was what she did. It was the hand life had dealt her. She could do this thing, this one thing, that would help them even if she couldn't do it for herself.

"I'll be there in an hour," she said into the phone.

Because she was never going to make it to Africa.

CHAPTER SIXTEEN

Roman sat in the driver's seat of the Challenger, studying his watch. It was 10 A.M. He was early. He had a meeting with Torrent and Tranquil at 1:00 P.M. over at Trout's. He had a hundred thousand in a briefcase in the trunk. His plan hinged on being able to convince these vipers he was the answer to their unspoken prayers. A moneyman who could legitimize their ill-gotten gains with the snap of a finger.

He closed his eyes.

He could see the blood running down Dante's arm after they cut off his pinkie. It reminded him of the blood on the cuff of his mother's scrubs that day.

"No," he said out loud.

The dreams of his mother had ceded their position to nightmares of Getty kicking and screaming inside the oven. In his nightmares the door flew open and Getty leapt from the oven covered in flames, fat flowing off his body like tallow from a candle, sizzling as it hit the concrete floor of the crematory. He'd woken up last night covered in sweat and clutching his pillow. He'd almost gone to Dante's room to get one of his pills, but he pushed that idea aside and just forced himself to go back to sleep. One of them had to keep their head even if what was rattling around inside it was abominable.

He checked his watch again.

10:05.

By the time he walked to the hotel and got up to the room it would be 10:15. That was the agreed-upon time.

In a way, this meeting with Torrent and his crew was similar to some of the high-pressure meetings he'd had throughout his career. There was a considerable amount of money at stake. He was dealing with "clients" who were notoriously difficult to please. He would need to maximize all his salesmanship skills to convince them to do what he needed them to do in the manner he needed them to do it.

One of his favorite movies was *Glengarry Glen Ross*. Al Pacino as Ricky Roma was the fast-talking, confidence-inspiring Lower East Side physical avatar of every great salesman he knew inspired him, but it was Alec Baldwin's Blake who was whispering over his shoulder when he entered boardrooms or private dens or sat down next to an Olympic-sized infinity pool with a man or woman who had never known want or wistfulness.

"Always be closing."

That was it, wasn't it? Yes, he was a money manager, but at his core he was a salesman. From the moment he entered that boardroom or that den or sat down in that Adirondack chair, he was giving his clients a message. Through his words, his body language, his clothing, even his goddamn shoes. He was closing the deal from the moment he shook their hand until he walked out to his Porsche.

"You can trust me. Not because I'm an incredibly virtuous person, although I'd like to think I wouldn't pass by someone in distress on the street. No, you can trust me because I want to make both of us money. I want to see your portfolio grow, I want you to see your money create a life for you that you've only imagined. And by doing so I get my commission fees. Because we both know this isn't an altruistic relationship. But that doesn't mean we can't be friends. Just because this is capitalism doesn't mean I don't care. But don't trust me because of that. Trust me because I like nice things. Trust me because I enjoy living in a condo with a private laundry service and access to a private chef. Trust me because my selfishness requires that I be successful. And me being successful requires I make your ledger blacker than night. It requires I make us both enough money that we become intimately familiar with the Cayman Islands.

"That's a joke, by the way."

By the end of his spiel the signature on the dotted line was a matter of fate, not chance. It was like gravity.

Most times.

Roman got out of the car. The run-down, two-level motel was out near the Skids, a few hops, skips, and jumps from the train tracks where his father had been nearly killed and where the police had found his mother's car. Those tracks, running parallel to the city limits of Jefferson Run like an artery, were purported to be haunted. When he had been a kid there were stories about a headless signalman or a brokenhearted young woman or young man who leapt in front of one of the six-ton engines pulling coal out of the mountains down to the ports in Norfolk or Newport News and passed into legend.

Those stories lost their resonance for him when his mom went missing. The vicarious thrill of a ghost story lost its appeal when your family had their own urban legend.

Roman walked across the decrepit asphalt bespeckled with tufts of brown grass and weeds forcing their way through leprous cracks. He went past the disinterested manager and walked around to the back of the motel. He checked his phone.

The text said *Room 213*.

He'd found her on an app that judiciously avoided the words "sex worker" or "escort." They used terms like GFE (girlfriend experience) and "sensual massage." Roman thought you could put whatever kind of wrapping you wanted on it, but you were still paying for access to someone else's body for sexual gratification.

Except that wasn't what he really wanted. Not in the way most people imagined it. He had communicated with "Naia" that his needs were unusually specific but he would pay a commensurate price for her help and discretion. He had assured her he would bring his own equipment, so early this morning he'd gone down to one of the city's two sex shops and purchased handcuffs, rope, a ball gag, and a cat-o'-nine-tails. He was a little disappointed by the quality of the items in the Love Hut. The cat-o'-nine-tails looked like it would fall apart with the first application, but it would have to do.

He wasn't ashamed of his particular needs and desires. He'd learned in therapy that sexual pathology can also be a coping mechanism. He got that. He felt guilt over his mother. That guilt informed the women he was attracted to and how he felt a deep, abiding need to be punished for something that ultimately wasn't his fault. It might not be everyone's cup of tea, but it wasn't perverse, it was preference.

Yet, lately he found himself considering the panic he felt when he couldn't get a session before a big meeting or an important decision. He felt like he was sliding down the slick walls of an abandoned well until he was able to secure that hour, that time, that moment when he gave himself over to that hallucinatory fugue state that existed between the raising of the lash and the sting on his skin. In that place where he paid recompense for his sins both real and imagined until the release came, heralded by cries and moans. He believed that release gave him clarity, sharpened his focus. But he'd begun to worry he was deceiving himself. That, like any other addict, he was justifying his obsession with false rationalizations. Perhaps there was no lucidity after he was freed from his bonds. Just relief as the denouement washed over him like a wave made of surrender.

Or maybe it wasn't that deep.

Maybe he just liked it.

He climbed the steps and walked down to Room 213.

Two hours later he was walking back to the Challenger with his bag of accessories and without any release. He threw the bag in the trunk and then got in the driver's seat and slammed the door.

He thought it was his own fault, really. He had a specific scenario that required an experienced dominatrix to navigate its circuitous vagaries, and the young lady in Room 213 was not up to the task. She kept apologizing as he kept trying to guide her through the steps he required to arrive at that place where he was in his body but also outside of it. Experiencing the pain but also in his mind observing it from an elevated vantage point.

"I don't know what you want. I don't get it. You just wanna fuck?" she'd said finally, her voice suffused with exasperation.

"No. I'll just pay you for the time. What's your Cash App?" he'd responded as he put on his shirt. Once the transaction had gone through, he gathered the accessories and left her sprawled across the bed. Part of the problem was she was too young. It instantly took him out of the fantasy. He realized an older woman was elemental to the fantasy.

He pulled out of the parking lot and headed away from the Skids, roaring over to the other side of town. The traffic lights were not on his side, though. He caught every red between Sycamore Avenue and Lillyhammer Street. When he got to the intersection across from the Church's Chicken he pulled out his phone and scrolled down to Miss Delicate's number.

The traffic light swayed slowly in the wind as his thumb hovered over her contact info in his phone. Her name was in all caps with a picture of a bruised pair of lips for her photo.

They'd never done a session over the phone. There had never been an instance where it would be necessary. Until today. That feeling of being in free fall that was strangling him was with him from the moment he woke up through the awkward fumbling session with Naia to this moment just a mile from Trout's.

He put the phone away.

He had a hundred grand in his trunk but he didn't have the most valuable commodity he needed.

Time.

He parked in the lot across from Trout's and grabbed the briefcase from the trunk. Trout's was located in the old commercial train station near the Route 643 that led out of Jefferson Run and into Warren County where Prosser State University was physically located, though everyone said it was a university in Jefferson Run because Warren County was so small most people forgot it existed.

Roman checked his face in the side mirror. He was wearing a light black pullover sweater and a gray blazer. He didn't want to look too professional, but he wanted to project an air of expertise. He didn't want to do anything to piss off Torrent and his psychotic little brother, but he also didn't want to appear weak or ineffectual. He needed to walk a fine line between confidence and genuflection. It really wasn't that different than meeting with any powerful client, except his clients in Atlanta wouldn't put a gun in his mouth.

He walked over the cobblestones that lined the street on this side of town as he made his way into Trout's. This part of Jefferson Run was what some folks called Old Town. Most of the buildings were over two hundred years old. They were a part of the original settlements erected by English settlers who had wandered up the river from Tidewater in 1745. Most students who came from around the country to attend Prosser State assumed the city was inspired by Founding Father and illegitimate sire of Sally Hemings's children Thomas Jefferson, but Roman had learned in school that the Jefferson in question was a particularly unruly donkey that had kicked its owner and escaped into the woods near the encampment that would become Jefferson Run. When asked about the whereabouts of the donkey, the owner (who'd lost an eye from the kick) was purported to have said, "I don't give a damn if Jefferson runs all the way to hell!!"

The name stuck.

Trout's had an upscale soul food atmosphere with leather seats in the booths that lined its cavernous walls and the smooth lacquered tables in the center of the building. A semicircle bar dominated the back wall. Overhead, the autumn sun filtered through massive skylights that were arranged in a circle on the domed roof. There was a catwalk that completed an elliptical path around the building, with the old upper deck platforms serving as intimate dining alcoves now.

Roman took two deep breaths, then let them out with measured deceleration. He could see the interior of the restaurant through the nine windows in the double doors at the entrance. He could see Torrent and Tranquil and Yellaboy, along with a couple of men he didn't recognize, sitting at a long table near the bar. There were two beautiful women sitting on either side of Torrent.

Yellaboy was sitting at the end of the table next to Tranquil, drinking a beer.

"This is what you do. This is what you do. This is what you do," he said in a barely audible whisper.

He opened the door and heard a chime ring.

A young lady with long honey-blond hair that matched her complexion and bright green eyes smiled at him from behind a small lectern.

"Table for one?" she said.

"No, I'm meeting some friends. I see them over there," Roman said.

That was the first of many lies he knew he'd be telling today. These men weren't his friends. They weren't casual acquaintances. If they allowed him to join their motley crew of killers and thugs he wouldn't be their business partner. He wanted to be their Chaos. He wanted to be their downfall.

Fuck them, Roman thought. Fuck every goddamn one of them.

He walked over to the table where the Gilchrist brothers were holding court. There were whiskey glasses in front of them and plates full of the remains of a fried catfish with the bone in, collard greens, okra and lima beans and corn. Half-eaten squares of cornbread littered the table like discarded Legos.

"Look what the cat dragged in," Torrent said.

"You want to talk out here, or is there someplace we can go?" Roman said. He kept his voice even and didn't even acknowledge Yellaboy, who was shooting furtive glances his way every couple of seconds. Roman could see him in the reflections of the forest of glasses on the table.

Let him be worried. That would come in handy later.

"Come on back. Y'all stay here," Torrent said to the ladies. He got up and headed for a door at the back wall near the end of the bar. His brother and Yellaboy and the two men Roman didn't recognize went through the door first. Roman felt his palms begin to sweat. He might walk through that door and never come back out. Or he might walk through that door and join this crew.

Either way, he had to move his feet.

He shuffled in behind the phalanx that had gone through that door.

Someone shut the door behind him. The room they were now in was an office. There was a metal desk in the back, a metal shelf with document boxes and large plastic binders. To Roman's right there was a threadbare black couch and a coffee table. To his left there were two recliners and an ottoman.

Torrent sat behind the desk. Tranquil perched on a stool to his left. Yellaboy took the couch, and the other two men each sat on a recliner.

"Talk, college boy," Torrent said.

Roman stepped forward and put the briefcase on the desk. When he moved to free the latches, Tranquil pulled a nickel-plated semiautomatic gun from his waistband and pointed it at Roman. It looked like the gun that had broken his teeth.

"Slow," Tranquil said. His voice had a dusky sound, like it was weak from being underused.

Roman forcibly controlled his breathing. His heart was beating a thousand miles a minute. He made himself not lick his lips or look away from Tranquil. His teeth started to ache, but he knew that was psycho-somatic. The implants didn't have nerves.

"I'm just going to open it. There's money in here and a box of ashes. That's all," Roman said.

When he said the word *ashes*, he heard a grunt from his right. He didn't have to look to know it was Yellaboy.

"Run me my money," Torrent said.

Roman eased his hands inside the briefcase, which looked more like a suitcase than Roman had realized when he had bought it. He pulled out five bundles of hundreds and sat them on the desk on the left side of the briefcase. His stomach was twisted up like a string of old Christmas lights. Tranquil was still pointing the gun at him. The expression on his face was surprisingly benign.

"I'm pulling out the box now," Roman said. Yellaboy let out a wheez-ing whistle. Roman thought if he didn't chill the fuck out he was going to get both of them killed.

He reached into the briefcase and pulled out the gray plastic rect-angle box that they used to pack cremains when they weren't going in a decorative urn. Many people who were going to spread the ashes in a river or in the ocean didn't bother with the expense of an urn. That was usually handled with the funeral home after the cremation unless the firm had their own crematory on site, and Carruthers Cremation Services never saw their clients.

He set the box on the table with a thump. There were indeed two sets of cremains in there. The box and its contents weighed around ten pounds. Roman used to be good at guessing the weight of the cremains as a kid. He could just pick up the box and get frighteningly close. His father would weigh the box on the scale by the prep station and announce how close he'd gotten. That was back when his father was required to weigh the remains for the state, a requirement Roman never understood. Crematories weren't required to do that anymore, but Roman thought he was still pretty good at guessing. Getty had been around five-six and probably 175 pounds. Splodie was a little taller and a little heavier. Their cremains together almost didn't fit in one box, but Roman had made it work.

"What the fuck is this?" Torrent asked.

"I told you. It's a box of ashes. It's Getty and Cassidy. Proof we held up our end of the arrangement," Roman said. He closed the briefcase and locked it.

Torrent picked up the five stacks.

"This is only fifty thousand. You promised us a hundred thousand, then fifty a month. Don't tell me you already fucking up our agreement," Torrent said.

Tranquil stood with the gun still pointing at Roman's head and then leaned across the desk and pressed the barrel against his cheek.

This was the most perilous moment. Meeting with a prospective client who was nervous or distrustful. A client who had been stung before or was convinced every money manager was a Bernie Madoff in disguise. This was where he reassured them while telling them exactly who the fuck he was.

"There's another fifty in the case. I can give it to you now or I can make it grow. I can make this money work for you. It's what I do. It's all

I do. I make money. Yeah, I get pussy every now and then. I like a good bourbon once in a while. But my thing, the thing I was put on earth to do, is make money. I promised you a hundred grand. I have a proposition for you."

"We already heard your proposition," Tranquil said.

Torrent held up his hand with two fingers extended.

"Let him talk. If I don't like what he say, you shoot him in the knee-cap. Every time it rain, he'll remember you," Torrent said.

Roman swallowed hard. He couldn't help it. The barrel of the gun was digging into his skin. All Tranquil had to do was flick his wrist, and he could open up the flesh on his cheek like he was a hog being led to the slaughter. Or he could just pull the trigger and send a steel-jacketed bullet through his skull and sear his brain like a branding iron.

He pushed those thoughts away and continued.

"Let me take that fifty and flip it. By the end of the week it will be one-fifty. You take it and cut us some slack for a few months," Roman said.

"You keep saying you good at making money, and I can't lie, I thought you was full of shit, but look at you here with this yard for me. How you gonna flip it? Tell me. Call it my need to know," Torrent said.

Roman stared at him. Now he was on his home turf.

"I'll take twenty-five and buy several shares of a cheap stock, and then I'll make a phone call to an associate of mine. They'll make a big noise about the company getting a large infusion of cash from an angel investor. It will blow the stock up. That'll give us seventy-five grand. That's called a pump-and-dump. I'll take the other twenty-five and I do a short sale," Roman said.

"What the fuck is a short sale?" Torrent asked.

"Sound like when they take Tank to a slave auction," one of the men he didn't know said. The room exploded in laughter. Roman didn't know who Tank was, but he memorized that name. It might come in handy later.

He leaned his head back.

Tranquil had to lean farther over the table to try to put the gun to his cheek again. Roman leaned even farther back.

"I can't talk with a gun in my face," he said.

He held his breath.

This was the moment. He wasn't disrespecting them, but he was drawing a line in the sand. Now he just had to see if he would get buried under it.

"Can't talk with a gun in your mouth neither, can you, nigga?" Tranquil said. He started to come around the desk, but Torrent waved him off.

"Chill. Go on, tell me what a short sale is. I got a thirst for knowledge, and a soft-ass college boy like you can be my tutor," Torrent said.

Gotcha, you motherfucker, Roman thought.

"A short sale is when I borrow stocks from a broker and turn around and sell them, and then I wait a few days and watch the price fall, then buy it back and give them back to the broker and keep the difference," Roman said. He studied Torrent's face. He could see the gears grinding in his head.

He cleared his throat.

"It's like if I borrow a pool stick from John Doe #1 that is worth a hundred dollars and I sell it to John Doe #2 for a hundred dollars, then I wait for John Doe # 2 to go through some hard times and I buy it back for seventy dollars. I've made thirty dollars. And then I give it back to John Doe #1. Think of the stocks as the pool stick," Roman said. "That's the legal way." Torrent nodded his head almost imperceptibly.

"Okay, you saying that makes me think there's an illegal way," Torrent said.

He was on the hook. Greed could make zealots out of heretics.

"The other way is you make a phone call and you find a stock that you know is gonna fall. Somebody's husband is cheating on them, so they don't carry a one on a spreadsheet. Somebody on that pipe, and they lie about their earnings, and it comes out when the market opens. Somebody was stealing from the till, and now the company about to go bankrupt. I know the people that know these things. I buy that kind of stock. In a week, *boom.* I make a hundred thousand on a twenty-five thousand investment because I know it's going to drop by more than seventy-five percent. Technically it's insider trading. That's the illegal part. Add that to the money I make from the pump-and-dump, and I get you your one-fifty."

Torrent stroked his goatee. "But if that price go up you fucked, right? And then you lose it all and then we have to take you out to the farm," he said.

Roman didn't know what the farm was, and he was sure he never wanted to find out as long as he was Black and breathing.

"Yeah. But that's not going to happen, because I know the people that know which stocks are going down. Just like I know the people who know how to make the stocks go up. Do you know how most rich people become rich people? They know sometimes you have to stretch a rule, and sometimes you have to break it. I'm the one that advises them when they should break that rule. And I'm very good at it," Roman said.

Torrent clapped his hands together and got up from his chair.

"Fuck it. Let's see what you can do. Either you make us the one hundred fifty or we take you out to the farm. Take our time with you," Torrent said.

"You don't wanna go to the farm," Tranquil said.

Roman felt a slick sheen of sweat break out over his chest and back, making his shirt stick to his skin like flypaper. This was the first step. He was almost in the door. Once he got in, he could set their house ablaze.

"All right, let me go finish my drink. I'm sure them thots done ordered another round of goddamn vodka and cranberry. They love that shit," Torrent said.

All right. I'll call you when it's done," Roman said.

"Don't call me, nigga, call Yellaboy," Torrent said.

At the mention of his name, Yellaboy nearly jumped out of his skin.

Goddamn it, chill the fuck out, Roman thought.

"Give him your number, Yella. I'll see you in a week," Torrent said.

"Yeah. One week," Roman said.

Everyone got up and Roman turned to go.

"Oh, one more thing. I almost forgot. Where the fuck is Splodie?" Torrent asked.

Roman felt his scrotum crawl up the crack of his ass. He turned back around and faced Torrent. He could feel every pair of eyes in the room on him except Yellaboy's.

Look at me, Roman thought. He's gonna notice if you don't look at me. He wished he had telepathy to make Yellaboy mean-mug him like the rest of the crew was doing instead of looking down at his shoes like he was a kid who had dropped his ice-cream cone.

"I don't know. Him and Yellaboy brought Getty and Cassidy to the crematory. They stayed until we finished and then they left and I had to let the ashes cool and then I packed them," Roman said.

"That's funny. Do you know what Yella said?" Torrent said.

Roman's mouth went dry.

This is how it ends, Roman thought. In the backroom of a soul food restaurant, face down on the cheap carpet with a bullet to the back of the head. He kept his face calm. One thing he learned in negotiation was don't give away your position. Don't panic until it's time to panic. He didn't know what Yellaboy said, but he couldn't imagine he told Torrent he'd left before the job was done.

He could read people. Wherever Yellaboy had gone, he didn't want anybody but Splodie to know. He wouldn't have told Torrent anything. Torrent was bluffing. He had to be.

Roman was betting his life on it.

"No, what did he say?" Roman said.

Torrent smiled.

"He said the same damn thing. Ain't nobody seen Splodie since the other night. That ain't like him. So I was wondering if y'all's stories gonna match. I guess y'all telling the truth, right?" Torrent said. He was smiling, but his eyes were cold as hailstones. He didn't trust Roman worth a damn. But he liked the idea of making easy money off the corner and out in the alleys. Roman could see that in those cold eyes.

"You think it's the Ghost Town Crew?" Yellaboy said in a watery voice.

"They would have took credit for it. Nah, I wanna find him, though. Talk to him. Make sure he ain't made no bad decisions," Torrent said.

"Like Getty did?" Roman said. He had to be bold if he was going to gain this maniac's trust.

"What about Getty?" Torrent said.

"Cop came to talk my brother because he went missing and they were friends. He told Dante that Getty was a confidential informant. So I guess it's a good thing he's in that box with his girlfriend," Roman said. He didn't put too much bravado in his voice, just enough sass to let Torrent know he was telling the truth and he wasn't afraid to share it.

"What your brother tell the cop?" Torrent said. His voice was almost metallic.

Roman could feel death all around him like a summer breeze. He was on fragile ground now. Every word he spoke now was like he was juggling a double-edged sword. He had to grab the handle, not the blade.

"Nothing. What can he tell them? What can I tell them? We put Getty and his girl in that box. That's what you wanted, right? For us to get our hands dirty," Roman said.

"Yella, did they really get their hands dirty?" Torrent said without looking at his underling.

"Uh, yeah. Me and Splodie had to push them a little, but they got it done," Yellaboy lied.

Wherever he went, he wasn't supposed to be there, Roman thought. He filed that away too.

"I heard Getty might have been a snitch. He's lucky y'all put him in that box. That was quick. Was it quick, Yella?" Torrent said.

"Yeah. Burned his ass right up like a goddamn marshmallow," Yellaboy said.

"Okay, then, see you in a week, college boy. Come on, let's get some of that Elijah Craig," Torrent said.

He walked around the desk and headed for the door. Tranquil took the money and put it in a drawer in the desk. Roman grabbed the briefcase and rose from his seat.

As they filed out of the office, there was a brief moment as quick as a cobra strike when Yellaboy and Roman caught each other's eyes.

Roman shook his head so subtly he might as well have not moved at all.

Yellaboy dropped his eyes first.

"Let me get your number," Roman said as he pulled out his phone. Yellaboy rattled off the digits and Roman saved them in his phone.

When he looked up, Yellaboy was looking at him with pupils that were as big as trash can lids. Roman had his back to the rest of the men who had filed out of the office. He moved his finger to his lips and made a *shhh* motion.

"Yella, you want a shot of this Elijah or what?" Torrent yelled.

"Ayo, for sure," Yellaboy said. He brushed past Roman and joined Torrent and his boys at the table. Roman turned and watched him take his seat. The waitress came over with a tray of shot glasses. Everyone at the table grabbed one and did a toast. They all took the shots to the head. Yellaboy glanced at Roman.

Roman imagined them all taking real shots to the head. He imagined watching them all fall like animatronic animals when someone turned off their switch.

He held on to that image as he headed for the door.

CHAPTER SEVENTEEN

Dante walked down the hallway of the hospital carrying a vase of flowers in his good hand and holding the string on a balloon with the words GET WELL SOON written on it in big eighties-style bubble letters. The nurse had told him that his father was still nonresponsive, and that was fine with him, because he didn't think he could have spoken to him without bursting into tears.

All these years of his monumental fuckups had culminated in one so gargantuanly horrific he could barely wrap his mind around it. Getty was dead. That dude Splodie was dead.

Murdered. They were murdered.

The words appeared in his mind like a neon sign. He'd murdered someone. He'd hit Splodie with a hammer in the back of the head. Watched his blood pool on the floor like spilled red wine. He kept seeing that blood everywhere now. He'd gone to the chicken place and gotten some tenders yesterday. When he'd opened the ketchup packet he'd had to stick his head out the window of Rome's rental car and vomit. He couldn't even look at a bottle of fruit punch in the raggedy market down near Tug's place.

He knew deep down inside he'd done the right thing. Cassidy didn't deserve to get burned alive because of him and Getty being the world's worst drug dealers. But he couldn't close his eyes without seeing Splodie's head splitting open like a piece of overripe fruit. Without hearing the way his chest rattled as his last breaths trailed out of his mouth.

Without the scent of him voiding his bowels filling his nostrils. He felt like his head was filled to bursting with these blood-soaked memories.

He stopped and leaned against the wall of the hallway. His finger had stopped throbbing and the stitches were beginning to heal. His mouth had filled with saliva and he was afraid he was going to throw up again, but he fought it back down and continued on to his father's room.

Roman was sitting next to their father's bed.

"I thought you was at the shop with Neveah," Dante said.

"Nah. Had to talk to Khalil about something in person. It's been a week since I met with Torrent and them boys. I got their money. The BBB are having a party at a private club tonight. I'm going to get us an invite to that party so I can give them their money. That'll buy us some time to make some moves," Roman said.

"I heard about it. I don't know if that's a good idea. It's Tranquil's birthday party. Can't you just drop the money off at Trout's and let it be? Them boys get wild when they party. They like to shoot their guns in the air for fun. I've seen them unload an AR-15 at a tree full of squirrels just for the fuck of it," Dante said.

"Khalil has been doing some recon. Torrent owns Trout's, but he has a front man named Josh Givens as the owner and manager. The place they having the party at, the after-hours spot the Kingdom, they own that too. They got three trap houses across the city. They have a street crew that runs the drugs through the houses. They also got a crew that steals and sells guns to some heavy hitters out of New York. They seem to be pushing the Ghost Town Crew out of Jefferson Run, but they ain't going without a fight. The main guys who are close to Torrent and Tranquil are D-Train, Yellaboy, Tank, and a couple of guys they call the Bang Bang Twins even though they ain't even brothers. Their names are Lucius and Lavon. They all going to be at that party tonight. I need them all to see me drop off a hundred and fifty thousand dollars. I need them to see what I'm capable of doing. I need them to start wondering if I can do the same for them. Do you know everyone under Torrent and Tranquil have to kick up more than fifty percent of what they earn slinging or running girls or running card games or moving guns? That's what we call wage theft in the business world. That's the kind of work conditions that will make an employee quit. Or put a bullet in their boss's head," Roman said.

Dante studied his brother's face. His light brown eyes seemed to be staring at something only he could see in the windswept recesses of his own mind.

"Rome, you been getting any sleep?" Dante asked.

Roman stroked their father's forehead.

"Sleep doesn't give me rest. I wonder if Pop is dreaming," he said. "I need you there tonight. I need you to be a witness. Then I need you to go tell the story."

"What story? You dropping a bag on these boys to get their mouths drooling?" Dante said. He stumbled, and the vase bobbled in his hand. He let go of the balloon and grabbed the vase as the balloon floated to the ceiling.

Roman took his father's hand in his own. "Are you high?" Roman asked.

"How else you think I came up here? How you think I could be in this room?" Dante asked.

"Why don't you sit down?" Roman said, still stroking their father's forehead.

Dante set the vase on the table next to their father's bed. He reached up and grabbed the string of the balloon and tied it to the neck of the vase. He pulled a chair from the corner and sat down across from Roman.

"Rome, what you and Khalil got going on? What do you need me to see tonight?" Dante asked.

"I'm working on things, Dante. Trying to get close to these boys. Trying to learn them. Like, for instance, Yellaboy is so nervous I think he pees his pants every time he's around Torrent and Tranquil. We still don't know where he went that night, but it must be something that Torrent would fuck him up over. The fact that they own these businesses through third parties means they are smarter than I thought. Splodie must have been one of his boys he trusted the most, because he hasn't given up looking for him," Roman said.

"All he gotta do is open that box. He'll find him," Dante mumbled while staring down at his father's hand.

"I know all that was hard for you. Splodie, I mean. How you doing? You ain't been home for a couple of days," Roman said.

"How you think I'm doing? Terrible. I'm taking enough oxy to kill a horse. I'm getting fucked up just so I don't go running down the street screaming every day," Dante said.

"It was him or us. I choose us. I'll always choose us," Roman whispered.

"You saying that doesn't make it any better, Rome. We killed people, Rome. That kind of thing comes back at you," Dante whispered back.

"You afraid of karma? Because I'm not going to let anyone put their hands on us again. If I gotta suffer karma for that, so be it," Roman said.

"It's not karma I'm afraid of. It's getting what I deserve," Dante said.

"Isn't that the same thing?" Roman asked.

"Karma is what comes back to you for what you done. Getting what you deserve is just what finds you eventually," Dante said.

"That doesn't happen to everybody. But we are going to make sure it happens to Torrent and Tranquil. I promise you that," Roman said.

"Don't do that," Dante said. He took his father's other hand and entwined his fingers in the old man's.

"Do what?"

"Make a promise we both know you can't keep," Dante said.

Roman sighed. "Neveah was gone this morning when I got up."

"It's Saturday. If her and Pop ain't backed up at the shop she goes out to this winery over in New Kent. She'll be out there most of the day," Dante said.

"That's good. She need to get away sometimes. I was talking to her about that the other night. She go with some girlfriends?" Roman said.

Dante shook his head. "Nev ain't really got no girlfriends, man. She go by herself."

Roman stared up at the ceiling. "I guess that's better than her going with that cop. He ever get in touch with you?" Roman asked.

"Nah. I been over at my friend Tug's house. I'm gonna be real, Rome, I'm not in a good headspace. Maybe I should skip that party tonight."

"You can't start acting different. We gotta pretend like everything is cool. We can't give them any reason to be suspicious of us. You're known as a party boy. You gotta keep that up. Like I told you, I need you there tonight. You know them better than I do. You not being there is going to be suspect," Roman said.

"You really made them a hundred and fifty thousand dollars?" Dante asked.

"Yeah. Making money isn't really that hard if you don't care about breaking the law and you don't get caught," Roman said.

They both went quiet. After a few minutes he heard Dante start to snore. His head was lolling to the side, but he still held their father's hand in his.

Roman let Dante sleep as they held their father's hands.

The Kingdom was a four-story former tobacco warehouse that dominated what passed for a skyline in Jefferson Run's north side. The exterior was composed of dusky red bricks bordering on maroon. The building sat at the corner of Marion and Lillyhammer, with the faded words BROOKS TOBACCO still visible on its west side. The Kingdom didn't have a parking lot, so Roman found a space one street over. He texted Yellaboy to tell him they were there.

Dante was sitting in the passenger seat with his head on the dashboard. He was tapping his fingers in time with the beat of a song playing on the XM radio.

"It's going to be all right. Don't be nervous," Roman said.

"Don't tell me to not be nervous. We going to a party with the people who fucked us up a week and a half ago, people who want to kill us so bad I think it makes their dicks hard, when I could actually be anywhere else. I could literally be spending my night cleaning up dog shit with a potato masher and I'd be having a better fucking time," Dante said.

"Trust me. It's going to be okay."

Roman texted Yellaboy and told them where they were. He got a single-letter text in response:

K

Roman put his phone back in his pocket and changed the radio station. The dulcet tones of "O-o-h Child" by the Five Stairsteps came warbling through the speakers. It was one of their mother's favorite songs.

"Change it," Dante said.

Roman did as he was asked without complaint or contradiction. There was no need to entertain a ghost.

A knock at the window, and there was Yellaboy standing next to the driver's-side door. Roman got out and went to the trunk. Yellaboy stood near him as he reached in and retrieved a paper bag.

"Here's what I got for Torrent," Roman said. He handed the bag to Yellaboy. Yellaboy took the bag and then reached in the pocket of his jeans. Roman's chest went tight, but then unfurled when Yellaboy pulled out two neon wristbands.

"Take this shit, man. Everybody gotta have one to get in," Yellaboy said.

Roman took the wristbands, then reached into the trunk again. He pulled out a plain white envelope. He handed it to Yellaboy.

"And a little something to you. We should talk sometime. Like I said, I'm good at making people money. No reason it gotta be just Torrent getting paid," Roman said.

"Hey, man, fuck you, okay? Splodie was one of my peeps, you hear me? If I ever find out you did something to him, I'll come to your house and light that shit up like a goddamn birthday cake," Yellaboy said.

Roman straightened his posture and looked Yellaboy in the eyes.

"I don't know what happened to Splodie, just like I don't know where you went that night. But I think you'd agree those are things probably best left undisturbed," Roman said.

Yellaboy scowled. "Stay away from me, man," he said as he started back across the street and down the alley. But he didn't return the white envelope.

Roman went around to Dante's door. He rapped on the window. Dante got out and stretched. He was wearing black fingerless gloves on both hands. The finger slot for his pinky was sewn shut. Roman figured he was trying to hide his stump.

I'm sorry, Roman thought. So sorry.

"That boy so tightly wound, if he fart too hard his eyeballs gonna pop out. I don't know what you playing at, but he ain't the one to help you," Dante said.

"He just a pawn. Fuel for the fire. Remember what Pop says," Roman said as he bent over and checked his reflection in the side mirror.

"You know when he says that he means us too. We burn too," Dante said.

Roman smoothed down the front of his shirt. "Yeah, but we're going to set them on fire first."

The Kingdom was one of several private nightclubs in central Virginia, a state that held on to blue laws longer than any state in the mid-Atlantic region. In the Old Dominion bars had to close at 2:00 A.M. and beer sales stopped at convenience stores at midnight. For the determined reveler, the only option besides drinking at home was visiting a private club. Private clubs consisted of members who paid for the privilege of patronizing an establishment that could stay open twenty-four hours a day if the members so desired. Beer, liquor, wine, and food could be served around the clock without violating Virginia's archaic hospitality regulations.

When they were kids, neither Roman nor Dante knew anyone whose parents belonged to a private club. A membership was one of those rarefied extravagances that their father ignored when he couldn't afford it and disdained when he could.

"I only been here once. I mean, shit be wilding in here. Just so you know," Dante said.

"I can handle wild," Roman said. Miss Delicate's face floated up out of the river of his memories.

The entrance to the Kingdom was a monstrous teak double door with huge polished brass doorknobs. Two bouncers as broad across their backs as grizzly bears patted them down and ran a metal-detecting wand over their bodies with indifference. Roman considered how easy it would be to smuggle a gun into the club, with such lax security at the front door.

They probably do it like that because most of the patrons are strapped to the gills, Roman thought. Once they passed the half-hearted security checkpoint, they were granted passage into the Kingdom.

The interior of the private club was more lavish than Candy's but still miles behind the more opulent clubs Roman frequented in Atlanta. The Kingdom was four floors of hedonism in the midst of a city on the brink of moral and financial collapse. A Circus Maximus in the middle of a fallen empire of glass and steel. The first floor was a lounge of leather-clad furniture and sandalwood paneling and supple lighting that gave the entire space a diaphanous sheen. Brown and black bodies gyrated on the dance floor or slid against each other in booths upholstered in sumptuous ebony leather. Hands reached under tables painted in dark walnut stain. Waitresses clad in minimal fabric that barely constituted a skirt and a top carried drinks to each table and booth, while the DJ played sensual R&B that pumped animal yearning through the speakers.

Roman made his way through the mass of bodies that felt like a living organism. A hundred-eyed, hundred-handed succubus and incubus that shared one body. He and Dante leaned against the bar and watched as a man dropped to his knees and pressed his face into his dance partner's crotch as she desperately pulled up her skirt. Even in the dim lighting Roman caught a flash of hair, a glimpse of full pouty lips, before the man's mouth found its home.

"I told you, they be wildin' up in here," Dante said. He turned around and motioned for the bartender.

"Let me have two Woodford Reserves on the rocks," Dante said.

"What's upstairs?" Roman asked as he leaned over and shouted in his brother's ear.

"Second floor is a smoke lounge. People smoking weed in them big-ass hookahs. Third floor is a straight-up orgy. Fourth floor is private rooms," Dante said.

"Where you think the guest of honor is? I don't see any of Torrent and Tranquil's crew," Roman said.

"Shit, they probably on the third floor getting that birthday sex in. That's where I'd be," Dante said.

Roman was going to respond with a pithy rejoinder when a tall, light-skinned woman with silky hair so shiny and long Roman knew it had to be a weave came up to Dante and put her arm in his.

"Don't tell me you up in here and just ignoring me!" the woman said with mock irritation. Dante smiled, the first time Roman had seen him smile since he'd lost his finger (*not lost, they cut it off*) a week and a half ago.

"Desiree Ottarson, as I live and breathe!" Dante said in a Foghorn Leghorn southern accent. Desiree threw her head back and laughed, and not for the first time Roman marveled at how charming his brother could be. It came natural to Dante, like breathing. Roman could do it, but it took concentration on his part. It was like he had to put on a mask. A balaclava of charisma that was ill-fitting.

"Hey, Rome, I'll be right back. I gotta go show Desiree how to shake it. She needs my help," Dante said.

"Boy, you ain't ready for all this," Desiree said as she glided to the dance floor and slapped herself on the butt with both hands.

"Lord is my shepherd, he know what I want," Dante sang as he followed Desiree to the dance floor. Roman watched them go with a smile on his face and an ache in his chest. That was the Dante he missed. The Dante he loved. He'd seen flashes of that Dante over the years. It was like seeing blue skies when the gray storm clouds deigned to part for a moment. Those moments lasted until the shadow of their mother fell upon him again and turned those storm clouds black as pitch.

Let him dance while he can, Roman thought. He deserves it. Just like Neveah deserves her peace.

"Can I have a gin martini? Light on the vermouth," Roman said as he slid his empty glass over to the bartender. The music switched from soft and sensual R&B to an old-school classic by Waka Flocka Flame, "No Hands." Desiree didn't appear to mind, the way she was still grinding against Dante, but Roman could feel a shift in the atmosphere. He watched as Torrent and Tranquil and their crew, including Yellaboy, the Bang Bang Twins, Tank, and D-Train, came down the stairs doing a synchronized dance, with Tranquil in the middle. They were wiping off their shoulders as they stepped to the right, then the left, in time to the beat of the song.

"GIVE IT UP FOR THE BIRTHDAY BOYYYYYY BBB!" The DJ announced with a full-throated enthusiasm that was worth every penny they were paying him. The bartender tapped Roman on the shoulder and handed him his martini. The BBB contingent commandeered the dance floor with a coterie of some of the most beautiful women in Jefferson Run.

Roman took a sip of the martini. It wasn't bad. The bartender had a heavy hand with the vermouth despite his instructions. He realized he was staring at Torrent and Tranquil and physically forced himself to look away.

There had to be a phrase or a saying that articulated the feeling one had attending a party thrown by and drinking the liquor of a man who had knocked out your fucking teeth a week and a half ago.

Roman took another sip of his drink and let it wash over his tongue. He'd once watched this nature special about Komodo dragons. The narrator detailed in an onerous voice how the Komodo dragon would bite its prey and infect it with its bitch's brew of venom and the bacteria that lived in its filthy mouth. Then the giant lizard would stalk its prey slowly, quietly, with patient resolve, until finally the prey toppled over, too sick to go on.

And then the Komodo dragon would begin to eat its prey. Alive.

That wasn't the part that had creeped Roman out, though. It was the ancient dead eyes of the dragon, as it followed its prey like a reptilian Javert, that got under his skin. Eyes that stared into the abyss and never blinked.

Do my eyes look like that, Torrent? Do you know I'm going to bite you and watch you fucking rot until I eat you alive? Roman thought.

"Why you looking so mean?" a voice said from his right.

Roman turned and saw a voluptuous young woman with a huge head of curly hair that was almost an Afro and the wide doe eyes of an anime character. She was wearing a tight yellow dress tied at the neck, with the back completely open, showing off her sun-face tattoo. The dress clung to her like an insecure lover. Judging by her complexion, she was either a white girl with a good tan or Latina with at least one parent descended from European explorers. The hair, the pretty light brown eyes, her luscious mouth that had broken into a wide grin, gave her a somewhat elvish appearance.

Roman liked that look. He liked it a lot.

"My drink is almost empty. It's a tragedy," Roman said.

"Well, I don't have a drink at all. Maybe if you buy us both something sweet we can avert this calamitous set of circumstances," she said.

Roman felt his face stretch into a grin.

He held out his hand.

"Roman Carruthers."

The girl took his hand.

"Jealousy Evers."

Roman raised one eyebrow.

Jealousy giggled. "My mama said between her booty and my daddy's eyes she knew people were going to be jealous of me, so she just went ahead and named me that and took away their power."

"Is that a real story?" Roman said.

"If it ain't real, it should be," Jealousy said.

Roman laughed. "What you drinking, Jealousy?"

"Can I get a mojito?"

"I'm going to resist the urge to ask, *Can you?* That sounds good, I'll have one too," Roman said. He ordered the drinks and handed Jealousy hers when the bartender returned.

"So, Jealousy, what do you do when you're not standing around looking gorgeous?" Roman said.

She took a sip of her drink. "Do you want to know my hobbies or what I do for a living or what I do when I take a mental health day?"

"All of it. Tell me everything," Roman said.

"Wow, a man who really wants to listen. You're sure you're not a cryptid?" Jealousy said.

"Far as I know, I've never been on a Patterson-Gimlin film," Roman said.

"Lawd, are we having the nerdiest conversation ever?" Jealousy asked.

"Not yet. We'd probably have to up the ante, maybe start talking about *Star Trek* or *Doctor Who* or anime first," Roman said.

"Anime, huh? Quick, tell me your favorite," Jealousy said.

"I'm partial to the old-school ones like *Ninja Scroll*," Roman said.

"You're serious, aren't you? Damn. You standing here looking all *GQ*, but you're a little weird, aren't you?" Jealousy said with a laugh. Roman rolled his eyes.

"I'm just teasing, we have that in common. If you tell me you're into cosplay, we may have to run away together," Jealousy said.

"I think that's where we diverge, sadly. It was fun while it lasted," Roman said.

Jealousy smiled. "Jealousy's my name, but my friends call me Jae," she said.

"Well, I hope we can be friends, Jae. I'm curious about what you do," Roman said.

"Oh, sorry, got sidetracked by the positive nerd vibes. Well, I mentioned some of my hobbies, but my day job is I'm an administrative assistant for the mayor's office. Exciting, I know. Try to contain yourself," Jae said.

"Actually, I do think that sounds interesting. I grew up here, and every mayor we ever had probably needed an army of assistants to keep track of their scandals," Roman said.

"Well, don't tell anybody I said this, but Mayor Gravely is slicker than an eel covered in baby shit. He won't get caught up," Jae said.

Roman howled. "I gotta remember that one."

"What about you? What is it that Mr. Roman Carruthers does to pay the bills?" Jae asked.

Roman swirled the ice cubes in his glass. "How long you been in Jefferson Run?" he asked.

"That's not an answer, Mr. Carruthers. I'm going to have to direct the witness to answer the question," Jae said.

Roman cast his eyes away. The DJ was now playing "When the Last Time" by Clipse. Apparently Tranquil was a fan of the Virginia duo, because he was sitting in a chair on the dance floor as three women took turns giving him a lap dance.

"No, I asked that because most people know what my family does. My father owns Carruthers Crematorium. It's been in Jefferson Run for a long time. It's actually kind of nice meeting someone who don't know about it," Roman said.

"Oh, that's y'all? I grew up in D.C. My mama and daddy broke up and my daddy came down here to Jefferson Run. He had some kids with a woman here. Unfortunately, our father liked to take things that didn't belong to him and he went away for a long time. While he was gone, we got to know each other a little bit. I got laid off from a PR firm in Maryland last year and needed a job, and they knew about a job in the mayor's office, so I came on down," Jae said.

"I'm sorry about your dad," Roman said. The story of his mother was right on the tip of his tongue, but he wanted to preserve this point in time a little while longer. Once the words came out of his mouth, they could never go back to when she didn't know his mother had disappeared.

"Yeah. It was tough. He, uh . . . he just lived a dangerous life, and, uh . . . it was . . . he's still inside. He'll be sixty-eight this year, and . . ." Jae trailed off, her voice fading away as the music reached a crescendo.

"I understand. My mom disappeared when I was sixteen. Nobody ever saw her again. People like to say our dad killed her, because why wouldn't somebody who owns a crematory use it to get rid of his cheating wife, right? Been twenty years, and people will still ask us to our face did our father kill our mother. That's Jefferson Run for you. They can never let the past be the past. I'm sorry if that's an overshare," Roman said.

Jae moved closer to him and leaned against the bar. "I think I started the oversharing. I'm sorry about your mom. God, we have too much in common. We should probably stop while we are ahead," she said.

Roman turned to look at her. "I mean, I don't think we should stop just yet. We probably have some more things to overshare."

Jae smiled. "You're trying to give Mayor Gravely a challenge for the slickest man in Jefferson Run, huh?"

The music changed again to a slow, sensual song. Roman was going to ask Jae did she want to dance, when he saw Torrent and Tranquil moving toward him. He steeled himself, but he felt a squadron of bumblebees erupt in his stomach.

"Jae, you know this fool?" Tranquil said.

"I know he bought me a drink and I know his family owns the crematory and I know he watched *Unsolved Mysteries* because he knows about Bigfoot. But that's all I know right now. I'll find out the rest later," Jae said. She smiled at Roman again. Roman returned it, but it felt hollow. Torrent and Tranquil were glaring at him.

Torrent slipped his arm around Jae's waist.

Fuck, Roman thought. She's his girl. One of them, anyway.

"Sis, let me talk to my mans here for a minute," Torrent said

It took every ounce of self-control for Roman to keep his jaw from dropping. Torrent kissed Jae on the cheek.

"Terrance, don't be an ass. We was just talking. You too, Tracy," Jae said.

"I ain't gonna do nothing. I just wanna talk to the man," Torrent said. Roman let the knowledge that his real name was Terrance and Tranquil's was Tracy sear itself in his brain. All knowledge was valuable. Jae was their half sister. They had the same father.

"Don't let them scare you. I'd like to continue our conversation. We can discuss your theories about the Loch Ness monster. I'm going to the bathroom. When I come back, y'all better not have run him off. I mean it," Jae said. She sauntered across the dance floor and headed for the restrooms.

Torrent stood in front of Roman stroking his goatee. Roman wondered if he knew how banal his villainous mannerisms were. He then immediately reevaluated that thought. He *was* a fucking villain.

"You trying to fuck my sister? Trying to get your lick back?" Torrent said.

Roman recoiled. "What? No, I didn't even know she was your sister until you came over here."

"He lying," Tranquil said. His voice was calm, but his eyes were charged like twin lightning bolts. Roman could see murder in those eyes, like seeing an alligator just under the surface of a lake.

"I'm not lying. I was just standing here and we started talking. I'll leave her alone. And I came to the party because I wanted to talk to you and make sure you got what I gave Yellaboy. Because I believe in trust but verify," Roman said. He was scared, but he was also pissed. These were dangerous men, killers without a doubt, but they were also cowards who ran an old man off the road and put him in the nether realm between life and death. Never mind what they did to him and Dante.

They tried to kill his daddy.

Torrent shook his head.

"All you do is talk. We got our money. You ain't gotta verify shit. But stay. Enjoy the party. Take Jae out if you want. I don't wanna hear her mouth about us scaring you off. But next time I see you, it better be because you dropping a tax payment or you taking my sister out on a date. I don't know how much longer I can hold Tranquil back from killing your ass," Torrent said.

"Look, what I wanted to say—"

"Did he stutter, motherfucker?" Tranquil said.

Roman felt Tranquil's bloodshot killing orbs bearing down on him but he had to press forward. It was now or never to make his case. Tranquil's rage was not more powerful than Torrent's avarice.

"I know a good business opportunity when I see one. If we can't talk here, we should talk soon. We can help each other," Roman said.

Jae sidled up to his side and bumped him with her hip.

"These two behaving themselves?" she said.

"I told you we just wanted to talk to the motherfucker. Come on, we're doing a tower of shots for Tranquil," Torrent said.

"Come on, Roman, let's do these shots. Then you can tell me why *Cowboy Bebop* is better than *Blade Runner*," Jae said.

"I think we are going to have to agree to disagree on that," Roman said.

Jae stuck her tongue out at him.

Torrent looked bemused.

Tranquil was incandescent.

Roman checked his Rolex: 4:00 A.M.

Dante was sprawled out on a couch with Desiree in a tangle of limbs. Roman went over to them and shook Dante. At first his brother pushed his hand away, but Roman was persistent.

"Get up. People are leaving," Roman said.

"Hmm . . . okay. Wait. Desi, get up," Dante said. He untangled himself from her long legs and got shakily to his feet. Jae came stumbling over and leaned against Roman. He thought he was the last sober person in the building. He'd cut himself off hours ago. Now the inside of his mouth was coated with the sour aftertaste of the last thing he drank, a poorly made old-fashioned.

"Lawd, I'm a lightweight. I only had three mojitos," Jae said as she held up four fingers. Roman shook his head. He liked her energy. Their conversation was smooth and uncomplicated no matter what they were discussing. After today he would like to see her again, but he wasn't sure that was going to be possible.

"Are you driving? We can give you a ride if you want," Roman said.

Jae waggled her finger at him while a wide grin ran across her face. "No, no, Mr. Carruthers. You're not getting this golden palace that easy. I'll call an Uber to take me home," Jae said.

"Wasn't like that at all, I—"

"Oh, you don't want to visit my golden palace?" Jae said, laughing. Roman turned and took her in his arms. He glanced over the balcony railing and saw Torrent and Tranquil and their entourage rousing themselves from the booth where they had polished off two bottles of bourbon and half a bottle of tequila. Roman had a feeling some of them would become reacquainted with those spirits as they prayed to a porcelain god this morning.

"I didn't say that. You never heard those words come out my mouth. I was only saying I wanted you to get home safe, is all. We don't want the palace to fall, do we?" Roman said. He wanted to kiss Jae, but he saw Torrent and Tranquil begin to make their way to the door. The crowd was spilling out into the night with destinations as varied as their intentions.

"Come on, let's get downstairs. We'll wait for your Uber with you. Make sure you're good," Roman said.

"A man as chivalrous as his name. Okay, my centurion, take me and release me from this garrison," Jae said. Roman took her arm and began to head for the stairs.

"Romans were not chivalrous. They were conquerors," he said.

"They were an empire that fell in sections. One unscrupulous emperor after another. Power without empathy leads to ruin," Jae said.

"You really are a nerd. Let's get you home. Dante! We going," Roman said.

"You an ass. But a cute ass," Jae said, giggling.

Roman helped her down the stairs, where they joined the mass of formerly animalistically aroused bodies as they spilled out onto the street. Roman watched the end-of-the-night traditions. Couplings agreed to in the opaque environs of the Kingdom were being enforced with varying levels of enthusiasm. From splitting the cost of a hotel to, "No, I'm tired, I'm going home."

Roman came outside with Jae holding his hand. Dante had left Desiree behind and was standing next to Roman. The crowd seemed in no hurry to disperse and stood on the corner, their incessant chatter creating an abstract soundscape on the street interrupted by the occasional passing car.

Torrent and Tranquil were down at the far end of the corner with their entourage, divided into two camps. There were the dancers who were still bopping and twisting to a beat only they could hear, and the dope boys who were bouncing off lampposts, random cars, and each other.

Roman thought they were ginning themselves up for a fight no one but they wanted to have.

"I gotta get me an Uber," Jae said.

"Let me get it for you," Roman said as he pulled out his phone.

"No, you don't get my address yet, Mr. Sasquatch Enthusiast," Jae said. She retrieved her own phone from her purse. Roman was typing away at a quick text message when he heard Torrent's voice cut through the chatter like a samurai sword.

"Hey, where the fuck Yella at?" Torrent yelled. Roman wondered whether the disappearance of Splodie weighed on him more than he'd initially revealed. Was Torrent embarrassed by another soldier seemingly skulking off into the night like a deserter from a faraway war?

"Man, fuck him, let's go to Waffle House," Tranquil said. He then started singing in a shockingly good voice a song where he used the melody from "Adore" by Miguel to articulate his love for Waffle House.

Roman put his phone back in his pocket. He and his trio were less than five feet away from Torrent and his bifurcated cabal. He moved away from Jae and closer to Torrent. Jae was typing into her phone and bopping her head side to side, making her curls move like seaweed.

Roman took another step closer to Torrent.

The crowd began to disintegrate as mini-groups broke off from other larger groups and the street began to empty.

Roman was right behind Torrent's group.

He closed his eyes and got ready.

He started counting. If he got to ten, then Khalil had called it off.

He got to eight when he saw the headlights.

A late-model sedan came roaring down Lillyhammer. The wheels squealed like suckling pigs as they made the turn and headed straight for the Kingdom.

Roman waited. He spread his legs and got into the barest of crouches.
He waited.
He waited.

Then, as the car was about to roll past, he screamed as loud as he
could:

"GUN!"

He reached out for Torrent's arm with his right hand and reached
behind him to grab Jae with his left. In one smooth motion he pulled
both of them down to the pavement with him like they were all struck
with the unexpected desire to pray.

The car came barreling by them. A blast of automatic fire cracked the
night like a stonemason's maul. The entrance to the Kingdom exploded
in a shower of splinters. The crowd screamed in unison and scattered like
atoms. Roman lay partly on Torrent and partly on Jae. Tranquil stood up
and fired the full clip from his semiautomatic at the rapidly receding car.
Roman raised his head and saw him standing in the middle of the street
walking and shooting as the car became just an echo in the dark.

Those who hadn't run began to rise from the concrete. Torrent
pushed Roman off him.

"Get the fucking cars! We going after this bitch!" Torrent said.

The BBB began to rush to their cars, but Tranquil stood in the middle
of the street, his still-smoking gun sending insubstantial tendrils spiraling
toward the sky.

"He gone," Tranquil said.

"Fuck that, let's get it," Torrent said, but Tranquil just shook his head.

"He turned off his taillights. He gone," Tranquil said.

Roman got up and gently helped Jae to her feet.

"You all right?" he asked.

"Yeah . . . I think so," Jae said. Roman saw she was shivering. He put
his arms around and held her close.

"Get up! Russell, get up!" a crystalline voice screamed into the night.
Roman looked over Jae's shoulder and saw an older woman trying to
hold up an older man. Roman had seen him earlier in the night giving
off old-school player vibes as he moved among the much younger crowd.

Roman pegged him for a once-upon-a-time ladies' man who had gotten into the hottest party in town on a hope and a prayer.

Rome saw the blood, and his first thought was Khalil had actually shot someone. But then he realized it was coming out of his nose like a fountain. The man was making wet gurgling sounds as he slumped to one side, putting all his weight on his companion.

Roman thought Russell looked like he was having an aneurysm. The blood, the partial paralysis, the way his eyes were bulging looked just like his great-uncle Everrett when he passed out at church one cold Sunday many years ago.

People just watched as the woman struggled to help the man to the ground. A few were filming the situation. Roman let go of Jae and ran over to the couple and helped the lady in her effort.

"I'm calling 911!" Dante said as he stood beside Roman. The man began to convulse, sending drops of blood spraying everywhere. Roman felt a few land on his face like the front edge of a summer rain.

"Russell!" the woman wailed as Roman tried in vain to hold him still.

CHAPTER EIGHTEEN

Roman woke up with Jae's body, fully dressed, curling into his like a cat. He could feel her warmth through his shirt like a heating pad on low. Her bed was a double, but it was short. He had to tuck his legs up so his feet wouldn't dangle. They had come back to her apartment near Millicent Avenue out near the bridge that took you into Warren County. Dante was on the couch, thankfully not snoring too loud. Jae turned to him and lay against his chest.

He'd texted Khalil after the ambulance came and carried the man who had collapsed over the Signor Regional Hospital. They hadn't even bothered to take him to the hospital in Jefferson Run.

That cake came out just right, Roman had texted.

Let's talk about cooking another one, Khalil had texted back.

After the drive-by but before the cops had arrived, Torrent had begrudgingly offered Roman his thanks. Tranquil kept his distance during their exchange.

"That was good looking out. Why'd you do that? If I owed a motherfucker what you owe, I wouldn't stop him from getting ventilated." He pointed at the holes in the front door of the Kingdom. "Them bullets could have solved all your problems."

"I wasn't trying to protect you. I just saw them coming around and I saw the gun. Wasn't about you at all. I just grabbed the people nearest to me. That was Jae and you. Could've been anybody. And you're right. It would've been better for me and my family if you had got hit. But I just happened to be standing near you. My bad luck I guess," Roman had said.

Torrent had chuckled.

"You different from me. Fool start blasting, you better look out for yourself," Torrent had said.

"Guess we different," Roman had responded.

He'd read a book once about sociopaths versus regular people, and one thing that stayed with him was how sociopaths lie versus non-sociopaths. The book said a sociopath doesn't have any difficulty lying because they don't have the same emotional responses as non-sociopaths. Essentially, they don't feel guilt. As an aside, the book said if you're a non-sociopath, the best way to tell a lie is to include as many truthful details as possible. It can help to mitigate your involuntary guilt responses.

So he'd told Torrent his version of the truth. If it had been a real drive-by and not Khalil purposely shooting over everyone's head, a few of the bullets finding a home in Torrent and Tranquil's faces would have solved a large chunk of his problems. But, like Khalil said, the remaining members of the BBB would have just assumed the debt.

"You have to take them all off the board if you want this to be done. Not easy, but not impossible," Khalil had said.

"Nothing is impossible. It just depends on how bad you want it," Roman had said.

The fake drive-by had served its purpose. Torrent owed Roman. Even if he didn't want to admit it. Now was the time to put part two of his plan in action. On one level the vast amounts of money they were bringing in presented a unique professional challenge. Roman knew there was no way they were laundering it all through Trout's and the Kingdom. They were spending a fair amount, but not as much as Roman had initially thought. They had nice but not extravagant vehicles. From what Khalil could figure, Torrent and Tranquil's house wasn't bigger than his father's. Khalil thought they had a lot of actual physical cash just floating around. The financial adviser in Roman considered that a waste. He could take that cash and turn it into long-term investments and short-term windfalls. He could use their ill-gotten gains as clay to build a financial masterpiece. Then use that masterpiece to engineer their downfall.

That was parts three and four.

The two thousand five hundred he'd slipped Yellaboy was just the start.

"You still here. I thought you and your brother would have slipped out as soon as my restless leg syndrome kicked in," Jae said. He felt her lips move through his shirt.

"Just waking up. Didn't want you to be by yourself. That was the whole reason we came over," Roman said.

"I know. And I appreciate you. I guess I can tell my friend Trina she can take 911 off speed dial since you and your brother turned out not to be creeps," Jae said.

"We are, we just hide it well," Roman said.

She sat up and scooted her butt back toward the headboard.

"I'm serious. I still have my dress and my drawers on. You didn't make it weird, no pun intended. I really did text Trina and told her you guys were coming over. Safety first," Jae said. She touched his cheek, then sighed. "I've been here long enough you'd think I'd be used to random drive-bys, but I've never been in one. I didn't want to be alone last night, but I wasn't feeling frisky either. You and your brother were actually gentlemen. That means a lot," Jae said. "You gotta be someplace? Like church or something?" Jae said. Roman noticed how she moved so that her back was to him and she was again lying on her side.

He liked feeling her near him.

"My daddy stopped going to church when our mother disappeared. Which meant we stopped going. I never felt the need to pick up the habit again."

"I usually try to make it to Gethsemane Baptist at least twice a month. After last night I should get up and go, since nobody got shot," Jae said. She yawned and pushed her body against Roman even more.

But someone got hurt, Roman thought.

When they had gotten to Jae's apartment, he'd gone in her bathroom and washed his face. None of Russell's blood had gotten in his eyes or his mouth, but the few drops that had hit his forehead had dried there. When he looked in the mirror, they looked like tribal markings.

Roman was not naïve enough to think his plan of going after the most dangerous gang in Jefferson Run wasn't a game with mortal stakes, but he wanted to ask the man in the mirror if he was prepared for collateral damage. He knew what that man would say, though:

It's us or them. I don't want innocent people to get hurt, but I don't want my brother or my sister or my dad to get hurt any more either. I'm sorry about Russell, but this isn't about him.

Roman thought there was fragment of his deeper self that was repulsed by that attitude, and frankly his more conscious mind was appalled, but his pragmatic soul thought he'd have all the time in the world to feel appalled later once Torrent and Tranquil and the BBB were a fading graffiti tag on another abandoned building. Getty, Splodie, Russell, Yellaboy, they were all tinder for the flames. That was the way he had to think about them, or he'd go insane.

"You can stay as long as you want, but I'm going back to sleep. I got a long day tomorrow. Those people from the state are coming," Jae said.

Roman put his arm over her waist. She put her hand on top of his.

"What people?" he asked.

"People from the state Office of Housing and the lieutenant governor. The mayor and some big-time real estate guys are trying to get some grants to revitalize the Skids. Bring in some apartments and fancy restaurants and all that hipster shit like they doing in Richmond," Jae said.

The wealth manager in Roman perked up at the mention of real estate investment. Most people thought of actual buildings as a solid investment, and they were in the long run, but state-encouraged construction projects not controlled by VDOT were basically money-printing machines. If you got the construction contract or the supply contract, you'd be swimming in cash like Scrooge McDuck.

Not to mention all the creative accounting measures one could take. There were the kickbacks, the skimming, the overly inflated estimates, the bloated budgets. If you knew where a project was slated to be, you

could buy up the cheap abandoned properties and sell them for exorbitant prices.

"Where in the Skids they planning on doing this?" Roman asked.

"Out there near where the Mason jar factory and the brake shoe
place used to be. Down there by the Greenhaven Apartments. I don't
know what they planning, but it must be big, because the whole office
has to be there, even the remote people," Jae said. Her words were coming out with a sleepy lilt.

"So if the mayor gets voted out, do you lose your job? Or do you
work for city hall?" Roman asked.

"I mean, yeah. Like, if he gets voted out the new mayor will probably
bring in his own staff. But according to the ladies I work with, the mayor
ain't lost an election since 2008. Gravely ain't going nowhere," Jae said.

"Your brothers have an interest in politics, huh?" Roman asked.

"You know they own that restaurant, right? Trout's? Like, they got
a guy to manage, but they own it. They've given the mayor money for
his campaign. They've worked together through the Chamber of Commerce. That's how they knew about the job. They know the mayor
pretty well. I guess he knows them too," Jae said.

"What's that mean?" Roman asked. He didn't want to push or seem
too eager to hear about Torrent and Tranquil. He liked Jae, he really did,
but she also obviously had intimate knowledge about a different aspect
of the BBB. He'd be a fool not to at least listen.

Jae turned over and put her hand on his cheek again

"I know they probably tried to scare you last night. And I know
you saw Tracy unloading on that car. You're not stupid. I wouldn't
have let you in my house if you were. They're my brothers and I love
them, but you don't want any parts of anything they got going on. I'm
glad they didn't scare you off, but now I gotta really go back to sleep,"
Jae said.

"Okay," Roman said.

He lay back against his pillow and a few seconds later Jae's body went
still. Her chest rose and fell with an easy rhythm and he knew she was
asleep.

He wished he could sleep, but his mind was awash in thoughts and images that made his skin break out in gooseflesh. The BBB and the mayor had a relationship. A major construction project was coming to Jefferson Run down by the Skids. Tidal waves of money were about to be crashing into Jefferson Run like a tsunami.

Enough money to buy the loyalty of all the king's men, Roman thought.

Jae pulled his arm tighter around her in her sleep.

Roman and Dante left Jae's around noon. He and Jae exchanged phone numbers and social media handles, the two opening salvos of a modern courtship.

"Any of these women your girlfriend or your wife?" Jae said when she perused one of his social media pages that was mostly photos from real social events with real people.

"You living up to your name now," Roman said.

"That wasn't a no," Jae said.

Roman walked over to her as Dante headed down to the car. He leaned down as she lay on the bed and kissed her.

"No. I don't have a girlfriend or a wife," he said.

Miss Delicate doesn't count, he thought.

"Okay, but if you're lying, I'm going to sacrifice you to the Mothman," Jae said.

"Moths don't have mouths. I think I'll be okay," he said with a wink before walking out the door.

Dante was waiting by the car. When Roman unlocked it he got in the driver's side. Roman paused. "You good?" he asked.

"Man, get in the car," Dante said.

Roman got in and they took off.

"That was you and Khalil, right? That's what you wanted me to see. How you saved Torrent's life. Big bad Torrent Gilchrist didn't get filled full of holes like a litter scoop because Roman Carruthers saved his life," Dante said.

"Something like that," Roman said.

"What was y'all thinking? What if somebody got shot? And Russell! Scared that old man so bad he dropped dead," Dante said.

"Pull over," Roman said.

"For what? So you can give me a speech about how this all my fault again?"

"Pull over," Roman said.

Dante grimaced and pulled into the Church's Chicken parking lot. Roman turned in his seat. Dante leaned his head against the window.

"Khalil shot that machine gun with one hand while driving an old-school Ford Taurus. He knows what he's doing. Do you? This the last time I'm going to say this to you. Because I don't have the energy or the time to keep discussing this. We are trying to fix *your* mistake. Now, you can keep questioning how I go about that, or you can help. But you can't do both." Roman said every word distinctly as he poked the dashboard for added emphasis.

"Now let's go home."

Roman turned around and faced the windshield.

Dante pulled back into traffic.

As they drove, the silence between them became a monolith made of recriminations and regrets. Whose specifically was a matter of perspective.

When they pulled up to the house, Roman saw a car in the driveway, but Neveah's truck was nowhere to be found. Dante parked to the left of the car, a plain blue Chevy Malibu.

"That's a cop car," Dante said before turning off the Challenger.

"How do you know?" Roman asked.

"All the license plates start with JR. They think they're unmarked, but everybody knows it," Dante said.

As if on cue, Chauncey exited the Malibu, while a white cop got out of the passenger seat. They walked around to the rear of the Malibu and waited.

"Don't get nervous," Roman said. They got out of the car and stood a few feet away from the police officers. Chauncey showed his teeth. Roman thought it was too predatory to be called a smile.

"How you fellas doing? You and I have met," he said to Roman, "but I haven't had the pleasure with your brother. Chauncey Mansfield, and this is my partner Joseph Neary." He held his hand out and Dante looked at it. He didn't extend his.

"All right. Well, fellas, last time was a courtesy call. This time it's official business. We're trying to find Mr. Getty, and now his girlfriend's mom can't find her, one Cassidy Gutierrez. Now, Dante, I know you and Getty were cool. Did he ever tell you he was a CI? Did he ever tell you he was working for us?" Chauncey said.

Roman could tell by the extra bass he was putting in his voice that revealing to Dante that Getty was a snitch was an attempt to scare Dante into saying or doing something incriminating. Roman also surmised the cops thought Getty was dead, or they wouldn't be putting a snitch tag on him in the street. He figured they thought, what difference did it make if he was face down in a ditch?

"He ain't never tell me no shit like that," Dante said.

"The two of you were at the BBB party last night. The one that got shot up. Drive-by at approximately four-fifteen A.M. Patrol officer took statements from everyone including you two," Neary said.

"See, I think it's curious that Mr. Getty has gone missing. He was your friend," Chauncey said, pointing at Dante. Then Chauncey pointed at Roman. "You're new in town, but you're his brother. Then the both of you happen to be at a party for the biggest, most dangerous crew of assholes and sociopaths in four cities. Who, coincidentally, Mr. Getty worked with and passed information along to us about for the last six months."

Roman held his gaze.

"I think you're the smart one. Tell us what you know. Did the BBB get rid of Getty? Did y'all help them get rid of the body? If you're being extorted, we can help. I don't know if you know who you're dealing with if you're dealing with the BBB. Terrance Gilchrist and his brother Tracy, also known as Torrent and Tranquil, also known as the leaders of the Black Baron Boys, sons of Horace Gilchrist, a former associate of Luther Barnes, Silk Perry, and the founder of the Black Baron Boys, currently serving life in Coldwater State Penitentiary. The BBB moves drugs through Jefferson Run, mainly coke but some Molly and heroin. They run guns up to New York along 95 and they traffic girls through the Kingdom and Candy's and truck stops from here to Maryland. And that's just the stuff we know about. Torrent and Tranquil are suspected to have ties to over a dozen murders. Look, let's get down to it. Y'all ain't about this life. You tell us what you know about Getty, and we'll give you some protection. You don't, and then Torrent and Tranquil are gonna kill you when they are done with you," Chauncey said.

"Are we under arrest?" Roman said.

Chauncey looked at Neary. A look of irritation manifested over both of their faces.

"Don't try to play hardball with us. We're better at it, and we play dirty," Neary said.

"I'm not trying to play hardball. But we've had a long night and we're both tired. Yes, we were at the party. As were hundreds of other people who probably knew Getty as well. It's Jefferson Run. Everybody knows everybody. I mean, we call it a city, but it's a little town in a big city's over-coat. We gave our statement to the patrol officers. So, unless you want to say hi to my sister, I think we're done and we're going to go inside and get some sleep," Roman said.

When he mentioned Neveah, Roman could have sworn he saw Chauncey's left eye twitch.

"Maybe we should take them downtown," Neary said.

"We're just going to tell you the same thing we just told you. And then if you keep interrogating us we'll just call our lawyer. Now, gentlemen, I'm about to pass out. Maybe y'all should be investigating who tried to kill Torrent and Tranquil last night and let me and my brother get some sleep," Roman said.

Chauncey walked over to Roman and leaned forward until their faces were barely an inch apart.

"When Torrent lets that psycho of a brother of his loose on you, you're gonna die wishing you'd taken my help," he said.

Roman held his ground. "I don't want to see you again unless you have a warrant. My sister may tolerate your inconsiderateness, but I won't," Roman said.

Chauncey grunted. "If I come back, I'll have the warrant and an extra-tight pair of handcuffs," he said.

Handcuffs don't frighten me, Roman thought.

"You gentlemen enjoy the rest of your day. Come on, Dante," Roman said. He went up the steps and into the house. As his head hit the pillow, he briefly pondered why he wasn't anxious talking to Chauncey and his partner. Was he too tired to be nervous, or was he operating on instinct like an animal?

Like a dragon.

CHAPTER NINETEEN

N eveah woke up, packed her overnight bag, which ended up being a two-night bag, since she'd spent the night at Chauncey's before leaving for the winery, and headed out the door of the cabin she had rented. The winery had a bed-and-breakfast on the grounds. In a moment of post-orgasmic naïveté she had asked Chauncey if he wanted to go to the winery with her and get a room there. His laughter had been the answer that slapped her back into reality.

Neveah got into her truck and drove down the winding pea-gravel-covered driveway until she hit Route 249, which took her all the way through New Kent County and back to the interstate. Back to Jefferson Run. Back to her brothers and her father and all the phantoms that haunted that city's crumbling streets. Back to Chauncey too, but he wasn't really someone she could return to, since they never really had each other in the first place.

Neveah saw a squirrel who apparently had a death wish run across the road, then stop on the double yellow line. She was able to swerve to the right, avoid the squirrel, and not kill herself in the process.

There was a white cardboard storage box full of documents sitting in the passenger seat. The box itself was crisp and white, but the documents within were weathered. The box shifted when she swerved, but she caught it with her right hand before its contents were spilled all over the floor of her truck.

Neveah pushed the box back in the seat. She briefly considered putting a seat belt on the box but decided she didn't need to add that to the list of things that made her feel ridiculous.

The exit to Interstate 64 was noticeably free of traffic this Sunday morning. Neveah was surprised she didn't have a wine hangover. She'd drunk one whole bottle of a stunning sauvignon blanc while she'd read over the documents in the box.

She'd wanted to read her mother's case file for years, but her father's adamant refusal to acquire it from the police made that desire an impossibility. He was her husband and her next of kin and the police quite naturally deferred to him and his wishes, even though he was their number one suspect in Bonita Carruthers's disappearance for a half a dozen years. When Neveah had called the Cold Case Division of the JRPD, she was shocked that they hadn't totally forgotten about her mother. People in Jefferson Run thought they remembered her but most only remembered her vanishing. They didn't remember her as a person, only as a salacious story. A priggish cautionary tale used to frighten young women and chasten young men. The cold case officer, Detective Kelly, knew so much about her mother it made Neveah tear up while they talked on the phone.

"She was a surgical tech at the hospital, right? We talked to all her coworkers again last year. You'd be surprised how many of them still work there. A lot of them coming up on their twenty or twenty-five years. Your mother made a big impression on those folks. They talked about how she was a great coworker and made this dish for the potluck . . . a cheeseburger casserole? They said it couldn't be beat," Detective Kelly said.

"Did any of them tell you they thought my father killed her?" Neveah said.

Kelly cleared his throat. "A few of them were of that mindset, yeah. A few of them thought it was a former employee of your father's, Oscar Conley. A few of them thought maybe it was a vagrant, a hobo your mom tried to help, since the car was found on the tracks."

"You know, there are days I wish I knew, and then there are days I'm glad I don't. As long as I don't, I can hold on to a little bit of hope. Enough to hurt. But that hurting, it makes you think she might still be out there," Neveah said, surprised at how easy it was to talk to this cop, and not her own brothers or her father.

"Hope isn't a bad thing, but sometimes trying to hold on to it is like trying to hold a baby bird in your hands. You hold it too tight, you crush it; too loose, and it freezes to death. They're both so fragile but I think they're both worth trying to save," Detective Kelly had said.

He'd met her at Trout's to give her a copy of the case file. He was a handsome man with a smooth athletic agility to his walk and a smile that made her wonder what his mouth tasted like. Taut dark brown skin stretched over a fit but not overly muscular frame. Neveah thought he probably worked out but not to the point of alpha-bro narcissism. He sat down at her table and slid the box over with a slight frown on his face.

"This ain't gonna get you in trouble, is it?" Neveah had asked, taking his grim countenance as a sign of concern for himself.

"No. I'm the only one working on these cold cases. And all these documents are copies. I have the originals back at the station. They just look rough because they been handled so much. Our filing department keeps getting moved around at the station."

Neveah raised an eyebrow.

Detective Kelly gave her a slightly chagrined smile.

"Our roof leaks. Look, I'm only going to say this because I've seen it so many times. You think you want to read this. You think you want all the details. But you don't. There is an image you have of your mother. It's the same image we all have of our parents. Once you shatter that image, you can never put it back together again. There are statements and affidavits in here that are not flattering to your mother or your father. I think you and your family have a right to know what the case looks like. I think you have a right to know what we know. I just don't know if you should," Detective Kelly said.

Neveah thought he was a kind man. A lovely man to look at across a table in a restaurant. The type of man who would hold the door for you or pull out your chair or ask you if you were okay the first time you had sex. The type of man she could never have because of what was in that box sitting between the two of them.

"Detective, I know my mother was fucking around and my father drank too much. But I really do appreciate you trying to spare my feelings," she'd said.

An hour after leaving the winery cabin, she was pulling off the interstate onto the exit that took her into Jefferson Run proper and near the train tracks where the police had found her mother's car that Sunday after she had failed to come home Saturday night. She drove up onto the gravel-lined access road that led to the switchyard where her mother's car had been parked, with both the driver and passenger doors open wide and a few drops of blood smeared across the steering wheel.

The police report noted the only fingerprints in the car were her mother's and her father's. The blood on the steering wheel was her mother's. There were fibers from a pair of her father's pants in the car. According to the report, they'd asked her father if he ever drove the car. He'd said he did from time to time. The report stated they'd asked him when was the last time he'd driven it. He'd said earlier that week. The report also stated that other than her mother's blood there was no usable DNA in the car.

That explained the fingerprints.

Neveah couldn't help but think that was mighty convenient.

She pulled up to the crossing gate and parked off to the side. She got out and pulled her fleece jacket tight around her shoulders. When the police came across her mother's car, it was sitting in front of the crossing gate. The service road wasn't open to through traffic. It was mainly used by the railroad mechanics and maintenance crews. It was also a well-known hookup location. At night it was as dark as a politician's soul. The lights from the switchyard were focused on the trains and the tracks, not the service road. If one parked a little bit farther up the road, away from the gate, they'd find the privacy they were seeking.

Neveah walked over to the gate and put her hands on the arm that spanned the opening. In the file, Oscar Conley had admitted that he and Bonita Carruthers had been having an affair for almost a year. The last time they'd been intimate had been the day she disappeared. She'd gotten off from the hospital and had breakfast with some friends from the night shift. Then she'd come to the crematory. Oscar said in his statement that Keith Carruthers had gone to Roanoke that day for some supplies for the second oven. Oscar had stayed at the crematory to man the first oven and try to keep them on schedule. He said in his statement that Bonita had arrived at the crematory around noon or so and they had engaged in sexual activity until about one thirty, when Oscar had left the crematory to go get lunch. Bonita had offered to watch the first oven and then shut down the crematory and wait for Keith to return, if Oscar wanted to take the rest of the day off. Oscar said he had agreed to this. The report stated the police had taken Oscar's fingerprints and DNA, but neither were found in Bonita's car. The report stated they had tried to test the one working oven for DNA, but there were too many immolated remains to get an accurate DNA profile. The report stated Oscar was a person of interest, as was her father, but ultimately there wasn't enough evidence against either one of them to make an arrest.

Neveah thought of her father's mantra, and flinched.

"I think . . . she was being nice. Even though we was doing something wrong. Bonita was a nice person. She just wasn't happy, ya know? Her and Keith weren't happy," Oscar Conley had said in his statement.

Neveah heard a long mournful whistle come from the west. A train was making its way out of the hills and coming down tracks that ran parallel to the James River, taking their wares down to the Chesapeake Bay by way of the Newport News port instead of the Norfolk one. The police theorized whoever had taken her mother had tried to park the car on the tracks to destroy evidence, but for some reason they had stopped short.

Neveah thought they had lost their nerve. All her life, one thing Jefferson Run had taught her was that a train was nothing to play with. Every kid in town knew a story about another kid who got hit on the tracks and was reduced to a slurry of blood, bone, and flesh. Those were true stories, not urban legends. Every few years Weldon brought them what was left of a body that the trains, those iron behemoths, had chewed up and spit out like gristle all across the tracks. Many times those bodies had barely walked the earth for more than a dozen years. Kids who wanted to try to beat the train to impress their friends. Who tempted fate and then were aghast that fate gave in to temptation and rendered their young bodies into tallow.

Neveah thought her mother's killer (*that was what he was; not her kidnapper, her killer*) had punked out when he couldn't wait for the gate to go up and then drive across the tracks. He'd gotten scared. He was afraid to drive around the gate. Afraid he'd get stuck and couldn't get out, because he knew what the iron behemoths could do to his stocky legs and ropy forearms and thick sturdy torso. He was a workingman, after all.

BonitaBonitaBonitaBonita. She walked back to her truck, got in, and closed the door. She turned on the radio and found a rock station on the XM and turned the volume up to the last number. She grabbed her steering wheel and, as loud as she could, she screamed. She screamed and screamed, bracing her feet against the floor and pushing her head back into the headrest. Screamed until her throat ached.

Roman woke up around 1:00 P.M. with the biting sting of a hangover needling his brain. He rolled over and got to his feet. He padded down the hallway and went to the bathroom and splashed water on his face. He peed, washed his hands, and headed back to the room. He heard the front door open and then close with a slam. He walked down the steps and saw Neveah coming up carrying a duffel bag.

"Hey, you okay?" Roman asked. He could see she'd been crying.

"I'm fine," she said as she brushed past him.

"You can do better than Chauncey," he said.

"What makes you think I want better? He's a piece of shit. I can't ruin a piece of shit," Neveah said. She went to her room and closed the door. A sharp pain shot through Roman's stomach hearing his sister say that with such conviction. He went down to the kitchen and put on a pot of coffee. He pulled out the burner phone that Khalil had purchased for him. He dialed the new number Khalil had given him. He answered on the second ring.

"How you doing, hero?" Khalil said.

"If it wasn't so many people out there, I would have reconsidered," Roman said.

Khalil laughed. "So, there's a single-story house over on Alberta Avenue that I'm pretty sure is one of their stash houses. In the last two days four different girls with perfectly legal cars that are almost too plain and nondescript have pulled around back of that old house under the cover of darkness to a single-car garage. The cars go in the garage, then the women walk out front on their phones and then a dope boy from the BBB shows up and they switch cars. Then about forty, forty-five minutes later, that car leaves. That old house got three guys in the front room. And one guy that's in the garage. I'm sure they are all strapped. When you want to do it?" Khalil asked.

Roman heard Dante stirring. He turned his head and saw him come down the stairs still wearing last night's outfit. He walked through the kitchen and headed for the front door.

"Where you going?" Roman said.

"I need to go see somebody about something," Dante said.

"You going to get high?" Roman said.

"Can't get nothing past you, Inspector Gadget," Dante said.

"Hold on, man," Roman said into the phone. He put it on the counter, then moved quickly across the kitchen, then the living room, and cut Dante off before he could get to the door.

"Those cops are watching us. You wanna get high, you wait till tonight. You can't be riding around in the daytime popping Molly and oxy with them looking for Getty. Why you think I started driving the Challenger? They know you. Now, you did good earlier today, but they pull you over while you zooted? While you're buzzed out of your mind? You might say anything. And that's not an insult, that's the truth, little brother," Roman said in a low voice. He did not want Neveah to hear them.

"I'm a grown-ass man. I go where I want to go. I'm not going to talk to no cops. You just said I did good earlier. Now I need to get out of here," Dante hissed.

"Dante, I love you, but we doing some serious business now. We're doing get-the-needle business. Ride-the-yellow-mama business. You fuck around and fuck up, and Khalil will make you disappear before Torrent and Tranquil can get their hands on you. He's my friend, but he is not going to prison for anybody. Go get Pop's bottle. Go back upstairs until I'm ready to go. You sip on that until the sun go down," Roman said.

Dante cocked his head to one side. "You think that's all I am? An addict and a drunk. Give me a bottle like I'm a baby and shut me up."

"I'm sorry. But you're running out of here like you're an addict and you need a fix. I know you're more than that, but I can tell you're hurting. I was only thinking that the liquor could dull the pain," Roman said.

Dante made a sound halfway between a chuckle and a groan. "You're so good at talking, even when I know you're full of shit I almost believe you. I'm leaving. You want to fight? I know you can probably whoop my ass, but I'm gonna leave when you're done whooping my ass. So, let me take the rental and go where I gotta go, and while I'm out I'll tell everybody how you saved Torrent's life. Nobody can spread a rumor like party kids," Dante said.

He leaned close to Roman's ear. "You would never let Khalil hurt me. I believe he's not to be fucked with, but I know you. That threat won't work," Dante said.

He grabbed the rental car keys off the hook near the front door and left.

Roman grabbed the phone off the counter.

"You still there?" Roman asked.

"Yeah. Your brother is hardheaded. I hope he learns to listen," Khalil said, and Roman's whole body broke out in a shiver so powerful it looked like a convulsion. Dante was right, he would never willingly let Khalil hurt him. But the matter might not be in his hands, if it came to that. He had to do everything to make sure that it never got close to that. They couldn't handle another lost family member who faded away into the ether.

"He's not going to be a problem. I'm taking a friend to dinner to-night. Then I think I'm adjusting my proposal to Torrent and his boys. Something has come up that might make things move a lot faster," Roman said.

"All right, what about the house?" Khalil said.

"Tonight. Do it tonight," Roman said.

"Okay. Hey, you got some extra cash left, right? I may need a little bit. There's a guy in D.C. who we can trust. I may need him for this," Khalil said.

"Yeah, that's no problem. I'm going to get you straight when all this is done too," Roman said.

"I mean, I usually have a nominal fee, but that thing you did for my mom when that guy stole her retirement savings? Nah, we good for a while," Khalil said.

"I appreciate that," Roman said.

"The service and loyalty I owe, in doing it, pays itself," Khalil said. "*Macbeth.*"

"You and Shakespeare, an unrequited love affair," Roman said.

"Willie Shakes, the Bard. People like to think of him as this snooty upper-crust dude, but he was writing for the people. He just happens to be the best to ever do it," Khalil said.

"I'm not going to argue with you. My degree is in economics and accounting. We'll meet up tomorrow and talk," Roman said.

"Bet," Khalil said.

Roman hung up and put the burner back in his pocket. He went and poured himself a cup as he pulled out his regular phone and dialed Jae's number.

Corey Gardner checked his phone. It was 10:00 P.M. He picked up his tablet and tapped the on switch. The screen came to life but was buffer-ing. He hit the tablet hard. The screen kept buffering. Alia had dropped the last shipment for the night, and now he had three hours before those boys from the north side of Richmond came through to re-up their supply. Any given night they could be sitting on as much as eight kilos of heroin. They were a warehouse for the wholesale product that the BBB sold. There were other places that were more trap houses than stash houses, but they only had stepped-on product. What Corey and crew sat on was nearly pure uncut brownstone.

Corey was one of four guards stationed around the house. He knew if Sway saw him watching a "comic book show," he'd flip the hell out. He would say they were supposed to be guarding. Corey thought Sway took this whole situation too seriously. Who was going to fuck with the BBB in Jefferson Run? Who had that much of a death wish? Corey knew cops who didn't want to cross the BBB. Why were they breaking their necks to guard a place most people were too afraid of to try to rob?

He tapped the tablet, then shook it. He was about to throw it across the room when the show started playing and he could hear the dialogue in his earbuds. He leaned back against the old, torn-out kitchen wall and put his feet up on the table.

The opening credits were almost over when he smelled the gas.

He put the tablet down and walked to the back wall of the demol-ished kitchen. He turned left and saw a three-foot-by-three-foot square covered by a blue tarp. This was the product. It was all there, which was good, but what was bad, incalculably bad, was the smell of gasoline that was so heavy he had to step back and catch his breath.

He gripped the AR-15 he carried like a lucky totem. That much gas, so virulent it was seeping through the drywall, meant someone was about to burn the house down. He tried to find his voice, to shout out a righteous warning like a war cry, but all that came out his mouth was a strange bleating that sounded like "Four" instead of "Fire."

Corey ran out the front door past Sway. He left his tablet but he didn't care. Sway followed him into the street under a sky so black it almost looked navy-blue. Finally he found his voice and screamed, "FIRE!"

The other two guards, Mezzy and Daquan, came out to the porch. Mezzy was about to berate Corey for playing too damn much when he heard what he described later as a *whoomp*, and then a fireball exploded out to the porch. Mezzy and Daquan went flying into the street. They both landed on skinned elbows and bleeding knees.

Mezzy hopped to his feet and began firing into the house. The barrage from his MAC-10 reverberated through the night with an idiot roar.

"Mez, who you shooting at? Stop!" Corey yelled.

They all stepped back, including Mezzy with a literal smoking gun. The house was fully engulfed in flames now. Then a second explosion happened, and the massive force of this detonation reduced the house to splinters.

Later, after they had been berated and threatened by Torrent, Sway told Corey he thought the second explosion was a grenade.

Roman was pouring Jae another glass of wine when he got the text. It was only one word:

barbecue

He put the phone down and poured himself a glass of wine.

"Everything all right? Your girlfriend need you to come home?" Jae said, smiling.

"I don't have a girlfriend. I've got a beautiful dinner date, though," he said.

"Boy, you too smooth. You bob and weave like Bruce Lee," Jae said.

"I love Bruce Lee. I read *Tao of Jeet Kune Doe* three times," Roman said.

Jae giggled. "You the only dude I ever met who talks about his book instead of his movies. I like that, though."

"Oh, I love the movies too. *Enter the Dragon* is my jam," Roman said.

"Did you and your brother try to fight like Bruce Lee?" Jae asked.

"Yeah, and we broke a toaster in the kitchen. We stopped kicking and started wrestling, and . . ." Roman's voice faded down to nothing.

"What's wrong?" Jae said, all the teasing gone. She reached across the table and grabbed his hand. Roman shook his head and squeezed her hand.

"Nothing. That toaster. We broke it, and my mom yelled at us so bad. Made up cuss words to call us. She never got to replace it. You know, it's little things like that, they make you think of her. She never got to replace her fucking toaster," Roman said. He was staring past Jae, past the maître d', past the front door with FOUCHE's written on the door. He'd taken her to Richmond to find a restaurant worthy of the dress she was wearing. Now he was staring all the way back in time to the week before his mother vanished. He could see her so clearly, her face contorted with anger and amusement. He heard her call him and Dante some variation of knuckleheads combined with a profanity that would make all three of them laugh.

"I miss her laugh," Roman said.

He put the phone in his pocket and shook his head, tossing the memory aside.

"Everything's good," he said. He squeezed her hand, then released her. He plucked up his glass like it was a brittle rose. "Here, let's have a toast to new friends and new experiences," Roman said.

"Are we just friends, Roman?" Jae said, peering at him over the top of her own wineglass.

Roman smiled. "Well, we sure aren't enemies," he said as they toasted.

Dante was sprawled across Tug's couch. His mind felt like it was wrapped in cotton gauze. He was watching some adult-themed cartoons while Tug and Raynell were in the kitchen arguing over the last piece of shoofly pie. Dulsi was curled up on the floor at his feet. They had shared half a bottle of Percocets. Dante had crushed them with two spoons so they could snort them to hasten the absorption into their systems. He apparently had more tolerance than Dulsi. She'd hit two lines and folded herself into a yoga-esque pose and gone immediately to sleep.

His phone began to vibrate in his pocket. He pulled it out, but he didn't recognize the number. He squinted at the screen. He didn't recognize the number, but he knew who it was that was texting him. No one called him Deedee but one person.

        Deedee I miss u

Dante held the phone in his hand, breathing hard as he stared at the screen.

Finally, as the light from the television screen bathed him in angelic blue illumination, he typed with one hand his short response:

                                        I miss u 2 Cass

CHAPTER TWENTY

"Roman, wake up."

Roman's eyelids shot up like a pair of roller shades. He sat up and rubbed his face with both hands. Jae was next to him, her hand on his shoulder. He turned over and took her hand as it slipped from his shoulder and kissed it.

"What time you got to be at work?" he asked.

"In an hour, but I have to get ready. I have to go from hentai temptress to professionally bougie. It's a process," she said. He raised her head with one finger under her chin and kissed her. Their tongues touched for the briefest of moments before he pulled away.

"I should get going, then," he said.

"I didn't invite you over because you bought me dinner. I just want you to know that. I'm not that cheap of a date," Jae said.

"I know. I think we're two nerds that kind of like each other. That lamb chop was good, though," Roman said as he poked her in the side.

"Boy, you stupid," she said.

A gentle silence fell over them like a plush blanket. It was the silence that could only exist between two people who had expressed in the most profane ways imaginable their admiration for one another.

Roman was a little astonished by how adroitly Jealousy picked up on what he liked. What he needed. There were times when he tried to express those needs to women who weren't a professional like Miss Delicate, and both he and those women became embarrassed by what he wanted. By what he craved.

Jealousy suffered from no such reservations.

They had gone back to her place after dinner and begun the tentative exploration of each other's body that is the hallmark of new lovers. As they kissed on the couch, as Roman's hand moved under her skirt, Jae bit his bottom lip and held it between her teeth for half a second. Roman made a noise in his throat and she released him with an apology.

"Sorry." She panted and leaned her head forward to taste his lips again.

"Don't apologize. I like it," he'd said.

Jae had smirked, her eyes shining under the soft light in her apartment. Roman thought they looked like cat eyes. Dangerous and wild. She ran her nails over his bare chest. His shirt had magically found its way to the floor. He felt those nails trail over his stomach. A flutter floated up from his belly to his chest.

"You like a little pain?" Jae asked.

Roman had leaned back and gazed at her. The question was somewhat ironic except she didn't know it yet. He liked the pain, craved it, needed its cleansing power. Yet he was always loath to confess that to a real lover. It was a level of intimacy he rarely approached with someone who wasn't a professional. Roman had enough self-awareness to recognize that type of intimacy lacked emotional depth. It satisfied his desires but didn't really touch his heart. It fulfilled a need, yes, but it didn't give him everything he wanted.

Not like this.

Roman had two specific types that he was attracted to usually. In a professional domme he liked women who were older, who were tall and athletic, even muscular. In short, women who bore somewhat of a resemblance to his mother. He knew a therapist could write twenty thesis papers on that particular desire. In his personal life he had a more diverse array of attractions. Usually the two sides of his lust were like the two sides of a coin. They never touched, never intersected.

Jealousy was putting the lie to that idea.

She wasn't older. She wasn't tall. She didn't resemble his mother in any way, but there was something about her that touched the glowing ember of his yearning and stoked it beyond measure. It was more than physical lust. That was there, of course, but it was *her*. Her essence, her mind, her laughter, the way she could make him smile in spite of the menacing black cloud he found himself living under since he'd returned to the place of his birth. Despite everything going on, when he was in her arms he felt safe.

He felt like he could trust her.

"Yeah, I do. I like . . . to be . . . punished sometimes," he said.

He waited for her to blanch at his request, but she didn't.

She licked her thumb and forefinger, then took his left nipple between them.

"Do we need, like, a safe word?" she whispered. Roman felt his skin break out in gooseflesh.

"Yeah. It's *flame*," he said, his tongue thick and heavy in his mouth.

The next thing he knew, his hands were behind his back and Jealousy was straddling him. They were both naked, their skin slick with a sheen of sweat. The heat radiating from her thighs made him feel as if he were going mad. The kind of madness that takes one over when lust begins to metamorphose into new love.

"Open your fucking mouth," she'd panted. They had used his belt to tie his hands behind his back. She'd grabbed his chin with her hand as she rode him, both of them gasping at the primal connection they were sharing.

"I'm gonna spit right down your fucking throat. You like that, dirty boy?" she'd said between exhalations.

"Yessss," he'd breathed out as his eyes rolled back in his head.

The night had only gotten better from there.

And now they were kissing again, gently, at her door.

"You want me to call you when I get off?" Jae said.

"I don't know if it's appropriate to have phone sex in the mayor's office," Roman said.

She rolled her eyes. "Boy, go on. I gotta get ready for work. Talk to you later," she said.

"You better," he said as he stepped backward through the doorway.

Roman drove home as the sun rose over the empty warehouses and unoccupied storefronts on the east side of town. He turned off of Lillyhammer and onto Lucy Boulevard. He was humming along with an old Prince song on the radio when he drove past the burned-out husk of a building on Lucy. The lot where the building once stood was cordoned off with yellow crime scene tape. Roman stopped at the traffic light and let his eyes crawl over the fragments of what was once a home that had transformed into a stash house and was now just a pile of cinders.

When the light changed, he touched the screen on the dashboard and called Dante.

"Rome," Dante said when he answered. Roman thought he sounded like he was speaking through a mouthful of suet.

"I need you to call Torrent and tell him I want to talk to him today around two P.M. at Trout's," Roman said.

"You better leave them alone, man. I heard they lost a trap house last night. Somebody blew that shit up like a piñata with C-4 in it. Heard it looked like . . ." Dante stopped talking.

"Make that call for me," Roman said.

"Was that you?" Dante murmured into the phone.

"Make the call, Dante." Roman touched the screen and the line went dead. The light turned green and Roman drove through the intersection. The black, charred shell rapidly diminished in his rearview mirror. Khalil didn't mention if everyone got out before he tossed a grenade into the inferno, and Roman hadn't asked.

He knew he couldn't enact his plan against Torrent and Tranquil with no one getting hurt. Blood had already been spilled. But the only people who were missing Getty were the police. No one was shedding tears for Splodie except maybe a mother who lied to herself about who and what her son was, or a father who pretended he didn't know his son was an orphan-maker and a widow-creator.

Roman turned off of Lucy and onto Sycamore Avenue, heading home. When he'd first seen Dante raise that hammer, he'd been convinced Dante had signed their death warrants. He wasn't so sure anymore. Splodie's death gave them a little weight to put on Yellaboy. Yes, he could push that weight back on their shoulders, but Roman was becoming convinced it wasn't nearly as heavy for them as it was for Yellaboy.

His therapist would have said he was compartmentalizing a tragedy. Roman was beginning to think the only difference between a tragedy and an opportunity was how much what was lost mattered. In Splodie's case, not much at all. It gave Roman the opportunity to make Yellaboy join his plan.

Neveah heard Roman pull into the driveway. When he walked inside, she saw him notice that she was smoking in the house, one of their father's pet peeves. But his current status made pet peeves inconsequential.

"How was the winery?" Roman asked.

"Fine. A few white ladies trying to escape their poor choice to get married because their husband could play Savage Garden on the guitar. Look, I want to show you something," Neveah said. Roman walked over and sat down across from her.

"This is Mom's case file," Neveah said, pointing to the document box and the pieces of paper lying out in front of her.

"Your friend get this for you?" Roman snapped.

"No. I got it from the cold case detective. It's a copy. He has the original," Neveah said. She pushed the box toward Roman. "You should read it."

"I don't even want to touch it." Roman said.

"Why? Because you know it'll tell you what you don't want to hear?" Neveah said.

"No, because I remember what they were really like. They argued, but they loved each other. There's nothing in that box that's going to change my mind about that."

"He caught her fucking around," Neveah said.

"What? Why would you say that?" Roman asked.

"It's in the file. Some dude named Lawrence Lee. He was out of town when she went missing. Pop caught them making out in the parking lot of the hospital one night. I guess he left us here and rode up there. She took her ring off before she gave him a hand job, though, so at least she was considerate."

"Shut up," Roman croaked.

"Look at this," Neveah said. She pulled an eight-by-ten photograph out of the box. She laid it on the table between them. Roman glanced at it but quickly averted his eyes.

"That's the driver's seat in her car. You notice anything?" Neveah said.

"What am I supposed to be looking for?" Roman said.

Neveah tapped the picture. "The seat. She how far away it is from the steering wheel? Mama was tall, but Daddy's taller," Neveah said.

"So? Whoever . . . took her probably moved the seat. I don't know why you draggin' all this up now," Roman said sharply.

"You're half right. Look again. The driver's seat is pushed away from the steering wheel, but it's sitting at a sixty-degree angle. Like whoever was driving had to lean backwards," Neveah said.

"I don't want to hear this shit," Roman said.

"All those years of lifting bodies turned Daddy's lumbar region to dust. Even now he has to drive with the seat damn near horizontal. The cops didn't know that. Nobody knew that but us. Remember how Mama used to tease him about it?"

"So what, Neveah? He drove the car sometimes," Roman said.

"He was the last person to drive that car, Roman. Not our mother. Him."

Roman pushed the picture across the table toward Neveah. "I'm not going to listen to any more of this."

"She was out here slutting around, and our drunk-ass father found out," Neveah said. Her tone was flat but her face was a storm of con-flicted emotion.

"*Shut up!*" Roman thundered. He got up and shoved his chair backward so hard it fell over. Neveah felt him rush past her. Heard him pounding up the stairs and then the predictable slamming of a door.

"Told you we were fucked up," Neveah said as she took one last drag. As the smoke spiraled out her nostrils, she took the cigarette from between her lips and squeezed the glowing end between her dead fingertips.

CHAPTER TWENTY-ONE

Roman pulled up to Trout's and headed for the door. The restaurant was closed on Mondays, but Dante had gotten Torrent to agree to meet him there.

"I called D-Train," Dante had said. "He made it happen, but he said Torrent was pissed about that stash house. Whatever you have to say to him, it better be good. I'm not playing, Rome. He killed a DJ once for playing the same song too many times in a row."

"He won't be able to say no to this," Roman had said.

"You think money is always gonna make motherfuckers do what you want them to do. But some people don't care about money, Rome. Some people are just fucking crazy," Dante had said.

"Even crazy people care about money, they just have to be reminded of it from time to time," Roman had said.

He knocked on the locked door.

D-Train came and unlocked it and let him into the restaurant.

Torrent was sitting in front of a large platter of crab legs. Tranquil was sitting next to him. D-Train went and joined them. A young kid was standing toward the back of the room. Roman thought he couldn't have been any older than fifteen or sixteen. There was another man Roman didn't recognize sitting at the table with Torrent and Tranquil and D-Train. The man had a reddish mark on his face that went from his forehead down to his chin.

Torrent used a pair of compound pliers to break the crab legs open and pull the meat from the cracked shell. The sound of the carapace shattering made Roman jump a little. He'd eaten his share of crab legs over the years but he'd never seen anyone pick crab meat with such ferocity. He could tell Torrent was in a bad mood.

That would make him more susceptible to what Roman was going to propose. Based on Roman's best estimate, Torrent might have lost over a million dollars in revenue. If Roman's plan worked, he would make ten times that.

"Can I sit?" Roman asked.

Torrent pointed a crab leg at the empty chair across from him. The platter of crab legs was sitting on a layer of newspaper spread across the table. Roman thought in a few years that might be the only reason people still bought a newspaper.

"One of the things I do for my clients back home is make sure that I keep them abreast of possible financial opportunities. Multiple fiduciary streams to diversify their assets. I was talking to Jae at the party the other night and she told me something I think could be a huge financial opportunity."

"You fucking her?" Tranquil asked.

Torrent turned. "Hey! Stop asking people that. It's fucking weird. I mean it." He turned back to face Roman.

"And you. This the last time we meet face-to-face. I don't care what opportunity you got, I don't need to see you. I just need you to bring me my fifty grand every month. You got three months free. If I was you, I'd be doing some of that money magic you always talking about. But I don't need to see your face. It makes me think you think you're smarter than me. I start thinking that, and then I want to smack you with a handful of barbed wire. So, go ahead. Say what you got to say. I give you until I finish this crab leg," he said as he cracked it with the pliers.

"The mayor is trying to get a state grant to revitalize the Skids," Roman said. "That means they are going to raise the rent of people that live in the trailer parks and the efficiency apartments to force them out. They are going to buy up all the businesses, like the barbershop and the used tire garage and the sex toy shops. Then they are going to knock everything down and build luxury apartments so that white hipsters can move in and open vegan matcha tea shops and vinyl record stores. Now, they might be possible customers, but they probably get their recreationals from a guy named Connor who lives in the Fan over in Richmond. And if all that money gets poured into Jefferson Run the cops are going to be under a lot of pressure to make sure that the corporations who are investing their cash into this don't have to worry about gangsters doing gangster shit. This new project can severely cut into your businesses, whatever those might be. But there is a way you can get ahead of it."

"That shit ain't gonna happen for five fucking years. Even if they get started today," Torrent said.

"Yes, that's true. But the contract bids are going to go in soon. Construction companies. Building supplies. Demolition crews. I looked it up for my own curiosity. This entire project is estimated to be seven hundred million dollars. That's divided among all the vendors that will be attached to it. Which includes the construction companies, the building supplies companies, and the demo teams. There are three construction companies that might get that contract. The building supplies are a bit more complicated because most of the ones around that could handle a project like this are national chains, but I did find two local franchises that would be in the running. The demo teams are a dime a dozen," Roman said.

"You think I should buy up these companies. But even if I did, that don't mean the city gives them the contracts, does it?" Torrent said.

You just bit on the hook, Roman thought. One of his mentors in the finance world used to say, "If they are asking questions, they are thinking about giving you their money. Don't say anything to disabuse them of that notion."

Roman leaned forward and interlocked his fingers.

"I'm going to make an assumption about something, and you can tell me if I'm wrong. Jae told me you got her that job in the mayor's office. Y'all are cool with the mayor. He did you a favor. I don't know why you're cool; that's none of my business. But if you happened to own those companies, I could see the mayor giving your bids his seal of approval. For a certain amount of compensation, of course. But you're looking at millions. That's not even talking about how much you can skim from upping the budget. Phantom charges. Kickbacks from subcontractors. It's literally a gold mine. I can manage it through my company back home. You can make ten times that fifty grand a month and still make money on the legal end, and I can get a commission on it. It's a win-win for everybody. You can even use this to help clean some of your money. Because, while you might have a friend in the mayor's office here locally, the state police are always looking for a fat rat to take down. They love doing those press conferences with all the confiscated guns and drugs. Trout's can only do so much," Roman said.

His mouth felt like sandpaper. He tried to not look at Tranquil, even though he could feel his eyes on him like a mouse could feel a hawk zeroing in on him. He knew he was pushing them, especially after they'd lost that stash house, but he had to project confidence if he was going to get them to go for it. Two weeks ago this same kind of speech had cost him his teeth, but now they knew he could deliver. That hundred and fifty grand he'd given to Yellaboy to give to Torrent had not only bought him time, it had purchased that most elusive of commodities.

Respect.

They knew he could back up all his claims with results.

But, Roman thought, where is Yellaboy?

"I guess you think you can tell me what to do with my money now? Last time you did that you got your teeth knocked out," Torrent said.

Roman thought every time he talked to Torrent he learned more about how he operated. What his thought process was like. Who he was as a negotiator. In college he'd learned there were five types of negotiation styles. Compete, Accommodate, Avoid, Compromise, and Collaborate. Torrent was a Compete style. He won and you lost. To this end, he used fear to keep you off your game. Terror was his main lever. And he could pull it anytime.

Roman had to convert him into a Collaborator. Make him believe they could both win, even if that was a lie. Especially because it was a lie.

"You know how they got Al Capone?" Roman said.

"Who the fuck is Al Capone?" the kid in the back of the room asked.

"Eddie, Al Capone was a fucking boss," D-Train said.

"That's Eddie Munsta. He's a baby gun-clapper," D-Train said.

"I ain't no fucking baby. I done put in work," Eddie Munsta said.

Roman knew what "put in work" meant. How old was Eddie? Maybe fifteen? A fifteen-year-old murderer with bodies on him, who didn't know one of the most infamous gangsters in history. Roman didn't know what was a worse indictment of society, the bodies or the ignorance.

"Taxes. Everybody knows that," Torrent said.

"This motherfucker clowning you," Tranquil said.

"No, I'm not. I saying that's why I'm so paranoid about cleaning money. I don't know what you're doing with your money, but I know that the DEA and the FBI watch people who look like us harder than they watch anyone else. And part of the way they stalk us is they follow the money. The cleaner you make your money, the harder it is for them to follow it," Roman said.

Torrent tossed the empty crab leg in the bucket next to the tray. He grabbed a wet wipe and cleaned his hands and his mouth. "Real talk. Getting those contracts is smart. Cleaning our money with them is smart too. You a smart nigga," Torrent said. "But what I can't understand is why a smart motherfucker like you wanna help me. I cut your little brother's finger off. Knocked out your teeth. Got your daddy laying up in the hospital in the deep motherfucking sleep. By the way, them implants is good work, though. If I hadn't seen your teeth on the floor, I wouldn't know they fake. A motherfucker do all that to me, I'm putting him on a T-shirt for his mama to wear to a candlelight service." He took a sip of his drink and studied Roman with his coal-black eyes.

"You don't want to put me on a T-shirt, Roman?" Torrent asked. Roman didn't smile, he didn't grimace. He kept his face as neutral as he could. He didn't slump and he didn't puff out his chest.

I want you to die screaming for what you've done to my family, you fucking asshole, Roman thought.

"Look, let's lay it out," Roman said. "I don't like you. I don't like your brother. But, like I said, my job, what I do, is find opportunities to make money, then I make that money make money. I love my brother. I love my dad. I love my sister. They mean everything to me. Everything." That was the truth. He was using that truth as the foundation for the lie he was about to tell.

"But that's personal," he continued. "And this is business, my kind of business. The best way I can keep you from hurting my family or me anymore is to make you a lot of money. If I get paid in the process, all the better."

Torrent picked up another crab leg. "Let me think on it," he said.

"This nigga so full of shit his eyes brown," Tranquil said.

"That's why I'm gonna think on it. That okay with you?" Torrent said. Tranquil grabbed a metal mallet with a head about the size of a beer can and used it to crack open a crab leg.

"That's all I can ask for," Roman said. Torrent didn't respond. Instead, he turned his attention to the man with the burn marks.

"Corey, come here," Torrent said.

Corey came up to the table and stood near Torrent's right side between him and Tranquil. Roman saw the outline of a gun under his T-shirt.

"You was in the kitchen, right?" Torrent said.

"Y-yeah," Corey said.

Torrent took the pliers and cracked open a huge crab claw. "And you say when you smelled the gas you ran out front and hollered to everybody to get out the house, right?"

Roman's stomach began to undulate. Corey couldn't see Torrent's face.

Corey couldn't see the rage in his eyes.

"You was out the house first, right?" Torrent asked. "That's what you said."

"Y-y-yeah, I was," Corey said.

"Then why the fuck you didn't run around the back of the house to see who was throwing gas on it?" Torrent said.

"Huh? I was . . . I mean, I was trying to get everybody out, Torrent!"

Tranquil grabbed Corey's right hand while D-Train got up and grabbed his left. Torrent relieved him of his gun.

"You think I give a fuck about them niggas in that house? I can get four of you motherfuckers anytime I want. Eddie Munsta would've gone around back, and he fifteen! You let somebody burn down a house that belonged to us! The BBB! I put that house in your hands. Well, you ain't gotta worry about that no more," Torrent said.

Tranquil took the mallet and smashed Corey's hand. Corey screamed, then whimpered, as Tranquil raised the mallet and brought it down again. Roman heard a muted snap and pop like his ears were full of water. He almost retched when he realized that was Corey's metacarpals breaking.

Tranquil hit Corey's hand again and again, staining one side of the mallet red, until finally Torrent tapped D-Train on the arm. Tranquil and D-Train let Corey go. He crumpled to the floor, holding his hand against his chest.

Corey, responsible for the stash house, Roman thought as he tried to memorize Corey's name and transgression. Torrent resumed eating like they hadn't watched his brother bludgeon a man's hand to mush.

"You want some of these crabs?" Torrent asked.

"My hand! My hand! It wasn't my fault! Oh shit, it wasn't my fault! I done pissed myself," Corey blubbered as he lay on the floor.

Roman swallowed the saliva that had filled his mouth.

This is all a part of his negotiation style, he thought. He thrives off fear. He uses it to manipulate you. He's smart, but I'm smarter. I have to be. God, I have to be.

"Nah, I'm good," Roman said.

"Get the fuck on, then," Torrent said as he cracked open another crab leg.

CHAPTER TWENTY-TWO

Dante ate a bowl of cereal while the late news droned on about violence in the streets. Dante thought violence was everywhere. Why should the streets escape its brutal embrace? He flexed his nub. It still hurt, but it was healing. The doctor had told him the stitches would melt, so he wouldn't have to return to the hospital. When the stitches started to bleed, the doctor didn't seem concerned.

"That's normal. Put it in some gauze," his nurse had said when he had called with his concerns. Dante had an irrational thought that the doctors and nurses had talked about him after they'd sewn him up and found him pathetic and irritating, and that was the real reason they didn't want him to come back.

He swallowed a spoonful of marshmallows, milk, and grains. He felt that way a lot about a lot of people. They didn't want to be bothered with him because by any and all metrics he was a disappointment. He even felt his brother and sister didn't want him around sometimes. Despite the fact that Roman was risking his life to try to clean up his mess. Or that he was fairly sure Neveah would literally kill a person to protect him.

He swallowed another spoonful.

The docs in rehab had called those thoughts intrusive, but he just thought they were pragmatic. It wasn't true all the time, but it was true enough of the time he should start adjusting to it. To that end he tried to make himself scarce, but then he found himself missing Neveah and

Rome. He'd missed Roman so bad that even before the shit with Torrent and Tranquil (his most epic fail) he'd considered driving down to Atlanta until his pragmatic thoughts interceded.

He thought he and Rome could have some fun. Women found Roman attractive from a distance but when they got up close and talked to him they found him fascinating. Didn't hurt he could talk about anything. Any subject that could be brought up in conversation, Roman knew something about it. Dante knew he wasn't bullshitting either. He'd seen him discuss his top ten hip-hop albums of all time, then turn right around and discuss the different types of escargots. You had to be careful, though, because if you let him go on too long he'd turn it into a dissertation and the women he'd brought over to your table would be nodding off.

"That's just the cornball in you. You can't help it," Dante would say when Roman's enthusiasm for how ball bearings were made would chase off another sexy vibing honey. Roman would punch him in the arm, but not too hard.

Dante finished his cereal.

He teased him, but he was proud of Roman. He always felt like those guys in that movie with that genius kid from Boston. His brother was wicked smart.

Dante took his bowl and put it in the sink. Neveah was upstairs in her room. He'd walked past the door a few times and noticed she was reading some papers from a cardboard box. She didn't mention it and Dante didn't ask, but whatever it was, she was taking it in like she was cramming for a formidable midterm.

Roman was hanging out with Jae. Dante thought she was the best type of woman for Roman. Someone to match his geek. After the shooting, when Rome drove them to her place, they had talked about famous assassinations. They even knew the correct dates.

"I can't believe either one of you have ever gotten naked with another person, if this is the highlight of your game," Dante had said, and Roman had reached over the seat to playfully swat at him. In that instant he forgot he was in debt to a pair of bloodthirsty lunatics. For a half second they were just brothers riding around the city with a beautiful woman.

Dante pulled the butcher knife from the chef's block. His father kept the knives razor-sharp. He didn't have the most healthy relationships with his children, but Keith Carruthers made damn sure they had sharp cutlery and clean dinner plates. Dante wondered, if his father really knew about his thoughts, both pragmatic and intrusive, would he leave so many sharp things around?

Dante touched the back of the blade to his wrist. He doubted if he did it that it would be much of a surprise to anyone. Oh, they would mourn, because all families mourn a loss, but wouldn't they be a little relieved? Finally, after all this time, the yoke would be taken from their necks. No need to look out for Dante anymore.

He turned the blade over so that the sharp edge lay against his skin. He pushed it just enough to see the flesh depress but not enough to break the skin.

Dante closed his eyes.

He didn't believe he would see his mother if he slid the blade across his veins. If he did, what would he even say after all these years?

He heard a key in the lock of the front door. Roman swung the door open with one hand while he carried a pizza box in the other.

Dante quickly let the knife slide out his hand into the sink.

"I got a pizza," Roman said.

"Really, I thought it was the nuclear lunch codes," Dante said, emphasizing the word *lunch*.

Roman made a show of rolling his eyes. "Half pepperoni, half everything else. Jae recommended a place." He set the box on the kitchen table.

"It was either Arturo's or Dolson's Pizza. And I know she didn't recommend Arturo's. Nobody goes there unless Dolson's is closed for the family's annual trip to Las Vegas," Dante said as he opened the box and took a slice. "You the only person that don't call me weird for liking everything, including pineapple."

"It's weird, but I'm used to it," Roman said as he bit into a slice with pepperoni and nothing else.

"Thanks," Dante said.

He looked at Roman. There's a thousand ways to die, he thought, but sometimes all it takes is one thing to make you want to live. Like your brother remembering what you like on your pizza.

Roman felt his phone ringing.

He sat up, blinking his eyes before giving in and rubbing them. He reached in his pocket and pulled out the phone. He noticed the time before he realized who was calling.

Two A.M.

He'd left Jae's early because she had to get up for work. She'd met him at her favorite after-work spot in Jefferson Run. Since he couldn't spend the night, they took the opportunity to put to the test the theory that the electricity and intensity of their first time together had been a fluke.

Roman was pleasantly surprised that it wasn't.

His chest still had some bits of candle wax despite him and Jae showering together. Or perhaps it was because of that he'd missed a few spots. He didn't care. He was enjoying getting to know her. He was also enjoying being a man in full, not having to hide facets of himself from someone who wasn't actively in the "scene."

As happy as he would have been to talk to her at any time of the day or night, it wasn't Jae on the phone now. He saw the initials YB come up on the screen. It took him a half second to realize it was Yellaboy calling him.

"Hello," Roman said.

"2234 Falmouth Road. It's in Warren County," the person on the other end of the line said. Roman had excellent recall that barely fell short of a photographic memory. The person on the phone was Tranquil.

"Is this the farm?" Roman asked.

"You don't want me to come get you," Tranquil said.

The line went dead.

Roman stood and went to the couch. He shook Dante, but only with enough force to shake him out of reverie.

"What's up?" Dante said.

"I need you to listen. I have to go. I'm going to meet Torrent and Tranquil at the farm. If I don't come back, you get in touch with Khalil and tell him go with Plan A. He knows where my safe is at my place. Tell him it's all his. He'll help get you and Neveah out of town," Roman said as he took out the burner and held it out in front of Dante.

Dante sat straight up.

"What the fuck are you talking about? You can't go to the farm. God-damn it, Rome, I knew this shit wasn't gonna work. Do you got a gun? Fuck, man, you can't go to that farm. People turn up after going to the farm and it looks like they got attacked by a werewolf. You can't go out there, Rome. Fuck it, I'll go with you," Dante said. Roman put his hands on Dante's thin shoulders.

"You can't go. If something happens, it's going to be up to you and Khalil to try and finish this. Look at me: if they were really going to kill me, they wouldn't trust me to drive myself to my own execution. This is some bullshit, but just in case something goes awry."

Roman stopped talking.

Neveah was on the landing.

"What the hell is going on? No more lies, y'all," Neveah said. She was in a T-shirt and sweatpants and a head wrap. Roman inhaled sharply. She looked so much like their mother, it was like Bonita was taking them to task for some foolishness.

"I have to fix something. Something that Dante messed up. I'll be right back. I gotta go to the ATM," Roman said. Part truth, part lie.

"We'll go with you," Neveah said.

"No, you won't. Nobody needs to see the manager of Carruthers Cremation Services paying off a drug dealer at two in the morning," Roman said.

"I heard you say something about not coming back. Don't fuck with me, Rome. If this feels that sketchy, call the cops. What if this is the people who slashed the tires on the vans or ran Daddy off the road? We can't . . . we can't lose you too," Neveah said.

"It ain't that serious, sis. I promise. I'll be back in an hour or so. Seriously," Roman said.

"If you ain't back by three thirty, I'm calling the police and saying you been missing for twenty-four hours," Neveah said. She shook her head and went back up the stairs.

Roman grabbed the keys to the Challenger.

"Remember what I said," Roman said in a hushed voice.

"Don't do this, Rome," Dante said.

Roman gave him a one-armed hug around the neck. "It's going to be okay. They aren't going to get rid of a golden goose."

"What if they don't think you're a golden goose? What if they think you're a fucking albatross?" Dante said.

"Either way, I'll spread my wings and fly away," Roman said.

Dante hugged him back. "Don't say nothing slick like that to them," he mumbled into Roman's neck.

The Challenger glided through the night as Roman crossed the bridge into Warren County and left Jefferson Run. The seats of the Challenger could be adjusted to make the lower lumbar region more comfortable. They could heat up or cool down with a single touch of the control screen in the center of the dash, but nothing he did could make the gun pressing in the small of his back feel natural.

He'd taken Dante's suggestion, if for no other reason than it gave him a fighting chance. In the last two private meetings with Torrent, they hadn't given him a pat-down. They obviously didn't see him as a threat. That was fine by him. Let them keep thinking of him as a pushover who would just take anything they dished out. A lot of finance guys in college read Sun Tzu's *The Art of War*. They thought it gave them an edge. To Roman most of it was common sense. Appear weak when you're strong? Anyone who had ever been in a fight could tell you that was how you got the drop on someone. Know your enemy and you know yourself? Another piece of wisdom that should be self-evident. Roman preferred another book of strategy by an ancient Asian warrior. *The Book of Five Rings*, written by Miyamoto Musashi. His sophomore roommate had given him a copy. He'd started reading it one night when one of his papers wasn't coalescing in his mind, and in two hours he'd read the whole book. It was barely over one hundred and fifty pages, but those pages held wisdom that he still thought about to this day.

"From one thing, know ten thousand things," Roman said as the GPS told him to turn down a dirt lane with a battered sign that said FALMOUTH ROAD. The one thing he knew was money. That gave him an insight about men like Torrent.

He'd seen the wheels turning in Torrent's head when he'd mentioned millions. Whatever was the reason for this invitation, it wasn't to put a bullet in his head. He knew this. He knew it because the one thing he knew better than anything else told him it was illogical for this to end with him bleeding out on the floor when they thought there was so much more money to be made.

If only he could convince his arms and legs of that so they'd stop shaking.

Roman came to the end of the dirt road and saw a massive three-story house backlit by a three-quarter moon rising up out of the darkness like some eldritch god. Off to the right of the main house there was a long house painted red that appeared pale and pink under the moonlight. Farther to the east there was a field of what Roman thought were probably collards. The crops had the wide leaf of a collard, but he wasn't a hundred percent sure. His grandfather had raised a garden, but that was a long time ago.

After his mother had vanished, his grandfather, her father, had let the garden go to seed. His grandfather never spoke of missing his daughter, Roman's mother, but his grief was deafening.

There were three cars parked next to the house. Two candy-coated old-school luxury cars. A Caddy and a Mercury Grand Marquis with tricked-out body work and rims wide enough, if you turned them on their side, you could eat dinner on them with a family of five. The third car was a black BMW. Roman shut off his lights and turned off the car. The yard went so black it was like Roman had closed his eyes. The moonlight seemed impotent in the face of the country dark.

There was a knock at Roman's passenger door. Roman jumped, but he counted it as a win that he didn't scream. He put the window down and D-Train was there leering at him.

"Come on," D-Train said. Another member of the BBB commanding him like he was a servant. Roman ground his teeth as he got out of the car.

Following D-Train toward the long house, he could hear the barking and yelping of dogs. Lots of dogs. By the amount of bass and volume in their barking, they were large dogs. Roman had an image of the body Weldon had mentioned enter his mind unbidden.

They got to the long house and D-Train entered through a door that was set off to the left of the main double doors. Roman followed him and stepped into a kennel with eight big cages on each side of the structure. Sawdust covered the floor as the powerfully built pit bulls in each cage barked and yelped and howled and panted.

Roman followed D-Train as he walked toward the back of the structure. Roman thought pit bulls had gotten a bad rap, ever since he was a child watching them be stigmatized on a local news station. They were strong, yes, but not in a markedly different way from dogs of similar size. Roman knew the dogs themselves weren't inherently violent or aggressive. They behaved the way they were treated. If they belonged to Torrent, Roman could only imagine what ethos they absorbed from him and Tranquil.

The two of them came to an open area in the rear of the structure. Torrent was there on his haunches petting a gray pit bull with a white belly and an enormous head. Torrent was scratching him behind his ears and rubbing his back while talking to the animal in a conciliatory tone that sounded like a foreign language to Roman when it came from Torrent. Tranquil was leaning against the wall of the structure drinking a beer in a dark brown bottle. At his feet were two of the biggest dogs Roman had ever seen. He couldn't see their muzzles, but he saw their brownish gray bear-like bodies stretched across the floor as their heavy tails slapped against the floor, kicking up clouds of dirt and sawdust.

"That's my good boy. Stop licking me, you goofball. You gonna have to get a job. You eat too much," Torrent said as the dog put its front paws on his chest and licked him on his cheek. Torrent kissed the dog's head and stood. Eddie Munsta was holding the dog's leash.

"Take him back to his cage. Make sure he got enough water. He stay thirsty, don't you, Zulu?" Torrent said as he patted Zulu on his head one more time.

Roman watched Torrent with Zulu like he was observing a wolf who had taken up crochet. He couldn't reconcile the maniac who had brutalized him and Dante with this man who was giving this beautiful dog all the love it could bear.

"These my boys," Torrent said.

"They look incredible," Roman said.

"People think we breed them for fighting, but I don't do that shit. I like dogs. They loyal. They don't care about nothing but you being they friend. And if they love you, they'll fuck up any bitch-ass punk that try to mess with you. Even a Chihuahua will fight to the death for they master. You stop moving for too long, a cat will eat you. A dog will stand guard over you till it's damn near starving. Too many cats in this game and not enough road dawgs," Torrent said.

When he said that, D-Train walked over to an object covered by a blue tarp. He pulled the tarp off and let it float to the floor

Yellaboy was in an old wooden chair with armrests and a high back that came to a point like church's steeple. Yellaboy's head lolled to the right, while his body slumped to the left. A pool of blood like a red oil slick spread out on the floor in front of the chair in a half circle. The zip ties around his wrists were the only things preventing his body from sliding out of the chair.

The brown-gray dogs pushed themselves off the floor and turned around so that they were facing him. He could see their muzzles were stained in crimson. One then rolled on its back to paw at the second one. They were playing like puppies.

The dogs had torn away most of the flesh from Yellaboy's shins. What was left were jagged chunks under the tattered rags of his blue jeans, which were now black with blood. Roman could see teeth marks on his fibulas and tibias. Roman tried to look away, but his eyes were drawn back to the body like flies to shit.

"He cried for his mama. They always cry for their mama," Tranquil said as he stroked one of the colossal dogs on the neck.

Torrent stood next to Roman.

"He gave it up," Torrent said.

Roman's whole body went stiff as a board. He didn't respond to Torrent's statement. One thing he'd learned the hard way in his profession was never to answer a question that hadn't been asked. He licked his lips and wished he'd put the gun in the front of his pants, not in the back under his T-shirt and leather jacket. He decided he had to ask a question of his own instead of answering one.

"Gave what up?" Roman said.

Torrent moved closer to the body so that now he was standing in front of Roman. Roman could hear Torrent's Jordans scuffing against the sawdust. At least he thought he could hear them. Fear had heightened his senses to preternatural levels. He could smell the cologne D-Train was wearing, the wet metallic scent of the blood on the floor. The acrid lupine aroma of the dogs. He could taste it in his mouth mixed with the arboreal flavor of the sawdust.

"He'd been chopping it up with some motherfuckers from the Ghost Town Crew. When they tried to take me out Saturday night, he was the only person from our crew that was nowhere to be found. Said they was offering him fifty grand to tell them who our connect was," Torrent said.

That's where you went that night, Roman thought.

Torrent stepped closer to the body. His shoulders were constricting and releasing. He lowered his head as he put his hands behind his back.

If he wasn't in fear for his life, Roman might have smirked just a bit at Torrent's narcissism. There were almost a hundred people standing on the sidewalk when Khalil decorated the front door of the Kingdom the other night. Yes, Torrent was the ostensible target, but he hadn't been the only person possibly in danger. But in his mind, it was about him and him alone.

"I been knowing Yellaboy since he was seventeen. His pops got killed over by a check-cashing spot. He had a kid about the same time. Little fucker stay sick. We put him on running with us. Then he goes and gets on the Ghost Town Crew's dick. He said he needed the money. Like we didn't put him on."

Torrent straightened his back.

"Dumb motherfucker."

Torrent faced Roman.

"We gonna get the construction company and the demo team. We don't need the building supplies if we charge the city through the construction company. You gonna be the face. I wanna see the official books and the real books. You can get your regular commission."

Torrent closed the distance between them in three long steps.

"That nigga was like family to me and I fed him to Hoss and Rosie like he was their favorite snack. You fuck me, and you'll be sitting in that chair. You try and fuck us over, I'll know. I always know. You'll be sitting in that chair wondering what happened to your nuts. And you'll bleed out right there like Yella did." Torrent snapped his fingers. The two giant dogs padded over to his side. He petted their heads as they sat on their haunches. Their yellow eyes bore a hole through Roman until he thought they could see through his chest.

"But not before you watch me feed your brother and your sister to my babies here," Torrent said. "D-Train and Eddie gonna help you get Yella in the trunk."

Later, as he drove back across the bridge and headed for the crematory, Roman thought about one of the lines from *The Art of War* that did ring true:

"The opportunity of defeating the enemy is provided by the enemy himself."

"You just handed me the shovel to bury you with," Roman said out loud.

Roman gazed through the windshield at a night that stretched out before him like a mural where the lights of the city were the perpetually open eyes of a thousand dying gods. He imagined Jefferson Run itself was one of those desiccated gods. A withered god who fed on blood and tears and agony. He could stanch the wounds of his city, if only momentarily, by taking Torrent and Tranquil off the board.

A king without a queen or pawns is just a piece of wood sitting on a board, Roman thought.

His daddy had taught him that.

CHAPTER TWENTY-THREE

Mike Handler knew he was a good man.

He went to church every Sunday at St. Anthony's Episcopalian Church. He coached his son's Little League team and was a supporter of his daughter's college volleyball team at Prosser State. He and his wife donated to the NAACP and the Literary Union of Jefferson Run. He was the owner of one of the larger employers still left in the city, Guardian Construction. He had more than one hundred folks who worked for him and depended on him. Most people couldn't imagine the stress he was under on a daily basis.

In the larger scheme of things, going to the top floor of the Kingdom once in a while was a minor transgression. It wasn't a brothel. No one could say he frequented a brothel.

He was a good man.

It was a private club with private rooms, and in those rooms there were sometimes women who would, for a fee, let you do all the things you couldn't bring yourself to ask your wife to do. Or maybe you had asked her and she had responded with virulent disgust. But it wasn't a brothel. They were explicit about that when you purchased a membership.

Because a good man wouldn't go to a brothel.

Mike was lying on his back, resplendent in postcoital glow. His skin reflected the magenta light that came from two heart-shaped LED lights on each wall above the king-sized bed. The lights were the outline of a heart that was designed to appear as if it were melting. Bethany, he thought she said her name was Bethany, had appeared cut from obsidian under those lights. Mike thought she could have been a movie star.

He checked his smart watch. Lisa had sent him a message about being safe and not drinking too much. She thought he was in Richmond for a Friday night drink with some of his executive staff. He texted her back assuring her he wasn't drinking a lot. He texted her that he'd only had two gin and tonics and he'd be home soon. He would leave in the next forty-five minutes. That would give him a plausible story about traffic in the capital city.

She didn't need to know the truth. What would the truth do except hurt her? And a good man didn't hurt the people he loved.

The door to the room creaked open as Mike turned over on his side and tried to strike a sexy pose, then immediately felt ridiculous and lay flat on his back. He was paying her enough that she could pretend to find him sexy. He didn't come here to work.

He'd expected Bethany to walk through the door after using the bathroom at the end of the hall. Instead, three men entered the room. The last man stopped and locked the door behind him.

Mike sat up and started to get out of the bed, but the last man through the door held up his hand and motioned for him to sit down. That man and the second man through the door were wearing hoodies and jeans. The first man was wearing a light leather jacket and a black turtleneck. It was the last week of September, but the weather was uncommonly cool in Virginia. It was making some of the large jobs his company was completing easier, but it would play havoc with some projects later in the year if this early winter weather continued.

"What's, uh, going on, fellas?" Mike said.

"Mr. Handler, can I call you Mike?" the first man said.

"I guess," Mike said.

"Mike, my name is Roman, and we have a situation here we need to resolve."

Mike sat back against the wall. This was a shakedown. He sucked at his teeth. This was the risk he took coming to a place like the Kingdom as the owner of a profitable business. He figured as long as the request wasn't too egregious, he'd pay it and go on with his life. Pay whatever they asked, within reason, and get the hell out of this room. If they didn't show him any photos or video, then the moment he walked out of here it was done. That was reasonable. He could accept that was the cost of his little dalliances. "Okay. How much to make this go away?"

Roman reached in his jacket and pulled out an envelope.

"No, Mike, we aren't interested in your peccadilloes. What we need is your signature. Now, this is a contract that transfers fifty-one percent of Guardian Construction to JCR Investments. Once you sign this, we'll be in business together, and business is about to get very good. You know the city is about to start taking bids for the revitalization project in the Skids. Now, you have your own demo crew. And a lot of the properties that have to be demolished have already been sold or will be sold shortly under eminent domain. So the demos can start relatively soon. Guardian is going to get this contract. And you're going to get a partner," Roman said.

Mike laughed. He laughed so hard, the sheet he'd pulled up to his chest fell down to his belly. As his laughter subsided, he wiped his eyes with the back of his hand.

"Fellas, I'm fully prepared to cut you a check to keep my visit here quiet, but I'm not selling more than half of my company. I have staff and employees to consider. I'll give you fellas points for audacity, though. Now let's get to the real brass tacks. How much is it going to take for me to get out of this room?"

A doleful expression took over Roman's face. He grabbed a metal folding chair from the corner and slid it over to the edge of the bed and sat in it. He leaned forward and pointed at Mike.

"Mike, I don't think you understand the situation here. This is happening. The only question is, does it have to hurt? Because these men behind me"—Roman gestured to the Bang Bang Twins—"they will make it hurt," Roman said.

Lucius reached in his pocket and pulled out a vise grip. He snapped the jaws together. The metal pincers made a harsh clicking sound that made Roman wince.

Mike scowled at him.

"You think you gonna just come in here and strong-arm me like I'm some big-head 'Bama negro that just got dropped off at the bus station? Fellas, my daddy started Guardian with two wheelbarrows and a dream. I have dinner with the mayor and the Chamber of Commerce once a month. I donate to the JRPD. Now, you want to make me pay a toll for that whore, I'll cut you a check right now. But you're not getting my company. And you can't kill me, because you need my signature on that bullshit contract. And if you come near me with those pliers I'll have the mayor and cops so far up your ass your breath is gonna smell like central Virginia bureaucracy," Mike said.

Roman sat back.

"Mike, who did you tell that you were coming here? Who knows where you are? And as far as the mayor goes, I have a meeting with him Monday. I can give him your regards," Roman stood. "Don't do anything where it's visible. He needs his hands to sign." He stepped aside and moved to the rear of the room. The Bang Bang Twins made a move for Mike.

Handler was a big man who had spent most of the summers of his youth carrying bricks and mortar and stirring concrete for his father. There was a time when he could bench four-fifty, squat six hundred, and carry two bags of cement on both shoulders. But he was fifty-five years old, and those summer days were forty years and many T-bone steaks ago. Lucius and Lavon grabbed him and pushed him down on the bed. He fought, but a hard punch to his exposed genitalia took all the fight out of him.

Lucius took the vise grip and unceremoniously grabbed a dollop of Mike's flesh just to the right of his belly button. Lucius squeezed the handles of the vise grip until it locked. A guttural groan erupted from Mike's throat. Blood, thin and watery as spring runoff, dripped from the jaws of the vise grip as Mike jerked and bucked his body, but Lucius and

Lavon each ran a solid 230. They held him in place like a butterfly pinned to a board.

Roman grimaced. The pain on Mike's face was biblical. His eyes were wide and his mouth was a twisted contortion that resembled images of Christ's suffering that were sculpted on four-foot-long wooden crucifixes in Baptist churches all across the South.

"Sign it, Mike. Please. Don't make us do this. Sign it, Mike," Roman said.

Mike continued to moan.

Lucius looked at Roman.

Roman nodded.

Lucius gave the vise grip a half turn.

Mike was a few shades lighter than Roman. The skin in the jaws of the vise grip had tawniness that was rapidly turning purple. Red streaks trickled down Mike's stomach and stained the bed. When Lucius gave him that slight rotation, Mike's voice went from a moan to a screeching howl.

"Mike, let's stop this, okay? Please, Mike," Roman said.

Lucius released the vise grip and moved them to a spot just near Mike's armpit. With a dispassion that bordered on tedium, Lucius grabbed a hunk of the meat of Mike's armpit and locked the vise grip in place.

Then he gave it a turn.

Mike screamed.

"The next one is going to be lower." Roman said.

"I'll sign!" Mike cried, as the blood began to flow.

Roman knocked on the door to Jae's apartment. She answered on the fourth knock. She opened the door wearing a baggy T-shirt and red and yellow floral pajama bottoms. It was 12:30 a.m. on a Friday night/early Saturday morning. The lights were low in her apartment, with most of the illumination coming from the television.

Roman stepped inside and closed the door behind him.

"Were you asleep?" he asked, even though he'd texted before he came over, after he had taken the papers Mike had signed to the safe at Trout's.

"Nah, just didn't want to appear too eager. You can't show how bad you need a booty call," Jae said. Roman laughed and pulled her to him by the tail of her shirt. They kissed languidly, with their lips pressed lightly against each other. Her mouth tasted like cherries and a bit of sweetness. When they parted, he noticed a glass of red liquid on the coffee table. Most likely it was Kool-Aid.

"This isn't a booty call. I want to spend some time with you," Roman said.

"While I'm naked, right?" Jae said as she fell across her couch.

"That's later. Right now I wanna lay next to you on this couch and you tell me about your day," Roman said.

"*You* wanna hear about *my* day? Before having sex? Wow, you're the brother from another planet," Jae said.

"That's a great movie. Directed by John Sayles, I think," Roman said as he spread Jae's legs and lay on his back, resting his head just below her breasts.

"Silly. You okay? I know I'm irresistible, but it's way late on a Friday night. You weren't out with your boys? Chopping it up at Candy's? Getting in that male bonding," Jae said as she stroked his head.

"Nah. My only boys are Dante and my friend Khalil," he said. He didn't think mentioning Khalil to Jae would be an issue. If they ever met, it wouldn't be until this was over. He grabbed her hand and took it from his head to his chest.

Over.

What was that?

When her brothers were dead? In jail? When his brother could walk down the street and not be afraid someone was going to snatch him off the sidewalk and take him to a farm where wolf-dogs would be waiting for him? In what world would he and Jae ever be able to be more than what they were right now, if he had to take her brothers away from her?

His father used to say how in the Bible it says that God destroyed the earth with water but the next time it'll be fire. One Sunday when he was a kid, before his mother vanished, Reverend Oakley Devlin preached from the Book of Revelation about the End Times. As they drove home from church in the minivan that doubled as a work van, his father, in that deep melodious voice of his, offered his opinion on the apocalyptic predictions they'd heard from the pulpit that morning.

"Scientists say millions of years from now, the earth's gonna fall in the sun. But if these politicians ain't careful, they gonna blow us all up long before that. Nuclear weapons go missing all the time. Either way, it's all gonna end in ashes," Keith Carruthers had offered.

Dante had burst into tears at the mention of the sun swallowing the earth. His father had to take them to the Tastee-Freez over on Sycamore to calm him down. Roman had been unnerved by his father's impromptu astronomy lesson, but once Dante started crying he pushed down his own anxiety so as not to give his parents even more to worry about.

He kissed Jae's hand.

The blood on Mike Handler's belly was the brightest red he'd ever seen. After he signed the contract, Handler had cried, much the same way Dante had all those years ago. They'd left Handler there, naked and bruised and bleeding, with half the company his father had built from nothing. Just like Keith Carruthers had done.

Roman closed his eyes.

Tonight he had stood by and watched a man be tortured into giving up his livelihood. Next he would most likely have a meeting with the mayor to discuss a bribe. He had killed a man and his brother had killed another. He'd engineered a fake drive-by that had put another man in the hospital. Roman knew he was doing this for the right reasons. Saving his family was the end, and the means were justified. But after all this was over, could it end in anything other than ashes?

"Let's go to the bedroom," Jae said.

"I have to tell you something," Roman said.

"Your wife needs you to come take out the trash?" Jae said. Roman could almost feel her smile. He sat up and moved her left leg over his head so that he could face her.

"Next week you're going to see me at the mayor's office. Remember I told you I'm here helping my sister out? Because my real job is a financial adviser? I'm going to be meeting with the mayor about expanding our business. I want to talk to him about whether he can talk to the city planning committee about giving us a variance. This was in the works before I met you. I just don't want you to feel weird about it. I didn't want to surprise you," Roman lied.

Jae shrugged. "Okay. But can I ask you something? A serious question."

"Sure. Anything," Roman said.

"How you know my brothers? I mean, we aren't as close as it seems, but I do know what they do, or what I think they do. I can't be involved with that. The other night just confirmed it for me. I mean, we all have the same dad, and I appreciate Terrance helping me get this job, but I'm not trying to live that life, and if you are, I don't think this is going to go anywhere."

Roman stroked her cheek. Her eyes were pleading with him to not be a part of her brothers' lifestyle. Another lie made its way to his lips. "They were asking about my wealth management business. I mean, I kinda know what they do too, and I got the feeling maybe they are looking to go legit. They didn't say that, but that was the gist I got."

"I don't even think that's possible for them. Our father had them in this life when they were kids. Terrance did two years in juvenile detention for beating up a kid who liked the same girl he did. Tracy has been in and out of jail. At one point him and our father were in the same jail. I don't know if they could leave this life behind if they wanted to," Jae said.

"In Atlanta, I've helped a few people shift from the street to the boardroom. It's not easy, but it's possible," Roman said. That part was true.

"You're telling me the truth?" Jae asked.

Roman kissed her.

"No disrespect to your brothers, but last year I made eight hundred thousand dollars. Legally. I don't need to get in bed with them. I'd like to get in bed with you, though," Roman said.

Jae kissed him back.

Then she bit his lip. Hard. Roman could taste a faint hint of blood. He grabbed her by her waist and picked her up off the couch. She held on to his lip until they fell across the bed. In the distance he heard a train cutting through the dark like a scimitar.

CHAPTER TWENTY-FOUR

The city hall of Jefferson Run was a ruined castle. It had been built by the Brighton family, the former Mason jar scions, as their main residence. When they closed the plant, the family moved en masse to New York City to live off their investments while the city choked on its newfound poverty.

The elevator let Roman out on the fourth floor. There was an office directly in front of him with several cubicles visible through a large picture window. There was also a sign that directed him to the mayor's office. He saw Jealousy sitting at her desk in her business attire. He wanted to wave at her, but her attention was focused on her computer screen. He decided he'd take her to lunch after his meeting was done.

He headed for the mayor's office. The signs directed him to take a left, then a right, and then one more right deposited him in front of a large oak door with a woman sitting at an even larger maple desk. She had long black braids interspersed with gray, and a narrow face that ended with a sharp chin.

"Can I help you?" she asked.

"I'm Roman Carruthers. I have a meeting with Mayor Gravely at eleven," Roman said.

The woman consulted an electronic tablet on her desk. She looked back at Roman, then consulted the tablet again.

"The mayor is on a call. You can have a seat and I'll let you know when he's available," she said.

Roman looked at his watch.

It was 10:59.

"All right," he said, stifling a sigh.

He took a seat and crossed his legs at his ankles. This was a classic power move. He had used it himself a few times. That didn't mean he had to like it.

Fifteen minutes later the receptionist called him up and let him into the office. She closed the door behind him as Roman walked up to the mayor's desk.

Mayor Gravely was a small, trim man with a gray box cut and small features that gave him a serious expression even when he smiled. He stood and extended his hand to Roman.

"Mr. Carruthers, nice to meet you. Melvin Gravely," the mayor said. His grip was firm but not intimidating.

"Nice to meet you, sir," Roman said.

"Please sit."

They both sat, and Mayor Gravely leaned back in his leather chair. Roman waited for him to ask him what he could do for him. This was the mayor's playing field; he'd follow his lead.

"So you're Terrance's new associate," Mayor Gravely said.

Roman hadn't expected him to confirm his association with the BBB so quickly, if at all. He sat forward in his seat.

"Well, actually I'm here as a representative of JCR Investments. We just became partners with Guardian Construction, and we wanted to inquire if there was anything you can do to assist us in acquiring the contract for the revitalization project in the western part of the city," Roman said.

Mayor Gravely smiled. "Son, we don't have to engage in strategic linguistic bullshit. This office is bug-proof. There are multiple sensors in here that would pick up a wire. Since none of them have gone off, let's talk freely, shall we? Mike called me Saturday and wanted to complain about his tummy hurting. Then I talked to Terrance, who explained what was actually going on. It's a smart move, and one I'm frankly surprised Terrance hadn't thought of on his own. He's a bright boy. He has a bit of a temper, like his father. Here's what's going to happen. Guardian will get the contract. Demolition can begin in three weeks. Actual construction will take a little bit longer, but we'll grease the wheels as much as we can. I'll get a fifty-thousand-dollar donation up front and then another when we get closer to starting construction. Those will be donations to my campaign. They should be broken up into four different donors. Now, whatever budgetary magic you have to do is fine, but if any state auditors come nosing around, you're on your own. This conversation never happened," Mayor Gravely said.

Roman sat back. "I guess we have it all figured out, then," he said.

"This is how things get done. This'll be good for us and for Jefferson Run. The state has money to burn," Mayor Gravely said.

Roman put his finger to his lips.

"You don't really believe anyone is going to move into these luxury apartments, do you? This is Jefferson Run, murder capital of the state, per capita. You've orchestrated this whole thing to get this surplus money from the state. Why do I think you, or a company reppin' you, owns a lot of property over in the Skids? The state will buy up those properties, and you make a nice profit there. Then of course you have your donations. Were you just waiting to see which construction company came through first?" Roman said with a slight smile.

There was something distasteful about Mayor Gravely that pushed a button in Roman. If Jefferson Run was dying, it was men like Torrent and Mayor Gravely who were the disease rotting it from the inside out.

Mayor Gravely steepled his fingers.

"You're a bright boy. But let me give you a piece of advice, son. If you can't stomach how the sausage is made, maybe just shut up and eat your fucking meal."

Roman and Jae went to the Mexican restaurant on the east side of town near the river. Los Plaza de Callao was housed in the former Tastee-Freez building. The previous drab blue-and-white building was now painted in vibrant orange and green and red. A tall wooden statue of a man in a sombrero stood outside the entrance beckoning patrons to join the festivities.

Roman and Jae sat near the window, even though the temperature was dropping precipitously. Roman touched the window and was taken aback by how cold it was.

"So much for global warming," he said when he removed his hand.

"I can't lie, I like it when it gets cool. The summer makes me melt. I hate walking around with titty sweat," Jae said. Roman busted out laughing. He'd only known her a few weeks, but he'd never been with anyone who made him laugh as much as Jae.

"You have to get you a big bottle of talcum powder. That's what my grandmother used to do. She'd go to church looking like she'd been juggling powdered donuts with her chest," Roman said.

Now it was Jae's turn to giggle. "You are so crazy. How'd the meeting with the mayor go? You think you're gonna get your expansion?" Jae asked.

Roman paused. He'd almost forgotten his lie. "I don't know. Maybe I should have offered him a bribe," Roman said.

"I know you joking, but . . . I don't think he'd turn it down. That man drives a Mercedes, while there's a pothole near my house you can swim in," Jae said.

Roman chuckled again. It seemed like when he was with Jae his cheeks always hurt from smiling so much. He picked up his menu.

"What you thinking about?" Roman asked.

"How you should spend the night tonight," Jae said.

He raised his eyes and looked at her over the top of the menu.

"We'll see," Roman said.

"We'll see? Boy, you better come get this," Jae said.

Roman was about to toss a bon mot at her when he noticed a big Bonneville coming down the street at a snail's pace. The Bonneville was a dark fuchsia with twenty-four-inch rims. It pulled up in front of a vape / smoke shop across the street. Recognition bloomed in Roman's mind like a moonflower unfurling its petals. Slowly at first, then as fast as a hummingbird's wings.

That was D-Train's car.

Roman watched as four men wearing Halloween masks in the shape of skulls got out of the car and stood on the sidewalk in front of the vape shop. All four of the men were holding guns. Roman wasn't an expert, but he thought they looked similar to the MAC-10 Khalil had used at the Kingdom.

The four men unleashed a fusillade of gunshots into the vape shop. Glass, bricks, and wood were all shattered and disintegrated by the un-yielding volley of shots. Everyone in the restaurant dived to the floor, including Jae and Roman. The attack seemed to go on for hours.

Finally the street went quiet.

Roman raised his head and saw one of the men painting a crude figure of a skull in a top hat on the building next to the vape shop with a can of black spray paint. The four men jumped into the car and left a trail of smoke behind them as they took off. Roman saw a woman stumble out of the vape shop. Most of her left arm was gone. Her face was awash in blood and her long black hair was sticking to her forehead. She went to her knees, then fell on her side in the middle of the street.

Dozens of people in the restaurant pulled out their phones. A few called 911, but most were filming the woman. Roman held Jae as she grabbed him in a bear-trap grip.

"I can't take this. I can't take this. I can't take this," she repeated like a mantra.

"Shh, it's okay. It's going to be okay," Roman said as he hugged Jae tight. It *was* going to be okay. Everything was going to be all right. That was the far horizon he had to focus on, even as bodies fell all around him like falling stars.

AFTERNOON

Roman is nervous.

Delia is sitting on the couch next to him while they watch a DVR episode of *American Idol* that his mother had set to record on Wednesday. She is only a foot away, but he feels like she is across the James River. She looks at him shyly. They both claimed to be experienced, but Roman knows he was lying and is beginning to suspect she was lying as well.

"I can sing better than that," he says as a particularly awful singer finishes his audition. Delia smiles and turns to face him.

"Prove it," she says, and Roman feels his stomach drop to the center of the earth. He has only sung in church, and even then he barely raises his voice above a whisper. He doesn't think he sings poorly, but he isn't ready to put it to the test in front of the most beautiful girl he has ever seen.

Later he will look back on this moment as the last time he was innocent.

"I . . . my voice ain't warmed up. But if it was, I could blow," Roman says. Delia scoots closer to him. He can smell her perfume. He'll learn later it's called Vanilla Fields. For the rest of life after this day is done, the smell of Vanilla Fields will make him nauseous.

"How do you warm up your voice?" Delia says. She still looks as nervous as Dante feels, but she's moved closer to him. His heart is bouncing off his rib cage like it's slam-dancing. He has never felt more excited in his entire life.

"I . . . make sounds with my mouth," he says, and almost passes out because of how inane it sounds. But Delia moves closer.

"What kind of sounds?" she says. She is barely an inch away from him now. He can see the dewy sheen of her skin. She has on cocoa butter lotion. He knows if he touches her she will feel as soft as anything he has ever put his hand on. He feels as if he is about to pass out and take flight at the same time.

He leans forward. The decision to do so is not a conscious one. If he had thought about it, he would have lost his nerve. It is an instinctual decision born of his desire to taste Delia's lips.

He kisses her, and she kisses him back, and then they are all arms and legs and deep breaths and hurried hands searching for buttons and zippers and flesh. Delia slips her tongue in his mouth and then bites his lip as it retreats. The pain is sharp and clear, but he is too excited, too overwhelmed, to even notice.

He does not know it has unlocked something in him. Something that will be amplified in the years to come by his memories of this day.

Delia grabs his left hand and slides it down the front of her pants, and what he finds there is warm and wet and he knows it will make him crazy when he puts another part of his body near it, in it.

And then the door slams open and Dante is standing there crying and hyperventilating, his nose coated in phlegm, his eyes red as a fire hydrant.

Delia jumps away from him as she buttons her jeans.

Roman is too discombobulated to zip up his own pants until he looks down and sees what's trying to escape. He puts himself away, pulls up his zipper, and takes a deep breath. He wants to yell at Dante, but the ferociousness of his brother's weeping makes him pause.

"What's wrong with you? Did somebody take your bike?" Roman says.

Dante shakes his head. Snot runs down over his lips. "I . . . don't . . . I can't . . ." Dante says, but he doesn't finish his sentence.

"Maybe I should go. Y'all need to talk," Delia says. She gets up, and Roman wants to tell her to stay, but Dante is scaring him. They will never resume their rendezvous. Delia will get shot in the thigh three months later and her parents will move away from Jefferson Run. Roman will lose his virginity two years later at a party in Richmond.

"Yeah, I'll call you later," Roman says.

Delia leaves, and Roman gets off the couch and approaches Dante. His brother is sensitive and is prone to cry at the most gentle provocation, but this is different.

"D, what's wrong?" Roman says gently.

"I . . . saw . . ." Dante says.

"Saw what?" Roman says.

"I . . . saw . . . Mama . . ." Dante says.

"Okay. You saw Mama. What happened?"

"I saw . . . Mama and Mr. Oscar," Dante says, and Roman feels like he has been tossed off the tallest building in the world and is speeding toward the pavement. The world fades away at the edges because he knows, knows in his bones, what Dante saw. He knows because he's seen Oscar stare at their mother. He knows because he has noticed how his mother looks at his father when he isn't noticing.

She looks lost.

Roman asks Dante the question that will change everything, but he does not know that yet. All he knows is he needs to hear it. He needs to hear what Dante saw so he can be wrong.

"What did you see Mama and Mr. Oscar doing?" Roman says.

Dante tells him that he went to the basketball court and played a few games until it got too hot and the game broke up. Then he tells Roman that he rode his bike over to the crematory. He figured his father would be there and maybe their mother too. She sometimes helped out after her shift. He would get a soda out of the fridge his father kept in the lobby and maybe beg him for five dollars so he could ride over to the McDonald's on Lillyhammer.

Dante says he got to the crematory and went around to the roll-up door in the back because even though his mother's car was there and Mr. Oscar's Jeep was there, no one was answering the door.

"I—I went around to the back and I—I heard noises. Like weird noises. Like somebody was yelling but like they was crying too," Dante says.

Then he tells Roman that he looked through the rectangular window in the garage door.

He tells him what he saw.

And Roman wants to cry too.

"Come on. We going back over there," Roman says.

"I don't want to. I don't want to go, Rome," Dante says.

"I want to talk to her, because it's a mistake. She'll just explain it's a mistake. She'll tell us that, okay? Stop crying, all right? We just gonna go over there and she'll explain it," Roman says.

He uses the bottom of his T-shirt to wipe Dante's eyes and nose. The snot sticks to his shirt, but he doesn't care. He only cares about stopping his little brother from crying, and hearing his mother say that what Dante thought he saw was not what he actually saw.

He wants her to lie.

By the end of this day, lies will become their love language. His, his brother's, and his father's.

His father's will be the boldest lie of them all.

CHAPTER TWENTY-FIVE

Neveah took a drag off her cigarette as she waited in her truck. The sign on the top of the hospital was lit up like it was advertising a casino, not a place of healing. She watched as nurses and doctors and orderlies and aides filed out the door as the shifts began to change.

She took one last drag off her cigarette when she saw Marion Carter come out the main entrance and head for her car. Neveah hopped out of her truck, stomped on her smoke, and made a beeline for Marion. The older lady waited by the car for Neveah.

"God, you look just like her," Marion said as she pulled her coat tighter. It was the first week of October, and the unseasonably cool September had given way to mostly temperate October. Neveah was wearing a fleece jacket over a Prosser State sweatshirt.

"Thanks for saying you'd speak with me. I know you're busy," Neveah said.

"Tonight's my bingo night, or I would have told you to meet me for a coffee or something. Oh, darling, what do you want to know about Bonita?" Marion said. Neveah thought Marion had to be at least sixty if she knew her mom, but she didn't look a day over forty. If it wasn't for the traces of silver in her hair she might have passed for thirty-five.

"Did she ever say anything about my father? Did she say if he was violent with her? Or did he ever threaten her?" Neveah asked.

Marion's face broke into a deep frown. "Oh, darling, your mama loved your daddy. And the way she talked about your daddy, he loved her too. He never laid a hand on her." Marion paused, turned her head back to the hospital, then back toward Neveah.

"But your daddy loved that crematory more. He worked morning, noon, and night to make it a success. Your mama was right by his side, but I think they lost their way to each other. She'd tell us how she did the books or helped your daddy with a really nasty case or cleaned up the ovens, and then she'd take a deep breath and say how your daddy didn't stop long enough to say thank you. It hurt her feelings," Marion said.

"So she wasn't afraid of him, even after he caught her with Lawrence?" Neveah said.

Marion puckered her lips.

"I think she was disappointed he didn't fight for her. Listen, darling, whatever happened to your mama, it wasn't because of your daddy. I believe that," Marion said.

"What do you think happened, then?" Neveah said. It came out harder than she had intended, but she let it lie where it landed.

Marion used her key fob to unlock her car. "I don't know, darling. I just hope wherever she is, she's at peace," she said before climbing into the car.

Neveah drove down Lillyhammer heading for Candy's. They were having Wild Out Wednesdays, where the drinks were half price. Her phone vibrated in her pocket. She took it out as she steered with one hand.

It was a text message from Chauncey.

where ru I'm free

Neveah typed with one hand.

im not

She turned off Lilyhammer and pulled into Candy's parking lot. The crowd was thin, but it was only half past nine. Neveah parked and went inside and sat at the bar. She ordered a gin and juice and sipped it through a straw.

Her phone vibrated again.

what does that mean

Neveah answered him.

it means im not free

Chauncey responded immediately.

fine

Neveah put her phone away.

"What in the wide world of sports is you doing here, sis?" Dante said. He sat next to her on a stool and spun around for one complete revolution. A white kid and black girl with him, her hair in two big Afro puffs, stood near the bar while Dante spun.

"I'm having a drink, since I worked nine hours by myself today. Is that okay with you?" Neveah said

"I'm sorry, Nev. I was helping my boy Tug with something. Tug, this is my sister, Neveah. This is Tug's girlfriend, Raynell," Dante said.

"Hey," Neveah said with a paucity of enthusiasm.

"We going to play pool," Tug said. He and Raynell melted into the crowd. Dante spun one more time on the stool. Neveah didn't bother to ask him if he was high. That was self-evident.

"All right, sis. I'm gonna go beat these fools at pool," Dante said.

"You see Roman today?" Neveah said.

Dante leaned against the bar. "He been hanging with Jae," Dante said, as if that explained everything.

"Dante, what do you remember about that day?" Neveah said.

"What day?" Dante said.

"You know what day," Neveah said.

Dante ran his hand over his hair. "I don't know, Neveah. I went riding my bike. I played basketball with Charlie and Stefan. I came home and Mama didn't," Dante said.

Neveah removed the straw and took a big sip of her drink.

"I can't remember what her voice sounds like," Dante said.

"What?" Neveah said.

"Her voice. I can't remember. I can remember what she looks like every time I see you, but I can't remember her voice. I'm a shitty fucking son," he said, his voice breaking.

"You're not a shitty son. We had shitty parents," Neveah said.

"Hey, hey, now, don't say that."

"Why not? It's true. Mama was cheating on Daddy. Daddy became a drunk. We had to raise ourselves," Neveah said.

"Hey, don't fucking say that. Daddy missed her. Yeah, he drinks too much, but he took care of us. He never got married again. I don't even think he ever fucked anybody else, so you just take that shit back!" Dante said. He took Neveah's drink and killed it in one gulp.

Neveah got up and tossed five dollars on the bar.

"You and Rome can keep putting him on a pedestal, but I'm done with that. Goddamn it, I can't even have a fucking drink for myself," she said. She pushed herself off the stool and headed for the door.

"Neveah, wait. I'm sorry. Let me get you a drink," Dante slurred. He followed her out to the parking lot. Neither one of them noticed the two Latino men who were walking in as they were leaving. Candy's wasn't a segregated club, but it was primarily a Black club. It was also where a lot of the BBB and their associates hung out when they weren't at the Kingdom.

Neveah rushed to her truck with Dante close on her heels.

"Neveah! I'm sorry! Please let me get you another drink," Dante said.

"Y'all keep defending him when he killed her, Dante. He fucking killed her. I know it. You know it. So does Roman. Twenty years we been lying to ourselves, and he been lying to us too. I'm done lying," Neveah said.

"What the hell are you saying? Daddy didn't kill Mama. What is you talking about? You talking crazy," Dante said.

Before either one of them could say another word, a crowd of people came running out of Candy's screaming and yelling. Dante and Neveah whirled around and saw people running into the street and down the sidewalk. Many of them were bleeding or had blood on them. A few people only ran a few feet before they collapsed, huge gashes on their backs or necks spouting blood like fountains. Dante saw Tug come running out carrying Raynell in his arms. There was a huge slash in her shoulder. Blood was pouring from the wound and spilling on the pavement leaving stains like a work of modern art. Tug ran across the street with Raynell.

As the crowd dispersed into the night, Dante and Neveah saw the two Latino men come out of the club. Each man was carrying a machete that was soaked with blood.

"Tripulación de la Ciudad Fantasma!" one of the men yelled as they took off through the parking lot and around the back of Candy's.

"Good God," Neveah said as she dug her phone out and dialed 911.

"I gotta go check on Raynell and Tug," Dante said.

Neveah grabbed Dante's arm.

"No the fuck you don't. You stay right here with me. What if them boys come back? No, you stay right here until the cops show up," Neveah said.

"They're my friends," Dante said. He tried to pull his arm away, but Neveah wouldn't release her grip.

"And you're my brother. Stay here. When the cops get here, we can go over there."

"Jefferson Got the Runs. That's where we live. Jefferson fucking Got the Runs," Dante said. He could hear Tug moaning Raynell's name as sirens cried out in the distance like clarions heralding the gods of war.

The JRPD came out in full force to investigate the rampage.

They blocked off the street while detectives questioned anyone who hadn't been able to escape before the patrol cars came flying around the corner. Yellow crime scene tape stretched from one end of the sidewalk to the other like decorations for a harvest festival. Neveah and Dante gave their statements near her truck as multiple ambulances ferried victims to the hospital. Neveah saw Chauncey talking to Dante's friend Tug while his partner was questioning one of the bartenders. He didn't look her way and she found herself relieved. She'd read in a book once that the opposite of love wasn't hate, it was apathy. She'd never loved Chauncey, but she didn't hate him either. She wasn't even apathetic.

She was done.

Neveah lit a cigarette and took deep drag and filled her lungs with smoke, then expelled it through her nostrils as Dante finished giving his statement.

Shit, she thought. Chauncey was making his way over to where she and Dante were talking to the patrolman. He had a smirk on his face but he didn't say a word to her. He approached Dante.

"Why is it here lately you or your brother or the both of you are in the vicinity whenever people are getting killed?" Chauncey said.

Dante hunched his shoulders. "Because we live in Jefferson Run?"

"You heard from Getty? Of course you haven't. He's dead, ain't he? You know what, I think you need to come downtown and explain to me exactly what's happening between the BBB and the Ghost Town Crew. You can start by telling me what happened to Getty and his girl. Then we can talk about what's you and your brother's relationship with Torrent Gilchrist." Chauncey said. He grabbed Dante by his collar.

"Why is my brother going downtown, when you got dozens of witnesses to what happened here. You taking them downtown too?" Neveah said.

Chauncey glowered at her, but she didn't care.

"Your brother is a person of interest in the disappearance of John Paul Mathias Getty and Cassidy Gutierrez. I'll be picking up your other brother too. Would you like to join them?" Chauncey said.

Neveah blew a cloud of smoke in his face. "Would you like for me to call your wife?" she said.

Chauncey's mouth opened but no words came out. Once he'd gained his composure, he turned to the patrolman who had been taking their statements.

"Give us a minute," he said.

The patrolman left and joined the other cops milling around the entrance of Candy's.

"You want to watch yourself, there. I'd hate to see you get taken in for a moving violation and then get stuck in a holding cell because your paperwork got lost," Chauncey said.

"And before they take me in, I'll screenshot every text you've ever sent me and forward them to your wife's social media accounts. All of them. Now, my brother was standing right here next to me when everybody ran out of the club. He didn't have anything to do with it. And you want to run him downtown because him and my other brother been in the fucking vicinity of a shooting or a stabbing or a bar fight or whatever the fuck is happening at any given moment in Jefferson Run? Like there ain't a goddamn murder or assault every five minutes here? Sounds like you want to make him a scapegoat for the police not doing their jobs. Go ahead, take him. By the time you get to the station, all your shit will be in the front yard and I hope it's on fire," Neveah said.

Chauncey ground his teeth so hard his jaw jutted out like it was trying to form a right angle. He let go of Dante's collar.

"You sure this is how you want to handle this?" Chauncey said.

Neveah tossed her cigarette on the asphalt and ground it out. "Come on, Dante, we're going home."

Dante got in the passenger side of the truck.

"You think about threatening me, you better make sure you got eyes in the back of your head, bitch," Chauncey growled.

"I'm not going to think about you at all," Neveah said. She got in the truck and shut the door. As she pulled away from the curb, she saw Chauncey in her rearview mirror, still standing there with his hands balled into fists.

That's where he belongs, Neveah thought. In my rearview mirror.

"He's a real piece of shit, ain't he?" Dante said.

"Yeah, he is," Neveah said.

"You didn't have to do that."

"Yeah, I did. It was a long time coming. It wasn't just about you. Anyway, nobody gets to talk shit to you except me and Roman. We've earned it."

Dante tittered in his seat.

Neveah looked at him, and he looked back at her.

Then they both burst out laughing.

CHAPTER TWENTY-SIX

Roman made his way down the stairs with a mouthful of cotton and a head full of ghosts. His dreams had been filled with people who had shuffled off this mortal coil. He chalked it up to the excesses of the previous night. And his guilt. His guilt was definitely a contributing factor.

He got to the landing and stopped short.

Khalil was sitting at the kitchen table.

"One of these days I'm going to ask you to show me how you do that," Roman said as he headed for the coffee maker.

"Ancient Jamaican secret. It's just you here this morning, so I figured it'd be safe for us to talk," Khalil said. He was wearing a black pea coat and a black knit cap. His locs hung to his shoulders.

"Neveah had to get an early start at the shop. I think Dante is hanging with his friend, the one whose girlfriend got stabbed the other night," Roman said. He set the timer on the Keurig and sat down across from Khalil.

"The pressure is getting to them. They've upped the security at the stash houses. The girls who drive down to South Carolina and come back with product now have a passenger. There's armed guards on the gun shipments that come in from Roanoke and Christianburg. How much longer you gotta pretend to enjoy partying with them before we make our next move?" Khalil asked.

"I need at least three more weeks. We sent the first invoice for the contract last week. Started the demo of the properties that I advised Torrent to buy and let the state buy them from him. Mayor Gravely got his first payment. They got me buying more pump-and-dump stuff for them too. Of course, that's for Torrent and Tranquil, the rest of the crew doesn't see a dime of that money," Roman said.

"How's that going? Working with them?"

Roman ran both hands over his face. "You know that quote from Machiavelli where he says it's better to be feared than loved? Because people might stop loving you, but if you make them afraid of punishment, they'll never stop fearing you?"

"Yeah. It's from *The Prince*," Khalil said.

"Torrent takes that shit to the extreme. Last night we were at the Kingdom celebrating the first invoice and how much money it was going to put in his pocket. Tank, one of the lower-ranking underlings, spilled his drink and a few drops got on Torrent's shoe. He had Tranquil pistol-whip him. For a spilled drink," Roman said.

"That's the pressure. Maybe we should turn it up," Khalil said.

"That ain't the pressure. That's who he is," Roman said.

"I knew a dude that used to work for this Miami cartel called the Machados. He told me something once that I think applies here. Men like Torrent, they don't respect anything or anyone. They'll kill you just as quick as they look at you because they can. Because somebody told them they were in charge. It's like the old Lord Acton quote about power. It corrupts, and absolute power corrupts absolutely. When you're working for men like that there's only one way it ends," Khalil said.

"In ashes," Roman said.

"That's one way to put it," Khalil said. "Love may not endure, but fear fails when a man's had enough. I wonder if Torrent's men have had enough yet."

The timer went off and Roman got up and poured a cup for himself and one for Khalil. He slid Khalil's cup over to him and took a sip from his own.

"Not yet. But we're getting there. I'm supposed to join them today and meet with the man who helps supply their operation. Their connection. Apparently he's heard about how good I am with money," Roman said.

Khalil set his cup down. "Supplies them with what?"

"Everything," Roman said.

"You need me to follow you?"

Roman shook his head. "No, Tranquil still doesn't like me, but I'm making so much money for them in a little less than a month they aren't gonna do anything to mess with that. I get the feeling that if a gun shipment went bad, that would put more pressure on them. Shit runs downhill," Roman said.

"Okay. I'll need two guys for that. Can you afford that?" Khalil said.

"Don't worry about the cost. I got it."

"Are we blaming the Ghost Town Crew for this?" Khalil said.

"No. I think we've done enough there. They can't win this fight. The BBB too much for them. Torrent's going hard at them. They on their last legs. We can just make it look random. It makes Torrent look weak," Roman said.

"There's a motorcycle club, the Rare Breed, where they move a lot of armaments. We could put it on them. That's a war on another front if Torrent decides to try and get back at them," Khalil said.

"Okay. That works," Roman said.

"If we hit the gun shipment, some people may not be making it home for dinner, if you know what I mean. You okay with that?" Khalil said.

Roman took another sip.

Over Khalil's shoulder there was a window that gave him a good view of the front yard. The lawn needed to be cut even though the grass was yellowing. His father's boxwoods needed mulching, the rosebushes on each side of the porch needed trimming. The grass was encroaching on the driveway even as the colder temperatures were settling in for the fall.

Roman didn't think his father would ever crank up his decrepit Wheel Horse riding mower with the three-speed clutch and cut his grass again. Spring would find him lying in repose while nurses trimmed his nails and changed his IV bags and his diapers as his body stubbornly refused to either let go or come back.

Torrent and his people did that to his father. All this may have begun with Dante, but it was Torrent and his broken psyche that put his father in that bed. They hadn't killed him, but they certainly didn't care if he lived or died. Now he was trapped between both of those states of being. Which in some ways was worse than if he had passed away on that lonesome set of tracks, crushed inside his van, a mile down the road on the very same tracks where his wife's car was found all those years ago.

Fate is like a train roaring down the track. There are times you can beat that train and there are times that train plows right through you. If Khalil was that train for some of Torrent's men, well, he wasn't going to lose any sleep over it. They sure as hell didn't lose any thinking about his father.

"You do what you gotta do," Roman said before taking another sip of his coffee.

The Osman Hotel's greatest claim to fame was a legend.

According to the story, Breece D'J Pancake, one of the finest writers many people have never heard of, spent the night in the Osman after a sojourn from UVA, in Room 127. The letters BDJP are carved in the trim where two walls meet in the corner behind a nightstand.

Or so the story goes.

Roman overheard the story as the desk clerk spoke with a guest checking in while he waited in the lobby with Torrent and Tranquil.

"I think this a bad idea," Tranquil said

"He said he wanted to meet him, so he gonna meet him," Torrent said.

Roman was sitting in a chair near a huge window while Torrent and Tranquil sat on a bench made out of bright pink molded plastic. Outside, traffic zoomed up and down Broad Street, the busiest street in Richmond. He scrolled through his phone until he found Jae's number. He sent her a text asking if she wanted him to make dinner for her tonight. She responded with a joke:

Or you can eat what my momma made.

The text came with a devil-face emoji. He sent back an angel emoji.

The playful electronic banter of a couple still finding the boundaries of their relationship.

Roman put the phone away.

He was lying to her. Despite those lies being in service to a greater good, they were still lies. Lies that were the shifting sand upon which they were building a relationship. Because Roman had to admit he wanted more than the frenzied couplings they had been sharing for the past two weeks. Jealousy was not only a woman who was open to his desires, she was also someone who was slowly finding her way into the damaged spaces inside him and making them whole again.

Yet here he was, risking it all for the chance to take down her brothers.

She'll be better off once they aren't a threat anymore, he thought. We'll all be. That lie was the easiest one to deliver because it was the one he was telling himself.

The elevator opened and a light-complected man in a black turtle-neck with a neck the size of a Clydesdale's exited. He made his way toward Roman and the Gilchrist brothers. He patted each of them down with his bear trap hands.

"Let's go," he said.

The man turned on his heel and headed for the elevator without any additional words of instruction. Torrent and Tranquil followed him, and Roman followed them. Once they were in the elevator, no one spoke as the bald man pushed a button that said RT. The car rose silently as one of those old-fashioned arrows at the top of the elevator denoted which floor they were approaching. When the arrow reached 14, the elevator stopped. The doors opened and they stepped out into an enclosed rooftop bar. A row of six custom-cut windows gave the bar patrons a panoramic view of the midtown Richmond skyline. Repurposed ware-houses and new office buildings stood shoulder to shoulder with eight-story-tall murals and dramatic architecture that highlighted the growing campus of VCU.

The bar was a mishmash of late-century modernity and postmod-ern sensibilities. Tongue-and-groove tigerwood flooring coexisted with form- but not function-friendly tables and chairs. The bar itself stretched the length of the space. Roman noticed they had a good selection of spirits, including a bottle of Pappy Van Winkle, which he knew retailed for twenty-five hundred dollars.

The setting sun was a yellow diamond whose facets were sparkling as it shone its dying light through the aforementioned windows. There were two people in the bar. The bartender, who had the demure demeanor of a man who had seen much and had the good sense to not see a thing, was wiping down a tray of glasses, and a man was sitting at a table near the last window.

Roman could tell the man was tall, maybe as tall as Khalil. His head was clean-shaven but he had a thick beard, with flecks of gray sprinkled in it like sugar spilled on a black tablecloth. The man was African American, a shade darker than Roman. He wore a charcoal-gray suit that Roman was ninety percent sure was a Huntsman tailored ensemble from the British tailoring house of the same name. Those suits started at ten thousand dollars. Purchasing one was on Roman's bucket list.

The man in the turtleneck walked over to the table where the man was sitting, stood behind him, and leaned against the wall. Roman wasn't an expert on guns or carrying them, but he was fairly sure the man against the wall had a gun in a holster clipped to his waist on the right side under his sweater. Virginia was an open-carry state, so that wasn't so unusual. Judging by the clothing he was wearing and the formality they had to endure to see him, Roman knew this man in the nice gray suit was someone either quite wealthy or quite infamous.

Or both.

"Y'all have a seat," the man said. It didn't sound like an invitation.

The three of them sat down across from the man in the suit. Roman thought he heard southeastern Virginia come rumbling out of the man's chest with the depth and volume of a narrator for a historical documentary.

The man placed his hands on the table and entwined his fingers. Roman noticed he was wearing a plain Timex with a leather strap.

He wears ten-thousand-dollar suits, Roman thought, but has on a two-hundred-dollar watch. The suit won't stand out to the uninitiated, and neither will the watch.

"Roman, Torrent tells me you've made him a lot of money on the Skids construction project. Almost enough to make up for him letting a stash house get burned down," the man said.

Roman took in everything the man said and the way he said it. Torrent had described him as a connection, a supplier, but Roman could see that this man was not Torrent's partner.

He was a boss.

"Yeah, we've been, um . . . doing well with that project," Roman said.

"Doing well? Don't sell yourself short. The demo contracts have already put seven hundred thousand in y'all's pockets, thanks to the inflated invoice you submitted. Mayor Gravely and I had a little conversation about it the other day. One of my interests outside of my normal business is real estate. Like this place," the man said as he spread his hands.

"You own this bar?" Roman asked.

The man gave him the barest of smiles.

"I own the building. Let's get down to it. I have a long affiliation with the BBB. We go way, way back. I knew their father, Horace. That association has been profitable for both of us, but it's a poor rabbit that only got one hole. I believe in diversification. I have my own money managers and they take care of my investments like good little white boys who are scared of their own shadow. And that's how I want them to be. They keep Uncle Sam or Johnny Law out my back pocket. But you're not afraid to, well, let's call it get creative with your investment advice," the man said. He leaned back in his chair and motioned for the man standing behind him. The man in the turtleneck came over and handed the man in the suit an envelope.

"Down in New Kent county there's a racetrack. They do horse races, harness racing, all that country-ass shit. There's an old boy who keeps coming to the races and keeps betting on the wrong horse. Instead of getting a new hobby, he took out a loan with some fellas that work for me. It's a shame, really. My daddy told me a man who can't control his vices is a slave to them. He said that right before he shot my mama in the face and ate the end of a shotgun. But I digress. Now, this old boy happens to work for the Virginia Department of Emergency Management. He's in charge of handling some of the money that they use to buy supplies for, what did he call it? Catastrophic environmental events. I want you to talk to him and help him get even more creative with his accounting practices. Do what you did for Torrent and them. Set up a fake company, have our old boy give you the vendor accounts for the supplies, then take that money and do your magic. Pretty simple, really," the man in the suit said.

Roman would have let out a sigh of relief if he didn't think the man in the suit might take it as a sign of weakness. This was actually pretty simple. He could set up a shell company in his sleep. There were other variables to consider, though.

"This old boy, like you call him, can he be trusted? Does he know if there are escalators built into the vendor payment system that will initiate an automatic audit? Can he make payments to offshore accounts? Those are all questions I'll ask him, but I want to make you aware of the risk involved here. I can insulate you from most legal ramifications, but if he gets caught and he starts talking—"

"He'll end up in multiple jurisdictions at the same time," the man in the suit said. There was a startling banality to the statement that made Roman's skin crawl. It was as if they were discussing how they took their coffee, not disposing of a dead body.

Not like you don't have experience with that, Roman thought. There was a certain hypocrisy in his disgust that he couldn't ignore.

I'm not like him. I'm not like Torrent and Tranquil. I don't enjoy it. I don't get off on it. And it'll never become normal to me.

"All right," Roman said. He was choosing his words carefully with this man, even more so than he did with Torrent and Tranquil. He reached for the envelope.

The man in the suit studied him. Roman couldn't tell if he was impressed with him or he was wondering how Roman's head would look on a pike.

"You ask good questions. People who are careless don't ask good questions. They can't think around corners. I'll give you three months to set up the dummy company, get the first payments, and for you to make the magic happen. Torrent said you gave him a fifty percent return. I'll expect the same. Of course, we ain't dealing with street money here. This is gonna be some seven-figure math. But you can handle that, can't you, Roman?" the man in the suit said.

"Yeah, I can. It's what I do," Roman said, his hand still extended.

"I don't think I have to tell you what happens if my investments don't find the same level of . . . enchantment, do I?" the man in the suit said.

"No, you don't," Roman said.

The man in the suit placed the envelope in his hand. "Good man. Let's get some food. The Salmon New Orleans is pretty damn good. I told the chef it better be, it's my favorite meal."

Later, after they ate and they were walking to their respective vehicles, Roman asked Torrent a question. "Who was that? He said he knew y'all for a long time. Is he like a relative?"

He knew damn well that the man in the suit wasn't a relative, but he was playing a trifle dumb. If he insinuated that Torrent and Tranquil were in any way subservient to the man in the suit, he thought Tranquil might shoot him on general principle. He was giving Torrent the room to tell him without feeling as though Roman was being disrespectful.

They were standing next to their cars in the public parking lot next to a bar called Garlands. Tranquil grunted at Roman's question. He got in the black BMW on the driver's side without saying another word.

"They call him Shade. Him and our pops used to be boys. Then our pops got locked up and Shade got rich. He gave my mom money while our pops was locked up until we was old enough to rep the set ourselves," Torrent said.

"That's a true friend," Roman said. Something passed over Torrent's face and Roman almost took a step back.

Torrent climbed into the BMW. "That motherfucker ain't got no friends. The devil ain't got no friends."

Roman went back to the house and found Dante there, sitting on the couch watching television. There was a large ceramic mug on the coffee table in front of him with a Punisher logo on it. The Punisher was Dante's favorite comic book character.

Roman remembered when he'd gotten that mug. Roman had won it for him at a county fair down in Mathews County when they'd gone to visit some of their mother's people the summer before she disappeared. Roman had won a basketball shooting game with two seconds to spare. He'd wanted a Spider-Man action figure, but Dante had wanted that mug so bad he couldn't say no.

He could never say no to his little brother.

"What's up? I thought you was over at Tug's place," Roman said.

"Yeah. I was. But the hospital called and said Raynell had took a turn for the worse, so he ran up to the hospital. I came back here," Dante said.

"I'm sorry to hear that," Roman said.

Dante didn't say anything. He took a sip from the mug, grimaced, and swallowed.

"You drinking while the sun still up?" Roman said.

"What fucking difference do it make, man? Raynell might die, Rome. All because of me," Dante said. He put the mug up to his lips and took a long swig.

Roman sat next to him. "It's not because of you. You put that blame where it belongs. On the Ghost Town Crew. And Torrent. And Jefferson Run. It's not your fault, okay?"

Dante smiled at him. "That's a nice thing to say, but that don't make that shit true," he said. The smile disappeared. "I gotta tell you something."

Roman crossed his legs. "Okay. What is it?"

"I heard from Cassidy. She wants to know if she can come home."

Roman felt his stomach begin to churn like it was making a batch of bad butter.

"And you told her that wasn't possible, right? You told her that the whole world thinks she's dead and she can't come back? That's what you told her, right?" Roman said. He kept his delivery even, but it was a struggle.

"I mean, I told her, but she didn't seem like she was listening. It was like it was, *whoosh!*, going right over her head," Dante said while making a flyover motion with his hand over his own head.

"Dante, she can't come back. Not yet. I'm getting close to fixing this for good, but if she comes back now, we're all dead. Everybody. You, me, Neveah, Daddy, everybody. You gotta talk some sense into her. Make her understand the severity of the situation."

"Roman, would you hurt her? You wouldn't do that, would you?" Dante said, and a sliver of ice slid through Roman's heart. Dante sounded as fragile as spun glass.

"Dante, I wouldn't hurt her, but I can't speak for Torrent and Tranquil. They see her walking, the first thing they are going to do is kill her as a matter of course. Because if you thought they were angry about you and Getty playing in their faces before, how do you think they are going to feel about us lying about killing her? Then how long you think it's going to take them to realize Splodie is dead? Dante, she cannot come back here. You make her understand it. If I have to give her some money, that's fine, but she can't set foot in Jefferson Run. Do you understand me?"

Dante picked up his mug. "I understand. I understand Raynell is fighting for her life with a gallon of somebody else's blood in her veins. I understand Getty is dead. Splodie is dead. Yellaboy. Four people from Candy's. The six people at the vape shop. I understand that there are sidewalks all around town stained with blood because I fucked up and you're trying to fix it. I'm not going to have Cassidy's blood on my hands too. Do you understand *that*? I'll talk to her. But if she shows up, we have to protect her. We have to."

He finished his drink. "I'm going upstairs."

He got up and stumbled past Roman as he headed for the stairs. Roman didn't watch him walk away. His head was full of images that were best left in his nightmares. Images of Dante tied to that chair at the farm. Images of Neveah, stiff and cold as a winter's morning. His father, eyes blank like marbles, his face covered by a pillow from some CNA or nurse who finds a debt they owe to a local dealer all forgiven if they do this one thing.

He closed his eyes and covered his mouth. He grunted so deep and so violently he sounded like a bear with its maw taped shut.

His phone, his regular one, vibrated in his pocket. He pulled it out and checked the screen. It was Keisha, his assistant. Roman answered the phone. His old life seemed so far away that it was like a dot in the distance across an endless sea.

"Hey, Keisha, what's up?" Roman asked.

"Roman, I hate to bother you, with everything going on with your dad, but President Taylor is freaking out about some investment plan he had with you, and then I got a call from the folks that rep the Atlanta Braves and they want you to have a meeting with some of their call-ups and rookies about wealth management, but the main reason I called is Lil Glock needs to talk to you. He said he's willing to do a Zoom. But he said it's a matter of life and death," Keisha said.

"I'm sure it's not, but when does he want to do this?" Roman asked.

"He'd like to do it now, if at all possible. I'm going to give you a little of the lowdown. He invested a lot of money to buy some abandoned apartment buildings back in his hometown in South Carolina, but it looks like it's a money-pit scam. The friend was supposed to be buying the buildings and renovating them, but turns out he owned the buildings and then basically—"

"Sold them to Lil Glock for way more than what they are worth and he has no intention of renovating them and selling them. He's probably gone with the money and deposited Glock's check in an offshore account or a double-encrypted Bitcoin account," Roman finished.

"Uh, yes, and now he wants to know how he can get his money back," Keisha said.

"How much?" Roman asked.

Keisha paused. "Four million."

Roman shook his head. "That's most of his liquidity. He sure knows how to make a beat, but he has no clue how to make a real estate investment. Give me about thirty minutes. I didn't bring my laptop. I have to go up to my dad's place and use his," Roman said as he rose off the couch.

He went out the door and headed for the Challenger.

Down the street, parked behind a boarded-up former title loan business that sat at a perpendicular angle from the Carruthers house, a nondescript dark blue sedan sat idling. The window rolled down and a telephoto lens emerged like a viper from a hole in the ground.

"Smile, you fucker," Chauncey whispered as he snapped photos of Roman, the Challenger, and the license plate.

CHAPTER TWENTY-SEVEN

Neveah parked her truck next to a large sign that said WARREN COUNTY SENIOR LIVING CENTER. Both Cs were missing from the woodcut sign. Neveah wondered had they fallen away or were they the culmination of a dare between bored kids in Warren. She got out of her truck and heard the gravel crunch under her feet as she walked across the parking lot. The senior living center was basically a series of one-room apartments laid out like a cheap motel.

And I've been to a lot of those, Neveah thought. Thanks, Chauncey. She walked down the crumbling sidewalk that ran parallel to a flower bed bracketed by landscape timbers that ran the length of the building. The early frost had killed most of the plants in the flower beds except for a few stubborn pansies.

Neveah stopped in front of 6E and knocked.

"Hold on, now," a deep voice said. She heard a television that sounded like it was on eleven rapidly decrease in volume. A few seconds later the door was opened by an older Black man with a wild gray beard and an equally unkempt tangle of gray hair.

"Lawrence? I'm Neveah Carruthers. I called you earlier," she said.

"Yeah, come on in," Lawrence said.

They entered his modest hovel and Lawrence shut the door. Neveah sat on a threadbare love seat and Lawrence plopped down into a decrepit recliner. The television was tuned to *The Price Is Right*. There was an aluminum TV tray in front of the recliner with a plate full of tater tots and fish sticks.

"I'd offer you something, but all I got is some beers and some lemonade that needs about a half cup more of sugar," Lawrence said.

"That's all right. I'm good," Neveah said.

Lawrence nodded like that was the answer he expected.

The television hummed with squeals and laughter as a young man did a cartwheel after correctly guessing the price of a box of microwave popcorn. Neveah watched as he sat in the driver's seat of a new Ford Focus.

"Popcorn must cost more in California. I would've guessed three ninety-nine," Lawrence said.

Neveah smiled.

"I guess you wanna ask me about your mama," Lawrence said.

"Actually, I wanted to ask you about my daddy," Neveah said.

Lawrence frowned. "I only saw him that one time. We didn't talk," Lawrence said.

"How long was you and my mother . . . involved?" Neveah asked.

Lawrence let out a deep sigh.

"It wasn't like that. That night was the first time we ever did anything other than talk. Your mother was a trip. Funny as hell. Kind, ya know? We used to go to lunch together sometimes, but not like boyfriend-girlfriend. We was hanging out. I never thought of her that way. I mean, your mama was beautiful, but I had a girl. I just liked being around her. Then that night, she started crying. I mean, I told all of this to the cops," Lawrence said.

"Some of y'all's coworkers thought y'all had a thing," Neveah said.

Lawrence tittered. "A lot of them old biddies was jealous of your mama. Nah, that night was the first time we . . . well, you know. She was so sad that night. She said your daddy didn't love her. He liked her, but she said he didn't . . . I mean, you sure you wanna hear this?"

"Yes," Neveah said, a little more forcefully than she'd intended.

"All right. She said they had stopped making love. Your daddy couldn't think of nothing but that crematory. She said she understood. He was trying to make a life for y'all, but . . ." Lawrence paused, and Neveah had the idea he was peering into the past like looking through a time portal.

"I can't remember her exact words but it was something like, what kind of life would they have if he loved the crematory more than he loved her. And then she started crying. I mean, she was bawling. And all I wanted to do was comfort her. I hugged her, took a bag of onion rings out her lap and hugged her. Next thing I know, we was kissing, and then your daddy was there. I ain't never seen a man look so heartbroken in my life. I don't know about no crematory, but the man I saw that night loved your mama and he looked devastated," Lawrence said.

Neveah steeled herself for her next question.

"You think he was heartbroken enough he would have hurt her?" she asked.

Lawrence seemed to melt into the chair. "I've asked myself that question for twenty years. I've asked myself what would I do if my wife was . . . with another man and I had access to a crematory." Lawrence paused.

"The thing that always got me was the look on his face. If he had come over and pulled me out my car and started swinging on me, I wouldn't have liked it but I would have understood it. But he just stared at us through the window. Didn't say a word. I gotta be honest with you. That shit scared the hell out of me. She, uh, had taken off her ring. The one with the heart-shaped diamond. When we, uh, you know. But when she saw your daddy, she slipped it back on while they locked eyes. I never seen people who look like they love and hate each other at the same time before. It was so strange. He was just staring at her. It was like I wasn't even there, and I didn't want to be there. For a minute I thought he was gonna pull out a gun and start blasting. Or break down crying." Lawrence sighed.

"Or both."

Lawrence tugged on his beard. "When I first heard that your mama had went missing, the first thing I thought was he'd killed her. That look on his face . . . Then I thought, maybe she ran away. Not from you kids but just from her life, ya know? I can't imagine what it's like living with someone you have love for but you ain't *in* love with them anymore," he said.

"You talking about my father or you talking about my mother?" Neveah said.

Lawrence yawned. "Eh, fuck, maybe I'm talking about both of them. What do I know? I'm just an old man."

Neveah thanked Lawrence for his time and went back to her truck. There was no one left to talk to except her father, and if the doctors were to be believed that wasn't going to happen for a long time, if ever.

She started her truck.

Her gut was telling her that her father had something to do with what had happened to their mother, but was that confirmation bias? Did she want it to be true so that she could finally have an answer? Or was her father a killer who had put her mother on a funeral pyre made of iron and fueled by propane? Everybody kept saying her daddy loved her mother, but that didn't mean he didn't murder her. She kept seeing that picture of her mother's car in her mind. She kept thinking about what Lawrence said about the look on her daddy's face. Was that look the last thing her mother saw? If her daddy did kill her mama, the closest he was ever going to get to paying for it was lying in that hospital not being able to move or speak until he died. The police weren't going to arrest him, her brothers refused to believe it. She was like Don Quixote tilting at a long-forgotten windmill.

"What the fuck am I doing with my life?" Neveah said out loud. There was no one to answer her, so she answered herself.

"Not anything that makes you happy," she said, and pulled onto the interstate.

Roman was at the crematory using his father's ancient desktop in what he was pretty sure was a fruitless effort to track down Lil Glock's partner to see if there was any way to get his four million dollars back. He had contracted an information-gathering firm that consisted of former hackers who, for a not-inconsiderable fee, would bend the rules of online privacy to find out anything about anyone. They were tracking Lil Glock's friend by his cell phone usage, credit card transactions, online purchases, even where he used music streaming services.

That was all well and good, but if he had put the money in a Bitcoin account, Roman knew it might as well be in a vault on the moon. Bitcoin wasn't registered with the FDIC. It wasn't really regulated by any one country or governing body. There was no one to appeal to in a formal legal setting to get Lil Glock's money back.

Roman sent a message to the hackers thanking them for their work and sending them an initial payment from his corporate account that Lil Glock was going to have to reimburse him for, regardless of whether he got his money back or not.

The legal avenues they had were admittedly weak, but there were other paths they could take if they could find Lil Glock's friend. Khalil could recommend people who would go and have a conversation with that friend with blowtorches and hammers and stun guns.

Roman caught sight of his reflection in the glass of the computer's monitor. Would he have even considered those kinds of methods a month ago? He wasn't naïve. He knew he'd been party to some advanced interrogative questioning before, but he'd mostly been in charge of the payment for such techniques. Not all of his clients were fake gangsters. They weren't street-level guys like Torrent and Tranquil either. They were corporate thugs who had no problem making that kind of call. He'd never been the one to order such persuasion. He'd always kept himself on the periphery of that kind of business. Kept his hands clean, for the most part, but behind every great empire was an even greater crime. Only now he wasn't the one cleaning it up, he was the one making the mess.

The doorbell rang. Before he could get up, someone rang it again. By the time he got to the door, they were leaning on it. He wasn't expecting any bodies today unless Neveah had forgotten to tell him. She'd seemed distracted this morning when she'd told him she had an errand to run.

Roman went to the door and looked through the peephole. What the fuck does he want? he thought.

He considered not opening the door, but then he thought it was probably better to tear the bandage off now instead of waiting until later.

"What can I do for you, Detective Mansfield?" Roman asked.

Chauncey came into the lobby of the crematory without uttering a word. Roman thought he was looking rode hard and hung up wet. Five o'clock shadow covered his face like a thin layer of scum on a pond. Bloodshot eyes seemed to have cratered into his skull. His clothes were wrinkled and hung on his frame like those of a scarecrow.

"I think you and I need to have a talk," Chauncey said.

Roman stood in the center of the lobby with his hands hanging loosely by his side. He didn't think Chauncey was here to arrest him. The aura was all wrong. He also was alone. He would have brought along his partner if they were going down that road.

"About what, exactly? I'm not trying to be rude, but I don't think there is anything you and I have to talk about. Unless you want to discuss the weather," Roman said.

Chauncey laughed. It was a bitter sound like the rattle of bones in a graveyard.

"I see being a smartass runs in the family. Your sister—"

"You thinking about saying something disparaging about my sister, let me stop you right there," Roman said. He didn't yell, but there was a finality about his words that made Chauncey pause.

"Well, I'm not here about her," Chauncey spat. Roman wondered if his wife had kicked him out, because, judging by his appearance, it was entirely possible he was spending his nights in his car.

Chauncey reached in his jacket and pulled out a tan envelope. "I'm here about this," he said, holding out the envelope.

Roman frowned. "If this isn't a warrant, I'm not interested," Roman said.

"Oh, I think you should be interested in this," Chauncey said.

Roman snatched the envelope from Chauncey. He opened it and saw it had a sheaf of photos. Pulling them out, he fanned through them like a deck of cards. There were pictures of him in the Challenger leaving the house, pictures of him at the Kingdom with Torrent, Tranquil, and the rest of the BBB. There were pictures of him with Jae leaving her apartment. There were a few pictures of Dante, but most of those showed him leaving a battered mobile home or the other popular bar in town, Cooper's Rest, obviously intoxicated. There were a couple of pictures of Neveah. Those made his vision go crimson around the edges, but he hid it on his face.

Roman slid the photos back in the envelope and offered them to Chauncey, who held his hand up and waved him off.

"Nah, those are for you. I got plenty of copies," Chauncey said.

Roman tossed the envelope onto the scarred coffee table in the middle of the lobby. He waited for Chauncey to tell him what he wanted. Because he was sure a want or a desire was going to be the next thing out of his mouth.

"I've been a cop for twelve years. There's a story that those pictures are telling me, wanna hear it?" Chauncey said.

"I have a feeling you're going to tell your story no matter what I say, so go ahead," Roman said.

"The story is a smart fucking guy who knows how to move money around comes home after his daddy tries to French-kiss a train and makes himself a permanent guest of the vegetable wing at the hospital. Once he comes home, his degenerate little brother runs afoul of a couple of vicious thugs and something goes down. Something bad. So bad, in fact, the degenerate's best friend and his girl go missing. And now the smart guy who's good with money is hanging around with these fucking animals and partying with their slutty half sister and making money for these fucks. Probably in exchange for them not butt-fucking his degenerate little brother with a forty-five-caliber pistol. How close am I?" Chauncey said.

"Like you said, it's just a story. Maybe you should write it down, send it to a website that publishes short fiction," Roman said.

"You're in bed with the BBB. Your brother is a known associate of the BBB. A snitch and his girlfriend are missing. Savion Graham, aka

Yellaboy, another known associate of the BBB, hasn't been seen in a week. His baby mama called the station saying he went out with some friends and never came home. Ever since you've come home, the streets have turned into Afghanistan. You're in this up to your fucking eyeballs and sinking another foot every day. How's that for a story?" Chauncey said. He put his finger in Roman's chest to emphasize his point.

Roman looked at Chauncey's finger. "I'm not a lawyer or a cop, but I think you should probably move your finger if you don't want me to call your brothers in blue and file assault charges," Roman said.

Chauncey laughed. He removed his finger. "You don't realize how fucked you are. Or maybe you do and you're scared shitless. The BBB are never going to let you go. Terrance Gilchrist and his psycho of a brother, Tracy Gilchrist, have been double-deep in the game since they were playing with Hot Wheels. Terrance committed his first murder at sixteen, but got off on a technicality when the main witness was found in the James River with a rat shoved down his throat and gutted like a fish. Tracy is two steps from being a serial killer. You're swimming with megalodons and you're a fucking guppy. Now, I don't know why you hitched your wagon to these two lunatics, but I know you know that the only way this ends is with you either in jail or face down in a ditch with two holes in the back of your head. These guys will squeeze you dry, and when you're no longer any use to them, they will snuff you out like a candle, because they don't believe in loose ends. Or maybe the GTC takes you out along with the Gilchrist brothers one night when y'all are leaving the club. Either way, your life will end like *that*," Chauncey said. He clapped his hands together as hard as he could.

"But I'm offering you a lifeline," he continued. This is a onetime offer and it won't be repeated, so listen up real good. Right now you're not the official subject of an investigation, but I can make that change overnight. Once that happens, it won't be long before I do get that warrant. I'll take you downtown and I'll make sure everyone sees me cut you loose. Especially Tranquil and Torrent. Won't be long before Torrent convinces himself you talked. Then he'll kill all three of you. Slowly. You'll die hearing Neveah call out for you, or your daddy, or both. But, you ready?

Here's the lifeline. You get me, let's say, twenty-five thousand, and I make sure your name disappears from any list of known associates. I sweep any possible investigation under the rug. Then you can be my new CI. We'll get you wired up and you can get us some evidence on Torrent and his gang of sociopaths for the probably hundreds of felonies I'm sure they have committed. I'll even plant some evidence on one of his other lackeys to take heat off you. Then you and your family can go back to your regularly scheduled dysfunction."

Roman cocked his head to the right. "Let me get this straight. You want me to pay you for the privilege of being a snitch? Then you want me to stand by while you set somebody else up to get fingered as said snitch?"

"Consider the twenty-five grand the nuisance fee for your sister trying to ruin my fucking marriage. It's this, or I go to Torrent and tell him you're a snitch anyway after I arrest you and make sure he sees you get out uncharged. Your choice, Roman," Chauncey said.

Roman shook his head. "I can't believe you're actually this stupid. Let me tell you what's really going on. I'm dating Torrent and Tranquil's sister. That's why you've seen me hanging around with them from time to time. As to my brother, I know he likes to party, and they are usually where the party is. Now, you and I both know what they do and how they do it, but that doesn't mean I'm a part of it or condone it. Jefferson Run is an incorporated city, but we both know it's really just a small town. We all know a lot of the same people. That's just how it is."

Roman put his hand on Chauncey's shoulder. "But now let's talk about you. You're not looking too good. Did your wife kick you out? What was it, did she finally catch wind of you hanging out with my sister? Did somebody finally tell her they saw you two together? But you're blaming her, like it doesn't take two to tango? I know that's gotta be rough for you, but I'm going to need you to keep my sister, brother, and the woman I'm dating's names out of your mouth. I'm not paying you anything, but I am going to do you a favor and not file a complaint with the chief of police for targeted harassment. My father is friends with the mayor, and I'm sure he wouldn't like hearing that the son of one of the most prominent members of what is left of the Jefferson Run Chamber of Commerce is feeling . . . unsafe. So why don't you go back to whatever hotel, hovel, hostel, or pay-by-the-day parking lot where you're resting your head at night and leave me and my family alone?"

Roman patted Chauncey's shoulder. "You have a good one, now," he said.

Chauncey smiled. "I hope you have a good lawyer. You're gonna need him."

"My lawyer's a woman and she's fantastic. Now I'm going to have to ask you to leave. I'm helping some clients remotely and I really have to get back to it. I'm assuming you have to get back to finding someplace to wash up when the parking meter runs out," Roman said.

Chauncey reached inside his jacket. "Fuck you," he said.

"Chauncey, you pull that gun out, you better fucking kill me," Roman said. The rage that was superimposed on that statement surprised him, but it was real and it was raw and he knew without a doubt he absolutely meant it. He was tired of this man. Tired of his condescending bon mots and his hypocritical priggishness that made Roman's stomach turn. Tired of his idle threats. Tired of his casual misogyny. Tired of his crassness. Tired of him wielding his badge like a club.

Most of all, he was tired of him disrespecting Neveah. So if Chauncey wanted to really get it on, then, by God, they could get it on right here and right now.

Chauncey must have seen that in Roman's face. Must have felt it in the death stare that Roman leveled at him as they stood less than a foot apart. Perhaps he'd seen that look before and knew how that story ended.

"You resisting arrest?" Chauncey said.

"Try me and find out," Roman said. Those were bold words to speak to a cop, but the moment Chauncey had asked for a blackmail payment, Roman had stopped seeing him as a police officer. He now saw him as a problem to be solved. What the solution was going to be was still to be determined.

Chauncey took his hand from inside his jacket.

"I can't get my money if I shoot your dumb ass. Besides, it's too much paperwork. I'm gonna give you a few days to think this over. Maybe then after you cool down you'll see how this is really your only option. We'll be talking," Chauncey said. He headed for the door.

Roman watched him leave. When he heard his car start up, he called Khalil.

"Pax Romana," Khalil said.

"We have a problem," Roman said.

"Well, that's okay. I wake up in the morning to solve problems."

"This one is bigger than usual," Roman said.

"All right. Let me get this thing straight tonight and we'll deal with it," Khalil said.

"What you plan on doing with the . . . items you're going to pro cure?" Roman said.

Khalil hummed for a second. "I figure I'll drop them off in GTC territory. They could use an upgrade over machetes."

CHAPTER TWENTY-EIGHT

Torrent came in the back door of Trout's, flanked by Tranquil and D-Train. D-Train locked the door behind them as Torrent stomped toward the kitchen. Standing in the kitchen were Roman, Tank, Eddie Munsta, and the Bang Bang Twins.

"Open the freezer," Torrent said.

Lucius opened the walk-in freezer and pushed the door back and locked it in place. A burst of cold air escaped. Roman wasn't sure if it was the cold air or seeing the two men sitting on the floor of the freezer naked and shivering that gave him goose bumps.

"Get 'em up," Torrent said.

"Why is this nigga here?" Tranquil said. Roman thought only he and Torrent had heard him, but then he saw D-Train smirk.

"Because somebody is going in the hotbox," Torrent said.

The Bang Bang Twins pulled the two men up off the floor and walked them out of the freezer. Roman saw dark pitch-black patches on their buttocks that looked like burned flesh. If either of them lived through this night, they'd have to get that necrotic, frostbitten skin removed.

Roman vaguely recognized both men from the Kingdom. The taller of the two called himself Wiz. The shorter man went by Cali, short for California, because he always talked about going to Los Angeles to be a rapper.

Roman didn't think he was going to make it. As a rapper or through the night.

"Which one of y'all was driving?" Torrent asked.

Wiz and Cali were still shivering so hard their teeth were chattering. Wiz turned his head side to side. His eyes were wild, like a rabbit caught in a trap.

"I—I—I was dr-dr-driving," Wiz said.

"So, what, you saw them roll up and you didn't drive through them motherfuckers?" Torrent asked.

"Th-th-they had b-b-bombs," Cali said.

"What the fuck you say?"

"We was coming down Route 794," Wiz said. "Got off Interstate 85 like you said. Coming down the back roads and shit was smooth. Us in the middle, Rashaun and Mezzy in the car in front of us, and T-Rock and Daz in the truck behind us. Us in the van, and then we see Rashaun's car blow up and go straight up in the air. Then like two seconds later T-Rock's truck behind us do the same thing. I swerve so I don't hit what's left of Rashaun's car and I go off the side of the road. Next thing I know, three white boys coming up on us and drag us out the van. Then they gone. Rashaun was still alive, but we couldn't get him out. The car was on fire. He was screaming and—"

Torrent interrupted his explanation, "I don't give a fuck about that nigga. He dead. What these white boys look like?" Torrent said.

Wiz licked his lips.

"They was wearing masks," Cali offered.

"Then how the fuck you know they was white?" Torrent said.

"They was wearing vests, like motorcycle vests. Said the RARE BREED on them. And they was talking white," Cali said.

"What the fuck is talking white?" Torrent said.

"Like they sounded like they was country singers," Cali said.

Roman had to admire Khalil's thoroughness. Wearing the cuts from a known MC, changing his voice and accent. His spec ops training was shining through.

"Rare Breed, huh?" Torrent said.

"Yeah, that's what they vests said," Wiz said.

Torrent stroked his goatee. "Who'd you tell?" he said.

"What? Tell what?" Wiz said in a quavering falsetto.

"Who'd you tell you was coming through Roanoke with a van full of AKs, motherfucker? AKs that was supposed to be going to some Dominicans that already coming down 95. Dominicans that I gotta call and tell them we lost they shit. So I'm gonna ask you again. Who the fuck you tell?" Torrent said.

"We didn't tell nobody shit!" Wiz yelled. His teeth were bared and his eyes were bugging from his skull. The kitchen went silent save for the humming of the freezer and the ticking of a clock on the wall.

"Then how'd they know you was coming up Route 794?" Torrent asked.

Wiz licked his lips again.

Tranquil stepped forward and pulled out his .45. "And why they let you live, then?" Tranquil said.

"No! Please!" Wiz screamed.

Tranquil put a round in Wiz's forehead. The sound of the gun going off inside, even in a cavernous space like Trout's kitchen, made Roman's ears pop. A fine red mist filled the air. Roman saw the fluorescent light dancing on the droplets. Wiz's body dropped like a bag of wet laundry. Cali turned to run, and Tranquil put two in his back. He fell face down, half in the freezer, half out, moaning like a wounded deer.

Torrent walked over to where he had fallen and kicked him in the ribs. Cali retched and blood came flowing out of his mouth mixed with vomit. When Torrent went to kick him again, he slipped on the slick floor made even more so by Cali's blood. Lavon caught him, and Torrent almost immediately shrugged him off.

Eddie Munsta tittered a bit. Like most fifteen-year-olds, seeing someone fall or almost fall tickled his funny bone.

D-Train punched him in the shoulder and Eddie cut off his giggle like he'd shut off a water faucet.

"Bang Bang, y'all get the plastic and wrap 'em up. Then put them in college boy's van. D-Train, you and Tank clean up this blood in here," Torrent said.

Tranquil put his gun in his waistband and turned to head out the back door. D-Train and Tank headed for the maintenance closet, while the Bang Bang Twins grabbed a roll of plastic sheeting from under one of the shelves in the kitchen that held the large soup pans and roasters.

Torrent went up to Eddie Munsta. He smiled at him.

"I almost busted my ass over there on that musty-ass motherfucker's blood," he said.

Eddie smiled back. "Yeah, that was—"

Eddie was standing in front of a long stainless-steel table that nearly ran the length of the kitchen. Various cooking implements were lined up on the table organized by their function. There were metal meat tenderizers and stainless-steel mixing bowls stacked inside each other. Strainers and sieves. Saucepans and large ladles and various tongs.

And knives. A huge butcher's block full of knives. Most of them had wooden handles, but a few had white fiberglass handles with a textured surface to ensure the user could get a good grip.

Torrent grabbed one of those out of the butcher's block and stabbed Eddie Munsta in the throat right below the chin. As he pulled the knife out, blood flowed down the front of Eddie's black T-shirt emblazoned with a red Prosser State Mighty Stag. Eddie stumbled and Torrent grabbed him by his hair, which was twisted into tight proto-locs, and stabbed him again and again in his chest and stomach until his body went limp and his legs could no longer support his weight.

Torrent let him fall to the floor.

"Oh, you ain't laughing now, are you, bitch!" Torrent howled at the rapidly cooling body.

No one moved. No one seemed to be breathing. Roman froze. He was wearing black latex gloves to help the Bang Bang Twins package Wiz and Cali. Lucius and Lavon had unfurled a length of thick three-millimeter plastic to wrap the bodies, but now they seemed immobilized. D-Train and Tank stopped rolling the mop buckets into the kitchen.

"Wrap his ass up too," Torrent said.

He followed his brother out the back door.

Later, as they loaded the three bodies into the Carruthers Cremation Services van, D-Train stopped and stared up at the night sky. The Bang Bang Twins had gone back to the Kingdom. Tank had already taken off to get his girl from work at the hospital. It was only Roman and D-Train left now.

"I used to fuck with his aunt. His mama died in a car accident. Eddie was like eight. His daddy didn't want him. Neesha, the aunt, she told me his daddy was married to some rich white lady up in Maryland. By the time he was thirteen he was running for us. Last year he started putting in real work." D-Train lowered his head, grabbed the handle of the rear door of Roman's van, and slammed it shut.

"The game is the game, ya know? You get down with this and you get capped, ya know, that's the risk you taking. Cops run up on you, then you might do a bid. But this? This was fucked up, man," D-Train said.

Roman watched as the big man's shoulders sagged under the weight of his own guilt. Roman sympathized with him. He was intimately acquainted with guilt. He knew the way it could crush you under its unyielding tonnage.

"When I was in business school, a professor told me a true leader will get you to the top of the mountain but he won't push you off the edge of a cliff when things aren't going well."

D-Train laid his hand on the door of Roman's van. "What you saying?" he asked. He barely moved his lips when he spoke.

"I'm not saying anything. I'm just making an observation," Roman said. He patted D-Train on the back, then got in the driver's side of the van.

As he drove away, he wondered if he should have shared a different quote with D-Train. This one was a Keith Carruthers original. His father had used it to explain why he was going to stop working for the funeral home and open his own crematory:

"Sometimes the man wearing the crown ain't the man that's supposed to be the king."

It was eleven by the time Roman got done with all three bodies. The ashes were still warm as he packed them in two urns after running the cremains through the grinder. He was sealing the second bag and putting it in the urn when an epiphany hit him like a cinder block to the face.

Eddie Munsta was fifteen. One year younger than Roman had been when his mother went missing. Eddie would never make it to sixteen. He would never graduate from high school or go to college. He would never get married or have kids. He'd be fifteen forever. Forever just gray sand in a plastic box on a forgotten shelf in the back room of a crematory where pain and misery and loss held court long after the flames that ate the dead had been extinguished. To Roman, it felt like life, existence, was a stygian wheel that had spun on a bitter axis and found Eddie at the same place where Roman had once stood. And while Roman had escaped with his life, in many ways he was just as dead inside as Eddie was in real life.

He sealed the bag and took the two plastic urns into the storeroom. He pushed them all the way to the back and pushed other urns in front of them that held the remains of people whose family members had elected to have them cremated, then decided paying for a cremation was a step too far.

He called Dante and got his voicemail. Roman sighed. He wondered, was this how Neveah felt when she couldn't get Dante to come and help her? He sent him a text telling him to lie low for a bit, that Torrent was in a foul mood, so he might not want to hit up the Kingdom for a while. He didn't tell him Torrent had stabbed a kid to death for laughing.

He could feel Dante was already on the edge of a breakdown. Hearing about Eddie would send him sailing over that precipice.

"Where the hell are you?" Roman said as he peered at his phone.

Dante read the text Roman sent, then set his phone back on the nightstand. The motel was only seventy-nine dollars a night, and it lived down to that inexpensive rate. Dante rolled over on his back and stared at the water stain on the ceiling. Cigarette smoke was fighting a duel with body odor for olfactory dominance. But the room was in a motel fifty miles outside of Jefferson Run at the end of a desolate section of Route 301 in a hiccup of a town called Aruna. A town that was no one's destination unless they were trying to hide out from their mistakes.

"Who was that?"

"Just my brother," Dante said.

Making mistakes is all I do, Dante thought as he turned over and took her into his arms. Rain, quiet as a secret promise, began to fall against the window, clouding Dante's view of the Honda in the parking lot with the huge spoiler.

CHAPTER TWENTY-NINE

Roman was making himself some pancakes when Dante walked through the front door. He walked past the kitchen and headed for the stairs.

"You look like you haven't seen the inside of your eyelids in a month," Roman said as he flipped a pancake. A few flecks of batter flew up onto his forearm as the pancake sizzled in the hot butter.

"Insomnia. A bad side effect of being scared shitless. The Black Baron Boys been on the warpath lately," Dante said.

Roman didn't comment on that statement because there was no debating it. Ever since they'd lost the gun shipment, Torrent had been in a near-constant state of unbridled fury. The BBB were on a rampage.

"How's Raynell?" Roman asked.

"Huh?" Dante said.

"Raynell. I figured you been over at Tug's place. You ain't slept here but two nights out of the last ten," Roman said.

Goddamn, Dante thought, he really do notice everything.

"Oh yeah. I mean, I went by there yesterday. She okay. I'm going upstairs," Dante said.

"All right."

Dante was halfway up the stairs when Roman asked him another question that stopped him in his tracks.

"You heard from Cassidy again?"

Dante stopped. He didn't turn around to answer Roman's question. "No, why?" he said.

"Just wondering. The mood Torrent is in, worst thing for everybody is her showing up in town because she miss her mother," Roman said.

"Yeah, well, I ain't heard from her. She probably halfway across the country by now," Dante said.

"I hope so," Roman said. He slid the pancake off the spatula and onto the others on his plate. He took the plate and sat at the dining room table.

"Rome," Dante said.

"Yeah?"

"You working on this, right? I mean, when you fix it, if you can fix it, she could come back then?" Dante said.

Roman dabbed at his chin with his napkin.

"It would probably be better if she didn't, but yeah, possibly," Roman said.

"Okay. I'm sorry for getting you in this," Dante said.

"It's going to be okay. I love ya, bighead," Roman said.

"Boy, if my head was as big as yours, it'd have its own gravity," Dante said.

"You better go on upstairs and lay down before I knock you out," Roman said as he smiled at his brother.

"I've heard anger management exists. You might want to take advantage of that," Dante said as he continued up the stairs.

He laughed as he said it, but if Roman had seen his face he would have thought his brother was about to burst into tears.

He went to his room and took out his phone. He had one new text message:

what he say

It was from Cassidy's burner phone. He texted back:

not yet. It's complicated.

Dante lay back across his bed. On the walls there were posters of popular hip-hop bands and some old-school shoegazing bands and a few pictures of superheroes from the latest film that held the title of summer blockbuster.

His father used to say this wasn't the room of a grown man. Keith Carruthers would stop at the threshold of the door, peek inside, and then shake his head reproachfully. Dante would be lying across his bed in much the same way he was now, and his father would intone with that Old Testament prophet voice of his: "You ain't twelve anymore."

And Dante would respond: "I ain't been twelve since the day Mama disappeared."

Then the two of them would stare at each other from across time and space like sentinels tasked with guarding the memory of the worst day of their lives until the stars fell from the sky. Eventually his father would look away and continue down the hall, muttering to himself about what he regretted and what he could have done differently, and Dante would reach into his nightstand like he was doing now, and grab a couple of strong edibles or ketamine tablets, and gobble them down with frenzied abandon until they wrapped him in their cotton-candy embrace and he drifted away to a place where the faces of his mother and father were hidden from him down at the bottom of a velvet hole in his soul as he floated among the ruins of his past, present, and what was left of his future.

As he closed his eyes and felt the hazy edge of consciousness fall away, he thought his father was wrong. This was the room of a grown man. A grown man who was a fragile assemblage of his worst impulses, but a grown man nonetheless. He was his father's son, after all.

Roman was washing his plate when his phone rang. He saw it was Neveah and answered, trapping it between his ear and his shoulder.

"What's up?"

"Can you come by the shop?"

"Yeah, I gotta come by there anyway. I'm using Pop's computer to work on something for a client. What, you need some help with something?" Roman asked.

"Something like that. I'm here now, if you can come on up," Neveah said. Before he could respond, she hung up.

Roman glanced at the phone before putting it back in his pocket. He knew his sister. Her hanging up like that meant she was upset. He wondered if Chauncey had tried to shake Neveah down with the pictures of him hanging with the BBB. Or maybe he had threatened her. Roman didn't think that was too far-fetched for a man like Chauncey. Roman grabbed the keys to the rental car off the hook, since Dante had the Challenger keys on him. He'd said something about needing the Challenger because he had to go see a friend on the other side of Richmond. He'd told Roman he didn't want to put all those miles on his rental.

Roman thought that was a rare instance of Dante being responsible, so he didn't argue with him. He got in the sedan and backed out of the driveway. As he pulled off, he reminded himself they had to get somebody to cut the goddamn grass.

Neveah was in their father's office when Rome got to the crematory. She was sitting behind the desk on the landline talking to what Roman surmised was the propane company. He stood in the lobby and waited for her to finish. His eyes were drawn to a photo on the wall in a large wooden frame. He'd noticed it before, but only in a subconscious way. The shape of the frame, the glare from the glass in the frame, even the images, were always on the periphery of his vision when he walked into the lobby.

Not today. Today he stared at the picture in the frame and was instantly taken back to the moment it was taken. It was the day his father and mother had officially opened Carruthers Cremation Services. It was a black-and-white photo, with his father and mother standing behind him and Dante and Neveah hitting a sassy pose. The five of them were in the parking lot. Over their shoulders, the crematory stood with its brand-new sign four feet above the top of the doorframe. White letters on a black background.

Oscar had taken that picture.

Roman wondered if his mother and Oscar had been intimate that day. Or perhaps later that night as his father was running up and down the highways and byways trying to secure contracts with all the funeral homes that didn't have their own giant immolation chambers.

If she was lonely, why didn't she tell him? And if she told him, why didn't he listen?

Neveah ended the phone call and got up from behind the desk. She walked out of the office and headed for the door that led to the oven room.

"Let me show you something," she said, and walked through the door. Roman followed her through the oven room to the storeroom in the back next to the cooler. She was standing in front of the shelf where the unclaimed cremains were held.

"Who's in them two urns back there?" she asked Roman.

Roman kept his face placid as he quickly came up with a lie.

"I found some cremains sitting back there near the hazardous waste bin. I figured they were some extras Dad had that he'd forgotten to run through the grinder. There wasn't a name on them or anything, so I ran them through the grinder and put them in two different boxes. I thought we'd figure it out when you did the yearly audit of the books," Roman said

"Okay. I just counted up the cremation crates. We're three short. You got an excuse for that too?" Neveah asked.

Roman silently congratulated himself on not using crates for Wiz, Cali, and Eddie.

"I don't know. Maybe Pop used them for those cremains that was near the hazmat container. Maybe he miscounted," Roman said.

Neveah walked over to where he was standing. They were close enough that he could smell the singed hair on her arms. The ovens were not currently in use, but he'd felt the heat from them as he passed them on his way to the storage room. She'd been working this morning, like so many mornings, alone. He'd been so focused on handling the pawns he'd been moving on the board, pawns used to try to secure his family's freedom, that he hadn't noticed the legitimate bodies from legitimate funeral homes in the cooler.

"Roman, you're lying. I know it. Because I know every inch of this goddamn place. I know every brick, every piece of drywall. Every nut and every goddamn bolt. I don't depend on Pop to count the crates because I'm the one that has to pay the bills. He works on the ovens. He keeps the cooler running. He has this little trick to keep the garage door from running off the track. I pay the bills. So I count the crates. I know how many remains haven't been picked up by a funeral home that got stuck by a family that decided maybe Grandma doesn't really need to have her ashes spread down by the river. Roman, you're lying to me, and I hope to God it's not why I think it is," Neveah said.

"Neveah. I'm not lying. And I know you keep things together around here. I'm telling you what I did. I saw those cremains and I put them in a couple of urns. I don't know why the crates are off. This is what happens when I try to help. I fucked something up, but that's all it is," he said.

Neveah grabbed him by his shirt. "Stop bullshitting me, Roman! This has to do with what happened to Daddy. And Dante's finger and your fucking teeth! Do you understand how much trouble we could all be in if you're doing what I think you're doing? We could go to *jail!*"

"What do you think I'm doing, Neveah?" Roman said.

Neveah let go of his shirt and stepped back.

"I don't even want to say it. But if Dante owes some drug dealers that you gotta pay off in the middle of the night, and now extra remains are showing up and crates are disappearing . . . destruction of a corpse without the authorization of the family is a felony. Destruction of a corpse to hide the commission of a crime is a class one felony and the Department of Health don't care if you did it to save your little brother's life," Neveah said.

Roman took her hands in his and gripped her tight.

"Neveah, I promise you . . . Dante is in trouble, but I'm fixing it. You don't have anything to worry about," Roman lied.

Neveah pulled her hands away.

"I don't have anything to worry about? Dante is in debt to the same people who probably tried to kill our daddy, cut his finger off, and beat the shit out of you both. I don't have anything to worry about? You and Dante are all I have. You're all I have, and you're telling me I don't have anything to worry about when you're paying off dealers for him and, what, getting rid of their trash? 'Everything burns,' right? Pop's famous saying. Oh my God, you stupid fuck, I can't lose you and Dante too. He killed her, Rome, he fucking killed her, and now you and Dante are playing wannabe gangsters, and I . . ."

Neveah started to sob. She pushed past Roman and went back to the lobby and out the front door of the crematory. Roman followed her as she jumped into her truck and started it. Roman went to the driver's side.

"Neveah, where you going? Come on, what are you doing?" he said. Neveah ignored him and put the truck in reverse and peeled out of the parking lot.

Roman hesitated for a moment before he hopped into the rental car and followed her. He hadn't seen her cry in so long, it unnerved him. She was in no shape to be behind the wheel. He had to convince her that nothing was going on so that he could calm her. Or at least put her mind at ease. He didn't know what he was going to say, but he couldn't let her think he was getting rid of bodies for Torrent. She didn't need those images, that knowledge, in her head. Neveah didn't deserve that. He was the one who had to carry that burden, not Neveah.

There were two vehicles ahead of him and then there was Neveah's truck. The four of them came up to the light at the corner of Industrial Way and Sycamore Avenue. He could see her taillights blink as she took her foot off the brake. She went straight, and the two cars in front of him turned right. He moved up and was directly behind her now. Roman flashed his lights, but Neveah ignored him. They crossed Sycamore and continued on as Industrial Way became Lucy Boulevard.

Roman flashed his lights again as they came up to the intersection of Lucy and Lilyhammer. To their right there was an empty lot that used to house an arcade back when they were kids. To their left was an appliance and furniture store that was holding on for dear life. Roman saw they had plastered FOR SALE signs across their windows.

Neveah stopped at the red light as Roman idled behind her. He saw her glance in the rearview mirror and shake her head. He flashed his lights and she flicked him off before putting both hands back on the steering wheel.

"Come on, just pull over, damn it," Roman said out loud.

As they sat at the light, traffic turning left onto Lucy Earl passed them on the driver's side. Most of the vehicles were box trucks or work vehicles heading for Industrial Way. There was a wrecker truck that passed them carrying a car that looked totaled to the junkyard. An HVAC van went by.

A late-model car with a garish purple paint job made the turn but then came to a halt. Roman saw that the driver was a Hispanic man. There was another man in the passenger seat and he thought there were two or three people in the backseat. The man behind the wheel turned and stared at Neveah's truck like he was studying it for his SATs.

Then he looked down at his lap.

Roman watched as the man tapped his passenger on the shoulder. The passenger held up a cell phone, touched the screen, then stared at Neveah's truck as well.

The traffic behind the purple car started going around him as the man flicked on his hazard lights. The light was still red as the two people in the back of the car lowered the window in the back and leaned out the door.

"No!" Roman shouted.

The two men in the backseat were leaning out the window holding guns side by side, aiming their weapons at Neveah's truck. Roman didn't know what kind of guns they were, but they looked like some type of semiautomatic rifle.

He slammed his gas pedal to the floor and aimed the rental at the purple car. When he rammed it, the speedometer was showing forty miles per hour. One of the men in the back fired off a volley of bullets, but Roman had pushed the purple car backward about a foot. The burst of automatic fire sailed over Neveah's hood and skipped across the pavement in the empty lot. Roman prayed Neveah would take off, and she did, running the red light and flying down the street.

The men in the car turned their guns in his direction, but he hit reverse and backed away from them as they fired haphazardly at his car. The windshield of the rental car erupted in a spiderweb pattern like a magic trick. Roman kept going in reverse as the purple car followed him down Lucy Earl. He tried to ignore the staccato reports as the men in the backseat kept raining shots in his direction.

The windshield exploded and shards of glass sliced into his forehead and scalp. He kept driving backward until he saw a delivery truck coming up behind him. Roman stomped on the brake and the purple car flew by him, the men in the back still firing as he ducked. The driver's window joined the windshield in the realm of the past tense. Roman rammed the gearshift into drive and took off down Lucy Earl. The delivery truck behind him tried to pass him as they raced down the street.

He blew through a red light and narrowly missed colliding with a white panel van turning left. He kept his foot on the gas until he didn't see the delivery truck or the purple car in his rearview mirror. He raced across town and headed home. The engine in the rental started to wheeze as it began losing power. A block away from the house, it shuddered and died in front of the In and Out convenience store. Roman let it glide into the parking lot until it came to a stop in front of the air/vacuum station.

Roman got out of the car and called Dante.

"What up?" Dante said. He sounded like he'd just woken up from a deep sleep.

"Where are you?" Roman said.

"Hey, what the fuck is wrong?" Dante said, now fully awake.

"Is Neveah there?" Roman asked.

"I don't know, I was asleep. Wait, I think I hear her downstairs. Neveah!" Dante yelled as Roman paced back and forth in front of the dead rental car.

Roman heard shouting and what sounded like crying and then a door being slammed shut. He could hear Dante speaking softly, then Dante was back on the phone.

"Rome, what the fuck just happened?"

"I need you to stay at the house with her. I'm down at the In and Out store. The rental is fucked."

"I'll come get you."

"No! Stay there. Don't leave the house till I get there. I need to make a few phone calls. Don't tell Neveah anything about what we got going on. I'll be there in about ten minutes. When we do talk to her, let me take the lead, okay?" Roman said.

"Rome, what is happening?" Dante said.

"Just stay there and wait for me. Ten minutes," he said.

He hung up on Dante and called Khalil.

"Marcus Aurelius," Khalil said.

"Where are you?" Roman said.

"I'm in my hotel . . . well, the hotel gym. What's up?" Khalil said.

"I think the Ghost Town Crew just tried to kill me and my sister," Roman said.

"Say what?"

"A car full of guys tried to shoot Neveah. They shot at me too, but we were able to get away. Them two guys you got to help you with that thing, you think they are available? I want one to shadow Neveah and the other to shadow Dante," Roman said.

"Only one of them is available. The other guy got a gig up in Detroit. You want my guy on Dante or Neveah?" Khalil said.

"Neveah. Dante knows what's up," Roman said.

"You want me following you?" Khalil said.

"No, I think I want you to follow somebody else," he said, before going quiet.

'What you thinking?" Khalil said.

"I think that problem set me up. When he came by, he was making allusions to me and my moneymaking abilities and how I was helping those guys out. I think he fingered me to the GTC. I think he was using the

GTC to set Neveah up too. Think of it from his perspective. I blow him off, so he's not gonna get paid. But if he sets us up with the GTC, then he either scares me into paying or he gets revenge on Neveah if they . . . ya know . . . if they get me, then he hurts her. For him it's a win, win, win," Roman said.

Now it was Khalil's turn to be quiet. When he spoke, it made the hair on the back of Roman's neck stand at attention.

"I can make that problem go away," Khalil said.

"Not yet. I want you to follow him. See who he talks to, where he goes. Get your other man on Neveah. I'm heading home. I gotta make sure she's all right. We'll talk soon."

"I'm on it," Khalil said. He hung up.

Roman put his phone back in his pocket. He took the keys from the rental and started hoofing it down the road toward the house. He looked back over his shoulder so often his neck started to hurt. The sidewalk ended about halfway to the house and so he was walking in wet grass and mud on the shoulder of the road. When he got to the house, he saw Neveah's truck parked nearly sideways and perpendicular to the Challenger. He walked up the steps and entered the house.

Dante was waiting for him in the living room. He was drinking out of the bottle again. Roman went over to the couch and plucked it from his hand and took a long swig. The scotch burned all the way down and made him gag and gasp.

"Roman, what happened?" Dante asked.

Roman took another sip from the bottle and handed it back to Dante. He sat down next to him on the couch. The scotch began to warm his body slowly, like the pilot light in an oven igniting a burner.

"I think the GTC tried to take us out," Roman said.

"*What?*" Dante said.

"Yeah. Neveah, she noticed some of the crates were missing. We were talking, we got arguing. She took off, I jumped in the car and followed her. Then when we was at the light a car full of GTC boys started shooting at us about a block from the shop," Roman said.

"Are you okay? You got blood on your forehead," Dante said. Roman thought he sounded like he was a kid again. He sounded the way he did the day their mother vanished.

"I'm okay. Was Neveah okay when she came home?" Roman asked.

"I mean, I guess. She ran upstairs like a scalded dog. She flew right by me. Rome, what is going on?" Dante asked.

Roman took one more drink from the bottle.

"I think Chauncey put them on to me. The GTC. He came by the other day trying to blackmail me for running with the BBB. He had pictures of me, of you. Of Neveah and the cars we drove. He had pictures of me hanging out at the Kingdom and Candy's and Cooper's Rest with Torrent and his boys. I mean, you take that and then you think about what happened between him, you, and Neveah at Candy's, she threatens him, well, I don't think you gotta be Sherlock Holmes to put it together," Roman said.

"Let me see if I got this straight. The cop that Neveah was messing around with tried to shake you down and you blew him off, and then a day or two later the GTC tries to kill you and Neveah? Roman, what are we doing? We should just leave town."

And, Roman thought, they possibly tried to kill us with the guns Khalil dropped in their neighborhood.

"We can't leave town, Dante. We're in too deep now. We have to finish it," Roman said.

"And when does that happen, man? When is it finished?"

Roman sat up and turned to face him.

"Do I have to remind you that all this is because of you? The brand-new teeth I got, you being a finger short, the two hundred thousand dollars I had to pull out of my savings, this real drive-by that almost killed me and Neveah, is because you wanted to play gang-gang. When is it finished? When we can walk down the fucking street and not look over our shoulders, Dante, that's when it's fucking finished. Goddamn it. You think I like this shit?"

"I think you know you're really good at it," Dante said.

"What does that mean?" Roman asked.

"I was over at Cooper's, and Tank and another Black Baron Boy was over there. They were drunk. They rolled up on me and told me about all the money you was making their boss. They were talking like you was spinning gold out of straw and shit. I know you, big brother. You love that shit, making money. You always liked it and you always been good at it. So, is you making them all this money, is that how it ends? You make enough and they finally let us go? Or do you keep spinning that gold until you run out of magic?" Dante said.

"Money is just a tool, Dante. That's all. When it ends, I'll let you know. You just try not to die until then. I'm gonna check my pants and make sure I didn't shit myself, then try and talk to Neveah," Roman said. He got off the couch and went upstairs.

Dante turned on the television. It was still early, but the local news had an 11:00 A.M. broadcast. He punched the number eight on the remote and the first thing he saw was a report about the revitalization project in the Skids. There was a segment on dogs that were available for adoption at the local SPCA. There was nothing about an assassination attempt near Industrial Way. Dante got his phone and checked social media. He went to the Jefferson Run page. The first post he saw recounted a shooting on Lilyhammer and the subsequent escape of the vehicles involved.

"Somebody almost got their cap peeled back on Lillyhammer and Lucy Earl. Streets is watching," one of the posts by someone named Duane Cross said.

"They crazy out there. Protect ya neck," a commenter opined under Duane's post.

Shit, it probably won't make the regular news, Dante thought. Nobody died. The veracity of that statement depressed him so much he decided to finish off the bottle of scotch, then go upstairs and eat another handful of edibles. His dreams weren't much better than the reality he was living, but at least in his dreams he wouldn't get shot.

"Neveah," Roman said.

He knocked on her door.

"Go away," Neveah said.

"Neveah, are you okay? Do you want to call the police?" Roman said.

The door flew open and Roman took a step backward. Neveah was standing there wearing a pair of ragged sweatpants.

"I pissed myself, Roman. Peed my fucking pants. I haven't done the laundry since they called me and said they were rushing Daddy to the hospital," Neveah said.

"Like I said, do you want to call the cops? We can file a report and—"

"You should stop lying. You're too good at it. How we gonna call the cops, Rome? What, I'm gonna tell them my brothers almost got me killed because they running the streets with some gang? How is that gonna work? Call the cops so they can arrest you? With Chauncey on the force, that's exactly what will happen. Listen, whatever you and Dante are into, stop it. Do whatever you have to do, but we can't go on like this. I won't. Do you hear me? I *won't!*" She screamed, and shut the door in his face.

Roman dropped his head.

"I'm gonna fix it, Nev. I promise. I'm gonna fix it," he whispered. He laid his hand on the door. He almost expected it to feel warm like a fire was raging on the other side, so intense was Neveah's anger. Roman grunted as if he were in pain. Her anger was justified, her disappointment was valid, and her fear was his responsibility.

He was scared too, but he didn't have time to be afraid.

The end was in sight.

CHAPTER THIRTY

Dante woke up to the sound of weed trimmers and lawn mowers and men joking with each other above the din of their machines.

He walked downstairs and peered out the front window. He saw three men in the yard. One was on a riding mower, one was carrying a Weed eater, and the third, a huge brother in a tank top, was mulching the hydrangeas and bougainvilleas and the rosebushes near the porch.

The commotion outside contrasted with the monastic quiet inside. Neveah had left around six this morning. Roman had rolled out around ten, and now Dante was getting up to meet the world at the crack of noon. He grabbed a bottle of water and headed out the door. He had a long drive ahead of him.

Roman had acquired a new rental after telling the cops his original one had been stolen, then ventilated out on Lucy Earl. Dante was blown away by Roman's ability to lie to the cops with a straight face. Anytime Dante ran into cops he felt like he couldn't help babbling. Getty told him once that he sounded like a Muppet when the cops rolled up on them.

In hindsight it was instances like that that proved Roman's point. Getty had not been his friend. If Dante was being honest (and why not? he was the only one here), he hadn't been Getty's friend either. If he had, he'd never started sleeping with Cassidy behind Getty's back.

But Getty was dead and he and Cassidy were alive and the nature of his and Getty's relationship was a matter best left to the trash heap of history.

Dante walked outside and hopped down the steps. The big brother in the tank caught his eye as he was heading toward the Challenger.

"Good morning. You Mr. Carruthers?" the brother asked.

"Um, nah, that's my pops, but that's also my brother. I mean, I guess he the one that got you guys. My pops used to take care of the yard, but Roman been talking about getting the yard done for a minute," Dante said. The brother got off his knees and wiped off his pants legs with hands big enough to palm a bowling ball.

"Oh, okay, well, let your brother know he can use our app to send us the rest of the payment. He put a deposit down, but we're gonna be finished today," the brother said. He brushed his hands off on the back of his khaki pants and held out one of his bear paws.

Dante took his hand and shook it. "Dante Carruthers," he said.

"Ike. Ike Randolph," the man said.

"That's an amazing tattoo, Ike. The guy and the little girl," Dante said. Ike flexed his bicep and the portrait tattoo seemed to come to life. It depicted a Black man and a little girl who might have been mixed smiling as they both looked off toward the right as if they were observing the slowly setting sun. When Ike flexed, their smiles seemed to get broader.

"Yeah. A guy down in Gloucester did it. That's my son and my granddaughter," Ike said.

"Oh, they look happy," Dante said.

Ike's face seemed to go slack. "They were," he said.

"Oh shit, man, I'm sorry. I . . . fucked up. My bad, man," Dante said.

"No, it's not. You didn't know. My son passed away, but my granddaughter is living with us now. She's . . . it's like he spit her out," Ike said.

"What's that? Under their portrait. Sorry, man, you ain't a book, I shouldn't be trying to read you," Dante said sheepishly.

Ike looked at the words under the tattoo of his son and granddaughter.

"Those are lyrics from a song my best friend liked. He passed away too," Ike said.

"Man, I'm so sorry. I shouldn't be so nosy," Dante said.

"It's fine. You mentioned your dad used to cut the grass. Something happen to him?" Ike asked.

"Yeah. He was in an accident. He's in a coma. They say he might come out of it in a week or he might never wake up. I mean, not great odds, I guess," Dante said.

"But he's still here. That's a good thing. Believe me," Ike said.

"At least he doesn't have to worry about me being a screwup. My brother got his own company, my sister runs our crematory. I'm just the disappointment of the family," Dante said. It felt strangely cathartic to actually say it to someone, even if it was simply this gardener with the scary hands.

Ike made his hand into a fist.

Dante took an unconscious step backward.

"If you really think that, talk to your family. It's never too late to change things unless you're in the dirt. But time is a wicked river. It will take you down the line before you know it. Talk to them now. I bet you they don't really feel that way. But . . . don't wait. Don't wait," Ike said.

"All right, man. Well, I'll tell my brother what you said. And thanks, man," Dante said.

"No worries, hoss," Ike said.

Dante backed out of the driveway and threw his hand up at Ike and his guys as he took off down the road.

If he ever slapped me, *I'd* apologize, Dante thought. Goddamn, he scary as shit. He headed for the interstate.

Dante wiggled his phone free as he drove and called Cassidy on her burner phone. He drove past the two motels still standing on the outskirts of town.

"They're some good places to get murdered," Dante murmured.

"Hey," Cassidy said.

"Hey. I'm on my way. You want me to pick up some pizza or something?" Dante said.

Cassidy didn't respond.

"Hey, you hear me?" Dante said.

Cassidy took a deep breath. "I'm not in Aruna anymore," she said.

Dante hit the brake and pulled onto the shoulder near the on-ramp to the interstate. Gripping the steering wheel with his right hand, he squeezed his phone with the left and put it back to his ear.

"Cassidy, where are you?" Dante asked.

A pause.

Another deep breath.

"I'm at my mom's," she whispered.

Dante put the phone in the passenger seat and stepped out of the car. He went around to the passenger side. He bent over and vomited up last night's dinner along with a few edibles and a half liter of bourbon. The bourbon was the worst. It burned all the way up his esophagus like he'd struck a fracking vein in his guts.

Dante wiped his mouth with the back of his hand and got back into the Challenger. He picked the phone up and put it to his ear one more time.

"Cassidy. You have to get out of town. You cannot be seen by anybody," Dante said. He spoke gently but precisely. He tried to imbue each word with a terrible seriousness. But as soon as she answered, he knew they were all fucked.

"I hid the car behind my mom's house. I was lonely, D. And I didn't know anybody out there. My mom says if we go to the police they can probably protect us. And you did what you did to protect me. They'll say it was self-defense," Cassidy said.

Dante let his head fall onto the steering wheel.

There were so many things that he wanted to say to Cassidy that he didn't want to say over a phone line. The panoply of bad ideas she had just enumerated was making his brain leak out his ears. Going to the police? Telling them he hit a dude in the head with a hammer? That his brother put Getty in a cremation crate, alive, and then set him on fire? That they then put Splodie in a crate and burned him up too? Hiding the fucking car behind her mama's house with that big-ass ugly spoiler on it?

He didn't think Cassidy was dumb. She wasn't. She was only a girl who had never had to worry about consequences and repercussions. She came from an upper-middle-class family like Dante, but unlike Dante, her family had never had to scrape and save and skip holidays to pay the bills. The common misconception about the Carruthers family was that they had always had a big house on the big side of town. Nothing could be further from the truth. He could vaguely remember having to eat potted meat and Vienna sausage for breakfast, lunch, and dinner.

Cassidy had never had to endure such gastric horrors. Her mom had retired from Prosser as an adjunct English professor. Her father lived in Philly as a music teacher but he was heavily involved in her life, if what Cassidy had told him was true. How she gotten with Getty was anyone's guess.

Dante bounced his head off the horn.

She didn't get it. This world they were in now, where committing murder was as commonplace as putting on a pair of shoes, where violence came down on you like sleet and hail and thunder all at the same time, where he and his brother had killed to protect themselves and now they might all die because Cassidy didn't seem to possess the instinct of self-preservation, this world was above her. It was too much for her tender soul.

"Cass, listen to me. You have to go back to the motel. Visit with your mother but then go back. Please. It is not safe here for you," Dante said.

"I think I can just stay with my—"

"Cass, they will kill you if they see you. Then they will kill us! Don't argue with me about this! This is for real. I'm not playing. They will kill us. You have to leave. Now!" Dante said.

He could hear her breathing, quick tiny inhalations that almost sounded like a whistle.

"Okay. Are you coming to see me?"

"Yes. Once you let me know you're back in the room. I promise I'll come see you," Dante said.

Nothing from Cassidy. There were volumes being said in that silence. He knew she didn't want to leave. It was like she lived in this blissful state of assumed invincibility. She couldn't conceive of someone wanting to hurt her. When they came for her this time, she'd scream like she did that night. A wild feral howl that asked an uncaring universe why this was happening. And the universe would do what it always did.

"Cass?" Dante said.

"I'm going. Let me say goodbye to my mom," she said.

"Okay, baby. Hey, I'll meet you at the room. Text me when you get back there. I'll bring some goodies and I'll spend the night again," Dante said.

"Yeah," Cassidy said.

"And, Cass? Don't call the cops, okay? That's not the move right now. We're gonna get straight, but don't get the cops involved, okay?" Dante said.

"Yeah," she said.

Dante licked his lips. "Message me when you get back to the room."

"Yeah. 'Bye," Cassidy said.

"'Bye, baby," Dante said.

And she was gone.

Dante tossed the phone onto the passenger seat. Traffic zipped by him as he grabbed on to the steering wheel like it was a life preserver. He had to tell Roman. He knew this, yet he couldn't seem to bring himself to let go of the steering wheel and do it. Was it because he'd seen how Roman had taped Getty shut in a box and set him on fire to protect him and Neveah?

He knew his brother loved him. He knew that he loved their father and he knew he loved Neveah. Dante also knew that there were terrible things done in the name of love. Abominable things.

Dante waited until there was a break in the traffic, then whipped the Challenger around and headed back to the house. He would wait for Cassidy to call him and tell him she was back in that small town. He'd wait all night if that was what it took. He'd stare out the window at the freshly cut lawn, and as it disappeared in the gathering dark, he'd pretend that Cassidy had the good sense to go back to the room. He'd wait and hope to be surprised.

But he didn't think he was going to tell Roman she was back in town.

Roman was waiting outside city hall as groups of city workers exited the building and headed to lunch. He was leaning against the new rental, a Camaro that he'd paid the up-charge for, and searched the crowd for Jealousy. Her thick curls made her stand out in any crowd, but he had yet to see her. As the last few employees exited the building, he got back in his car and called her. He knew a phone call was gauche in the latter days of this social experiment called dating, but she wasn't answering his text messages.

The phone rang and rang. Roman was about to hang up when she answered.

"Hey," he said.

"Hey," she said back.

"I've been texting you."

"I know."

"Is something wrong?"

When Jealousy spoke, he could hear the tears in her words. "You lied to me."

"What? I told you I'm single," Roman said.

"No, I asked you were you working for my brothers, and you said you were advising them about going straight, right? That's what you said," Jealousy said.

"Yeah, that's what I'm—"

"Tracy told me you work for them. He told me you're cleaning their money for them. He told me you help them make more money than they ever seen just slinging. He told me Terrance wants to make you a part of the fucking crew!" Jealousy said. She was openly weeping now, and another piece of Roman's tortured heart shattered in his chest.

"Jae, listen, I can explain. I swear it's not—"

"All I asked was for you to tell me the truth. That's all. Goddamn it, I was falling in love with you, and you lied to my fucking face. Don't call me anymore. Don't text."

"Jae, listen to me. I am doing some of that work for them, but it's all in service of creating a legitimate business for your brothers. I'm trying to help them get out of this life!" Roman lied.

"They're my brothers and I have love for them, but I don't want the blood on their hands on mine. How can I hold you if your hands are soaked in that same blood? I can't have this in my life, Roman. I can't have you in my life. Not like this. Please don't contact me anymore," Jealousy said.

She ended the call.

Roman shook his head and tapped his phone against his skull. He knew Tranquil didn't like him, but he didn't think he hated him so much that he was willing to sacrifice his sister's happiness. Roman raised his head and looked at the third floor of city hall. Jealousy was up there crying because he'd lied to her. But that lie was one of many he was willing to tell to save his family and protect her. Because he thought he was falling in love with her too.

And Tranquil had torn all of that asunder just to spite him.

"You ain't seen spite yet, motherfucker," Roman said to himself.

He got in the rental and pulled out of the parking lot. He drove over to Cooper's Rest and posted up on a stool near the end of the bar. The bar was full of the lunchtime crowd that filtered in from the strip mall down the street. There were a few old-time pros in there sitting at their favorite spot along the bar like they had been placed there by a royal decree.

Roman ordered a scotch neat and sipped it as he tried to figure out a way to get Jealousy to talk to him without being creepy or demanding. He knew she needed some space, but he also knew she still had feelings for him. He wasn't ready to give up on that yet. Not until he had a chance to tell her how much she meant to him.

There were times after his mother vanished that he didn't know if he deserved love. He had dived into a life of casual connections or professional companionship because the idea that he was worthy of love was a notion that was slipping through his fingers as the years flew by like sand sifting through a sieve. Bit by bit, grain of sand by grain of sand, it had waned from his soul.

Then he met Jealousy.

A woman who accepted him, challenged him, made him smile. How could he give up on that because her brother wanted to be an overprotective cliché?

Roman sipped the scotch and stared out the front window of Cooper's. Traffic was light in this part of town like it was light over on Industrial Way. The outer edges of Jefferson Run were where the symptoms of a dying city were most visible. The Skids, Industrial Way, and the end of Sycamore Avenue. They were the canaries in the coal mine that everyone seemed to be ignoring.

Roman finished his drink and ordered another one. There was a part of him that dreamed of grabbing a gun and walking up to Torrent and Tranquil and pulling the trigger until it went *click*, but he took another sip of his scotch and suppressed that urge through a sheer act of will. That was the fool's path. He couldn't win a one-on-one shoot-out with those two like he was Doc Holliday.

He needed more guns.

And he was close to having them.

He took another sip and watched a few cars drive by as the lunch crowd kept flowing in off the street. A couple of Torrent's boys walked in and nodded at Roman as they headed to one of the back booths. Roman finished his drink and threw a fifty-dollar bill down. The last thing he wanted to do after Jealousy breaking up with him was sit in a bar and pretend he wanted to drink with two lower-ranking members of the BBB. They didn't deserve his best performance.

Roman headed for the door. As his hand gripped the weathered brass handle, his heart jumped up into his throat like a startled rabbit.

Splodie's Honda drove past Cooper's heading toward the other end of Sycamore. That was BBB territory.

Roman left Cooper's Rest and deliberately kept his pace slow as he walked to his car. Once he was inside, he called Dante.

"What up?" Dante said.

"She's back. Have you been in touch with her? Did you tell her it was okay to come back? Because it definitely *isn't* okay," Roman said.

"Rome, I didn't tell her to come back. How do you know it's her?" Dante said.

"You're not stupid. How do you think I know? She's driving the fucking car," Roman said.

"Fuck. I don't know, man. I didn't tell her to come back," Dante said in a singsong tone that Roman recognized. It was the same tone he used the first time their father found weed in his book bag.

"Dante, you didn't tell her to come. But did you know she was here?" Roman asked, but in truth it wasn't really a question. He already knew the answer. He didn't feel angry, but resentment like hot steam from a kettle rose through his body from the bottom of his feet to the top of his head. How could Dante be so reckless? So thoughtless? So utterly senseless?

"Roman, I didn't know she was coming. I thought I saw the car this morning, but I wasn't sure," Dante said in that same singsong style.

Roman decided to let it go. What Dante knew and when he knew it was irrelevant now. What mattered was getting Cassidy out of Jefferson Run before someone from the BBB saw her and Torrent took them all out to the farm.

"Can you talk to her? Get her to leave? Like, yesterday?" Roman said.

Dante breathed deeply on the other end of the phone. "I'll try."

"Don't try. Do it," Roman said.

He hung up and immediately called Khalil.

"Veni, vidi, vici," Khalil said.

"Where you at? You in the Run?" Roman asked.

"Yeah, checking on our problem," Khalil said.

"Meet me over at the construction site in the Skids. Burnt Mill Road. There's a warehouse scheduled to be demolished. Park up the street and—"

"I know how to get in places without being seen, Rome," Khalil said, and not for the first time Roman reminded himself to never get on the wrong side of Khalil Sanders.

Khalil was sitting on a stack of pallets when Roman got to the warehouse. He was wearing a black leather jacket, jeans, and black rubber-soled shoes. Roman was getting better at spotting guns, and Khalil had one on a shoulder rig. Roman knew from previous conversations he had at least two more and a Ka-Bar on his person.

"What's the sitch? By the way, that's a joke. I hate people who say shit like that," Khalil said.

"Remember that girl we told you about? Getty's girl?" Roman said.

"Yeah, Cassidy," Khalil said.

Roman wiped his chin with his left hand. "She's back in town. I just saw her driving Splodie's car."

"That's bad," Khalil said

"Yeah. If Torrent sees her and that car, he'll know we lied. He'll kill all three of us," Roman said.

Khalil hopped down from the stack of pallets. "He'll try," he said.

"Even you can't protect all three of us at all times. I talked to Dante. I told him he has to convince her to go," Roman said.

"But you don't think he will," Khalil said.

"I don't know. I don't know if he can," Roman said.

"So what are we talking about here, Roman?" Khalil said.

Roman leaned against the stack of pallets. The interior of the warehouse had been mostly gutted. The wiring and the metal girders in the ceiling had already been harvested. The entire revitalization project was an exercise in living up to the adage, "Tear it down to build it back up."

Roman didn't know how much he believed in that old axiom. In his experience, things rarely were the same after the tear-down part of that proverb. Most of them came back as a Ship of Theseus. Fundamentally the same, but different in ways that were imperceptible.

He was trying to tear the BBB down and bury it, not build it back up.

He couldn't do that if he was gristle in the jaws of Torrent's wolf-dogs.

"I'm gonna tell you what the car looks like. I need you to talk to this girl. Put the fear of God, and if not God, the fear of Torrent, in her. She has to leave town. Now. Today," Roman said.

"And what if she doesn't want to go? What if she just won't listen? Because, I gotta tell you, Rome, it seems you made a pretty convincing argument the night you burned her boyfriend alive. I don't know if anything I say is going to be better than that," Khalil said.

Roman lowered his head.

The concrete dust that covered the floor reminded him of ashes. Cold ashes that were sapped of their warmth. Ashes as cold as the grave.

"She has to go. One way or the other," Roman said.

Khalil angled himself so he was leaning against the stack but looking at Roman.

"Just so we're clear, because I don't want any daylight between us on this. If she doesn't get it, if she doesn't leave, you want her to go. Is that what you're saying?" Khalil said.

Roman put his hand over his mouth for a moment. It was an unconscious movement. It was as if his body wanted to stop the words he was about to speak from ever being heard.

"She can't be here. Whatever you have to do to make that happen." Roman paused.

Dante had saved her life once. Dante, who didn't like to squash a bug, had taken a hammer and caved the back of Splodie's head in like an overripe melon. He hoped she had enough sense to save herself this time. A tiny clarion inside his head roared that he was crossing the Rubicon. There were lines you couldn't uncross. But he knew that was a lie. In reality there weren't any lines. There was just a dichotomy. Either Cassidy left town, or he and his brother and his sister were killed. Either Getty was burned alive, or his brother died. Either he did the things that needed to be done, or his family would never be safe. There were no lines, only choices.

Us or them.

He had already made his choice.

"Do it," he said.

CHAPTER THIRTY-ONE

Neveah sat at the foot of her father's hospital bed in a chair that was about as comfortable as she was at a formal dinner for the Jefferson Run Chamber of Commerce.

She got here just after visiting hours started for the morning. The nurses said there hadn't been any significant change in his condition. The doctor said they were fast approaching the time to talk about long-term care facilities. Neveah knew her father's insurance wouldn't cover that, but their house was safe because Keith Carruthers had put it in her and Dante's names five years ago when he turned sixty-five in anticipation of a moment exactly like this one.

"Something happen to me, I don't want no nurse taking what we built," he'd said as he had her and Dante sign some papers.

What you and Mama built, she thought.

"When I got my first period, we were still in the trailer in the Skids. Mama found me in the bathroom crying, with blood on the seat and on my thighs. I knew I was supposed to get one, she'd told me what might happen. But it was so heavy the first time. Goddamn, it freaked me out. It's one thing to talk about it, but seeing blood pouring out of you is something else. She found me crying on the toilet. She cleaned me up, taught me about maxi pads, and told me, 'I ain't gonna tell you that you're a woman now. Being a woman is more than just getting your monthly. But things have changed. And you have to be mindful of that.' And I asked her what things, and she said we would talk about that later.

But we never did," Neveah said. She got up and went to her father's bedside. She leaned over until her mouth was an inch from his ear. She smelled the antiseptics they wiped him down with and the acidic odor of urine from his catheter.

"You took that from me. Because she was fucking around. You could have let her go. She didn't want you, but that didn't mean she didn't want us. And you killed her for it," Neveah said.

The door to the room opened and a nurse came in carrying a tray with three IV bags on it. She set the tray on a table by the bedside.

"Can I squeeze in here for a minute? I'm sorry," she said. Neveah moved to the side. The nurse came around and started changing out the bags.

"What are those?" Neveah asked.

"Oh, one is a solution to keep him hydrated. One is a nutrient-rich drip to keep his calorie intake up, and the last one is a blood thinner to prevent clotting." The nurse's name tag said DOROTHY.

"I didn't know he was on a blood thinner. I keep track of his medicine. He mostly is on blood pressure med and some potassium and magnesium supplements," Neveah said.

Kept track of that for him just like I kept track of everything else, she thought. For the man that killed my mama.

"Oh no, we put him on a thinner because sometimes when people are in this state they can develop blood clots. Don't worry, we made sure to flush his system before we gave him the thinners," Dorothy said.

"Flushed his system? For what?" Neveah asked.

"To get rid of any medications that might have had an adverse interaction with the blood thinner, like aspirin," Dorothy said.

"Oh."

"I want you to know we are doing our very best for your father. I've seen you here a lot. I can tell he is so important to you. We are doing all we can for him," Dorothy said.

"Thanks," Neveah said. Or, she thought, you could stop. Stop doing all you can. Let him slip away. Let my mama wave at him from heaven as he goes to hell.

"I think I'm going to go. Let you do your work," Neveah said.

"Do you want to say goodbye before you leave? They can hear us, even if it's just a whisper. Some patients have come out saying they heard everything," Dorothy said.

"I already said what I wanted to say," Neveah said.

As she walked through the parking lot, she pulled out her cigarettes and lit one. Overhead the clouds were rolling in like a blanket made of gray wool. She smoked as she leaned against her truck. She didn't think she'd be coming back to the hospital. Later today, before she left for the winery, she'd call the doctor and tell him to start the process of putting her father in a long-term care facility. Let them clean him and care for him and feed him that baby food slop she'd seen going in through his feeding tube. If he was out in Warren County at the Warren Convalescent home or outside of Richmond in Midlothian or Laburnum, she wouldn't have to go visit him and pretend she cared if he lived or died.

There were times over the years when she felt like she had been forced to give up her life, like some conscript in an army of one. A guard compelled to be on watch against the fall of the House of Carruthers. Morning, noon, and night. Twenty-four hours a day, seven days a week. Run the business, pay the bills, try to keep Dante sober, try to keep her father from going off the deep end, try to keep Roman from forgetting them.

Neveah tossed her cigarette on the ground and stubbed it out.

No more. Not ever again.

Her watch was at an end.

Bruce Wallis pulled up to the cobblestone-lined parking lot across from Trout's already regretting agreeing to work a double shift. At least the temperature was dipping into the sixties, so the kitchen wouldn't be as hot as the surface of the sun. Bruce hopped out of his car and jogged across the street to Trout's. He was just about to knock on the door for Josh to let him in when he heard a commotion around the corner. It was a cacophony of what sounded like moans and conversation mixed inexplicably with laughter and a few pleas to the Lord.

Having lived in Jefferson Run for the last four years, Bruce knew it was the wiser course to just ignore the hubbub and carry his ass to work. Except he saw a few people he knew coming from around the corner shaking their heads in reproachment.

"What's happening over there?" Bruce asked Tyler, one of the assistant prep cooks.

"Ghost Town Crew fucked somebody up," Tyler said.

"What, there's a body over there?" Bruce asked.

"Nah, a car. Splodie's car. Shot all to hell and back," Tyler said.

Bruce had a moment when he thought he might pass out, but then the moment faded.

Bruce wasn't in the "game," but he also wasn't a fool. He knew who really owned Trout's. The guys who came in and never paid for anything but sometimes left huge tips. Torrent and Tranquil. The Gilchrist brothers and their crew. Splodie was one of the guys in that crew. If that really was Splodie's car and it actually was full of bullet holes, life in Jefferson Run was about to become exponentially more dangerous.

"Where is it?" Bruce asked.

"Around the corner in front of the old grocery store. I don't know how they got it there. It's so full of holes it looks like a chunk of Swiss cheese on wheels," Tyler said.

Bruce took off in that direction. "Fucking hell," he said when he turned the corner.

Splodie's Honda was being held together by dew and dust, apparently. The body of the car was perforated with bullet holes the size of Bruce's index finger. The windshield had shattered inward. Bruce didn't walk all the way up to the car, but he had better-than-average vision, so he could see that the driver's seat was soaked in a burgundy substance that stained the white fabric. On the hood someone had spray-painted a crudely drawn outline of a ghost. The same tag was on what was left of the driver's door.

Tyler was standing by the front door of Trout's when Bruce came back. He had a pensive expression that Bruce thought he probably shared.

"The BBB gonna tear them boys up, ain't they?" Tyler said.

"Yeah. Let's hope we don't get caught up in the crossfire. Come on, let's get to work," Bruce said.

Torrent was drunk when Roman arrived at the bar in the Kingdom.

He was in a booth flanked by D-Train, Corey, and Tank. His Afro was askew and his normally freshly ironed white button-down shirt was wrinkled and untucked from his jeans. He had his feet up on the table and was drinking from a large cut-crystal glass.

Tranquil was nowhere to be seen.

Roman thought wherever he was, anyone at that location was having a bad day.

"College boy. Sit your ass down," Torrent said.

Roman's grandfather, his mother's father, had grown up in Red Hill County as a hog killer for a slaughterhouse. He used to tell stories about men who hadn't known how to use the bolt gun correctly and how those men ended up with a few chunks missing from their hands.

"Ain't no more dangerous animal than a wounded one with teeth," his grandfather used to say.

Torrent was wounded and his teeth were sharp. His pride was wounded because the GTC had dropped off Splodie's car around the corner from what everyone knew was his place. His heart was wounded because it seemed like he really cared about Splodie, inasmuch as he had the capacity to care about anyone who wasn't named Tranquil or Jealousy. But it was his spirit that seemed to be the most grievously injured. Roman thought he saw exhaustion on his face. An existential malaise that was seeping through his pores as much as the gin he was guzzling.

"I wanna ask you something," Torrent slurred.

Roman pulled a chair from one of the tables and sat down at the booth. Torrent swung his legs around and leaned forward to glare at him. Roman could feel his wrath like the heat from one of the ovens at the crematory.

He truly is capable of anything right now, Roman thought.

Another thing his grandfather told him about animals was that meeting aggression with fear was a recipe for disaster. "You gotta stand your ground or they'll be bearing you under it," his grandfather had said.

Roman didn't lean back. He gave Torrent his most neutral expression. Torrent put his finger in Roman's face.

"What the fuck did Splodie say to you when he left that night? Did that nigga tell you where he was going? Don't lie to me, college boy," Torrent said. Spittle flew from his lips and landed on Roman's brow.

"He didn't say anything. We finished putting them in the oven and then he left. He didn't tell us where he was going and I didn't ask," Roman said.

Torrent didn't look away, but Roman thought he was not seeing him right now. His eyes had a faraway dreamy quality that mostly was from the liquor, but Roman thought it was also partly from long hours of staring into the abyss. Violence exacts a heavy toll on every man who spills blood. If one is judged by his eyes alone, Torrent's bill was coming due.

In more ways than one.

"The Ghost Town Crew gonna feel it today," Torrent said.

"Feel what?" Roman asked.

"My foot on their necks," Torrent said.

He chugged his glass, then held the glass up for another.

"I let Tranquil loose on them. Them niggas ain't gonna be safe nowhere. Tell me how much money we make this week off that construction gig," Torrent said.

"I've deposited another hundred thousand in that account I made for you. Also I made an agreement with Shade to take a small percentage from the shell company I made for him to put in your accounts," Roman said.

Torrent's eyes went bright like stars.

"You talking to Shade behind my back?"

Roman felt his balls tighten, but he answered him.

"No, he wanted an update on things, so I told him. He called me but I never gave him my number, so I assumed you told him it was okay to talk to me." That was the truth. He hadn't called Shade, Shade had called him. But the nature of the conversation was wide-ranging.

Roman didn't think Torrent needed to know how wide-ranging.

"I don't trust you worth a fuck. You're too smart. But you ain't smarter than me. I know you hate me, nigga. It's like *Star Wars*. I can feel it in the air," Torrent said as he waved his left hand in front of Roman's face. "But you an earner. I'll give you that."

Torrent rubbed his face with his left hand.

"Get the fuck out of here. Go make me some more money, college boy," Torrent said. Roman got up without saying a word. He nodded at D-Train, Tank, and Corey. Then he turned to leave.

"I think you lying about Splodie. But you didn't kill him. The Ghost Town boys did that, and they gonna fucking pay, my word is my bond," Torrent said.

Roman paused. "I'm not lying. But you're right. I don't like you. But I don't have to if I'm making us money. That's my bond," Roman said.

He left.

Esteban Trujillo executed a deft spin move as he weaved around his friend Diego Diaz with a soccer ball. It was chilly, but that was okay, since Esteban had a tendency to sweat copious amounts. They were playing four-on-four in Coleman Park near the west side of Jefferson Run. There were bigger parks on the east side, but Esteban knew better than to step into BBB territory. He didn't run with the Ghost Town Crew, but a lot of his friends did, so he just stayed on the side of town that had more people he knew. Esteban was majoring in environmental sciences at Prosser State. He planned on leaving the Run as soon as he graduated.

He just loved playing pickup soccer on a cool, crisp Saturday morning with his friends. There were a few girls sitting on benches near the field, but most of them were the girlfriends of guys in the GTC, so Esteban made sure he didn't stare at them too long. A quick look here and there was okay, though.

At least he hoped so.

He was spinning around Gabino Rodriguez and heading for the net when he heard the first shots. A discordance that ripped through the atmosphere like a bag of nails in a washing machine. Esteban stopped and turned, trying to figure out where the shots were coming from, when four steel-jacketed rounds from a Heckler & Koch MP5A3 tore through his forehead and lower jaw. His body crumpled to the grass, joining everyone on his team and three members of the opposing team. And two of the five girls sitting on the bench and a random man walking his dog.

The dog ran off but returned minutes later to the man's side.

It was still there when the cops arrived.

The police were still processing the crime scene when they got another call of shots fired. This time it was at the home of Tommy Hernandez, second-in-command in the GTC and cousin of Ernesto Salaazar. Tommy was celebrating the quinceañera of his niece when six men on motorcycles rolled up and sprayed the whole party with semiautomatic gunfire. By the time the police arrived, Tommy, his niece, and seven other partygoers were dead.

At the same time, three blocks from city hall, the Jefferson Run Vape and Tobacco Shop exploded. Witnesses said one minute the shop was there, the next minute it was a pile of rubble and glass. The explosion blew out the windows of the restaurant across the street and devastated the empty sandwich shop next to the vape store.

"What the fuck is going on?" the arson investigator asked a detective.

"Feels like Torrent Gilchrist is settling some debts."

The night came, and with it, mercifully, a modicum of peace on the streets of Jefferson Run. A light rain moved across the city like it was crying over the blood on its streets.

Roman was on a video call with Lil Glock, admonishing him for making such a large investment without consulting him, when he heard the doorbell. He paused his conversation and went to answer it.

He peered through the peephole, then opened the door.

Dante came in soaked to the bone and smelling like a bourbon distillery. He stumbled into the lobby and fell across the couch.

"I can't find her," he said. The words came out sideways, but Roman understood him. He'd had a lot of practice talking to his brother when he was drunk.

"What you mean, you can't find her?" Roman asked.

"Cassidy. I've been calling her all day, and nothing. Then they found that car over by Trout's. You seen the news? Torrent went off. Seven people dead at the park. Fucking kids' party got shot up. They blew up the vape shop. That shit's gone. Poof!" Dante said, blowing air over his outstretched fingers. The missing pinkie had healed over, but he still wore fingerless gloves with the pinky finger hole sewed shut.

Roman sat down next to Dante.

"Why don't you stay here until I'm done, then I can drive us both home? Neveah is down at the winery. We could order some pizza, get a movie off Netflix."

"She's dead, ain't she? Those fuckers killed her, didn't they?" Dante said. He began to cry, huge teardrops running down his face and disappearing in the water already on his skin.

"I . . . I think so. We told her to leave town, Dante. Sounds like it wasn't the BBB that did it, but riding around in that car . . . that was a bad idea. I'm sorry. I know you cared about her," Roman said.

"Rome, is it almost over? When is it gonna be over?" Dante asked. The pain in Dante's voice broke Roman's heart all over again.

He put his arm around Dante and pulled him close. The scent of the whiskey was strong, but not as strong as his love for his brother.

"Soon, little brother. Soon," Roman said.

He let Dante fall asleep on the couch while he finished up with Lil Glock on the video chat. Once he felt that he had appropriately chastened the former-drum-major-turned-gangster-rapper, he went into the oven room.

There was a crate sitting on the lift. Roman had gone into his dad's computer and ordered a pack of cardboard cremation boxes without telling Neveah. He knew he'd need a few more of those boxes before all this was done.

He grabbed the handle of the lift and pushed it up to the oven. He opened the oven door and lined the lift up with the rollers inside.

He looked over his shoulder. The door separating the oven room from the lobby didn't have a lock, so he had to be quick in case Dante woke up and wandered back here.

He pulled the top back.

The body in the crate had a placidness that was rare on the faces of the dead. The mouth and eyelids were completely closed. Her long hair draped down over her shoulders like a tidal wave of black water. Her bearing was that of someone simply asleep.

"I'm sorry," Roman whispered.

He replaced the top and shoved the box in the oven.

JUNE 6, 2004

EVENING—INTO THE NIGHT GONE BLACK

Roman rides with his brother on the handlebars of his little brother's bike as they make their way to the crematory. The street where it's located is not yet called Industrial Way. Today it's called Seventh Street. Most of the streets in Jefferson Run that don't have names will get new monikers in the next twenty years. Numbers will be replaced, as will streets named after Confederate soldiers. Those rechristenings will come with their share of controversy, but by then Roman will be in Atlanta at the University of Georgia, dating one of his professors.

He doesn't know any of this, of course. He can't see the future. If he could, he would turn the bike around and go home and watch the Cartoon Network with Dante. But that is not the path that they are on today.

The crematory looms ahead of them like a great brick citadel with cylindrical chimneys as ramparts. There is no smoke billowing from them now but the scent of burnt remains, bitter and coarse, fills the air. It is a scent that Roman and Dante will encounter so often they will cease noticing it.

But not today.

Roman parks the bike and lets it lean on the kickstand. He doesn't want to go in here. He doesn't want to confront his mother. She is, like his father, a larger-than-life figure in his mind. Not quite a superhero, but more than just another person. She's his mama, and she is beautiful and fierce, and he loves her dearly. But he loves his little brother as well. An idea that his mind is not yet ready to embrace or articulate drives him to walk to the door and enter the crematory.

He doesn't need to see stuff like that, is how the idea appears simplistically in his mind. Later, when he is a man, he is able to put more context and nuance to the idea:

Children should be protected from the lives of adults. Especially from the private lives of their parents. Children should be allowed to exist in a state of constant unawareness when it comes to what their parents do inside or outside the bonds of marriage. That sacred covenant is between God and man, but Mother and Father are gods in a way, and they have a sacred covenant with their children. To keep them safe, to do no harm, and to allow them to be children as long as they can.

But that is not what he is thinking at sixteen years old.

All he is thinking is that his brother came to him crying because he saw something he shouldn't have and somebody has to do something about it. He subconsciously knows it won't be his father. He doesn't understand everything that is going on between his parents, but he knows that his father, while physically present, is always away. Building, dreaming, planning their future. Even at the expense of their present.

But this is another idea he has not learned to articulate yet. It is just a feeling that permeates his bones and sits in his belly like a cinder block.

Roman grabs the doorknob and finds it unlocked. He twists the knob and enters the lobby. Dante is behind him, not crying but also not speaking. He doesn't want to be here either. He doesn't understand what he saw, not really, but he knows that what his mother and Oscar were doing was something that she wasn't supposed to do with someone who isn't his father.

They go through the lobby into the oven room.

For as long as he lives, this is how Roman will remember her.

Tawny brown skin as supple and soft as the petals of a magnolia flower. Her eyes are so light they appear gold. The way the setting sun shines through the skylight makes them glow just a bit.

She is in her scrubs, but it doesn't seem possible that she just got off work a few hours ago. Her face is beautiful. The smile is like sunrise, like Christmas morning, like every good thing he's ever known all at once.

He doesn't know it, but it's her smile that he will miss the most. No other smile will ever make him feel the way his mother's does.

"Now, what y'all two doing up here? Come to beg some money to go to the new McDonald's? I bet that Church's is mad they opened up across the street. They might jump Ronald," Bonita Carruthers says, and laughs at her own joke.

This is the memory that Dante will cry over, the one that haunts his dreams and his waking hours. The sound of his mother's laugh. It is pure and it is good and he will never find its like again.

Their mother frowns when they don't share her laughter. She studies them. She knows something is wrong. She knows her boys.

"Y'all all right? Roman, what is it?" Bonita says.

Roman can't speak. He is here now and the words won't come. He didn't know how hard this would actually be and he isn't prepared for the enormous sense of sadness that is filling his chest.

But where he falters, Dante in his innocence cuts to the heart of the matter.

"I saw you with Mr. Oscar. I saw you through the window. You was bent over and he was behind you and he was doing stuff to you," Dante says.

Bonita's face caves in on itself like a falling star. And Roman knows she is going to try to lie, but the truth is on her face, and that makes him even sadder. The words she is about to say don't matter. He sees the truth in her eyes, in the crease in the middle of her forehead. In the way her mouth hangs slack.

"Oh, baby, that wasn't what . . . it isn't like that. That's not what . . . you don't know what you saw," Bonita says. That last part, six simple words, cracks open a fissure in Roman's soul that will never heal. Rage as white-hot as burning phosphorus flows through his body.

Disillusionment, a word he doesn't yet know, fills his heart to bursting. In his view, with those six words his mother, the queen of their family, has tossed her crown in the trash.

"He knows what he saw. Why you lying, Mama? How could you do this to Daddy? *How?*" Roman says. His words sting his mother. He can see how they make her flinch as he speaks.

But Bonita Carruthers is not a woman to let her children talk to her that kind of way, even if she may be in the wrong.

"You need to watch your mouth, boy. I'm your mama. You don't come up in here disrespecting me. Grown people business is grown people's business, and children ain't got no place in it," she says.

"So grown people can just be hoes and nobody supposed to say nothing?" Roman says, and instantly realizes he has entered an undiscovered country. A land of fallen idols and deposed emperors. A realm that each child must one day traverse. A journey that takes you from seeing your parents as infallible to recognizing them as all too human. For most, that journey ends with a wistful kind of acceptance. We love our parents not because they are perfect but because they persevere despite their imperfections. We all fall short of grace, but the beauty lives in the attempt.

Roman and Dante will never get to cross that valley from idolatry to understanding. It's not meant to be. Not for them, not for Neveah, and not for Bonita.

His mother slaps him. It's quick and it's hard and it hurts. His right cheek feels like a bee landed on it and killed itself to make him scream. He doesn't fall down or stumble. At sixteen he is already five-foot-nine and a solid hundred and sixty pounds. He will eventually reach six-foot-one. His cheek is burning like he had laid his head against the back of one of the crematory ovens.

He reaches out and grabs his mother by the arms.

There will never come a day when he will answer why he did that. He will tell himself it was a reflexive response. In the years to come he will try to accept the idea that he was defending himself. There will be times he will try to convince himself he was going to hug her. As if his embrace could quiet the disorder between, around them. As if his sixteen-year-old mind had thought so deeply about how to respond to the first time his mother had laid her hands on him.

What happens next will forever be hidden behind a long black veil for both of them. In Roman's mind it will always appear as a scattershot reel of images illuminated by a white strobe light. He will have no confidence in his recollection and he will never ask Dante what his perspective was at the time. It's not a conversation either of them wants to have.

If he could find a place to see that moment for what it really was, it might give him a modest dose of absolution, but he will never find that place as long as he lives.

His mother tries to pull away from him. She is shouting, cursing, but Roman is giving her words back to her with even more venom. He is screaming about his father, about Dante, Neveah, and finally himself. They are struggling, not fighting exactly but something even more primal. A physical expression of their shared pain and resentment and loss.

Dante appears, inserts himself between them, implores them to stop, to please stop. Roman has a moment of clarity, and as his mother pulls away with one last herculean effort he lets go of her arms as Dante is pushing him backward. He has a realization that he is in fact on the verge of fighting his own mother. A mother he loves fiercely despite the words he has said or the things that Dante has seen.

He lets go and she falls.

Neither he nor Dante will ever truly understand how it happens. Both of them, in their most agonizing nightmares, will only ever see her falling, hands outstretched, her face full of surprise, her mouth a wide O.

Then their nightmares will end. Neither will be able to remember the sound of her head hitting the corner of the worktable where the cremains are ground into powder and packed in plastic bags that go in plastic urns. But the moment will live with them forever in their subconscious. Years from now, Roman will have to run to the bathroom at a hibachi restaurant when the chef slaps a piece of premium filet mignon on the grill. The sound of the meat hitting the metal will unlock this moment in the lost chambers of his mind and he will lean over the toilet bowl retching and crying and not really knowing why.

They both watch as their mother's body falls to the floor. Blood as bright as a flame pools around her head on the floor like a halo. Her eyes remain open, as does her mouth. Her tongue rapidly begins to lose its color as her heart slows, then stops.

They go to her then and try to awaken her, pulling on her body, smothering her face with kisses. Pleading with her, with God, with anyone for her to get up, to please get up, Mommy please *get up*!

They stay there until it's dark. Until their father returns. They see him cry silently, tears like cut glass rolling down his cheeks.

He sends them into the lobby and tells them to stay there while he takes care of this. His wife, their mother, is gone, but her body remains.

They can hear the oven ignite through the door.

Then Keith Carruthers walks into the lobby.

"We can't never tell nobody what happened. Nobody. Not even Neveah. If anybody find out, they'll take y'all away. They might even put us in jail. This is ours. We have to bear this. No one else."

"It was an accident," Roman says. His voice is flat and whispery.

Keith grabs him, hugs him tight. Roman can feel his father's heart beating through his shirt. He smells of liquor and cigarettes and Brut cologne.

"I know that, boy. I know. I know," Keith moans.

Dante comes to them and Keith embraces both his sons. He holds them so tight that it's hard to breathe. Roman cries into his father's chest. He will always remember the spots of blood that inexplicably landed on the cuff of her pants. Blood drops that looked like a henna tattoo.

There will be days and nights when he will think he's never really taken another full breath ever again.

CHAPTER THIRTY-TWO

Roman swung by the hospital on his way to lunch with Shade in Richmond. He was carrying the information for the crypto account he had created for Shade's shell corporation. He was going to give him the account numbers, then discuss a few other things with him.

Pertinent things.

He went to his father's room and saw that they were packing up some of his things. Two nursing assistants were putting his father's get well cards and flower vases with dry dead roses and marigolds in a plastic tub. Roman stopped a nurse as she was coming out of the room.

"Excuse me, why are you packing up my father's things?" Roman asked.

"He's being transferred to a convalescent home," the nurse said.

"What? Are y'all just giving up on him?" Roman said.

"The doctors have talked with your sister about his long-term prospects and she and the doctors agreed this was the best course of action. She didn't discuss it with you?" the nurse asked.

"No, she did not. Who do I need to speak to in reference to putting a hold on any transfers until I talk to my sister?" Roman asked.

The nurse frowned. "Dr. Naquin or our social worker would be the best people to talk to, I suppose," she said.

"Okay. Do me a favor? Put my father's things down." Roman turned to the nursing assistants. "Right now, please."

He called Neveah before his meeting and directly after, and she didn't answer either time. He called her again as he drove to the house. Finally, as he was pulling in the yard, she answered.

"I'll be home in a few days," she said into the phone.

"I'm not worrying about when you come back. I need you to explain to me why you're sending Pop to a nursing home without talking to us," Roman said.

"Oh, like you talked to me about whatever you and Dante are doing that got me shot at? Like that, Roman?"

Roman bit down on the inside of his cheek. "Are the doctors giving up on him? Is that it? Are you giving up on him?" Roman asked.

"I'm not giving up, I'm thinking of myself, for once. It's been over a month. His insurance is about to run out. The doctors don't think he's going to come out of it. I can't work myself into an early grave to keep paying for these hospital bills."

"I can give you money," Roman said.

"Rome, I love you, but I don't think I want the money that you're making nowadays. This is the right thing to do. For him and for us. Are you gonna take him home? Wipe his ass? Change his feeding tube? Because that's what's in his future. I'm not trying to be gross, I'm trying to be real," Neveah said.

"I'll do anything for him. I'll move goddamn heaven and earth for him. But that's not the problem here. We're a family. When it comes to Pop, we should all talk about this. He . . . deserves better," Roman said.

"Does he?"

"What the fuck do you mean by that?" Roman asked.

"I'm not getting into this with you. But the man you keep putting on Mount Rushmore probably burned our mother up in that crematory he loves so much. So I'm sorry if I'm not feeling particularly charitable," Neveah said.

Roman closed his eyes so tight his cheeks hurt.

"He did not kill her. Neveah, I'm not . . . I'm not judging you for wanting your own life. God knows you deserve it. And the thing with Dante is complicated and I'm sorry we haven't been more open, but this is Pop we are talking about. The hospital can give him the treatment he needs. Nursing homes are fine for people who have nowhere else to go or no one to help, but there are three of us. We can figure something out. Please. Let's talk about this," Roman said.

"Rome, if you want to figure something out, go ahead. But I've made my decision. You want to keep him in the hospital or bring him home, that's on you. I mean that. I'm not gonna be a part of that. You know how hard it is to move a body that's dead weight, right? Imagine doing that all day every day until one of you shuffles off. Because that's what it's gonna be when the hospital bills are growing faster than your bank account and you have to bring him home. You need to think about this. I'm gonna go. There's a kayak thing down here at the winery on the creek. Like I said, I'll be home in a couple days," Neveah said.

Roman shook his head. "Okay. We'll talk then."

"I mean, I've said what I have to say, but we can talk. I'm gonna go," Neveah said.

"I love you too," Roman said.

"I know. 'Bye," Neveah said.

He'd expected them to argue, but there was nothing she said that he could dispute. Caring for his father at home would be a massive undertaking. Hospital care was not an unlimited resource. But he couldn't accept that they were giving up on their father. Keith Carruthers had one of the strongest wills he had ever encountered. He could not convince himself that his father was done fighting. Not yet.

Roman went into the house. Dante was sprawled across the couch. Two empty bottles of Jameson were on the coffee table. Dante sat up and waved at Roman.

"Greetings and salutations," Dante said.

"You had anything to eat yet?" Roman asked.

"I had . . . one Pop-Tart and then I had a bottle of Jameson to wash it down with," Dante said.

"Dante, I'm worried about you. This is a lot, man," Roman said.

"Yeah, it is. A lot of whiskey, a lot of drugs, a lot of dead people around us. A lot of 'it is what it is,'" Dante said.

Roman sighed.

"We are very close to being done with this. I need you to hold it together a little bit longer."

Dante laughed. He threw his head back and howled. "No, we're not. I told you, you like this shit. You're good at making them money. You like getting in there and moving it around like it's Monopoly. You ain't fixing this, you're a part of it," Dante said.

Roman blinked. "I'm fixing something that you did that almost got our father killed. That got your finger taken off. I'm here trying to make this right when I could be back home in Atlanta."

"You got Cassidy killed. I fucked up with Torrent and them and trusting Getty, but if you hadn't offered to burn up their problems they would have never brought them to us. You wouldn't have had to kill Getty and I wouldn't have had to crack Splodie open like a Brazilian walnut," Dante said.

Roman came over to the couch and got down on one knee. "I want you to listen to what I'm about to say. I hope it cuts through all this liquor and the ketamine and the Molly and the heroin and whatever the fuck else it is you're on. You're my brother and I love you, same as I love Neveah, but you, you're the reason Cassidy is dead. Because you couldn't keep her from coming back here. You're the reason Pop is about to get moved into a nursing home. It's you. You keep fucking up and we keep cleaning it up and then you just keep fucking up again. It's a never-ending cycle of excuses and mistakes that become habits because you keep doing the same shit. I love you, but I'm tired of it. Yeah, I'm good at making money, almost as good as you are at fucking things up. So you don't get to ask for my help and then question the way I give it. I don't ask why you're like this and I wish I could do something to . . . just . . . make you better, but I can't, so all I can do is try to save your life," Roman said.

Dante smiled.

"You don't know why I'm like this? It's because of my original fuckup. The Prime Fuckup. The original sin. Say it. I know you think it. I know Pop does. Say it, Rome. Say it to my face. Say it's my fault that she's—"

Roman grabbed him by his throat with both hands. He got to his feet while still holding Dante's neck and pulled him off the couch.

"No. No. I'm not going to say that, because we're not going to talk about that. That . . . was not your fault. It was not my fault. And we're not gonna fucking talk about it. Not now, not ever. You hear me? Do you hear me?" Roman said through clenched teeth.

"I miss her too," Dante gasped.

Roman let him go. Dante fell back on the couch.

"Stay here. Sober up," Roman said.

"Where you going?" Dante asked.

"You're right. Time to end this," Roman said.

He walked to the front door.

"Hey, Rome, Rome! Don't do something that you're gonna regret. I'm sorry. You're right. It's me. It's my fault. I told her everything was going to be all right and it wasn't. And she died, just like Mama. I'm sorry, Rome. I'm sorry. Don't go get hurt. Please just stay here," Dante said through a mouthful of tears.

"Wait for me here. Don't leave the house," Roman said. "And, hey, I'm sorry. I shouldn't have said that. We all make mistakes. None of us are perfect. But I promise I'm going to keep us safe. You just stay here, okay?"

"Okay. You ain't gotta apologize. I know it's true," Dante said.

Roman walked back over to the couch and tapped Dante's forehead.

"Look at me. You're not a fuckup. I was mad about something else and I took it out on you and that was wrong. I'm gonna go. You just chill out here for a minute."

"All right. Rome? I know I disappoint you, but thank you for never giving up on me," Dante said.

"I could never give up on you, Dante. Never," Roman said. "I gotta go."

He walked out the door and hopped in the Challenger.

"Goodbye, Rome," Dante said.

Chauncey was finishing a beer when his cell phone rang. "Yeah?"

"It's Roman Carruthers. I need to talk to you."

"Well, look who's come around. You got my money?" Chauncey said.

"Look, I can get the money, but shit is about to go down with Torrent. He's losing his mind. He blew up that vape shop. Those kids at the park? And that party? That was all him. Look, I can't do this anymore. I can't be a part of this. I need your help," Roman said. His voice shook as he spoke.

"What you want from me, man? I want my money," Chauncey said. Sharon had finally served him yesterday at his mother's house, which he couldn't stay at for long because his sister and her rug rats were living there.

"I can wear a wire, but there's supposed to be a sit-down out in the Skids at a warehouse. The GTC is supposed to send a rep and Torrent and Tranquil and his crew are gonna go and try to broker a truce. You could be there with some recording equipment. Get a bunch of evidence, I guess, and then you can arrest them later. Then I can get your money once they are locked up. It's not safe if they are still walking around," Roman said.

"Why don't you just call the JRPD? They can offer you protection," Chauncey said.

"Because they won't keep my name out of it. You will. Because you want your money," Roman said.

Chauncey considered what pretty boy was talking about. He turned it over in his mind for about a minute, trying to see all the angles. Finally he smiled and spoke into the phone.

"Give me the time and the place. I'll get there an hour early and set up," Chauncey said.

"Okay. Come alone, man. These guys hella paranoid. They get a sense something ain't right, they'll kill both of us," Roman said.

"Don't worry your pretty little head. You just be ready to write my check," Chauncey said.

"You get them arrested, you'll have it by the end of the next day," Roman said.

"Text me the info."

"All right. Thanks man," Roman said.

"Just text me the info," Chauncey said.

He hung up.

Roman put his phone back in his pocket.

The rook, he thought.

Torrent and the BBB were ordering another round of drinks and another order of catfish when Roman walked into Trout's. Torrent seemed in better spirits since decimating a large portion of the GTC. Roman could only hope it would sustain him through this next conversation.

"Can we talk? In the back? It's important," Roman said.

Torrent took a shot off of a tray one of the waitresses was carrying as she passed by his table. Tranquil stared at Roman with his lifeless mud-brown eyes.

Roman did his best to ignore him.

"What's so important, college boy? Have a drink. Everything is copacetic," Torrent said. He was in a better mood but was tipsy.

Roman leaned forward and dropped his voice.

"Somebody from the GTC came by Dad's place today trying to recruit me," Roman said.

"Say what?" Torrent said.

"They stopped by the crematory today. Can we go in the back and talk?" Roman said.

"Yeah, come on. Fuck," Torrent said.

In the back office Roman sat in a chair across from Torrent's desk. D-Train, Tank, Corey, and the Bang Bang Twins formed a semicircle around the desk.

"A guy who said his name was Carlos Veracruz came by and said he heard I was making a lot of money for you, and he was wondering if I wanted to work for him and make him some money. He said I'd get to keep more of my end if I worked for him. He said that if I was interested I could meet his boss tonight. He said his boss was Ernesto something. So, I told him yeah, I'd like to talk to him, and now I'm here telling you," Roman said.

Torrent interlaced his fingers and laid his hands on the desk.

"Didn't these boys try and kill you and your sister? Why would he try to get you to work for him?"

"I don't know. Maybe now they trying the honey, since the vinegar didn't work," Roman said.

"So, why did you decide to tell me? You could have just said no and kept it moving," Torrent said.

"Because I'm not stupid. I didn't want it to get back to you that I had been approached. Because I don't want me or my brother or my sister to get killed," Roman said.

"What time you supposed to meet him tonight?"

"Nine. The old tobacco warehouse in the Skids."

Torrent tapped his fingers on the desktop.

"You think we should pay this motherfucker a visit tonight?" Torrent said to Tranquil.

"The GTC is just about dead. If it is Ernesto, he ain't got enough soldiers or enough guns to hold out much longer. The Run belongs to us. I don't think you need to cut the head off this snake when the body is already dying," Tranquil said.

Torrent tapped his fingers.

"Yeah. But if it is Ernesto and we tap him, it's a message," Torrent said.

"The vape shop was a message too," Tranquil said.

Torrent rolled his head from side to side. Roman heard the joints in his neck cracking.

"Fuck it. We cut the head and make sure them motherfuckers dead. All right, college boy. Be here around eight. We gonna see what's good with Ernesto. Come on, let's go finish our drinks," Torrent said.

As they filed out of the office Tranquil passed Roman. "Sorry about you and my sister. I thought she knew what was up," Tranquil said.

Sure you are, you fucking psycho, he thought. "Don't worry about it," he said aloud.

"I wasn't going to," Tranquil said.

Roman left Trout's and drove out to the crematory. He parked the car and went inside. He went to the office and got his father's gun from the safe. He put it inside his jacket pocket. He walked into the oven room and stood in the center under the skylight.

The full moon shone down through the ancient glass like a beacon from a distant ship. Neveah had picked a good week to finally take a vacation. The cooler was empty and they hadn't received any calls from any of the contracted funeral homes.

He wasn't religious, even though he had attended church as a child. His father went mostly out of habit, and when the crematory took off he stopped going altogether. This building had become his sanctuary. No fire-and-brimstone sermon could match the radiant heat of the two ovens. This building, the site of so much of his own personal agony, was a church of sorts for his father.

Roman prayed a dark prayer:

No matter what happens tonight, Dante and Neveah will be safe. Torrent and Tranquil won't threaten my family anymore. I've failed so much, done things I regret, things that make me ill. But please let me do this one thing right. Mama, if you can hear me, watch out for me tonight. I miss you so much. I can never be sorry enough. Please watch out for me tonight.

He walked out to the car. Before starting up the Challenger, he texted Khalil.

we good

Khalil responded immediately.

you know it

Roman fired up the Challenger and peeled out of the parking lot, roaring through the night like a rider on a steed that had never known defeat.

Roman had lost a lot in life, but he knew one thing.

He'd never been defeated.

CHAPTER THIRTY-THREE

Dante pulled up to the auto body garage and parked the rental across the street. He was listening to the nineties hip-hop channel on the satellite radio. "My Mind Playing Tricks on Me" by the Geto Boys was blasting through the speakers, making the glass in the windows tremble.

Dante took one last swig from a bottle of the cheapest bourbon he could find. He took a small pill bottle out his pocket and did two lines of crushed Percocet. He reached in the glove compartment and pulled out a Desert Eagle .380. The gun looked like it belonged on top of a tank. He'd borrowed it from Tug, who wasn't in any condition to ask too many probing questions. Raynell was still in the hospital in the ICU. So when Dante asked him about his piece he handed it over with no more concern than if Dante had asked to borrow his favorite video game controller.

"I gotta go talk to a dude about something," Dante had said.

"Yeah, all right, man," Tug had said, and went back to staring at his phone waiting for any updates on Raynell. Dante had gotten up, tucked the gun in his waistband, and headed for the door.

"Hey, Tug, thanks for everything, man," Dante had said.

"Yeah, man, see ya later," Tug said.

"Yeah, man, thanks again," Dante had said.

He left humming the song "What About Your Friends" by TLC.

The auto body shop was over on the outskirts of the western edge of Jefferson Run. You drive one more mile, you enter Chesterfield County, like you can enter Warren County if you drive east over the bridge.

Dante looked down the street, which became a two-lane blacktop road that drove you out of the city into a county. There was an obvious line of demarcation between the city and county. You could see it where the trees held court on each side of the road. That started where the streetlamps stopped.

A few of the streetlamps were actually working tonight, but they were dulled by the light from the full moon. Dante took another drink from the bottle. It made his chest tingle.

When he was a kid, that last streetlamp in this part of town was the border of his territory. His mother had told him he couldn't ride his bike past that point. The traffic in Chesterfield was too dangerous, she would say. He never expected that boundary to hold him here for thirty-four years.

The song on the radio changed. It was an old R&B hit. "Old Time's Sake" by Sweet Sable off the *Above the Rim* soundtrack.

The old times. The before times. The times that didn't give him nightmares.

He reached into his pocket and pulled out an old Instamatic photograph. His dad had spent about a grand on those cheap disposable cameras when he was a kid, documenting the construction of the crematory.

He held the picture up to his face.

It was him and Roman and Neveah and his mother and father after church one Sunday. He and Rome were wearing clip-on ties and Neveah had on a beautiful yellow dress and her hair done up in two big Afro puffs.

His mother was exquisite. His father was standing behind her with his hand on her shoulder. She was laying her hand over his. She was wearing that heart-shaped diamond ring that his father had bought her. It was small, but the clarity must have been off the charts because it glittered in the picture.

He was making a silly face in the picture. Rome was serious as always. Neveah was looking off to the right. He couldn't remember why.

He put the picture back in his pocket.

He racked a bullet into the chamber of the Desert Eagle.

He took several deep breaths. In and out. In and out.

"I'm sorry, Cassidy. I let you down," he said out loud.

Dante got out of the car.

"Ernesto Salaazar, I am here for you. Come on down, motherfucker!" Dante screamed. His voice echoed up and down the street but dissipated as it reached the trees.

The last streetlight blinked out like a lantern being extinguished as shots rang out through the night.

Roman parked the Challenger next to Torrent's BMW. They had met at Trout's, then driven out here to the Skids in a caravan that sliced through the night like a dagger. He got out and buttoned his jacket. There were streetlamps near the warehouse, but they had blown out years ago and no one had bothered to replace them. The moonlight gave the street and the warehouse and everything in the immediate vicinity a purplish hue.

Roman waited for Torrent and Tranquil to get out of their car. D-Train, Tank, Corey, and the Bang Bang Twins had driven over in D-Train's late-model Caddy. They were already out of the car. The wind had dipped down from chilly to downright cold.

Finally Torrent and Tranquil got out of their car.

"Is there lights in this motherfucker?" Torrent asked.

"Yeah, the power is still on," Roman said. "I got the key from the demo team. This is the next structure to be knocked down. I turn the light on when we get in. I've been coming by checking on things. I guess we go in and just wait for Carlos and Ernesto."

"Yeah, let's wait for them," Tranquil said.

Roman didn't slow his stride, but there was a note to Tranquil's tone that gave him a moment of concern. Was it sarcasm? Was this sociopath capable of sarcasm? Roman unlocked the side door to the warehouse and went inside. He ran his hand along the wall and found a switch. One-third of the warehouse became illuminated under a set of sallow overhead lights enclosed in wire cages. The light allowed them to see, but since the warehouse only had windows in the rear of the building which created an alley with another old warehouse, Roman wasn't that concerned about anyone noticing their meeting.

Torrent and Tranquil entered, followed by the rest of their crew. Roman went over to a stack of pallets and leaned against them with his hands in his pockets. His breath created small white plumes in front of his face like miniature clouds.

D-Train was the last person through the door. He pulled it shut behind him. He moved to stand next to Torrent and Tranquil. That was when Roman noticed he was alone on one side and the rest of the BBB were on the other side. In between them were a couple of piles of trash and debris like small yurts.

Roman didn't think they were bulletproof.

"What time Carlos and Ernesto supposed to get here, again?" Torrent said.

"Nine. So in about thirty minutes," Roman said.

Roman hoped Chauncey had the good sense to hide himself behind some of the stacks of rotting burlap sacks in the rear of the building. Or the abandoned machinery toward the far left wall. As long as he was in the building things should be okay.

Hopefully.

Torrent cleared his throat.

"You know I ain't never trust you, but I was beginning to like your ass. I even thought you was good for Jae. But you just another college boy that thinks he's smarter than me," Torrent said.

"What? What are you talking about?" Roman said.

Torrent smiled.

"Chauncey, you can come out now," he said.

Roman let his mouth hang open as Chauncey came out of the shadows. He wasn't carrying any type of recording equipment or video camera or anything of the like. He was just grinning at Roman as he stood off to the side but parallel to the BBB.

"We had a deal, you piece of shit!" Roman yelled.

"I made a better one with Torrent. Nothing personal. Well, it's a little personal. Your sister ruined my life. One of my fellow officers overheard her talking in the parking lot of Candy's, that night GTC hit it. She told my wife. Now I don't get to see my kids. I don't get to go in my house that I fucking paid for. So, after we finish here she's probably gonna get a visit from these boys," Chauncey said.

Roman forced himself not to pull his gun and shoot Chauncey where he stood.

"Chauncey came by after you left. We came to an understanding. He's suspended right now, a little morals violation got him caught up. Your sister wasn't the only honey he was banging, ain't that right Chauncey? A little meter maid blew up his spot," Torrent said.

Chauncey didn't respond.

"But now he's gonna help us pin a lotta shit on you, and that'll help him get back on the force. Then we'll have a friend there and in the mayor's office. So, thank you for that," Torrent said.

"You gonna kill me without asking Shade for permission? I'm making money for him too. You forgot about that?" Roman said. A vibrato entered his voice because he was shaking.

"Shade don't run this. I do. I'll explain to him what happened. He'll get over it. That motherfucker get over anything if it keeps him from pulling a bid. I told you, Roman, you ain't smarter than me. But you wouldn't listen. Some motherfuckers always wanna test shit. Well, a hard head make a soft ass, as my mama used to say. D-Train, will y'all punch this motherfucker's ticket, please?" Torrent said.

Roman knew he'd say that. Torrent might have Chauncey in his back pocket, but he still wasn't going to commit murder in front of a cop. Or let his brother do it either. Even though Roman could see in Tranquil's eyes he wanted to, real bad.

D-Train pulled his own gun out and pointed it at Roman.

Roman locked eyes with him.

Tank, Corey, and the Bang Bang Twins pulled their guns as well.

"Nighty-night, bitch," Torrent said.

Roman lowered his head.

"Okay. Okay. Do it. Do it now," he said.

D-Train, Tank, Corey, and the Bang Bang Twins spun around and pointed their guns at Torrent and Tranquil.

A moment as brief as a hiccup passed before it was apparent to Torrent what was happening. Confusion washed over his face, then was quickly replaced by rage.

"Nigga, who you pointing a gun at?" Torrent screamed. Chauncey's smile faded away like a ghost in the morning light. Tranquil reached for the small of his back, but Lucius put his gun against the side of his head.

"D-Train, how much money I put in your savings account?" Roman asked.

"One hundred thousand. Plus help setting up an IRA," D-Train said.

"Corey?" Roman asked.

"Seventy-eight thousand, and then got me and Mom invested in a motherfucking mutual fund," Corey said.

"How you doing, Tank?" Roman asked.

"Man, homey got me in on that deal with Shade. Got enough to put my niece on a four-year ride at Prosser State," Tank said.

"We got enough to buy a bar in Richmond. Got in on that mutual fund too," Lucius said, speaking for the Bang Bang Twins.

"Between Shade's deal with the state and the regentrification of the Skids, we gonna eat real good for a real long time. No more pump-and-dumps, no more playing with the SEC. We're all going to eat real good. Nobody is going to have to take your crumbs anymore," Roman said quietly.

"This how it going down? You think this is how it's going down, after all I've done for you motherfuckers? And talking about Shade? You think he gonna let this shit slide? Bitch, you don't know who you dealing with!" Torrent yelled.

"Terrance, he already got permission," Tranquil said.

Torrent whipped his head to the right and looked at his brother. Understanding flooded his face. He turned back to Roman.

"He said as long as it's clean he was okay with it," Roman said.

He took a step forward.

"You tried to kill my daddy. My brother. Me. You made me lower myself to your level. Wallow in the dirt and mud with you until I don't know if I'll ever get clean. But now we balance the books. Tonight, all debts are paid," Roman said. He stared at Torrent until he started frantically looking around for, if not an escape, a reprieve, but the men who stared back at him gave him no hope of that either. Roman stepped back.

"Look what you did to my hand, motherfucker," Corey said.

"You bust me in the fucking head for spilling a drink. Who does that, man?" Tank said.

D-Train steadied his gun hand with his left hand. "You shouldn't have killed Eddie, man. He was just a kid. He didn't deserve that."

"Fuck this," Tranquil said. He grabbed his .45 from his waistband.

Before he could fire, Lucius pulled the trigger.

And then the rest of them followed suit. The shots created a violent symphony that filled the vast space inside the warehouse with a cloud of dissonance.

The Gilchrist brothers fell together, Torrent lying across his younger brother. Trying to protect him to the end. Tranquil was as silent as his name implied, but Torrent was coughing, blood flowing over his lips and soaking his chin.

"You . . . mother . . . fuckers," he wheezed.

Roman walked over to where he lay.

He reached inside his jacket and pulled out his father's gun.

"You're not going to end up on a T-shirt. No one is even going to know you're gone. Not for a while. By the time they realize, there won't be any candlelight vigils. There are only a few people who are going to mourn you, and even they didn't really want to be around you," Roman said.

He pointed the gun at Torrent's face.

"What's . . . gonna . . . happen . . . to . . . my . . . dogs?" Torrent said.

"You ain't gotta worry about that anymore," Roman said.

He swallowed hard.

"To be a king, you have to think like one. You have to do king shit," his father had told him when he was teaching him how to play chess.

Roman pulled the trigger.

Torrent's cheek imploded as he went still.

Chauncey was holding his hands up in the air.

"Look, we can work something out. I mean, you can't kill a cop! Not with that gun. They're gonna trace it right back to you. All of you!" Chauncey squealed.

"You're right. I can't kill you with this gun," Roman said.

He held up his hand, extending his index finger toward the ceiling.

Then he pointed down.

A bullet, noiseless, as quiet as the grave, flew through the air, through a window in the rear of the building, and entered Chauncey's skull at three thousand feet per second. Chauncey collapsed like a bag of laundry tossed on the floor.

"Who did that?" D-Train asked.

"My insurance salesman. Let's get them in the car. Lucius, y'all go to Chauncey's car and take the money out of my trunk. Make sure you spread it all over the car and the coke, okay?" Roman said.

"You got it," Lucius said.

"D-Train, make sure those dogs get to good homes. Just sell them at the farm. Don't let a shelter get them, okay?" Roman said.

"Yeah, no problem," D-Train said.

Thank you, Mama, Roman thought. Thank you for looking out for us for one last time.

By the time everything was put in place and cleaned up it was midnight.

Roman drove back to the house and parked the Challenger in the driveway close to the porch. The rental was gone. He figured Dante hadn't heeded his warnings and had gone out or over to Tug's place. Neveah was still at the winery, so he had the house to himself. He went inside and got a bottle of water out of the fridge and sat down on the couch.

He thought of calling Jealousy, but he decided against it. He could just feel she needed more time. He turned on the television and started flipping through the channels. He landed on the Cartoon Network and let it stay there. His brain needed simple, easily digestible content. He chugged the bottle of water and leaned his head against the back of the couch.

He felt himself drifting off when his cell phone rang.

He grabbed and checked the screen. It was a Virginia number, but he didn't recognize it. Who would be calling him this late? Then his mind went to Neveah and he immediately answered.

"Hello?" Roman said.

"Is this Mr. Roman Carruthers?" an official voice on the other end asked.

"Yes?" Roman said.

"Mr. Carruthers, I'm sorry to have to call you this late with . . . I unfortunately have to inform you that I am from the medical examiner's office."

"What is . . . Why are you calling me?" Roman asked.

The official voice paused.

"I'm sorry, but we have your brother's body here. He had you listed as his next of kin on the information card in his wallet. I'm so sorry, but we need you to come and confirm the identification."

Neveah's phone vibrated against her back. She had fallen asleep with it in the bed with her. She regretted not putting it on silent. She grabbed it, saw it was Roman, and almost hit ignore, until she noticed it was four in the morning.

"What is it?" she said.

"Come home. I need you to come home," Roman said. He sounded strange. As if he were far away from the speaker.

"What? Is it Daddy?" Neveah asked. She had worked around death long enough to know certain early-morning calls or late-night ones could only be for that one specific reason.

"No, please, Neveah, just come home," Roman said.

A hole the size of the world opened up in Neveah's belly.

"I'm on my way," she said.

Roman was waiting for her on the bottom step of the porch. He was sitting there with his head in his hands staring down at the gravel of the driveway.

"Rome, what is it? What happened?" Neveah said.

He raised his head. He was crying. "They killed him. They killed him."

"What? Who?" Neveah asked as the pit in her stomach grew even more wide and deep, because she knew who he was talking about but a part of her mind said if he didn't say it, if the words didn't come out, it wouldn't be true.

"Dante. He's gone, Neveah," Roman said.

And they ran to each other then, grabbing each other in an embrace that only those who have lost a sibling can understand.

Jealousy got up and looked at her phone. It was six in the morning and someone was knocking on her door like they were trying to knock it off its hinges. She walked through her apartment and looked through her peephole.

"Roman, go away, I'm not talking to you. Please go," she said from her side of the door.

"They killed my brother," he said.

Jealousy's breath caught in her throat. She pulled the door open, and there was Roman, his eyes red, his clothes in disarray.

"What did you say?" Jealousy said.

"They killed him," Roman whispered.

Jealousy reached out for him and pulled him into her apartment and shut the door. He grabbed her ferociously, and they both sank to the floor. He was trembling and crying and talking into her neck.

"What am I supposed to do now? They killed him, Jae. Shot him full of holes. They had me look at him, and they massacred him. They massacred my brother. What am I supposed to do now? What do I do, Jae? I don't know what to do."

"Oh, baby, just let me hold you. Just stay here with me, baby. That's all you gotta do. I'm so sorry. Shhh. Just stay here with me, baby," Jae said.

Outside, it began to rain in earnest, the rising sun hidden behind gray clouds that swirled across the sky. Jealousy held Roman, and Roman cried and cried, his tears more voluminous than the rain.

Neveah was drunk.

She'd grabbed a jar of moonshine from her father's private stash in the shed out back and had started drinking as soon as Roman had left for parts unknown.

She took a long swig of the 'shine and let it burn her all the way down to her toes. The house felt empty, endlessly empty, like it would never feel full of life again. Dante was dead. Those words didn't even make sense to her.

She went to get up from the table, and the jar of moonshine slipped from her grasp. The jar shattered, soaking her pants with corn liquor and bits of glass. Neveah stared down at the mess and suddenly she was unmoored. She slammed both of her fists down on the table and swept the dishes and the fake-fruit centerpiece onto the floor.

She started to scream. To wail. To howl. She went to the sink and pushed the drain tray onto the floor. Dishes broke and shattered and spilled across the floor like confetti.

She spun around and found herself face-to-face with the teddy bear cookie jar. They used to joke about it being a decapitated bear when they were kids. Then their mother disappeared and they stopped joking. But her father still kept the damn thing with its creepy eyes on top of the fridge.

Neveah grabbed the bear off the top of the fridge and raised it above her head.

"I hate this fucking thing!" she screamed.

She hurled it to the floor.

It splintered into a thousand pieces.

She'd expected it to be empty, but it wasn't.

She stared at the contents of the jar and recognized them for what they were. She'd seen thousands of the same contents over the years. To an untrained eye it might appear to be sand, or dry cement, or perhaps even cat litter. But she knew what it was, knew it like she knew her own name.

Neveah went to her knees. She pawed through the contents, ignoring the ceramic shards. Ashes. Cremains. The sum total of a human being's body after immolation. Her numb fingers fell upon a hard twisted piece of metal. She picked it up and held it to the light. The metal was melted into a near-question-mark shape. At the bottom of the question mark there was a burnished heart.

CHAPTER THIRTY-FOUR

Roman came home two days later.

He'd spent those two days with Jealousy, trying to navigate this new reality where his baby brother was dead and his sister wasn't answering his calls. He'd gotten in touch with Weldon to go and receive Dante from the medical examiner. He would handle the cremation, but he couldn't bring himself to pick him up and pull him off that slab where his body was resting.

When he walked into the house, Neveah was sitting at the kitchen table. She was smoking in the house, which was something she didn't normally do. Roman guessed the old rules didn't really matter much anymore.

He joined her at the kitchen table.

"I've been trying to get in touch with you," Roman said.

"I needed some time," Neveah said.

"Yeah. So, I guess, do we want to do a service? I guess we could do it at Weldon's place. I don't know," Roman said.

"I didn't want to call you on the phone and tell you this," Neveah said. She took a long drag on her cigarette. "Pop died last night. They say it was an abdominal aneurysm." Her tone was even, but her eyes were wild.

"What the fuck did you just say?" Roman said. He thought he was going to pass out. The room was spinning. His chest was as tight as a drum.

"Yeah, they called me this morning. Like I said, I didn't want to tell you on the phone," Neveah said.

"What caused the aneurysm?" Roman asked.

"I don't know. Maybe someone gave him some aspirin or something that fucked up his blood thinners. Who knows?" Neveah said.

Roman looked at her. She looked at him. A thought entered his mind, and he desperately pushed it away. He couldn't even begin to think thoughts like that. Not now. Not ever.

Roman was spiraling. He fell across the table and let his head hit the smooth wooden surface. He blindly reached out for Neveah and she took his left hand.

Then he felt her place something in his right hand.

Roman raised his head and brought his right hand to his face.

There was a twisted sliver of gold with a heart-shaped diamond on one end like the head of a stick pin. Roman dropped it like it was liquefied molten steel.

"Where did you get that?" Roman said.

Neveah picked up a paper cup that was sitting on the end of the table. She stood up and poured the ashes on the table.

"He killed her, Rome. He killed her and put her ashes and her ring in a goddamn fucking *cookie jar!*" Neveah roared.

Roman pushed himself away from the table, away from those ashes, and stood as well.

"What . . . he didn't kill her," Roman whispered. He couldn't take his eyes off the ragged pile of ashes in the center of the table.

"Roman, open your fucking eyes! That's her ring. Those are her ashes. That's our mother! The sick fuck kept her above the goddamn fridge!" Neveah said. Her face was a vulpine mask.

"He didn't kill her," Roman said.

"Why won't you see the truth? It's here! It's right in front of you, and you gonna keep defending him. He killed our mom!" Neveah said. Her voice cracked.

Roman raised his head and they locked eyes.

"He didn't do it. I'm telling you," Roman said. "He didn't do it."

Neveah recoiled in horror until the small of her back hit the sink. She dropped her cigarette on the floor and put both hands to her mouth.

Roman came around the table and took her hands in his own.

"It was an accident. She fell, and Daddy . . . she was cheating on him, the police would have arrested him. Or us. It was an accident. We were arguing, and she fell. It was an accident. He didn't kill her, Neveah. He wasn't even there. Dante saw her with Oscar, and I . . . It was an accident," Roman said for the first time in his life.

"I did it for nothing," Neveah murmured.

"What? What did you do? What are you talking about?" Roman asked.

"Get off me!" Neveah moaned. She pushed Roman away and raced up the stairs. Roman stood in the middle of the kitchen clenching and unclenching his fists as his whole body trembled.

Neveah came back down stairs carrying a gym bag. She rushed to the door. Roman chased after her, calling her name.

"Neveah, where are you going? Please, where are you going? *Neveah!* We are all we got. We're all that's left. Where are you going? Please, we're all we got!" Roman said.

Neveah stopped.

She turned to face him.

"Then we have nothing. I have nothing. We are nothing," Neveah said.

A few moments later he heard her truck start, and then she was gone.

OCTOBER 26

NIGHT

Roman stands in the middle of the floor surrounded by D-Train, Corey, Tank, the Bang Bang Twins, and the rest of the BBB. He is talking to them about how he plans on incorporating their profits into his company to make the money legitimate. He explains that he will be returning to Atlanta for a time and that D-Train will be in charge until he gets back. He tells them when he comes back, he and Khalil will help them reshape the BBB. No longer will they be having shoot-outs on the corner. Their actions will be precise, efficient. They will bring a business mindset to the street. Nights in Jefferson Run will be quiet from now on. He says this even as he thinks of the call he got last night from Khalil saying that he'd finally caught up with the man who had robbed Lil Glock and had convinced him to return the money with the help of a straight razor and a bottle of rubbing alcohol.

Corey asks what are they going to do about the remnants of the GTC. He says the streets are saying they are trying to regroup.

Roman goes to a cremation box sitting on the body lift and opens it. He grabs a latex glove from the workbench and puts it on and reaches inside the box.

He pulls out the head of Ernesto Salaazar.

"That's not going to be a problem," he says, before tossing the head back in the box and pushing the box into the oven.

He comes back to the center of the room and explains that he will be hiring attendants to work at the crematory. His sister is no longer a part of Carruthers Cremation Services. The BBB will deal with him and him alone if they have "materials that need disposal."

"Everything burns," he says. As the words come out of his mouth, he thinks of his father, his brother, his mother. He can see flames blooming behind the tempered glass of the oven door like furious red-and-orange roses, burning for Salaazar the same way they did when they devoured the three people he loved more than life itself.

He thinks of Neveah. Of love blackened and blistered and turned to ashes.

Corey asks another question, and Roman pauses.

"You're asking a lot of questions. You don't need to. I'm telling you how things are going to work. I'm telling you how I'm going to make us rich. You keep asking questions, you're gonna make me nervous. You make me nervous, and you might be carried out in one of these," Roman says and he tosses an empty plastic urn at Corey's feet.

Corey stops asking questions.

Before Roman can continue, the doorbell rings.

He tells the crew to be quiet and goes to answer the door in the lobby.

It's Jealousy.

She comes inside. She asks him if he has seen her brothers. He moved in with her after the memorial services for his brother and his father. He's told her he plans on selling the house, and she supports his decision. She says she wasn't worried when she hadn't heard from her brothers for a few days, but now it's been two weeks. Roman had told her he wasn't working for them anymore, and his actions since the morning he came to her have proven that fact.

He has taken Torrent and Tranquil's kingdom and made it his own. He will never work for anyone ever again.

But she tells him she is afraid. She's scared. She knows what they do and she is afraid something has happened to them. And then today she couldn't get in touch with Roman, so she just came here to talk with him, the way he had come to talk with her when Dante died.

Roman hugs her and tells her he is having a meeting with the guys who are going to run the crematory for him now that Neveah has left town. He stares into her eyes and assures her that her brothers will show up eventually.

"Wait for me here in the lobby, and then we'll go and we'll have dinner, and tomorrow we'll file a police report, okay?" he says. He kisses her, and she subconsciously bites his lip. In public they are boyfriend and girlfriend, perhaps soon to be fiancés, but in the bedroom, in the dark, she's Mama and he's her dirty boy and she loves both versions of him more than she's loved any other man in her life.

"Five minutes," he says, and he goes back through the doorway.

Jealousy stands there looking at the door for a few seconds before she goes back outside. There are four cars in the parking lot. She recognizes those cars. One of them, the Caddy, belongs to D-Train. She knows he worked for her brothers.

She walks around the corner of the building to the roll-up door that Roman has told her is how they bring the bodies into the crematory.

She goes to the narrow rectangular windows in the garage door and peers inside.

She sees the man she loves talking to a group of men with their backs to the door. Behind him the oven has roared to life. Bright orange flames illuminate Roman's figure from the back, creating a silhouette effect. She can no longer see his face.

The flames glow white-hot through the tempered glass in the center of the metal door of the oven. Those flames behind him evoke a painting she likes called *The Fall of the Rebel Angels* by a painter whose name she can't recall. It shows the defeat of Lucifer, who thought it was better to reign in hell than serve in heaven.

As she stares through the window, she is reminded of something her brother Terrance used to say about a man he told her was a business associate when she asked if he was a family friend. "The devil ain't got no friends."

Jealousy looks at the man she loves. She looks at him holding court among these other men whose bearing is that of supplicants. She touches her belly and thinks about the possibility of a life growing there. She's two weeks late, and she is almost never late.

She stares through the narrow windows at the fire blazing behind the man who may be the father of her child.

She thinks of her brothers.

Of the veil of serenity that seems to have fallen across Jefferson Run in their absence.

Of something Roman has said to her more than once.

A tear runs down her cheek as she whispers softly.

"Everything burns."

ACKNOWLEDGMENTS

As writers, we always try to push ourselves to surpass the most recent versions of ourselves. That's a task that is impossible without an incredible supporting cast.

Thank you to Josh Getzler, the greatest agent in the world.

Thank you to Christine Kopprasch, an editor without peer. Look at us now, my friend!

Thank you to the wonderful community of writers who read *King of Ashes* as it made its way from a nebulous idea to an actual novel: Chad Williamson, Nick Kolakowski, Paul J. Garth, Rob D. Smith, Bobby Mathews, Holly West, and a special thank you to Jordan Harper. You were right, Hoss.

Finally, for Kim. She knows why.

ABOUT THE AUTHOR

S. A. Cosby is a *New York Times* bestselling writer from southeastern Virginia. He is the author of *All the Sinners Bleed*, which was on more than forty Best of the Year lists, including Barack Obama's, as well as the Edgar Award finalist *Razorblade Tears*, the Los Angeles Times Book Prize winner *Blacktop Wasteland*, and *My Darkest Prayer*. He has also won the Anthony Award, ITW Thriller Award, Barry Award, Macavity Award, BCALA Award, and Audie Award and has been longlisted for the ALA Andrew Carnegie Medal for Excellence.